Jane Linfoot writes fun, flirty fiction with feisty heroines and a bit of an edge. She lives in a mountain kingdom in Derbyshire, where her family and pets are kind enough to ignore the domestic chaos. Happily, they're in walking distance of a supermarket. Jane loves hearts, flowers, happy endings, all things vintage, and most things French. When not on Facebook and without an excuse for shopping, she can be found walking or gardening.

@janelinfoot
@janelinfoot
/JaneLinfoot2
janelinfoot.co.uk

Also by Jane Linfoot

How to Win a Guy in 10 Dates
The Right Side of Mr Wrong
High Heels & Bicycle Wheels
The Vintage Cinema Club
The Little Wedding Shop by the Sea
Christmas at the Little Wedding Shop
Summer at the Little Wedding Shop
Christmas Promises at the Little Wedding Shop
The Little Cornish Kitchen
Edie Browne's Cottage by the Sea

A Cosy Christmas in Cornwall

JANE LINFOOT

OneMoreChapter

One More Chapter
a division of HarperCollins*Publishers*
The News Building
1 London Bridge Street
London SE1 9GF

www.harpercollins.co.uk

This paperback edition 2019

First published in Great Britain in ebook format by
HarperCollins*Publishers* 2019

A catalogue record for this book
is available from the British Library

ISBN: 9780008356316

This novel is entirely a work of fiction.
The names, characters and incidents portrayed in it are
the work of the author's imagination. Any resemblance to
actual persons, living or dead, events or localities is
entirely coincidental.

Set in Birka by Palimpsest Book Production Limited, Falkirk,
Stirlingshire

Printed and bound by CPI Group (UK) Ltd, Croydon CR0 4YY

For Yoyo, my wonderful Old English Sheepdog,
beside me all day, every day, fifteen
lovely years together.

The strongest blizzards start with a single snowflake …

Wednesday

11th December

1.

Be Jolly

'Could there be a better present for the woman who has everything?'

I'm smiling across at Merwyn in the front seat and, as I take in the words *Cockle Shell Castle* carved into the monumental gateposts, I'm so excited I'm finding it hard to breathe. Then I ease my car through the gateway and onto the winding approach, and as we round a bend and the pale walls and castellated towers come into view, washed in moonlight, I can't help letting out a gasp. I've held my anticipation in check for six whole hours since we left London, but now we're here there's a butterfly storm in my tummy. In the pictures the castle looked wonderful, but in the flesh, above the twinkle of the dashboard fairy lights, it's more magical still. As I pull the car up by some big square planters and gaze up at the building, it's one of those rare moments in life when it feels like I'm actually living in a fairy tale.

'Christmas in a Cornish castle by the sea has to be *the* perfect gift. It's as if those small-paned windows are drawing us in. We're just *so* lucky to be here.'

After *so* long in his doggy travelling harness, Merwyn's side eye tells me he's less enthusiastic than me. He may look like a messy brown floor mop more often than he looks like a dog, but in his *Yappy Christmas* neck tie he's beyond cute, and he's been surprisingly good company on the way. He never grumbled once about me playing non stop Christmas tunes and singing along to *I Wish it could be Christmas Every Day*, which would be my tag line if I had one. George, my ex, would never have put up with non stop Pirate FM either; sometimes it's good to make comparisons with the past and come out ahead.

'Come on, time to stretch your legs, we have to go round the back for the key.' I drag on my coat and pull my woolly bobble hat further down, clip on Merwyn's lead, and let him scramble out over me as I open the car door. Then I grab the wodge of instructions and follow his bounds.

As we pass a studded front door that's big enough for a giant, I feel as if I should be pinching myself to be sure I'm not dreaming. Then an icy blast of air slices up under my fake fur jacket, whips straight through my chunky fair isle jumper, and saves me the trouble – anything this freezing has to be real.

And just in case anyone's wondering who this woman who has everything is, it definitely isn't me. *Hell no!* It's my best friend, Fliss's, older, more successful, and seriously driven sister, Liberty Johnstone-Cody. Libby is one of those amazing multi-tasking entrepreneur super-mums who started a decade ago with a new-born, a toddler and an idea for a baby carrier, and went on to take over the world.

Just to get things straight from the start, where Libby is fabulous at amassing and seizing the day, I'm more of an accidental dropper. I got as far as a steady boyfriend, but I managed to lose him. One time I was going to buy a very small flat, but then I didn't. This time last year I had an awful disaster it's very difficult not to think about. Let's just say, right now I'm trying really hard to do better.

I do have a job I used to love, as a visual merchandiser at *Daniels*, which is a family run department store tucked just behind Regent Street in London. My mum calls it window dressing but I actually style and build displays. But along with everything else, that's gone a bit pear-shaped lately, since Fliss, my best friend who works in the same team, went on two lots of maternity leave in quick succession. The first was very much planned, the second was a disaster because it happened too fast. But that's what life's like for Fliss and me; we have calamities but we have so many of the damned things, mostly we grit our teeth and try to ride those catastrophe waves. Whereas lucky old Libby wouldn't recognise a setback if it slapped her in the face, because, quite simply, she doesn't allow negativity into her life.

Libby actually grabbed this two week rental in a Cornish castle for Christmas within six seconds of it appearing on Facebook Marketplace. She bought it herself, because that's what she's like, and got her husband Nathan to pay for it afterwards. But it's only *slightly* less romantic because of that. Sometimes we women have to do things for ourselves, and there's nothing wrong with that. Realistically, Nathan's a high flying banker who struggles to find time to go home to see his kids, he's not going to have space in his day to mess around on Facebook. And buying your own present might mean you forfeit those two seconds of amazement when it arrives. But the plus side is you get exactly what you want and you're never disappointed. Best of all, you're in control. And for Libby control is a must.

That's the other thing about being a hot shot business mother of four, nurturer of kids *and* a burgeoning business, running through life at a million miles an hour with all her hands full, while juggling fruit at the same time. These days it's not enough to *be* one, she has to show the world she's doing it too – if the social media posts aren't there, whatever she's doing may as well never have happened.

So Libby pulling off a fortnight over Christmas in a castle will be entirely wasted if she doesn't get the word out – she *has* to get those Instagram photos loaded. And not only that, every single one *has* to look more amazing than anything anyone else is posting. No pressure there then. Which is basically where I come in – I'm here to style the arse off Libby's Christmas, and to make her uploads look prettier than everyone else's.

A few years ago, Fliss would have been the obvious choice for this job. But she's up to her ears in sleepless nights and stroppy toddlers, and – she won't mind me sharing this – multi tasking just isn't a thing that's working for her. She's barely made it out of her pyjamas in three years. Which is why Libby turned to me.

When she marched into *Daniels* a month ago like a pocket-rocket begging me to help style her castle Christmas, waving her arms and tossing around words like 'sumptuous' and 'luxurious', I was off to Human Resources to beg for time off faster than you could say 'ramparts'.

Just to give you a picture, Fliss and Libby are both teensy, neat, and various shades of blonde, depending on the week. With my gangly frame I feel like the big friendly giant when I'm next to them. And it's worse still since I had a car accident this time last year and cut my face really badly. Since then I've had to grow my cute dark haired pixie cut into one of those straight-ended wavy bobs that's hell to maintain and isn't quite working, and then top the whole lot off with whatever hat works for the weather. It's not that I'm making light of the accident, because how could I when the man who was driving the car died in it, but the only way of coping I've found has been to throw myself into work. So for me the offer of working over Christmas felt like a life saver.

With twenty-four days still left to take before March, HR could hardly refuse me the time off. Libby promised me a wodge of cash too, but, I have to be honest, I'd have come without. Not being rude to my mum and dad, because I was so grateful for the way they came to the rescue last year. But I couldn't face another Christmas in Yorkshire with them and the grans all worrying about me. And with Libby giving me the chance to help add all the trimmings to her Cornish house party I'm counting on her making so many demands there won't be any time at all for me to think about how awful December was last year.

But the great thing is, if we're talking professional expertise, Christmas is my speciality area. In retail we're planning for next Christmas while the current one's still going on. Behind the scenes in *Daniels* it's Christmas most days of the year.

Libby, being the wheeler dealer she is, insisted on having a few extra days added onto the let at the start, which to be fair probably wasn't *that* difficult to do. We all know December's a slack time for holiday rentals, people are too busy with parties and preparations to go away. So I've come on a couple of days ahead of the rest of the party to be here for any deliveries.

As Merwyn and I make our way around the side of the castle, the moon is shining like a spotlight through the bare criss-crossed branches of the trees, and the crenellations at the top of the tower walls are pale against a black sky spattered with stars.

I'm actually looking for someone ... I glance at the paper ... called Bill. Not that I'm ageist, but aren't most castle caretakers as old and decrepit as the buildings themselves? I'm mentally preparing myself to fall over someone stooped, white haired and wrinkly at any moment. Or maybe I've been watching too many Disney films.

After a full day of driving I know Merwyn's enjoying the walk, and I know castles ramble, but I hadn't expected it to be quite so far between the front door and the back. The terraced house I grew up in had its front door on the side, and its back door round the corner only a few feet away. My dad used to joke that if he chose his spot carefully he could answer both doors at the same time. Although if this place boasts that it sleeps twenty-five in ten glorious bedrooms, they have to fit in somewhere.

As we make our way further, the moon is washing the lawns with pale grey light, and the shrubbery is casting long shadows around the edges – I don't think I've ever seen moon shadows before. And over the sound of Merwyn's snuffles and the buffeting of the wind I'm catching a few notes of music. It's funny how little you need to hear before you can pick out a tune. It takes about a second to know it's that song where they repeat 'Happy Christmas' in Spanish over and over again, and end with the words '*bottom of your h-e-a-r-t*'.

My ex, George, had it down as the most maddening Christmas song ever, and after five years with him I found myself thinking the same. As you do. It's certainly not the kind of song I'd expect anyone like Bill to listen to. He'd be way more likely to go for Frank Sinatra. Or Eartha Kitt singing *Santa Baby*. I only hope this Bill hasn't gone out after we've come so far. As we get closer to the end of the wall we're following the music gets louder and there are prickles of annoyance stinging the back of my neck.

And then we turn the corner, and as I take in the wide courtyard, its beautifully laid stone flags flooded with the kind of soft yet brilliant light that comes from expensive designer spots, my jaw sags. There are carved stone benches around the edge, hewn oak posts and pergolas, and in the centre of it all there's the biggest hot tub I've ever seen. And lounging in the corner behind the steam clouds, muscular arms outstretched along the tub sides, there's a guy. And even through the soft focus of the mist I can tell there isn't going to be an ancient wrinkle anywhere in sight.

Phwoar. On second glances make that *P-H-W-O-A-R*.

Thank Christmas those completely uncharacteristic thoughts didn't get as far as my mouth. It's just, even though I work in high end retail, I don't bump into beautiful, sexy, dark-eyed tousled-hair, stubble and cheekbones every day. More to the point, now it is laid *this* bare in front of me, my alarm bells couldn't be clanging any louder. It's great to look at raw power and beauty for a few seconds, in the way you'd enjoy watching a tiger from behind a barrier wall, a moat or two and a thick sheet of safety glass. But you totally wouldn't want to meet it head on in the wild.

He's shaking back his hair, rubbing the water out of his eyes, then his brows knit into a puzzled frown. 'Hi, can I help you?'

My mouth's still hanging open. 'I seriously doubt it, unless you can tell me where Bill is.'

As his frown softens his flinty eyes soften too. 'It must be your lucky day ... *I'm* Bill ...'

Then as his low laugh hits my ears and his eyes lock with mine my heart stops because this isn't just a random hot guy swishing about in the waves – this is one *I know*.

Oh crap.

I swallow hard and slam my mouth closed just in time to stop my lurching stomach from escaping to turn cartwheels across the stone pavers. The hair might be longer, the face more worn, and initially I was thrown because I've never seen him naked before. But of all the guys I could do with never meeting again ... *in the world* ... *ever* ... this is the one. If I'm honest it's a long story I hadn't ever expected to confront again ...

Chamonix, January 2013. My one and only time skiing with George, sharing a ski lodge with his friends and friends of friends. Or more accurately, me spending shedloads I could not afford, then doing everything *not* to ski. Riding the lifts, trying the hot chocolate in every cafe, but mostly tucked up by the log fire reading, while the rest of them did the kind of moves out on the slopes that made me question why they weren't all in the Olympic squad.

George and I were a few months into living together, he was just starting to break out with the kind of dick head behaviour he'd kept hidden up until then. And all of it given a worse twist when I took an early flight, knocked on the chalet door and it was opened by this hunk in socks called Will ... *the guy in the hot tub here ... eeeeeek* ... who ... well ... you know those moments when your insides totally leave your body because you fancy someone so much?

We had this delicious time making the fire together before the rest of the party arrived. However cosy and picturesque you think checked wool sofas, sheepskin covered floors and pine clad walls with a view of distant snow covered mountains could be, times it by a hundred and then you'll get the idea of how blissful it was.

But I was with George, and I hate people who cheat. So obviously I had to hide what was simply a very bad case of totally misplaced attraction. But my body had other ideas. The whole ten days I kept catching myself arching my back, maxing out my 'open and available' body language when I didn't mean anything of the kind. Truly, those super-thin Merino wool base layers did nothing to hide my horribly big boobs, I was practically pushing my nipples into this poor guy Will's face non-stop.

And then there was the laughing. That was the other unfortunate thing – we got jokes no one else did and cracked each other up the whole time. I put the whole thing down to that glass of free fizz I had on the plane that got me off on the wrong foot.

But now, looking at him in the hot tub all these years later, this guy Will has moved on from the past so far he's actually changed his name to Bill. It wasn't as if we knew each other well, we were simply accidental chalet mates for a really short time. Considering I look so very different – and so much worse – with my new hairstyle and what it's hiding, the fact there was so much drinking he'll most probably have the same alcoholic amnesia I do, and seeing that I didn't even figure on his radar in the first place – I'm guessing he'll have no idea who I am at all today.

All I have to do is stop my heart from clattering louder than skis being banged together and we'll be back to how we were – me accidentally letting out a misplaced gasp at some tanned pecs through the steam. And then we'll move on.

I clear my throat, desperately try to reconnect with my dignity so I can take this back to a more businesslike place. 'So let me introduce myself properly, Bill, I'm ...'

The crinkles at the corners of Bill's eyes in the tub are unnervingly familiar as he raises his hand and cuts me off. 'Hold it there, you don't need to tell me, there can only ever be one Ivy Starforth.' His lips twist. 'You *do* remember me, right? I'm Will Markham, we met in Chamonix ...'

I take a moment to let my stomach hit the floor and bounce back into place again. Then I try to minimise the damage. 'Yes, but you're the one who's being confusing here – I once knew a dry, much more dressed, banker called Will. And now I'm faced with a very damp Bill outside a castle – what's that about?'

'People called me that when I moved to Cornwall.' He gives a sniff. 'And is your husband with you too?'

I'm struggling to keep up here. 'Excuse me?' If he hadn't called me by my *actual* name I'd think he'd got the wrong person.

He's frowning. 'You *do* have one?'

It's a relief we're so far away from reality. However much he once tied my libido up in knots all those years ago, we're talking financiers here. This one's so superior he assumes he knows my marital status better than I do. I hope Merwyn's taking this in so I can check back with him later, because I'm struggling to believe it's happening.

'Last time I checked, I didn't have a husband – not as far as I know.'

'When was that?'

'Five seconds ago.'

One eyebrow shoots up. 'Well, how good is that? Huge congratulations, Ivy Starforth, on *not* being married.'

I'm momentarily putting aside how surreal this is. He seemed so convinced about my husband. As for me, I'm not proud of that afternoon we spent alone at the chalet. In fact I've managed to lock it away in the filing cabinet in my memory bank that's got a huge notice on telling me never to open it again. It's not that anything awful happened, because it didn't. At least not in real life, anyway. It might have in my head occasionally afterwards – maybe a few thousand times – simply because ever after that holiday, whenever the going got tough it was useful to use him as my go-to, cardboard cut-out, idealised fantasy man. But that's the whole point about out-of-reach dreams – they're what you use to get you through, you have them safe in the knowledge that they aren't real and never will be. You certainly never expect to be embarrassed by barrelling into them head on in out of the way Cornwall, for goodness sake.

But there we were in Chamonix. George got some last minute session work and had to rebook his flight. Will had turned up early too while everyone else was working all the way to the end of Friday. Which left him and I chatting as we waited for the others to arrive. That's all we did. But somehow he was so laid back and all over nice, not to mention the hot part, it left me wishing like hell that this could be the guy I was with rather than the one who was currently winging his way through the air on the FlyBe jet for the winter holiday of a lifetime he'd persuaded me we couldn't miss out on. Which, as was usual with George, I ended up not enjoying very much in the end.

Getting trapped in a few hours of domestic fantasy never happened to me before or since. I've always blamed it on the holiday thrill and too much mulled wine. We certainly haven't clicked again here. Quite the opposite. My immediate subliminal reaction was to pick up on how up himself Will was, and that was when he was practically submerged. Which just goes to show how unreliable first impressions from seven years ago can be. And how a few timber plank walls and the warmth from burning logs can totally blur your judgement. And leave you feeling guilty for the treachery for years after, because, truly, I'm not that kind of person usually. I rarely fancy anyone. I also pride myself on being loyal and faithful and steadfast and honest, which is why I was so appalled and ashamed of myself for that afternoon.

Bill's closing his eyes even more now and his voice has softened. 'It's amazing to see you again, Ivy, why did you wait so long to get back in touch?'

I manage to get over the liquid brown warmth of his gaze enough to get the words out. 'I'm not here on a social call, Will – I mean Bill – or whoever you are.' Hopefully that's shown him how little I've thought about him since 2013. Truly, Fliss doesn't even know about him, and I tell her all my secrets. If he or anyone else ever found out the truth I'd die of shame. 'This is a total coincidence, one of those "small world" moments ...' I'm dying at how trite I'm sounding '... I'm here for this year's Christmas rental.'

His eyebrows shoot up. 'Shit. Right. *Really?* Surely you can't be, you're a day early!'

He's just got that air that suggests no one ever contradicts him so I force myself to stand my ground. 'It was Mrs Johnstone-Cody who made the booking. Just so you know, she never makes mistakes, we are due today.' Just saying. After three hundred and fifty-odd miles, I'd rather not come back tomorrow. Beautiful people stuff up too sometimes, and he has to be the one who's wrong here.

A perplexed look crosses his face, then it's gone. 'Well, whatever day it is, it's great to see you, Ivy.' That's the thing with super-attractive people like this – they mess up – then they move on seamlessly like nothing happened. His hand comes towards me, and I stare at it in horror for a second, then step close enough to brush the end of one dripping finger.

'Now you're here, how about coming in for a dip?'

I can't believe what I'm hearing. Castles, hot tubs, delicious guys coming out with the most ridiculous suggestions? It's like I dropped into an episode of *Made in Chelsea*. 'Absolutely not. Thanks all the same.' I'm up for fun, but even I draw the line at jumping into a bath with someone I'd once have had difficulty keeping my hands off. Especially when he's still hot as ...

'Your loss, it's wonderfully warm, the bubbles are just starting to come through.' As he dips down and re-emerges his muscular shoulders are tanned and gleaming under the lights, and his gaze is soft yet intense. And from the one slightly closed eye, I know he's laughing at me.

I'm from the north, my mum and dad had tiny horizons, I didn't hit the bright lights of London until I was in my twenties, so I'm used to cracking people up with my lack of social polish and the way I say 'bugger' not 'bogger'. Come to think of it, me being a hilarious northerner was probably why there was all that laughing in Chamonix. If posh people taking the piss is what I've come to expect, it doesn't mean I like it. If Bill's like the rest of George's extended social circle he'll be one of those entitled guys who were weaned on champagne and assume the rest of the world was too. The kind who don't even know what a back door is, let alone how to use one. Those cheekbones are the giveaway. That accent. I know it's wrong to judge, worse still to write people off without knowing them properly, but after the way George walked out on me, any guy with tuned-up vowels can't be trusted.

'I'll take your word for that.' It takes me a second to change the subject. 'So what's with the music?'

'*Feliz Navidad*? It's so much less obvious than your usual Christmas tunes.' Even though he's pulling a face, he still looks like perfection on a stick. 'On repeat in an attempt to get in the festive mood.'

That's one way of looking at it. George saw continuous repetition as lazy, and a total lack of musical creativity. But there you go, it wouldn't work if we all liked the same. George was entitled once, but by the time he hit thirty he'd fallen on hard times, which was where I came in handy. As a temporary interim. A stepping stone. A door mat to use on his way to better places. If I needed a lesson that normal people need to stay away from rich people, George was it. The minute he got his break he left me for someone more suited to his new, moneyed life. And things went seriously downhill after George. So far down they ended in the accident.

Nowadays I put all my energy into riding a better wave, and believe me, that doesn't include guys. Especially ones who talk like they've swallowed a plum and luxuriate in bubble baths in Cornish castles when they know damned well they should be leaping out of the water and sorting their guests out.

But before you think I've written off the whole south of England, I haven't at all. Meeting Fliss and being welcomed into her very southern family gently opened my closed northern eyes in the best possible way and I'll always be grateful for that. Fliss wasn't only my bestie and my party partner and next-room neighbour at uni. She was also my social translator. She held my hand as I discovered the scary world of student London and later hauled me up into my job at *Daniels*.

And thinking of nicer things, one mention of the 'f' for 'festive' word, and I'm glancing up, appraising the pergola. Okay, I put my hands up, I can't help it, it's my job. However slick and polished the outdoor space is already, in my head I'm already up the stepladders, festooning it with fairy lights. Pink and turquoise strands hanging from the wooden poles, moving in the breeze. They would work amazingly.

'You haven't got around to the decorations out here yet?' I'm stating the obvious, expecting him to say it's his last job, and maybe to share what he's planning.

'Decorations?'

I'm taking in his blank stare when two things hit me.

First, even though Merwyn is standing next to me, staring at Bill even harder than I am, I'm not actually holding his lead any more. *How did that happen?* And second, since I moved in and braved the crackling static of that finger touch, my (early Christmas present to myself) Russell and Bromley Chelsea boots (off eBay) have been kicking up against a towel. Except now I'm looking more closely it's not just a towel. Dropped across the top, there's also a pair of cotton boxers.

'Ok-a-a-a-y.' My voice has gone all screechy and as the words *naked hot entitled hot man of my personal dreams in a hot tub* zip through my brain I'm suddenly sweating inside my fair isle. As I look at the boxers, then look at Bill, Merwyn is following my gaze. And over the tub edge I can see Bill doing the same. There are times when the only way forward is to ignore the roaring of blood pounding through your ears and simply come out and say it like it is. So I take a deep breath and press 'go'. 'You're not actually wearing any clothes in there are you, Bill?'

Bill's grin is unrepentant. No surprise there then. 'Good call, Ivy, I am totally in the buff here, thanks for getting that one out into the open.' On the down side, him coming clean is even more disarming than plain old arrogant. 'In my defence, I have to say, whatever Mrs Johnstone-Cody understood, *I* wasn't expecting guests until tomorrow.'

I sniff. 'I'll take your word for that too.' It's good that he's switched back to super-pleased with himself.

'Great.' Nice recovery there from Bill, we both know it isn't at all. 'So if you'd throw me the towel and my – ahem – shorts, we can fast-forward to your welcome tour.'

It's a relief we finally got as far as him mentioning showing me round. 'Lovely, I'll do that now.'

Merwyn's giving me one of his 'I don't believe a word and neither should you' looks, but I'm not going to tell him off for cheek because Merwyn and I need to present a united front here. I'm in enough shit with my misplaced, completely inappropriate and bloody alarming flutters without starting an argument with the dog.

As I dip down towards the towel I'm mentally assessing the size and how much mannequin coverage it would offer if it were on a display in a *Daniels* department store window. Transposed to a Cornish courtyard, and the body I've been undressing in my head for years, the answer is, *nowhere near enough*. And then there are the – ahem – shorts. I've had plenty of practice after years of picking up George's underwear. But as my hand reaches out towards the shorts the pale blue checks look as expensive as Bill does, and the thought they actually belong to him makes me freeze for long enough to mouth a silent O-M-G in my head.

And how I'll come to regret that OMG. One moment of hesitation on my way down, and Merwyn picks up on it. He sees the minute space in time as a challenge, and goes for it. One dart, he's grabbed the shorts, a swift turn and he's off across the courtyard. Two more delighted leaps, then he's shaking the life out of the boxers, haring off into the shadows with the towel and dog lead trailing behind him.

I run as far as the courtyard corner and see him disappearing into the shrubbery, but it's no use going further because he thinks it's a game. The more I chase the faster Merwyn will go.

'Well, I did not see that one coming.' As Bill shakes his head, there's no clue if he's being ironic or straight. From my experience it takes more than a pair of lost boxers to throw these hard-boiled guys off kilter even if the boxers are disappearing at a hundred miles an hour into the night.

'If you'd had a decent sized bath sheet it would have been too heavy for him to do that.' Just saying. So he knows for the future. But I can't blame this on anyone other than me. Merwyn's my dog, I have to take full responsibility here. Well, he's not *actually* mine, but there's no time to go into that now. 'Give him a minute, he'll be back.' Or at least that's what I'm banking on. What Merwyn hates most is being ignored, hopefully he'll reappear any second to see why I'm not joining in the fun.

Bill's got one eyebrow raised. 'Time flies when you're in a hot tub, you could come in for a dip while we're waiting?' This is exactly what I meant by hard boiled – totally unflappable, ignoring the concerns of the entire rest of the world, getting straight back to his own hedonistic priorities.

'For the second and last time, I'm *NOT* coming in. Thanks all the same.'

'Message received, loud and clear. In which case I'll use the time to suggest you settle into a room in this part of the house tonight, then I'll show you around the rest in the morning.'

'Fine.' There's no point in arguing. He's also called it a house not a castle, but I'll let that go for now. It's one more sign he's used to a place the size of Downton Abbey.

'There's food if you're hungry, wine if you want to unwind, or if you want to get completely wiped out there are vats of gin.'

Seriously, as if the signs weren't all there already, you can't trust anyone who offers you that lot. 'For a handyman you're really going the extra mile.'

He's looking at me through narrowed eyes. 'Let's hope you still feel that way in the New Year when you're writing your review.'

'Actually, I've got supper in the car.' It may take a couple of days to stop my insides feeling like hot syrup sponge every time he looks at me. Hopefully by the time everyone else arrives at the weekend, I'll have had so much practice I'll be entirely impervious to his charms.

'I'm pleased to hear it.'

When was I ever this confused about someone being serious or joking around? 'You do have a microwave?' My mouth's watering at the thought of my mac and cheese ready meal, I'm so pleased I bought the big size.

'That wouldn't be very authentic.' The uncertain frown is back, making furrows on Bill's forehead.

I can't stay silent about this. 'Said the man in the twenty-first century hot tub.'

'Don't worry, Ivy-star, I'm sure the Aga will do the same job.'

Ivy-star is Fliss's nickname for me which came from the first boss we had at *Daniels* who used to bark, 'Ivy Starforth, what a *STAR!*' every time I had a good idea. I'm flinching that Bill's remembered George calling me it enough to pull it out here seven years on. I'm still standing mentally scratching my rather bemused head, desperately trying to pull my wobbly bits together when I hear the sound of paws galloping on gravel.

'Merwyn!' I brace myself to swoop him into a 'welcome back' body slam. Somehow as I'm squatting trying to dodge the licks we end up on the floor, but at least I've got him by the collar now. As I scramble back to standing I can't help feeling proud to be proved right. 'See, I told you he'd be back.'

'Covered in mud, without my shorts or my towel, I might add.' Bill's shaking his head. 'Do you know how much Calvin Kleins cost? I can't afford to let dogs bury them.'

'Down to the last penny as it happens. I also know Calvin Klein doesn't do boxers in that particular check. Never has, as far as I can remember.' There are advantages to knowing your way around the entire men's underwear department inside out. Strictly business of course. As for Merwyn, his cute brown furry face is caked in dirt clumps all the way from his nose to his ears. His paws and legs too. He has to have been digging. I've never actually seen him this filthy, but I'm not going to play it up. So for once he'll have to go without a telling off. 'Someone's going to need a bath.'

Bill gives a grunt. 'Let's hope he's less water averse than you.'

It's been a very long day. I'm still reeling at the shock of finding Bill/Will here and there's a limit to how much a woman can take. To be honest, I wasn't completely certain Merwyn *was* going to come back. But now he has, all I want to do is clean him up then collapse into a comfy chair. Preferably at the opposite end of the castle to anyone called Bill. As blasts from the past go, this is the equivalent of that Icelandic volcano that erupted and brought worldwide air travel to a standstill due to the dust in the atmosphere. The aftershocks from this could go on for weeks.

'Isn't it time we were going inside?' I'm screwing my eyes closed, slipping off my jacket and thrusting it in Bill's direction, because someone has to move this on here. It might as well be me. 'Just get out of that tub and wrap up anything that matters in my coat. Tell me when you're covered, and I'll follow you in.'

I swear I did not foresee the view of rippling butt cheeks that offer was going to result in. Or how disturbing I'd find it to see my furry navy blue cuffs bumping off his calves as he ran. Or think about the water marks on the lining. But sometimes you have to take short cuts and live with the consequences.

We're just coming up to a broad planked, disarmingly normal-size back door when Bill reaches up to a little niche in the stone, and the music stops. But instead of the expected silence of the middle-of-nowhere in the countryside, there's a peculiar sound – a kind of weird repeating rumble, like the wind in a storm, only louder.

'Oh my, what the hell is that noise?'

Bill gives me a hard stare that's very uncomfortable. 'That's the waves crashing up the beach, it's what you get if you stay in a castle by the sea.' And then he laughs, which is somehow even worse. 'Welcome to Cornwall, Ivy Starforth, I hope you won't be grumbling about it because that's one noise we can't turn off.'

And when I hear that low rumbling laugh, and see the light dancing in those dark brown eyes, I have the strangest feeling we might *all* be in big trouble here.

Even Libby.

Thursday

12th December

2.

Merry and (not so) Bright

The last thing I do after I've bathed Merwyn and before my phone battery dies is to text Fliss:

Arrived safely, currently tucked up in castle listening to sound of sea, more soon xx

It's short, but it feels like the best cover-all until it's light enough to check out both the details and the bigger picture. Seeing as we share all our worst moments she'll be desperate to hear about every last caretaker horror too, although I'll be missing out the full implications of where he fits in. But I'll save all that until I've got a better idea of what's here. Then I go up to my teensy room by an even tinier kitchen staircase and when I crawl into bed I barely notice that it's less fortress, more seventies pine lodge. Actually I do, because that's what I'm like, but by that time I've given up giving a damn, and anyway this is only a temporary bed in the caretaker's flat. I admit that I fall asleep wondering about how Will slash Bill came to be here. When I wake up ten comfy hours later I'm actually thinking even if I am offered a princess and pea four poster mattress stack later, I'd be mad to give up on the memory foam.

By the time Merwyn and I have done a morning circuit of the castle grounds, the kettle's boiled on the Aga, and soon after I've filled up my insulated reusable coffee mug. A couple of cranberry and macadamia nut breakfast bars later, I've come round enough to perch on a stool at the kitchen bar without falling off. I'm just checking my phone when Bill walks in.

'Morning, Ivy, how are you today?' He's taller and all-over bigger than I remember, with his shoulders bursting out of his Barbour jacket and his denims tight across his thighs. 'You do know you're wearing your hat inside?'

I've had ten hours to bolster my defences, so when I'm faced with the overall hunk effect this morning I'm ready to take refuge in flustered grumbles. But my heart sinks that this is where he's landed.

The hat ... Well ... that ... I've been wearing seasonal variations ever since I cut my face, even at work. My hair's grown to a rather ragged side parted bob, but I still need a hat to keep my swept over fringe in place and hide the long jagged red scar that curves from the middle of my forehead and down to the start of my right ear underneath my hair. I try not to dwell on it or tell people about how it happened. But as I close my eyes for a fraction of a second to blink away the pictures whirring through my brain, my head starts to spin so fast I have to cling onto the work surface to steady myself. A year on, I've pretty much got the flashbacks under control. But when they happen, like they are now, there's nothing I can do but go with it.

Suddenly I'm in the car again, careering backwards through the darkness as we leave the road and start to roll. By hanging onto the granite of the island unit really hard and locking my neck I might be able to stop the images flashing through my brain before the bit where it feels like we're being spun in a washing machine ... before the part where the tree branch crashes through the windscreen ... before the glass explodes and comes raining down like a storm of tiny diamonds. Before the bit where I'm reaching out in the blackness, finding the warmth of Michael's shoulder rammed against the steering wheel. Asking him if he's okay. Racking my brain as to how to get someone I've only known for an evening to stop sleeping and talk to me. How I can't move, all I can do is count the tracks, because even after the car has been tumbled over and over the early hours radio is somehow still playing. And I keep on asking him to wake up, but he never replies. Because what I don't know yet is that he's never going to talk or wake up again. Because his neck's broken and he's already dead.

'Ivy, are you okay?' Bill's voice cuts through the darkness in my head. 'I was asking about your hat. You *do* know you've forgotten to take it off?'

I ignore the bit about the hat, drag myself back to the kitchen, and go with the rest. '*Message failed to send.*' I remember now, that's what I was about to say. 'It's not the best start to the morning, but I'm sure I'll get over it.'

As for the accident, one lift back from an early Christmas party wasn't ever meant to go so wrong. A whole year on, I still can't rationalise that I walked away and Michael died. The only way I can attempt to live is by not thinking about it every waking minute. And the best way I've found to do that is by working non-stop and trying my best to do things for other people, not myself. If I put all my effort into making

Christmas for Fliss and Libby and their families wonderful, for a few days it'll let me blank out the terrible bleakness of the mistakes I made that night.

Bill blows out his cheeks. 'Messages failing is a Cornish thing. Don't worry, by the time you go home, you'll be used to it.'

'You're saying there's *no signal?*' I can't believe what I'm hearing, although it's less of a surprise that he's shrugging off someone else's problem. It's a good thing I skipped the niceties, there's no time to lose on this. It's also a relief to have wrenched myself out of my own personal abyss of blackness and get back to the mundanities of other people's everyday concerns.

'It's more that the signal comes and goes, you have to move to find the hot spots. The top of the south tower's usually your best bet.' Again, he's a lot less concerned than he should be.

I let out a snort but I'm not letting him off the hook because I'm feeling really indignant on everyone else's behalf. 'I can see why you had peak-time availability. How do you cope living here?'

He pulls one of those perfect-on-a-stick faces. 'I find the views and the size of the kitchen more than make up for the lack of communication technology.'

Which reminds me, I've been so tied up with the unimportant distractions, I missed out saying how wonderful it was to peep out of my bedroom window when I woke up and see the lawns behind the castle running straight out onto a long sandy beach with the sun glinting off the pale blue water beyond. Through the wide kitchen doors there's a similar vista, out onto the wide sweep of the bay, and a distant cluster of buildings which must be where I saw the lights from my room last night.

I take the long way round the kitchen island to avoid passing him, and end up where I've got a better view through the kitchen doors. 'Is that the nearest town along there, then?'

As Bill's lips twitch into a smile, for some ridiculous reason I'm reminded of that fragrance ad where the guy walks through and the women all fall down and have orgasms. Which isn't the best thought to end on when he's opening his mouth to say something.

'St Aidan village is just around the bay, and to answer every Londoner's first questions, it's fifteen minutes' walk along the beach, and it has all the bars, fish and chips and surf shops most people need, complete with a double dose of picturesque.'

I ignore the jibe about 'most people' and grin down at Merwyn who's leaning against the legs of my stool. 'There you go, that's a date for later this afternoon.' Merwyn's got my back here.

As for Bill's kitchen, it might be short of a microwave, but it's got two four slice Dualit toasters, a massive Aga, an island unit and a long table as well as some chunky distressed leather sofas. Not forgetting a high slanty ceiling and lashings of characterful beams. Bill's right – if I were a handyman and this was where I lived, even if my second home was Downton Abbey, I would *not* be giving my notice. At the same time, if I imagined his house – if I'm honest, I have done every now and again – it wasn't ever like this. There's just something very impersonal about what's here. As I scan the walls and shelves for clues about his life there's *nothing* to land on other than the fact he must like toast.

'So if you're ready, I could show you around now?' Now

he's less hidden behind steam clouds I can see his stubble shadow is bordering on a beard, and his brown hair is just as wavy and crumpled as it was last night. When his gaze locks with mine, I'm suddenly so hot I'm wishing I'd saved my polar bear white fluffy polo neck for later.

'Great idea, I thought you'd never ask.' I ease myself down to follow him, and as I gather up Merwyn, his lead and our coats and pull down my hat I glance at my phone and see it's already past ten. 'It's lovely to find loaded people in the country really do start work half way through the morning.'

Bill shakes his head then strides out through the hallway and towards the back door. 'Speak for yourself, some of us have been up since five bottling and dispatching gin.'

'Yeah right, and I'm a Cornish man.' Apart from the bullshit, I have to put him right here. 'Sorry to challenge your view of stereotypes, but not everyone in London is totally obsessed with designer gin.' When our *Daniels*' stylist team voted four years running to have our winter party at an après ski venue, gin palaces weren't even in the running. We can all personally vouch for the awfulness of a gluwein hangover, but we still go back again and again simply because the memory of drinking it is so warm and cosy.

Bill's swinging a bunch of keys in his hand and as we go through the hot tub courtyard and around the side of the castle he's talking over his shoulder. 'Most people prefer to go in through the front entrance for maximum effect, I take it you won't mind conforming to *that* stereotype?'

I'd sort out an equally snarky response. But by the time I catch him up the gigantic front door is already swinging open.

'Come in, and welcome.' Lucky for both of us, he's slipped into 'castle guide' mode. 'Guests usually leave the main door unlocked, and use the key code on the inner door of the porch.'

As he holds the doors open for me I do a big jump to get past him as fast as I can and move through into a huge hallway with a bumpy stone floor and a staircase so huge and chunky that it appears to be hewn from entire trees. For a fleeting moment I'm surprised the giant Christmas tree isn't here yet, but then we are a day earlier than he expected so I move on to other thoughts. Like how I can't begin to imagine the size of the chandeliers with a space this enormous. But when I look up to check them out, instead of a cascade of glistening crystal there's a cluster of large bare hanging light bulbs with glowing yellow filaments, and a tangle of wires looping around above them.

'I see the light fittings are on-trend rather than traditional.' Despite half choking with the shock of it being so different from the image in my head I'm trying to see them through Libby's eyes – and failing. It's all so much rougher than I was expecting – somehow I hadn't expected the inside walls to be the same stone as the outside ones.

Bill nods. 'The electricians went for low impact, low energy solutions throughout.'

At least the shock of what's here – or what isn't – is taking my mind off the shadows of his jawline and the women in the perfume ad. Whatever it was I reacted to in Chamonix, he hasn't lost it, more's the pity. It doesn't feel like the right moment to ask where the sumptuous wallpaper is. Even plaster on the walls would have been good. I'm desperately crossing my fingers for a more 'cosy' feel in the next room.

'Come through and see the chill out areas ...'

As I look at the back of Bill's Barbour there's a niggle of doubt at how wrong that sounds so I'm trying desperately to think back to the pictures Libby sent me. For now I can't remember any more than the gorgeous outside shots, then close ups of things like cushions and pillow tassels, candlesticks and corners of picture frames. Then Bill steps out of the way and reveals acres more stone flags and rocky walls, and a space like a gallery with some angular leather sofas, a couple of coffee tables, a square alcove off and, if welded steel is your thing, a rather beautiful side console unit. And it's so pared back, there's still no clues at all about the guy himself.

He leads the way and I follow him through to more gallery space. Then he turns and says, 'Okay, that's your lot, if we go on up to the first floor, I'll show you the bedrooms.'

Looking around the bedrooms with a 'perfume ad of the year' model and the body I've personally hijacked to inhabit my secret dreams all these years was the bit I was expecting to feel really wobbly about. Frankly, I was hoping to put it off for longer, but there's a more immediate worry. 'But what about the rest of the reception rooms?'

He smiles. 'People are always fooled, the usable space inside castles isn't that big. At least it means we can crank up the heating and beat the draughts.'

That glimmer of good news about the inside temperatures hasn't stopped my heart plummeting. 'What?'

'Cockle Shell Castle was built as a folly. It's impressive from the outside but it's not meant for housing battalions.'

Or large house parties from London, even? 'Just show me what there is.' As for where the hell the library and the dining room are, I can only hope they're upstairs too.

When he opens the doors to four first floor bedrooms, it's less of a shock to find the same emptiness as down below – simple beds, shower rooms and not much else. Calling it stylish would be going too far, but somehow I'm past making comments. By the time we're coming down from a higher floor the same as the first, but with lower ceilings, I'm getting my brain into gear. The number of bedrooms is right if I add in the ones on my staircase, but the rest couldn't be more wrong. Libby was hoping for a house stuffed with two weeks' worth of opulent photo opportunities. More importantly, so was I. With what there is here, even adding in a present mountain, once I've done the stone wall and window photos we'll be just about done.

Worse, now Bill's staring at me. 'You're very quiet?' It's a question not a statement.

To be honest I'm shocked he's noticed. 'It's not very festive for a Christmas let.' I try again. 'It's very basic and bare.'

'Right.'

'I mean, you are aware how much she's paying for this?' It was a well-leaked secret, so everybody else does. I know Libby thought it was a steal, but to ordinary mortals like Fliss and me it was an eye-wateringly massive amount. When Fliss stretched for her mortgage she didn't factor in two babies, and I'm equally broke. Signing an extended lease in an area a lot further upmarket than my means was all about pleasing George. And more fool me for doing that.

Bill's coming over super-arrogant now which is a sure sign he's on the defensive. 'Obviously I know the price, I took the booking.'

I'm going to have to spell it out. 'Well, minimalism used to be great, but in London we came out the other side of the "empty" tunnel and maximalism rules now. For this kind of money we expected spaces rammed with gorgeous stuff.'

'Really.' This time it's a statement, not a question. 'Well, wherever *you* are on your style cycle, what *we* offer is accommodation for stag celebrations, and they're usually delighted with what's here – no neighbours to annoy, plenty of space to party, very little to break. And then there's the gin too. Wherever *you* stand on gin, the stags never turn it down. The castle suits them down to the ground. Which to be fair is where most of them end up.'

I ignore that he's banging on about gin again, and brace myself to break the news. 'We booked for a Christmas house party in palatial surroundings, decorated to the hilt with festive bling.' Whatever he says, I know that because I've seen the place settings in pictures.

He lets out a breath. 'Christmas crackers. Someone called Nathan messaged, there was no specific request for decorations at the time of booking.'

It can't go without comment. 'So you just thought you'd take the frankly *humungous* amount of money and run?'

'Not entirely.' From the way he's shuffling from foot to foot, I've hit a nerve.

One thing's still puzzling me. 'I mean, where the hell's the wallpaper?' It was definitely on the pictures Libby put up on our secret Pinterest page, I've been flicking through them non stop since they arrived. Of course! How could I be so dense? I get out my phone to check them, then groan as I realise my mistake. 'Where's this signal hot spot you were talking about? And I need the internet password, please?'

'You don't get it do you, Ivy?'

I ignore the way my tummy flips as he turns to me, because I'm boiling inside on Libby's behalf. 'Get what?'

If Bill wasn't so unconcerned, I'd swear that was an exasperated head shake. 'The whole castle is an internet-free zone, that's one of its biggest selling points.'

Holy crap. 'There's no wifi *ANYWHERE?*'

'Guests love the freedom an enforced break gives them. With walls this thick wifi wouldn't be practical anyway.'

I'm trying to get my head around this. 'There must have been a mix up, there can't be any other Cockle Shell Castles, can there?'

Bill's eyes are flinty. 'I thought you said Mrs Johnstone-Cody didn't make errors?'

'But if she had ...?'

He sighs. 'There's a rather bijou Cockle Shell Hideaway up the coast from Port Isaac. Decorated to the nines and then some. But they're such different places, you'd never confuse them.'

Not so you'd think. But I'm imagining Libby doing her two second check before she booked and leaping on the first gorgeous pictures she came across. If the words Cockle Shell and Cornwall were enough to confuse Google Images, what hope did Libby have? She'd be dizzy with the coup she was pulling off, and probably doing ten other jobs at the same time too. Maybe if she'd been multi-tasking less she'd have jumped to less wrong conclusions.

'Well, we're here now. This is the one *Mrs* Nathan Johnstone-Cody booked.' The hot tub's swanky. And the outside's spectacular, even if the inside isn't, so I might as well think positive thoughts. Christmas dinner out on the front lawn might work. At least that way even if the turkey was cold we'd still get some awesome shots against the castle facade. Which reminds me ...

'We haven't seen the kitchen yet?' I round on Bill expectantly, and Merwyn does too. For a small dog he's got a remarkably large vocabulary. Admittedly it's mostly food based.

'We *have* seen the kitchen.' Bill's face creases into a two second laugh. And then when I don't join in his smile fades to puzzlement again.

I know he's wrong on this one. 'We definitely haven't.'

His face splits into a grin as he tries again. 'Where do you think you ate breakfast?'

Oh my days. For all the reasons. 'But that can't be the kitchen, you said that was *your* kitchen. Where's the *proper* kitchen?'

He's staring at me now. 'No, there's definitely only the one kitchen. Stags don't often eat in, but when they do, that's definitely the only place they do it.'

'You *are* joking me?'

He's staring at me like I'm the one who's being dense here. 'Think about it, I'd hardly have all those chairs around the table just for me would I?'

'B-b-b-but …' I'm so shocked, I'm having trouble breathing. I know this isn't completely my disaster. But I'm invested, I'm here. And way worse, I'm the one who's going to have to break this to Fliss and Libby. And then try to sort it out as best I can so twenty people can have at least some kind of happy Christmas. And then something worse hits me and lets me find my voice.

'So you'll be in the house too? Cooking your porridge, lounging on the sofas, plunging in the hot tub with not nearly enough clothes on. It isn't an exclusive let at all is it?'

He's blowing out his cheeks. 'It's more of an Airbnb model than a proper let. I like to be here to make sure things don't get out of hand. But mostly I'm here so when there are problems, I'm on the spot to sort them out.'

'*Problems …?*' The word hangs between us.

Bill shrugs. 'An ancient building is like an old car – full of character and idiosyncrasies, it might run for years with no trouble. On the other hand, it might not. And I'm here for those times.'

Oh fuck. 'So not only has Libby rented a castle that's only slightly more comfortable than a multi-storey car park, now it's a car park whose barrier is liable to stick!' Suddenly the lack of squishy furniture and Christmas deccies seems like the least of our difficulties.

Bill's looking impassive. 'If you need gin to bring you round, you only have to say the word?'

I know I shouldn't be losing it, and I don't usually, but just this once, I can't help it.

'I'll take fairy lights or pine trees or four posters or candles.

Even Santa on his effing sleigh would be *really* useful. But for the last and *FINAL* time, I don't want any of your *SODDING GIN*!' It comes out really loud, and it echoes round the castle walls and bounces back up off the floor, then resonates off the ceiling. Then I collect myself. And when my voice starts again, I'm back to talking quietly. 'Thanks all the same. Drinking myself under the table isn't going to help anyone here. Merwyn and I are going to go for a walk. Unless there's anything else you have to add, we'll talk to you more about this when we get back.'

For once Merwyn is a little star. One twitch on his lead and he's marching in step beside me out into the hall. I have no idea why I'm almost crying here. I take a moment to make sure my hat is pulled down past my eyebrows to avoid the horror of it blowing off, and I'm heaving open the front door when I hear Bill's cough.

'There is *one* last thing ...'

Surely there *can't* be. 'And ...?'

'We don't accept dogs.'

Of all the bombshells so far, for me personally this is the worst. I stop for long enough to roll my eyes at Merwyn and to mutter *You absolute effing arsehole* under my breath. Whatever I said about 'Made in sodding Chelsea' types, I wasn't expecting this. It was obviously too much to expect he'd make allowances for knowing me. But if he wants a fight, I'm happy to give him one.

Then we stride on outside, the salty sting of the wind hits my cheeks and the humungous castle door slams behind us. And a few seconds later we're out on the beach.

3.

Fa la la la la (or maybe not)

'Is everything okay?'

By the time we next see Bill, Merwyn and I have been blown all the way to St Aidan and all the way back again. Thanks to a well-timed snack rescue in St Aidan and the kind of planning you can only do when you're half running, half falling along the sand, we're now curled up back in the kitchen feeling more collected than before. So instead of yelling *THERE'S NO FURNITURE OR COMFORT OR INTERNET OR DECCIES OR DOGS, HOW THE HELL CAN ANYTHING BE OKAY?* I just sniff and stay completely silent.

It was a bracing walk, with the wind smashing into our faces, so I have to admit it's way cosier watching the cobalt blue sea dissolving into wiggles of white foam rolling up the beach from the comfort of the sofa in my case, with a frothy hot chocolate. Or in Merwyn's case, from his Christmas Tree rug with the pompom edge, on the polished wood plank floor.

Bill's taken off his Barbour and is resting a denim-shirted

shoulder on the wall as he studies us. 'You seemed a little bit over-wrought before, that's all.'

Over-WROUGHT????!!! So like a guy to imply it's the woman who's being unreasonable when he's the one who's responsible for every aspect of the panic. I make my voice airy, because there's only going to be one winner here. 'St Aidan was pretty, thanks for the recommendation.'

Not that Bill can take any of the credit, but there were the cutest white painted cottages with grey slate roofs stacked up the hillside, narrow cobbled alleyways winding up between the buildings, postage-stamp sized views of the jewel-like sea, and brightly coloured boats bobbing in the harbour.

'It was very Christmassy too.' We even saw a pony and trap, driven by Santa and an elf, its bells jingling as it sped off around the bay. Every shop window was festooned with decorations, and there was a wedding shop with snowy lace dresses, trails of frosted ivy and the kind of twinkly ice-chip fairy lights that take your breath away. Not that I'll ever be needing a shop like that myself, but I couldn't help but sigh at the prettiness.

But Bill must know that there are outdoor Christmas trees every few yards around the harbour and all the way up into the town too. Despite his 'decoratively significant' two week let, for some reason he hasn't felt inclined to follow that festive lead.

He tilts his head on one side. 'So, did you call in anywhere?'

'We popped in the Hungry Shark, it's dog friendly, *and* it has free wifi.' I stare at him pointedly. 'Just saying. It *is* possible to find both only a mile down the beach.' I also discovered they do mince pie muffins to die for, and I had two, but given who he is and what he's not done, not to mention his 'don't give a damn' attitude, that's one tip I won't be passing on.

He nods. 'The hot apple punch there is good, you should try that next time.' His eyes go just a little bit darker as they narrow. 'I can't promise it tastes half as good as those vin chaud cocktails we drank in Chamonix, but I reckon they must have had magic mountain dust sprinkled in them.'

I don't even have to think hard to bring back the heady mix of warm cinnamon, Cointreau and mandarin, but I'd never tell him that. I'd also rather not let him know that I'd be a lot more comfortable if he wasn't dragging things up from so long ago. I mean, I thought women were the ones who nailed every detail of distant memories. It's quite a shock when a guy pulls one out. 'Probably all down to those rose tinted holiday ski goggles you were wearing.'

He lets out a low laugh. 'As I remember, you were wearing those too.'

'No, mine were definitely genuine, see it like it is, bog-standard Raybans.' Jeez, I need to move this on. But I'm not going to tell him I had two of the punches he mentioned, or who knows where he'll take that to.

I was trying to pluck up the courage to send Fliss the '*Houston, we have a problem*' text. I'd planned to ping that off the minute I had signal, then follow up a few minutes later with a call. If there had been one bit of bad news I could have done it. But after everything I discovered earlier this morning, it felt like too much of a disaster avalanche to drop onto Fliss when she has so much on her plate at the moment. Not only has she got two babies to deal with, but her husband Rob has been causing her to worry recently too.

Fliss and Rob are one of my favourite ever couples, simply because they seem so much more right together than on their own. From their meeting in a cupboard playing sardines at a party, past an Eiffel Tower proposal, their huge and wonderful farm meadow wedding, through to Rob delivering Oscar on his own in the bathroom when the hospital had sent Fliss home – they've been there for each other in the most incredible way. For my money, two people consistently appreciating each other is a very rare thing, but these two have that in spades. Or at least they have done for the eight years they've been together. When everyone else ran out of dizzy love a few months in, until very recently they were still solidly head over heels. Rob's so reliable, and laid back and supportive and always there, for a guy he seemed too good to be true. But nothing less than Fliss deserved.

Obviously George coming home ridiculously late, and being vague with his replies and turning up on Facebook at places I didn't even know he'd been to happened so often I'd have been more surprised if they hadn't. But Rob's always been so consistent, if his heart misses a beat Fliss notices. It's not that she's clingy or possessive because she's really not. It's more that they're so in tune she picks up on the smallest variation. And lately there have been a few instances. Singly I'd have sympathised and forgotten them. But there have been enough now to set my pre-alarm bells ringing. And even though there's nothing so extreme to make it okay to bring it up with him, there are certainly enough to send her round the bend with silent worry. And kick herself for not getting rid of all that baby weight she put on, and not getting dressed for three years and forgetting about sex. And doing all the things it's okay to do when someone really loves you enough they won't give a damn.

So, I hold my hands up – I chickened out and I've come back to reassess. Before I launch the bad news dump on Fliss, I want to see if I can improve the situation.

'So what were you saying about Merwyn earlier?'

It seems like a good place to begin. When life puts brick walls in front of you, you can turn around. Or you can knock them down and march on forwards. That's the kind of person I am. It's not always easy, but that's the outcome I'm trying for here. And Lord Arrogant would do well to note, my demolition hammer's at the ready. I might have been soft and naive back in the day in Chamonix, but there's been a lot of water under a lot of bridges since then.

I'm deliberately personalising this by calling Merwyn by name, so I give the dog in question a nudge with my toe and make sure he sees me get a doggy chocolate out of the pocket of my jeans. I stopped short of the emotional blackmail of dressing him up in his super-cute Santa suit which makes everyone melt, but when he sits up and blinks those soulful brown eyes of his and offers his paw, he's equally irresistible.

But Bill's not even looking our way. 'Well behaved dogs are by prior arrangement only, Merwyn isn't on the guest list.'

Damn. If I'd known this before I could have rung ahead or even tried to hide him, not that I'd have managed that. I might as well come clean. 'He was always invited, but he was only available to come at the last minute.'

Bill's blinking at us now. 'Keep going.'

I'm trying doubly hard here, not to be distracted by the views, and not to lose my cool no matter how annoying he is. 'He belongs to my neighbour, Tatiana, she's a model, I'm his stand-in mum when she works abroad.' I can see I'm not making any impression. 'He's a kind of a dog share.'

Bill's frowning. 'Still not getting it.'

'Tatiana got a last minute job and flew off to Prague, there was no one else to look after him so he's here with me.' I'm throwing in all the details to make him understand. 'Merwyn begged me ... he was wearing his Santa outfit ... I couldn't refuse.' That's how I know how effective it is.

Bill's raising his eyebrows. 'So this wasn't another of Mrs Johnstone-Cody's oversights?' He's so condescending.

'Merwyn's all down to me.' Merwyn's eyes are still popping, his gaze welded on the chocolate drop, but I hadn't counted on him drooling quite so much. I'm going to have to grovel fast before he dribbles all over the rather expensive-looking floor. 'I'm sorry, I assumed dogs would be welcome, they are in all the best on-trend places now.' Flattery's not working so I try again. 'It's a big castle, he's a little dog.' I almost add *so get over it*, but I manage to bite it back. Instead I get a tissue out of my pocket and try to mop the slobber puddle off the floor without Bill seeing.

Before I know it Bill's standing in front of us, handing over kitchen roll, studying me through narrowed eyes. It's actually more like an in depth examination than a look.

'So you lost the pixie haircut you had in Chamonix?'

Damn, I was hoping we'd get Merwyn the 'all clear' before

we moved on anywhere else. What I want to talk about is Merwyn's free pass to a castle Christmas, not sodding hair-styles.

Bill's stare is so piercing it's as if he's turning me inside out. 'It made you look like Audrey Hepburn in her elfin period. You wore your hat less then too.' He blinks at me. 'Come to think of it, you've had it on ever since you got here. Are you cold?'

However persistent he is, I'm not giving anything away. 'I'm fine, it's just with longer hair I get more bad hair days that need covering up.' Even if he caught me off guard there I'm so pleased with that reply I throw in a bit more. 'You know what it's like, all this damp sea air and salt, it's a nightmare for messy bobs.'

'You've still got a look of Audrey, even in that woolly hat with the huge furry pompom.'

I let out a hollow ironic laugh. 'That's a bonkers comparison. How did you even ski if you're *that* blind?' I can't say how nostalgic I am for my lovely cropped cut. Or how exasperated I get trying to make my longer hair behave. Now he's mentioned it, I'm tugging the sweep of my bob fringe down under my hat making sure it's covering the side of my face properly. 'You're right though, I only grew it about a year ago.'

The corners of his eyes crinkle. 'Both ways really suit you. To my mind dark brown hair is very underrated.' His face breaks into a grin as he reaches across and gives the strand below my ear a playful tug. 'And longer is good because it's easier to pull.'

'Stop that!' I lurch sideways.

'What?' His lips are twisting into a smile and his laugh is low. 'It was one little tweak, there's no need to jump all the way to St Aidan.'

That's what he thinks. From the shivers radiating across my scalp and zithering down my spine, St Aidan is probably five miles too close. And just because he says something nice doesn't make him any less arrogant. In fact in this case it only reinforces how great he is at telling lies. I mean, in all our years together George never mentioned Audrey once. Now I've got my shuddering under control I need to turn this back onto Bill.

'You've changed a bit yourself.'

He grins and rubs his fingers through his tousled curls. 'Waving goodbye to Will and his short-back and sides means a lot fewer trips to the barbers.' His eyes narrow. 'There's plenty to pull too, help yourself, any time.'

I shake my head at Merwyn to hide that I'm even tempted and let out a snort. 'That's one thing I definitely won't be doing.' And hopefully that's an end to it.

It's not as if we ever met up with any of the holiday people again after we got back home. I decided afterwards that George must have blagged his way into that chalet in the same way he did with everything else in life. But if Bill's intent on raking over the past, I might as well find out what happened to the super-attractive solicitor who spent the entire holiday throwing herself off her skis and into his path. 'Weren't you with a woman called ...'

He rolls his eyes as I hesitate. 'You're thinking of Gemma. We weren't actually an item, at the time I think I was probably trying my best to avoid her.'

'Omigod, yes, Gemma c-c-c –' For once I manage to stop before the worst comes out. If I'd given her her full 'cow-face' title Merwyn might be banished for ever. It's important to say, we didn't call her anything that rude lightly. Looking back, that was probably an offence to cows. But she pushed the other eleven of us to the limit by being the chalet-mate from hell – using all the hot water, always grabbing the best shower, hogging the steam room, stealing other people's cake from the fridge, drinking all the wine, taking the last milk, making nasty comments about everyone else's bums in ski pants, not to mention their thighs, party dresses, career progress and their sex toys.

I pick myself up enough to carry on. 'Gemma was the super-pretty one.' It's probably only human to remember the worst bits. Her faking a broken ankle on the slopes so he had to take her to hospital. Doing the same pretending to fall downstairs. 'Good job avoiding her, I'd say that was a narrow escape. She was hard work, hideous even.'

He pulls a face, then he goes on. 'Well, she got me in the end, we did go out eventually.'

I'm smiling. 'Haha, you nearly had me there.' And then I see he isn't laughing. 'Shit, you really did get together, didn't you?' I've no idea why there is a stab of jealousy shooting through my chest big enough to wind me. I mean, he was bound to be with someone, and that was never going to be me. But even though Gemma was super-attractive with a high flying job, I'm still reeling, simply because she seemed so calculating and blatant for someone as warm as he was. But as my mum and gran always say, if a woman sets her sights on a man and is determined enough, she can usually get him in the end.

'We actually got together shortly after Chamonix. Gemma wasn't too keen on life down here, but luckily we'd kept our London place, she's working back there for now.'

'So you're still in touch then?' Why the hell did I ask that? It's obvious they are.

He gives a hollow laugh. 'I hear from her most days, yes.'

Can you kick yourself and die inside all at the same time, because that's what I'm doing now. 'I'm soooo sorry.' It isn't nearly enough. 'Double sorry. Triple, even.' And I'm also waving goodbye to every chance of clemency Merwyn had.

Bill's still staring at me like I'm Exhibit A. 'It must be my turn for a question now. So if you and George aren't married you must be having the longest engagement ever? Or else you got married and divorced? I mean, he *was* your fiancé?'

I have to put him right on this. 'There was never a wedding or even an engagement.'

'Really?' He's screwing up his face like he doesn't believe me, then he blinks and carries on. 'My mistake then.' From the way his brows are knitting he's definitely confusing me with someone else. And people like him never admit they're wrong, so there's something very odd going on here. 'So where's George now?'

I should know the answer to this. 'New York ...'

'And you're flying out for New Year in Manhattan as soon as you're finished here?' Bill might not be giving much away himself, but he's certainly big on filling in my backstory.

I shake my head and rack my brain. '... or it could be Los Angeles.'

Bill gives a sniff. 'I take it from the confusion that it's not a long distance relationship?' From his smirk I'd say he has to be looking down on my lack of geographical knowledge too.

'No, George and I are ancient history.' At least this has taken the heat off my earlier blunder.

'Great.' For a second Bill's beaming at me, then he pulls a face. 'Except, it possibly isn't so great for you.'

'This is why it's good to talk about the future, not the past.' I'm hoping that'll put a stop to him banging on about ski lodges and let me get back to my current, most pressing problem. 'So is there any good reason dogs aren't allowed in the castle?' If I hadn't put both my size sevens (on a good day, sometimes I have to admit to an eight) in it so wholeheartedly, I might have been able to fall back on the shared history I'd rather forget. As it is, I'm fighting this at a disadvantage.

Bill blinks as if he's having to drag himself back to the moment. 'It's an insurance issue. It's a very ancient structure, we can't have dogs running wild.'

I think we both know that's bollocks. 'So you're happy for the place to be wrecked by party revellers, but a tiny dog, who wouldn't harm a fly, let alone a battlement, is banned?' My voice has gone high with disapproval. It's Bill's turn to look vaguely embarrassed, and I'm not going to waste that show of weakness.

'A castleful of shit-faced stags or a small dog? I know who I'd rather let to.' I'm about to pull out my trump card. 'Merwyn doesn't drink either. He's completely teetotal.'

Bill's wincing. 'Shit-faced. That reminds me, there's the poop issue too.'

Damn that I'm the one who brought this up. But we're covered here. 'Merwyn and I come armed with value-range sandwich bags, we scoop before the poop hits the ground. Every time. And we have baby wipes for squelchy days.'

Bill holds up his hand. 'Stop! That's way too much information if you're not a dog person.' And in a nutshell, that's the issue.

At least we know. Arrogant *and a dog detester*. How did I get him so wrong? As if he wasn't bad enough already, he just went down another lift shaft in my estimation. Merwyn's at his most adorable, waving his paw in the air, quivering with choccie-anticipation. But Bill's oblivious, so I'll have to try another route.

I have one last weapon so I clear my throat. 'Dogs aside, you've done a top-price Christmas let to someone expecting the full works. I wouldn't like to be in your shoes if Libby turns up and finds the castle is bare. You need my help here, so you might need to ease up on the anti-animal thing.'

Bill's squinting at me. 'Sorry?'

It never fails to surprise me when someone thinks that people who can afford to pay too much for things won't want value for money. From what I've seen working at *Daniels* the people with the biggest bank accounts are always the pickiest. What's more, they can also afford the redress when things go tits up. I'm just surprised that Bill, being one of 'them', doesn't know the score here.

I'm going to have to tell it to him like it is. 'I have to warn you, Mrs Johnstone-Cody's nothing like your no-fucks-given easy-to-please stags. When she sees the lack of space, luxury, privacy, decorations and authentic four-posters, she's not going to be a happy bunny.' I pause to let that sink in. 'That's definitely an optimistic view. Libby's larger than life, and she doesn't take prisoners. Realistically her explosion could blow the roof off – off the castle *and* whatever business you're running here.'

I have to admit most of what I know about Libby is what I've heard second hand from Fliss. She's a couple of years older than us so when we went to stay with Fliss's mum when we were at uni Libby was already off living her super-expansive and very charmed life. But the stories from Fliss about Libby's latest exploits have kept me shocked and impressed in equal measure for years.

Bill groans. 'If you're more than five feet tall, ancient four posters are a pain in the butt. And however hard Mrs JC stamps her feet, I can't make the castle any bigger – it's the size that it is, end of story.' The way he's rolling out the excuses with that sarcastic tone, he has no idea of the shit storm that's about to hit him.

'But there are things you *could* do?' If I'm pushing him, it's only for the sake of Merwyn's Christmas.

He's straight back at me. 'If Mrs JC seriously wants to lug in all her own wood *and* keep the very temperamental fires going, good luck to her with that one, I'm happy to make myself invisible.' His expression hardens. 'But if I'm banned from my own kitchen, she can forget borrowing my internet.'

My mouth's dropped open. 'But you said there wasn't any?'

'There isn't. Not in the public areas.'

Oh my. If I'm going to have to crawl on the floor here to beg, I'm going to have to do it. I *NEVER* use my womanly wiles to get what I want, I'd *NEVER NEVER NEVER* flirt with a guy like Will. I mean Bill. Except in my head, obviously. Or when I accidentally got all breathy and chesty in those Merino wool incidents, but I swear they weren't planned. But for something this important, this one time, I'm desperately channelling my inner Audrey.

'I need to upload pictures to Instagram as they happen, or no one will see the Johnstone-Cody Christmas. It's my responsibility to deliver fabulous photos and I'm getting paid for it. Without internet I might as well not be here, I'm totally stuffed. I know it's a first world problem, but I need this job.'

I can see him soften a little. Then he says. 'There's ten meg in my room.'

'Excuse me?' I have no idea what he's talking about.

'Ten megabytes per second – that's how fast the internet works. And there's signal in there too.'

'*WHAT?!!!*' When he invited me to share the hot tub it was a flat out *NO!* If he invited me into his bedroom to use the internet, however undressed he was, I'd have to shut my eyes tight and dive straight in even though I'd despise myself for it. But I draw the line at pleading stares. 'So, can I borrow it or not?' I'm aware my glare's coming out a bit fiercely. 'Occasionally? By arrangement? When you're not in there?' I'm going for broke here. 'I *am* saving your life here with my insider information, don't forget.'

He's shaking his head. 'Sure. Fine. But don't tell anyone else.'

I'm with him on that. 'Especially not the kids, or they'll be in there twenty-four seven.'

It was a throw away thought, but I'm delighted I said it, if only to enjoy the horror spreading across his face. 'There are *KIDS?*'

'Only nine of them.'

His voice rises to a shriek. 'But we let to adults, nothing about this castle is child-friendly.'

I shrug and try to look less shocked than I feel. 'Another bit of small print you should have checked before you grabbed the cash. It's too late now, they're coming, you'll have to upgrade accordingly.' If he's a dog hater and a child hater, I can't imagine how this will ever work out. No wonder the place is so bare and lacking in any traces of emotional warmth. Whatever I picked up on all those years ago, I got him totally wrong. The man obviously has no empathy at all.

But at the same time I've made two unexpected leaps forward. There's actually no need for Bill to hide anywhere, because how many of Libby's friends will have their own dedicated wood delivery person? I'm wondering how Bill would feel about smartening up a bit so we could pass him off as a butler in a few of the photos.

Now I'm sensing I've got the upper hand, I'm throwing it all out there. 'So what about the deccies, then?'

This time his groan's louder still. 'I'm a straight guy, I struggle garnishing a cocktail. Ask me to tinsel up a castle, I haven't got the foggiest where to begin.' Which proves he knows one twinkly word, so he's not *quite* as clueless as he's claiming.

'There are always attics rammed with cast-offs in the houses by the sea in Enid Blyton books.' The more I think about it, the more it goes with the territory. And if we're stuck with an arrogant arse like Bill, who's so far failing miserably with this let, we might as well make the most of whatever trappings we can get our hands on. 'Don't you have a loft we could plunder?'

'You know the top floor's full of bedrooms.' That's it. Then he takes a deep breath and wrinkles his nose. 'There *is* some of the old tat we pulled out of the castle – that's over in the coach house, but I swear none of it's usable.'

I sit up straighter. 'You'll be surprised what you can make use of when the going gets tough. And Christmas trees would make a huge difference too. It's my job to make things look pretty, if you'd stop channelling your inner Scrooge, I'm *sure* we could sort this. Believe me, anything that stops Libby having a meltdown will be more than worth the effort. She and the kids are arriving late Sunday. If we work our socks off from now until then, we can turn this around.'

Bill rolls his eyes, then does another shudder at the mention of the children. 'When you put it like that, what are you waiting for?'

Time for me to drop my very own bombshell. 'I can only stay if Merwyn does.'

'Why did I ever start this?' Bill's growling through gritted teeth. 'You'll have to keep him out of the distillery. The kids too.'

'Obviously. Merwyn hates distilleries anyway.' I'm not going to admit that yet again I have no idea what the hell he's talking about. What distillery?

Bill looks as if he's close to having smoke coming out of his nostrils and his ears. 'Fine.' It's obviously nothing of the kind, but this is his bed, he made it, he has to lie in it, or however the saying goes. 'I'm not happy, but you've got me over a barrel here – Merwyn can stay.'

And finally, a result! 'Did you hear that Merwyn, you got your invitation to Christmas at the castle!' I let him snaffle his chocolate drop, and he's so ecstatic that he leaps up on the sofa, jumps straight onto my knee and smothers me in sloppy doggy kisses.

Bill's face is crumpling in distaste. 'Two conditions – no dogs on the sofas and definitely no dogs on the beds.'

It's not that we aren't going to be respectful. But Merwyn and I both know, Bill's in no position to make rules here. And the faster he realises that, the better we'll all get on.

As for me, there was a train wreck roaring towards me at a hundred miles an hour and somehow I've managed to avert it. It's not that I care about this for myself, it's more that I want to make things perfect for Fliss and Libby and everyone else who's coming down. It's going to be a huge challenge to keep this on track. It's going to be hideous doing this with Bill around. But right now, with three days ahead of me, an empty castle, and carte blanche to fill it with Christmas, I couldn't feel any more focussed on the job in hand.

I whistle Merwyn, then beam across at Bill. 'So where's this coach house then?'

4.

Hello cold days

Merwyn and I are following Bill around the front of the castle, and when my phone rings it's such a surprise, I almost drop it. When I see who's calling, I wish I had.

'Libby! Lovely to chat, how can I …?' I notice Bill slow to a halt ahead of me.

Libby cuts me off in mid sentence. 'There are packages on their way as we speak!!' Forget EE, her booming voice is loud enough to have carried all the way from London on the wind. 'I've been trying to get you all morning, have you had your phone switched off?'

'Great news on the parcels, the signal's patchy, that's all.' My bad luck to hit a hot spot now. If she's going to ask about the castle, I have no idea what I'm going to say.

'So how's the castle?'

My stomach drops. 'Practically on the beach, can you hear the sound of the waves?' I push my phone high in the air.

Whatever surf splashes she's picking up, she's shouting over them. 'How about inside, is it gorgeous?'

Yards ahead Bill turns and raises an expectant eyebrow.

What can I say? She won't want to hear the truth, I don't want to lie, so there's only one option. 'You're breaking up ... sorry ... I've lost you ...' I press the red circle on my screen, then switch the phone off completely.

Bill sends me a disbelieving frown. 'You find signal and then end the call, what's that about?'

I'd call it a survival tactic. 'I'll talk to her when I know what there is to work with.'

He pulls a face. 'Don't hold your breath.'

We have a couple more false starts before we make our way along the path through the shrubbery beyond the side of the castle. Twice more we set off and both times we're stopped by van drivers with clipboards and sheafs of papers and parcels to add to the pile in the castle hallway.

As we finally head off Merwyn's skipping along at my side, his tail waving like a flag, it's as if he's decided that now he's officially on the guest list he might as well look like he owns the place. I pull my hat down more securely to keep out the freezing wind gusts, and get a first glimpse of the coach house buildings through the foliage. They're long, low and barn-like, but with their dark slate roofs rimy with salt and the late afternoon sunlight reflecting off the shimmering silver of the sea, they make a dramatic group against the fading sky. By the time Bill's pushing open the wide door at the end of the longest building, he's still chuntering.

In Chamonix Will was good tempered, and in my head that's how he stayed. I can't help being taken aback by how grouchy the passing years have made him.

As he flicks on the lights, he lets out a sigh. 'Okay, knock yourself out.'

I'm staring around a wide space lit by the flat glare of strip lights, up to the rafters of a high slanting roof, taking in shelves full of boxes and lumpy tarpaulins. 'Go on then, show me what's under the dust sheets.'

He sniffs as he lifts up a corner. 'Bits of furniture, general rubbish, they're hardly going to satisfy a high end customer are they?' His eyes flash. 'And there's definitely no child equipment either.'

As I swoop in on an ancient leather armchair, I can't believe what I'm looking at. 'How many of these have you got?' I'm holding my breath, hoping there might be a pair to go either side of one of the fireplaces, or to tuck away to make a cosy corner in one of the tower alcoves.

Bill frowns. 'There's loads, but none of them match and they're all scuffed.' He's saying it like that's a bad thing.

'That's not a scuff, it's patina.' I lean forwards and breathe in the deep waxy smell of the hide. 'Better still, Libby's going to love them.'

'And some are velvet, not leather.'

I try not to melt into a silent pool of stylist happiness. 'And what's in the boxes?'

Bill takes a couple down and pulls them open. 'Mismatched crockery and old jars, the kind of rubbish that's no use at all.'

I'm staring down at the prettiest assortment of plates and dishes but now I know they're here I don't need to keep contradicting him. 'And you're sure it's okay to use this stuff?' As I take in a nod I can hardly believe my luck.

Further along the shelves we find hanging candle chandeliers, a whole load of plant pots, storm lanterns, ancient kitchen utensils, old baths and enamel jugs. Propped up against the walls there are step ladders, hundreds of pictures and photographs in frames, endless boxes of books.

I reckon this lot will more than take care of the accessorising, but I'm not going to put him out of his misery yet. 'The stuff here will go part way to saving your neck, what about the rest?'

'There's *more*?'

Okay, I'm mean, but I'm truly enjoying another appalled squeal. 'Even if we raid the grounds for twigs, we're still short of Christmas trees, candles and a million tea lights.'

He lets out a groan. 'The Facebook ad was one desperate moment – I never thought anyone would *actually* bite.'

I'm not interested in details – he got himself into this mess, now he needs to sort it. 'Well, we're onto damage limitation now. So do you have a budget?'

His voice is dry. 'Not really.'

I'm searching his face for clues as he swallows. 'Not really, because you haven't thought about it, or not really, meaning there's no money?' He doesn't look dodgy, just beaten.

'Realistically I can throw a hundred at it.'

'Jeez, Bill.' It comes out as a shriek.

'And I have a mate with a Christmas tree plantation, he might give us some mis-shapes.' He takes in my horrified look. 'Or a discount.'

He's taken Libby's money with no plans to put in the extra effort and he's not getting away with this. But there's a flip side too. His accidental advert ended up giving me my chance to make Christmas wonderful for everyone. As Fliss knows, I've jumped at the chance to prove that everything that I touch doesn't have to turn sour. The accident happened at the end of a horrible year that began with George walking out. Then the whole of last December was a blur of hospitals and police interviews and Michael's funeral and visits to the scene of the accident. When so many things have gone wrong I'm starting to feel that it's all down to me. Being part of a lovely Christmas, if only from the outside, would give me hope that I'm not destined to wreck and ruin everything I go near. But that's the last thing I'd ever tell anyone else. Especially Bill.

'Lucky for you, I know all the best fairy light suppliers and their discount codes. We should get onto that straight away.'

He's wincing. 'Like ... now?'

As for me inviting myself into his bedroom this soon, I'm going to have to grit my teeth and go with it. And pretend he looks like Quasimodo.

Friday

13th December

5.

Make it a December to remember

When I'm woken by hammering on my bedroom door on Friday morning, it's so early that when I pull back the curtains it's not even light enough to see the sea.

'If you want to choose trees, I'm leaving in five.'

'And I love you too, Bill.' I don't. At all.

Despite my groans and Merwyn's yawns and dirty looks we pull on our clothes and do a dazed run-in-the-dark round the lawn. By the time Bill's battered pick-up rattles to a halt by the front door we're standing, backs to the gale, coffee in hand, watching the dawn light send luminous pink streaks across the pale grey sky.

Bill throws the door open. 'I brought the Landy, hop in.'

I lift Merwyn up into the cab and heave myself in after him. 'So what are we listening to? Apart from the banging of metal panels, I mean.'

Bill pulls out of the entrance gateway onto the lane. 'Pirate FM's obscure festive half hour, it's quite a challenge to hear the awful tunes that didn't make it. We'll be there in forty.'

My eyes are barely open, but as the road winds back to hug the coast I'm sitting back basking in the sound of some band singing about *Puppies for Christmas*, and it's magical to see the breakers crashing relentlessly up the beach as dawn lightens to day.

Bill finally showed me to his room and the wifi yesterday evening, after my dinner of Aga baked potatoes. It's on the ground floor, tucked away beyond the stairs that lead up to mine and as empty and pared back as the rest of the place. If I was hoping for a glimpse of the real guy in there, I was truly disappointed. I can completely see that he'd strip back the rest of the castle so the stags don't crush the ornaments as they fall over, but in his room you'd have thought there'd be a flash of something – anything – more individual. I understand not everyone wants to be like Fliss and I and have every drunken moment from our youth emblazoned across the walls to remind us of the fun times we had and how crazy and alive we used to be. But there aren't any photos or any personal touches at all even on Bill's bedside table. No birthday cards, not a single postcard or memento to express that he has a private life or indeed a past. There's nothing. It's as if his backstory and history have been completely wiped out. There isn't as much as a paperback here, not even a print on the wall. It's as if someone's come and very carefully wiped away every trace of his past.

I'm not being nosey, or judging here. I'm just really puzzled that someone who I once glimpsed as such an outgoing, fun and rounded guy should be living this stark and sterile existence. I mean, I did get a glimpse in his suitcase in Chamonix, it was as full of shit as mine, his room too. So it's not that he's an anal tidying minimalist who travels through life with nothing, because he's not. Even if he did think he was better than people, he didn't deserve this. There has to be some rational explanation for the vacuum, something more than the castle being newly converted.

Whatever the explanation, he didn't touch on it last night. He was in and out and mostly left me clutching my laptop, perching on the edge of his king sized bed which is so high I only had one toe on the floor. Obviously Merwyn insisted on coming too, so we took his furry tree rug for him to lie on and had to promise he wouldn't try to clean his face on the pristine pale grey duvet cover.

The moment I put in the password a hundred emails from Libby pinged in, all of them delivery notifications, and all duplicated in the matching texts that popped up on my phone too. Then I rushed off a Facebook message to flag up to Fliss and Libby that the interiors we've been mooning over are the wrong ones and that what we have here is more-tower-less-frills. Then I called Fliss a few minutes later, certain by half past eight her kids would be asleep. They weren't.

I love Oscar and Harriet to bits, but they're the kind of insomniac babies who drink milk non stop, scream really loudly and never close their eyes. The theory that second babies are easier hasn't worked for Fliss either, which is why popping out number two has almost pushed her over the edge. Oscar was easily three before I saw him fully zonked out and that was only with chickenpox and after Calpol, which if you don't know is squirted into their mouth from a syringe, and the baby equivalent of a tranquiliser dart. Fliss swears all that saved her as a mum is the phone app she works with her nose at the same time as clutching both kids, which reads advice out loud and plays soothing tunes.

If Fliss ever actually gets her nose onto her phone when I ring her, there's a five second window to talk, so when she answered I didn't mess about.

Unlike her babies, she always sounds super-sleepy. '... Ivy ... fab ... just feeding Harriet ...' Nothing new there then.

I fired out the words '... stylish ... stony ... sparse ... small-but-snug ...' then threw 'staff' in as an inspired afterthought. Then I blurted. 'I've taken full charge of the deccies too.' And damn for putting my head on the block there.

I could hear Fliss musing over the sound of Harriet's sucking noises and Oscar banging the life out of what might have been a drum, or possibly the patio doors. 'Sparse ... how?'

Another damn for that one. 'Don't worry, it'll be full by the time you arrive.'

'Brill ... we'll see you Sunday ...' And then there was a clatter of the phone being dropped, Fliss was telling Oscar not to lick his mango yogurt off the TV screen, and we got cut off.

I must admit, conversations like this make me view the super-cute baby clothes in *Daniels* in a whole different light – the kind that has me whooshing off to *Pet's Corner*. Five seconds listening to life on Fliss's sofa is enough to remind me crooning over the tartan velvet coats and diamanté dog collars is a whole lot safer. Even if they cost ten times more than the human versions they're cheap at the price when you consider what they're saving you from.

After that I took refuge in shopping for the castle and by the time Bill wafted back in again my online baskets were overflowing. I trotted out my favourite festive mantra, 'You can never have too many candles, or ribbons ...' then tossed in a couple of kiddie ones just for the pleasure of seeing him shudder again, '... or fire guards or high chairs ...'

It must have worked, because he pulled a face at the checkout totals, paid by one-click PayPal, then disappeared. I'd gone in armed with my strongest cinnamon candle, worried about how I'd cope with his scent when we were poring over the screen together, but as that bit turned out to be complete wishful thinking on my part, I never got to light it.

But this morning, in spite of the mix of dust and oil and wax jacket in the front of the Landy, as I watch his hands wrestling the steering wheel around the twisty country lanes between fields and hedges that are monochrome in the cold morning, there's more. In fact the man-scent wafting my way is so delicious I'm already working on excuses to get into his bathroom to check out what it is he's wearing. I know I'm taking an extended break from dating, and the women in Men's Fragrances at *Daniels* are great at splashing them around. But if I ever spot a new one in the wild, I like to get it in my notebook for future reference. A boyfriend in my future definitely isn't a priority. But in the unlikely event I did get one, decades down the line etc. etc. – *please, oh please let him smell like the inside of this Landy cab does now* – end of Fairy Godmother message. And the fastest way to make that happen is to find out what Bill's aftershave bottle looks like.

I might have to fall back on the doggy choc trick – throw one into Bill's bathroom then dive in after Merwyn to drag him out when he chases it. I'm working on the finer detail of the plan, when I notice Bill's braking, and glancing over at me.

'We're here, you might like to wake up.'

Shit. I try for nonchalant and remind myself not to breathe in too deeply. 'Just thinking about delicious smells.'

'Like pine needles?' The rough piece of board with a spray painted Christmas tree outline and an arrow we're trundling past and a very bumpy lane that finally ends in a car park full of potholes suggest his mate in the trade is as cut price as he is. Merwyn's bobbing up and down as we stop, then as I open the door he sees the puddles and he looks doubtful.

'Your call, Merwyn.' I shout to Bill behind the pickup. 'He doesn't like getting his paws muddy.'

Bill's eyebrows shoot up. 'Except when he's burying my shorts, then apparently he doesn't give a damn.'

'Would you like me to order you some more?' I've no idea why I'm offering, the way Bill left them lying around, he was asking for them to be run off with.

'You're okay, they weren't my best ones.'

'Definitely too much information.' As I clamp my hands on my ears Merwyn decides he'll join us after all, and jumps into my arms.

From the way Bill's rubbing his hands and taking long strides down the car park he's either wanting to get this over with or he's taking charge here. Or possibly both. 'So are you looking for Norway spruce, Nordmann fir, or something more exotic? It's all about the needle drop, you do know that?'

As Merwyn and I pick our way between the puddles I have to ask. 'So when did you become the expert?'

There's no crack in his confidence. 'Since I phoned up to arrange it. We pick up the smaller ones here, I'll pay for them all when they bring the big one for the hallway. So do you want one more or two?'

I'm hoping he's joking. 'If you've sorted the huge one, we need a medium one for the kitchen, two more for the chill out spaces, some for the tower rooms and then another ten for the bedrooms.'

'That many? *Really?*' Bill's horrified expression matches his squawk.

'They're the fastest way to get the festive feel.' I'm taking this to him. 'Unless you've come up with a better idea?'

As expected, he doesn't take me up on that one. 'No doubt you want the fancy ones?'

This time I'm thinking of the minuscule budget and the bigger picture. 'A tree is a tree. Let's get as many as we can of the cheapest.' I know he's being tight, but if they're freshly cut the plain ones will easily last us until Boxing Day. 'Unless you want them to double up for your New Year lets too?'

'Hell, no.' He strides further along the yard, to where there are trees propped against the fence.

'That way there will be more cash to splash on the rest of the deccies.'

'You mean this doesn't end here?' He just gives a disgusted

head shake. 'Hurry up and grab them then, I haven't got all day.' He picks up two by their tips and swings around.

'Not so fast.' I take in his look of incomprehension. 'You can't just take any, they're not all the same.'

'You just said, a tree is a tree.'

I'm enjoying breaking it to him. 'We have to choose the prettiest ones. Let's start with the smaller ones for the bedrooms. Hold them up one by one, turn them around, and I'll say yes or no.' I have to admit I'm loving how much he's hating this.

By the time I've carefully selected sixteen trees the pile is huge. Bill looked like he lost the will to live some time ago, but I'm flying because suddenly Christmas feels so much closer. I slip Merwyn's lead over my wrist and wrestle as many trees into my arms as I can, which turns out to be three.

Bill's staring at me. 'But you don't have to ...'

'I lug stuff around all the time at work, I've got this.' It's not a technique that would comply with any of *Daniels'* manual handling guidelines, but hey!, this is Cornwall, it's the holidays, rules are made for breaking. It's always great to shock guys who assume women can't lift anything heavier than a lipstick and by the time I set off I'm pretty damn pleased with myself. I'm half way back to the car park when I hear Bill's shout.

'I-v-yyyy ...'

My mouth is pretty full of pine needles. 'What now?'

'You're going the wrong way.'

Unbelievable. He comes out with the name Fraser fir, and now he knows it all. I can't see past the branches, but I spin around anyway. 'Wrong way *how*?' Of course I'm going the right way, when I looked three seconds ago the Landy was still in the same place.

I'm not the only one who's confused as I hesitate. Below the branches Merwyn's on his fully extended lead running backwards and forwards in ever crazier circles. Then I try to take a step, and my foot won't move because Merwyn's lead is tightening around my ankles. 'What the heck ...?'

One minute I'm storming down the car park, the next I'm wobbling. It's one of those moments when I know I'm going to fall, I can feel myself toppling, and there's nothing I can do except tilt, and follow the trees forwards.

'Waaaaaahhhhh ...!!!!'

The next thing I know, there are pine needles sticking up my nose, my body's rocking on a springy cushion of spruce and my legs are sticking up behind me, and I suspect they must be waving wildly too. And Merwyn is next to my ankles, still attached, and barking like a mad thing.

'Bill!!! Help!!!!' I'm yelling and trying to kick, but my legs are stuck. 'Come and h-e-e-e-l-p me!!!'

There's a low laugh behind me. 'Hold it there, I'll just get a few more pictures.'

What? 'Forget effing pictures, come and untie me *NOW*!!!' I push spikes out of my mouth, unstick my hat from the prickles that are pulling it and drag it down as far as I can over my face. As I roll sideways off the branches, if it wasn't for the freezing water seeping around my bottom I'd be hot to the point of exploding.

Bill's laughing so much he's staggering towards me. 'One

more. Sitting in that puddle next to your tree pile, that's the best one of all.' Then he slides his phone into his pocket and holds out his hand. 'What?' He's trying to look innocent.

'Taking pictures, instead of helping me up, that's what.' Seriously, if he doesn't stop the doubled up laughing soon he's in for a swipe on the head with a Nordmann spruce.

'You're the one who wants stuff to load to Instagram. That sequence is pure gold.'

I'm despairing at how little clue he has. 'That's *nothing* like what Libby wants.'

He pulls me to my feet even though by now, obviously, I'd rather he hadn't. He's still laughing, watching me as I pull stiff soaking denim off my legs.

'What, don't tell me *your* boxers are muddy too, would you like me to order you some more?'

I take a deep breath and give him my best glare. 'Have you finished?'

The way his eyebrows go up is really annoying. 'There is one more thing ...'

I'm almost roaring. 'What?'

'Two, actually.'

I roll my eyes.

His lips are twisting. 'If this is a taste of how this Christmas let is going to be, bring it on.'

I'm growling through gritted teeth. 'It's not. At all. I will *personally* guarantee, the rest will be perfect beyond the point of boring. And?'

As he tilts his head, he has dimples in his cheeks. 'There are trolleys further along ... for carrying the trees.' His eyes are mocking. 'And a machine that pulls the branches into a net to make them neat for travelling. So they're easy to carry and they'll fit in the pick up.'

'Know it all.' *And damn.* For every part of this. But mostly for what the slices in his cheeks are doing to my stomach. It's not that I'm usually bossy but he seems to have forgotten who's in trouble here. 'Well what are you waiting for? Get a trolley then.'

6.

If in doubt, add glitter

'I thought Christmas was meant to be about the people?'

This is Bill, later on Friday. And, yes, I *am* talking to him again after the tree toppling fiasco, but only because if I want to get this show on the road, I *have* to.

Finding a well equipped laundry room next to the enormous pantry helped. And while my puddle soaked clothes were being washed and dried I found a stripy blue apron, a whisk and a frying pan. After inhaling a stack of pancakes dripping with warm maple syrup I was back in the game but this time with a whole new strategy – in future I will *not* be taking shit from castle personnel.

So we have a castle hallway stacked with trees in nets, and we're now in the coach house checking the pile of furniture that I've spent the last couple of hours sorting out to take over to the castle. And I'm half way to thinking, so long as I keep Bill *very firmly* in his place (and out of my head) I might just be able to pull this off.

I'm looking up at him from the leather armchair I'm testing

out. '*Of course* it's about the people – any *people* who sit in this seat will be super-comfy.'

He gives me an exasperated look. 'But surely what matters is the company *not* the trappings?'

I can't let that opportunity pass, so I round on him. 'In which case, why are *you* spending *your* Christmas at work with strangers?'

That question turns his pissed off expression even darker. 'Christmas is a write off for me this year, I don't care what I do.'

Of course, we've ruined his Christmas being demanding and having a party that includes nine kids instead of a minibus full of stags. How did I not get that before? After jumping in with both feet last time, I'm feeling my way with this. 'So Gemma won't be here then?' For everyone's sakes, given what hard work she was back in the day, I'm desperate he's not going to say she will.

'Gemma's off on a winter holiday.'

I suppose it's pointless both of them having to lie low at the castle looking after a yawny Christmas let. Us writing off his Christmas probably explains his attitude, but he's the one who chose to do it.

'My dad will be around though.' There's that twist of his lips again. 'So long as I let him out of his tower.'

My mouth drops open. 'You keep your dad in a …?' Then I see from the glint in his eyes – of course he bloody doesn't. I'm kicking myself for being so gullible. This has to be him breaking the news of another guest in what's getting to be a very overcrowded castle. 'Someone else we'll be sharing the toaster with?' *And shit to that thought.*

'Nope, for once you're wrong. He usually eats breakfast in his pyjamas, in his motor home beyond the coach house.'

'Camping? *In winter? IN THE GROUNDS?*' This place just keeps on giving. I mean, why the hell is he not at Downton Abbey or whatever their stately pile's called? This quest for the simple life is all the fault of a certain Duke, abandoning his palace and decamping to a farm cottage next door to Sandringham. Take it from me, I shared a teensy bedsit with George once, after the first couple of days, the novelty of waking up where you can reach the kitchen sink to put the kettle on from the bed is less than thrilling.

Bill's laying down the reassurances. 'It's warm in his motor home, and handy – he helps out here too.'

'Well, that sounds as if it's going to be fabulous for all of us.' *Not.* It's yet another eccentricity to hide from Libby.

Bill nods at the heap of furniture and boxes that I've piled up by the door. 'I'll get him to bring this lot over to the house first thing tomorrow, then we can get it into place.'

'That sounds like a plan.' Anyone else, I'd feel guilty for my mean thoughts, but this may not be the worst news.

A text came through from Fliss when I was in Bill's shower earlier – *obviously* I wasn't going to let an opportunity like that pass me by, me not traipsing mud from the car park all the way upstairs was the perfect opening for me to get into Bill's bathroom. Except I still have no further idea what he's smelling of. However spartan the rest of the place is, his man-perfume shelf is rammed. If I'd even begun to work my way through them trying them out I'd have had total nose confusion. I didn't just make it up, that is a real thing, the *Daniels*' girls on perfume talk about it all the time. But sadly I'm still without my hot tip for my notebook.

According to Fliss's text, Libby is so stoked at the idea of her own handyman there's a good chance that will totally make up for the lack of deep pile carpet. If Bill's dad is going to be knocking around the wood baskets too it's going to be double the fun. Especially if their shared gene pool means he's equally decorative.

As for the butler shots I know she'll be setting her heart on, more mature might be better still, so I may as well test the ground. 'So how does your dad feel about dressing up?'

The cloud that passes across Bill's face says it's an instant thumbs down. 'Sorry, but there's only room for one Santa in St Aidan. Gary from the jingle bells pony cart gets very cross about imposters.'

Weird, but fine, Santa was way off what I'm after anyway. 'We definitely don't want to upset any locals.' As he didn't dismiss it entirely it's worth another try. 'But if red coats are out, an evening suit might work?'

His voice shoots up. 'If you knew my dad, you would *not* be asking that. *Don't catch me, don't change me* free spirits don't dress to order, he's all about wild hearts and the open road.' He takes a second to blow out his cheeks. 'If you want a guy in a tux, you'll have to sweet talk me.'

I ignore that my toes just turned to hot syrup. 'That's not a thing I'll be doing any time soon.'

'Great, well in that case, let's look at this lot.' He's scowling at my accessorising heap. 'I simply can't see how shitloads of superfluous ornamentation are going to give anyone a great time.'

Which goes to show how very wrong first impressions can be. He was such a happy guy all those years ago by that alpine fire, there was no sign whatsoever he'd turn out this grumpy. Me not getting what my most secret inner self wished for back then saved me from the hugest heap of trouble. All I can think is that over the years, having him all to myself in my head, I must have gradually changed him, whittled him into someone else entirely. I've somehow built him into someone very different from the guy himself. It was bound to happen. That's the trouble with fantasies, when you give them free rein they travel a long way from their real life counterparts. They never talk back either. Which is possibly why having too many of the damn things isn't ideal.

I'm going to have to put him right on that all-encompassing comment though. 'If you create the most magical setting imaginable, those *all-important* people enjoy it so much more.'

'Excuse me for missing there was so much alchemy involved.' It's that snarky tone and – oh joys – he's shaking his head again. And to think I thought him being an anti-child dog-phobe was as bad as it was going to get.

I have to stick up for #TeamChristmas. 'We're creating memories that will last a lifetime, you can't put a price on that.' I stand up, give Merwyn a tickle to remind Bill we're two against one here, and start to search for containers to put the trees in. 'A castle and a beach is already fabulous, but overlay it with candlelight and pine needles, cranberry cocktails in frosted glasses, warm baked cinnamon biscuits and gingerbread houses, the distant sound of Santa's sleigh bells, and it'll never be surpassed.' My eyes are probably sparkling too much as the images of present piles and frosty mornings flash through my head, I might be giving too much away here, but I don't even care.

Bill's blowing out his cheeks and sounding disgusted. 'You've really fallen for the whole *stockings hanging by an open fire* thing haven't you?'

My shriek of protest comes out louder than I'd planned. 'And I'm completely happy with that. Some people live for summer, my time is December.' Or at least, it used to be. And then something beyond the pile catches my eye. 'Are they what I think they are?'

'Traditional alpine toboggans? Just like we had in the mountains.'

I ignore the last bit because I really am gasping with excitement. 'You have *that* much snow here?'

He gives me a hard stare. 'Why the sudden interest? From what I remember in Chamonix you prefer to stay indoors.'

Once again, I'm quietly cursing his recall. 'Those mountain ski runs scared the bejesus out of me, even the nursery slopes were too steep, but in any other situation snow is dreamy.'

His eyes have locked with mine. 'So that finally explains why you concentrated on the hot chocolate, not the black runs. Why didn't you say? I'd have helped you.'

I may as well be honest, even if I wasn't then. 'I was enough out of my depth as it was, I'd rather have dived head first into a snowdrift than admit I couldn't ski.'

He shrugs. 'I did come back early every day so you had company.'

I'm not sure he's thinking of the right holiday. 'I thought you came back so you could grab the steam room first?'

His head is tilting. 'That was Gemma, not me. When she wasn't falling over in front of me she pretty much superglued herself to my snowboard, that's why we always arrived back together. But I came back to see you.'

I'm blinking. 'Sorry?'

'As I remember, I especially liked your jumpers.'

I can feel my eyes stretching open as I shriek. '*What?!!!!*'

'They were really nice. Everyone else was in ski jackets, you were always in your base layer.'

I'm still squeaking in shock. 'Jeez, Bill.' Then it hits, from the way his eyes are dancing, this has to be a total wind up.

'I liked how you made me laugh too.'

I let out a groan. 'Please tell me you're joking me.'

'Of course I am, all I ever wanted was to get in that sauna. That's why I was always hanging round the fire telling you my best jokes, they can't have been very good if you can't even remember them.'

I can feel my lips curling even though I'm trying to stop them. 'What's the difference between a snow man and a snow woman?' And more fool me for encouraging him here.

'Snowballs.' He gives that resonating low laugh. 'Something tells me you know a lot more than you're letting on, Ivy Starforth.'

Oh my days, now he's tied me up in knots again. I've no idea what he means, so to save my sanity I'm taking this back to where we left off. 'If you gave us a snowy Christmas, you'd be off the hook with Libby.'

He's back to staring at me in that same, slow way he has. 'I'll talk to Tomasz Schafernaker and see what I can do.'

'Who the hell is ...?'

'He's a meteorologist.' He's tilting his head, looking down on me through those narrowed eyes again. 'The BBC weather man.'

Forget the protests about how bloody condescending he is, there are way more important questions. 'There's *really* a chance of snow?'

He gives a shrug. 'It's not unknown.'

'We'll have all the sledges then.' I'd love snow so much, I'm not even daring to think about it, so I'm moving this on. The thing is, for me, in a world where lately it feels like nothing can be relied on, Christmas is the one certainty I can cling onto. I know the recipe to make Christmas work. Other things spiral out of control and my life comes crashing down. But so long as I have enough lamella and berries, I should be able to win with Christmas and everyone else will get the benefit.

'It's a simple equation – the more glitter you throw at Christmas, the more enjoyment you get back. Name me *anything* else *that* sure to pay off?'

He shoves a couple of galvanised buckets at me. 'It's an awful lot hanging on one day. And it's not *that* healthy to be *this* obsessed with perfection.'

I have an answer for that. 'Unless you're talking gin.' It's a stab in the dark but as he's always banging on about it, I suspect I've got him.

'Gin's different.' It's as if he's woken up for the first time. 'Obviously when you make it, you're bound to strive for the ultimate, you wouldn't do anything less. Or at least, I wouldn't.'

I shrug. 'So, you're hung up on gin, for me it's Christmas.'

There's a new light in his eyes. 'Now you've mentioned it, I might as well show you the distillery, it's only next door.' He's so enthused, he's already set off. 'Don't worry, I'll give you the shortened version of the tour.'

'Why not?' I'm going to have to do this sometime, so I try not to let my eyes glaze over as I follow him out into the fading daylight. Hash tag, I'd rather be sleeping. Just saying.

7.

Let the fun beGIN ...

I follow Bill as he hurries along the outside of the coach house building and when he pushes through some wide glass doors, the dimly lit space I'm staring around is as big as the building we've come from, with the same high ceiling following the slant of the roof. But in here the stone end gable has been completely knocked out, and instead there's an immense glass window looking straight down onto the beach and out to sea.

'Great view!' I can't deny him that one. The late afternoon has leached away the colour and the edges have blurred, but I can still make out the muted blue of the sea broken by lines of breakers frilling up the sand, a sky streaked with silver. Pin pricks of lights coming on around the edge of the bay, the twinkly cluster that is St Aidan. Then as Bill snaps on the inside lights, the outside darkens, and I'm suddenly blinking at reflections off a polished concrete floor, and flashes from some very shiny copper cauldrons and pipework and dials set back in the corner. The tangy salt and seaweed smell from outside has given way to the heady mix of fresh paint and neat alcohol.

'So you weren't joking, you really do have a still?'

The weary boredom on his face has turned to illuminated bliss. 'We're only a couple of years into production but Cockle Shell Castle gin's already winning awards.'

I pick up a bottle from a shelf and turn it over in my hand. 'Star Shower – the name's cool.' That's as much as he's getting – the silver and rose gold and pink stars on the label are lovely, but I know better than to heap on the praise.

The way he's suddenly jumping from shelf to shelf, he couldn't be more animated. 'That one's got a raspberry burst to it, Shining Comet's got an orange hint. We use juniper berries from the gardens and we're developing other flavours too. The rhubarb and lime's almost ready to go.'

'We?' There's no sign of collaborators. Apart from the equipment and shelves of glasses and bottles the space is almost empty.

He coughs. 'At first I had help with the marketing, but now it's just me.'

I'm gazing around. 'You ... and some very smart glass tables and Philippe Starck ghost chairs.' See-through perspex with a hint of Louis Quatorze, they're still one of my favourites from *Daniels*' furniture department. The last thing I was expecting to get in Bill's distillery was furniture envy.

'They're for the tasting sessions, I liked the way the transparency of the tables echoed the transparency of the gin.' If only he'd applied half this much inspiration and attention to *our* deccies.

'I don't suppose …' I'm kicking myself for sounding this tentative, so I try again. 'I may have to … actually I'll be stealing them for a few days.' Well, two and a bit weeks actually.

'What for?'

'For dining at the castle over Christmas.' I can mix and match with extra chairs to make up the numbers, but that won't matter.

He's looking at me like I've seriously lost my marbles. 'Only one hitch with that, Ivy – there isn't a dining room.'

'One end of the bit you call the chill out space? Obviously we'd keep the plastic away from the roaring fires.' If we overcome the melting risk, they'll be sensational. I'm chipping away. 'The whole transparency thing … echoes of icicles … how amazing the chairs would be, draped with fairy lights? They're exactly what we need to transform those – ahem – empty spaces.'

'Two hitches actually.' He lets out a breath. 'Glass tables, and all those sticky kiddie fingers? How's that going to work?'

I'm cursing his stubbornness when my second brainwave hits. 'Imagine the Christmas tree in the entrance hall decked with miniature gin bottles and sea shells.' I'm searching his face for a positive sign. 'The tables and chairs are just the start – we could fill the entire castle with transparent gin-themed decorations?' See what I'm doing here? Weaving the furniture into the vision. Taking Christmas back to his adult-only comfort zone. 'We'll take our lead from the stars on the gin labels and have bright orange and cerise pink as our theme colours.' I'm doing this so wholeheartedly I'm actually getting carried away on my own wave of enthusiasm.

And finally, he nods. 'You could be onto something there,

Ivy-star.' Then he sweeps up a glass from a tray. 'Let's drink to that!'

Just when it was going so well, my heart comes crashing down to my boots again. 'I'm actually on a break right now.'

His voice shoots up. 'From *alcohol*?'

'That's the one.'

'But you can't be. Think of all those toffee vodkas we had by the log fire ... you can't give up anything that delicious.'

This time I clamp my mouth closed before it drops open and try to laugh this off. 'They could explain the blurry judgement.' Now I come to think of it, the caramel flavoured alcohol might explain why I remember that delicious feeling of my toes turning to syrup. But I need to call a halt to all this reminiscing. 'Can we please stop wasting time living in the past. If we're going to sort out a fabulous Christmas, there's no time to lose, we need to get on.'

'So what happened?' He's frowning. 'You refused my offer of a drink two seconds ago, that qualifies as the present.'

He's got me there. But if I fill him in with the middle bits, at least I'm being open and honest, and it's a darn sight less dangerous than talking about ski lodges. 'After George there was too much drinking, too many awful dates. I'm taking a holiday from all of it.'

Actually it was so much less fun than I'm making it sound. But when George left almost two years ago now there was this crazy voice inside me, telling me I'd thrown away my fertile years. The more desperate I was to find someone new, the more impossible it was. And the worse the guys became, the more reason I had to throw down the shots.

If I'm honest the accident was the culmination of that very awful time. It was the bottom of a very deep trough, the turning point. But anything that tragic is very hard to move on from. So long as I throw myself into doing things for my friends rather than for me, and pretend to the outside world that everything's okay, I can just about hold it together.

Bill shrugs. 'Sleeping with strangers, Tinder's got a lot to answer for.'

As my eyes pop open my protest is loud. 'Actually I *didn't* do that.' Mostly not, anyway. Mostly I passed out way before I got anywhere near their beds. 'But eventually I got a wake up call that made me rethink all those poor choices.' I'm trying for my best super-confident beam, knowing it's coming across more wild eyed than I'd like, and that I'm sharing so much more than I should. And knowing that if I hadn't been in that awful state, Michael would probably be alive now.

That's not something I'll ever leave behind, it's a weight I'll carry with me forever. However much I pretend I'm fine, which I have to do for other people, I know I'll never get past the guilt. But that's something I've got to lock up deep in my heart, something private for me, my very own penance. The only way to explain it is that it feels like a rock sitting inside my chest. I can't let it spill out and bring other people down. But I know that it will stay there forever, because I really don't have the right to be happy again. And I'm completely resigned to not being.

'So here I am, there are lots of things I don't do for now, neat gin's only one of them. But it's all working out really, *really* well.'

'I'm pleased to hear it.' He swallows and looks like he'd rather be anywhere other than where he is. 'It explains why tinsel's become inordinately big in your life.'

Could he be any more patronising? 'No, I've always been the same with tinsel.'

He's still going. 'How about we take the buckets over to the castle on a trolley and wash them instead?'

At last there's an offer I can't refuse. The distillery was supposedly a doggy no-go area, so I've been pretending Merwyn wasn't here, but if we're leaving I can talk to him again. 'Time for a walk?'

His tail shoots up, and he skitters towards the door, claws slipping on the gleaming floor.

8.

Surprise surprise

Wandering towards the castle as the sky darkens with the crash of the waves echoing in the distance and the lights shining on the front doesn't get any less thrilling. But however picturesque it is, as I hang on to Merwyn *and* make sure the bucket stacks don't topple off the trolley, I'm reminded again that real life is a lot less perfect than fairy tales. I actually love trundling gear around, ideally I'd be the one hauling the trolley. But you know what guys are like? Even though George rarely ventured into a supermarket, the once in a blue moon he did, he *had* to be in charge of the wheels. And as Bill is head of ops *and* arrogance personified, I don't get within a country mile of this trolley handle.

Instead of minding, I'm thinking ahead to dinner, and the spag bol I left bubbling on the Aga. The only flaw in my plans for an evening on the kitchen sofa sorting out lists is that Bill could be crashing around in my space.

Bill pulls the trolley to a jerky halt in front of the house, and as I make a lunge for the falling buckets he's staring at a huge, shiny, black four by four.

'Looks like Jeff Bezos is out making the Amazon deliveries himself today.'

'It's good of him to take the parcels round the back, fingers crossed he's bringing fairy lights.' I realign the pots and we set off again. 'And please let's avoid sudden stops like that in future.'

As we round the corner at the rear of the castle the courtyard is already flooded with light, and the trolley lurches again. This time the buckets go clattering across the stone flags and I'm cursing Bill's bad cornering as I chase them across the lawn. It's only when I've finally collected them all that I turn and see the reason they fell – the package stack he swerved to avoid is as big as a wall. As we manoeuvre around the boxes I'm looking at Merwyn.

'So where did the driver go?'

I'm noticing the steam coming off the hot tub, when there's a high pitched giggle. Then a cloud of blonde curls bobs up over the edge and I do a double take. 'Miranda?!?!' Seeing as she's Libby's mum, just in time I manage to stop myself being super-rude and asking what the hell she's doing here.

She picks up a champagne glass from the side and takes a swig. 'Ivy! You're looking beyond cute in your woolly hat! And after everything that's happened too, it's so lovely to see you're here and looking so well.'

You know what mums can be like, even other people's, bringing up all the stuff you'd rather not talk about. And as if it wasn't enough of a shock finding Fliss and Libby's mum here ten days earlier than she's pencilled in on the arrivals list, a second later another head bobs up beside her.

Miranda's waving her fizz. 'Top tip, if you travel with champagne and glasses like we do, you'll never go far wrong. We thought we might as well make ourselves at home and have a dip while we waited for you to get back. There's someone here I've been dying for you to meet – Ivy, this is Ambrose.'

This is the first I've heard of Ambrose, but whatever. As I coax Merwyn forward so I can reach his dripping fingers and try not to tread on their clothes pile, I'm aware I've been here before.

'*Enchanté*, Ivy.' Ambrose's voice is as deep and luxuriant as his tan, even if his greeting is a bit naff. He flicks an iron grey curl back off his forehead then picks up his own glass and dips his shoulders back under the water.

As I launch into the introductions I refuse to sound disappointed that someone else has arrived. I mean, I'm not, so why would I? 'So this is Bill the castle caretaker, and Merwyn, who's slightly Tibetan and currently a contender for the cutest dog in the world.'

Bill's cough is low beside me. 'So long as he's not burying your underwear.'

'If you're wondering why we're here so early ...' It's a relief that Miranda's read my mind and is talking over Bill. When she breaks off to smile at Ambrose, she's looking as if she could eat him whole. And then go back for seconds. '... well, it's a complete secret from Libby, but Ambrose and I thought we'd snatch a few romantic days here on our own before the family arrive. You won't tell on us will you?'

Ambrose steps in to help. 'You know the first rule of house parties ... the early birds get the best rooms.' He laughs. 'But you must do, you're here. And Miranda isn't settling for anything less than a four poster master suite, by the way.'

Miranda's eyes are such a startling blue, and so full of warmth and concern, I can completely see why she's rarely without a husband. 'You look worried, sweetheart. It is okay for us to be here?'

'It's fine.' I take a deep breath and decide to go for a white lie. 'The last let needed the place empty ...'

Miranda jumps in before I finish. 'Oh my, was it for a photo shoot? No wonder either, the place is amazing.' She nudges Ambrose so hard he almost slides off the shelf at the side of the tub. 'We said it looks pretty enough to be a film set, didn't we, Ambie? It's just like the castle on *Frozen*.'

It isn't at all. This one's way prettier, but I'm not going to argue. 'So long as you don't mind that we're still moving things back in?' We're here to make dreams for guests, not shatter illusions, so I don't say any more.

I've known Miranda years, ever since Fliss and I were art students at St Martins in London and we used to go to stay with her in her flat in Brighton. As a mum she's a bit off-the-wall, if only because ever since their dad died when Fliss was ten she's been a stalwart mum, but as Fliss always says, she's gone through her men like a dose of salts. But other than the revolving-door guys, she's always the same – generous and warm, laid back, welcoming and fun, easy to be with, and we all love her to bits. I take it from the bare third finger on her left hand that's dangling over Ambrose's bronzed shoulder, and his absence from the guest list, that he's a relatively new addition.

Her love life was going through such a turbulent patch when Fliss and Rob were getting married, in the run-up to the wedding they gave up trying for a definite name, and just put *Mother of the Bride's plus one* on the table plan. Whoever it was she brought – none of us are that good pinpointing names, except Libby who writes everything down which takes the pressure off everyone else, including Miranda, because they know they can always check in her archives – the first and last time Fliss met that one was when he turned up on her wedding photographs and the top table.

Miranda's beaming. 'Of course we don't mind, we'll help won't we?'

Judging from his white knuckles on the tub side, this time Ambie's ready for the nudge she's about to give him. He grins at her. 'When we're not in here, we will.'

Miranda's locked her gaze elsewhere. 'He's joking, Bill.' Her laugh is low and chesty. 'I'm an artist, I'm very creative, I don't mind rolling up my sleeves.'

Ambrose's laugh is a low echo. 'You can say that again.'

'Not appropriate, Ambie.' There's a throaty peel of laughter and a gigantic wall of water splashing over the stone flags as Miranda shoulders Ambie off the tub shelf and he disappears below the waves. As Ambie splutters his way back to the surface, Bill is still getting the benefit of her cherubic full-beam smile with an extra dose of static crackle. 'Did you see that, Bill, that's what happens to men who don't behave.' Miranda folds her arms across her chest squeezing her more than ample bazumbas and cleavage into view above the water-line. 'Don't worry, we won't let you down.'

You only need to see the look on Bill's face to read the writing in his invisible thought bubble.

FUCK!!! FUCK!!! and WHAT THE FUCK?!!! There might also be a teensy whimpering *Get me out of here!* too.

'Okay, Bill?' As I give him a nudge, he comes to and gives a cough.

'So, just to be clear, there's no smoking in the castle, the courtyard, or the car parking areas.' The furrows in his brow deepen as he eyes her tobacco tin and Rizla papers next to the towel. 'Or the coach house ... or the distillery.'

I'm beaming to cover my own WTF? 'And thanks, Bill, for that lovely welcome.'

Miranda's still twinkling at him. 'But roll ups will be fine, won't they? Because they don't *actually* count as cigarettes?'

He hasn't even flinched. 'Roll ups are banned too. And any tab ends go in the sand buckets by the doors, we don't want you dropping them around the grounds or on the sand.'

Miranda's winking at him in mock horror. 'What, you own the beach now?' She's such a tease.

Bill's not seeing the funny side. 'It is with the castle, yes, but we do let people walk on it. But not if they drop cigarette ends.'

She's completely unbothered. 'I eat little boys like you for breakfast, Bill!' There's another chortle. 'But I'll let you off today. And you can tell whoever is king of your very lovely castle that we'll behave impeccably.'

Bill carries on as if he hasn't heard. 'No horseplay in the hot tub either. If we get ice on the courtyard, the hot tub will be emptied. Immediately. And just out of interest, for the record, are you wearing swimsuits in there?'

I put my hand over my mouth and hiss 'hypocrite' at him under my breath.

'Bill, you are *such* a spoilsport.' From the sparkle in her eyes, Miranda is loving this. 'Skinny dipping in the hot tub is my *favourite* Christmas thing.'

Bill's completely cool. 'In which case, you'll have to find a different hot tub somewhere else. This one is only available for non-naked guests.'

'Fine, no need to get your Speedo's in a twist.' It's rare for Miranda to look like she's beaten. But behind the steam clouds, beyond the two angry red circles on her cheeks, she's as deflated as a popped balloon because she's offered Bill her palmful of goodies and he's flatly refused to eat out of it. And I've never heard her sound snappy before. She's holding her hand out. 'I take it you provide endless supplies of fluffy towels? In which case, please would you get us some. Unless you'd rather we came inside as we are?'

At which point, my hopes for Christmas take another nose dive.

All out war between Bill and Miranda won't be pretty. It wasn't even on my list of stuff to worry about. But realistically, if Bill's taken five minutes to fall out with Miranda who is easy, what the hell is going to happen when Libby's sleigh slides into town?

Saturday

14th December

9.

Happy landings

With everything there is to do in the castle, and Libby arriving tomorrow evening – pause for a silent scream at that – when I wake up early on Saturday morning there's so much adrenalin pounding through my system it's impossible to stay in bed. As I get dressed Merwyn is giving me his 'just no, totally no' look from the comfort of his squishy red velvet sleeping cushion. He is obviously bullshitting because even though I set off without him he still reaches the bottom of the stairs before I do. We're even more wide awake after our scamper along the beach by phone-light. The wind is icy, but the sound of the waves pounding and the frothy water rushing up over the sand and onto our feet seems so much louder in the dark than it does in the day.

Whatever Bill claimed about his dad's breakfast habits, when we get back to the kitchen the toasters are full and there's a tall man in orange woven Aztec joggers watching toast on the Aga top too. Then as he turns to grin at me his smile is a livelier, more lived-in version of Bill's, and I get the full effect of his long straggly hair and the two dangling beaded braids that swing around as he moves his head.

He's straight in with the introductions. 'Hi, I'm Keith, better known as Keef the reef, or Bill's dad. And these …' He waves a hand at the crowd around the table who look like they all shopped at the same place as him when they bought their clothes thirty years ago. '… are Rip, Brian, Bede, Taj and Slater, my crewmates from the *Surf 'til we die* club.'

I'm blinking at silver ponytails and grey grizzly beards of all lengths from stubble to full and bushy, taking in lashings of thong necklaces and shell bracelets, faded ripped denim as weathered as their faces. From the tangles of their hair I'd say none of them visit the barbers except to buy salt spray.

Bill raises an eyebrow beyond the kitchen island. 'The name's ironic, obviously they'll never die, because they're way too busy rocking their hang fives and helicopters and riding their party waves.' There's an amused twist to his lips. 'He looks nothing like me, that's because he's adopted.'

My brows are knitting together. 'Really?'

Keith's face crinkles into a grin. 'The first rule of the castle – never believe Bill's bollocks. Toast, Ivy?' The cuffs on his faded peach *Rip Curl* sweatshirt are hanging in shreds as he hands me a plate and two perfectly browned slices. 'We'll finish our coffee then we're all yours.'

With Keith's easy charm and an offer like that, they can make as much toast as they like. Any time. And then some. It's a shame Miranda's not here to join in the fun, but no doubt she'll catch up with us later.

The first thing she and Ambrose did when they came in

yesterday evening was to complain about the cold. Once Bill turned the heating up they headed off upstairs with snacks and many bottles of champagne, while we stayed in the kitchen and opened the box stack.

The surf crew waste no time. Before I'm spreading my fourth slice with – totes delicious – motor-home-made orange and gin marmalade, they're already zooming between the coach house and the castle in a variety of colourful but surprisingly shiny vans. If you want something shifting fast, ask a silver surfer. Just saying. By the time I've humped the deccie supplies from the kitchen to the front hall, they're streaming in, filling the place with comfy chairs.

When we've made the most of every cosy corner in the downstairs and the towers and the chairs are still coming, I lead the way up to the first floor.

'So where would you like them?' Keef-the-reef strides off the top step, braids flying as he swings his tub chair round.

I'm counting on my fingers working out, and when I look up there are chairs and surfers lined up all along the landing. 'I think two in each room on ...' I break off as I hear a strange moan.

'Yes?' The guys are all staring at me expectantly over their chair backs.

'We should have enough for ...' There's the same noise again, this time louder.

I'm a designated first aider at work so I'm staring round the faces checking for grey complexions and heart attacks, and it's there again. 'Is everyone okay, can anyone else hear ...?'

'Grunting. And banging.' Keef's exchanging glances with Taj. 'Probably nothing to worry about, let's push on.'

Bumps in the night – or actually the day? Bill's dad desperately pretending they're not there? I wasn't born yesterday, this has to be a cover up!

There's another loud clatter, and as my blood runs cold it all falls into place in my head. 'It's haunted isn't it?' My voice rises to a wail. 'It wasn't the wifi at all, there was Christmas availability because the place is full of poltergeists and no one wants to stay here!'

Of all the problems yet, this is the worst. The rhythmical way this ghost is banging now, it's going to take more than a bit of garlic and a sprig of sage to scare it away. We've got children coming too. My mind's racing ... how the hell do I organise an exorcism at short notice with no internet ... and do they even work anyway?

Which is the perfect point for Bill to arrive and plonk his chair down next to Keef's. 'What's happening here ... *what the hell is that noise?*'

As Keef tilts his head his braids fall across his nose. 'The sound of ghostly removal men?'

Taj nudges Keef. 'If you ask me, those moans are a lot more earthly than spiritual.'

I go rigid as the banging gets faster and faster, then a series of banshee shrieks sends ice through my veins.

Keef puts down his chair and sends me a wink. 'That DO NOT DISTURB sign might be your clue. The rumpus they're making in there, that sign should be on the other side of the door.'

Oh my days. 'That's Ambrose and Miranda?' I'm not sure if this is better or worse but either way I'd welcome a hole to crawl into. Just this once I'm turning to Bill. 'But aren't monumental castle walls meant to be sound proof?'

It's one of those awful times when we should be running but instead everyone's feet are welded to the floor. We're all standing, staring at the sign, when the handle begins to rattle. A second later the door bursts open and one electric purple furry mule appears, followed by Miranda yanking on the ties of her slinky pink leopard-print dressing gown.

'Sound proof? It's nothing of the bloody kind! We could hear every word you lot said, talk about wrecking the moment!' She's tousling her curls with her fingers, chortling as she sweeps her smile along the row of chair carriers. 'No harm done, I forgive you, but only because you're all so sun tanned, strong and handsome.' As she pauses to let the full effect of her charm seep in, her gaze has stopped short of Bill. 'I'm Miranda, by the way. So do any of you hot hunks fancy making me a tea? Or joining me for a dip in the tub?'

Looking along the line of jaws on the floor, if I don't whisk them away fast I'll lose my entire work force. 'Not right now, we're off to the top floor, we'll have to catch you later.'

She rounds on me as she sweeps towards the staircase. 'Don't forget me, sweetheart, I'm dying to get stuck in remember.'

'Great.' I knew I could count on her. 'I was thinking garlands for the ...' But she's already gone.

As the others trundle on up the next flight of stairs Keef the reef's patting me on the arm. 'We'll shift the rest of this furniture then get straight on with the trees. Don't you worry, Ivy, we surfies travel with fairy dust, your castle will be sparkling by tonight.' He sends me a wink. 'And not a ghost in sight, I promise.'

Bill's still choking into his sleeve. 'Nights in a haunted castle, I'm definitely missing a trick there.'

Obviously I don't reply to that. But if this is the beginning, I'm seriously doubting we're going to make it as far as the end.

10.

It's beginning to look a lot like Christmas

While Keef and his surfie crew carry on ferrying from the coach house, I race around dropping boxes of lights in each room in readiness for the trees, adding throws to the ends of the beds from a pile of lovely fifties print curtains I came across, and spread jars of lights around the windowsills to make up for the lack of curtains. By the time I've distributed a big pile of woollen rugs around the easy chairs, and thrown fairy light strings around the mirrors, it's feeling twinkly and a lot more welcoming.

It's one of those days when I'm so busy, the clock on my phone's leaping forward by hours not minutes. By the time I head back to the kitchen to tie up little bunches of pine and juniper twigs with orange and pink bows to hang on the doors, it's already early afternoon and there's still no sign of Miranda. The surfie crew are finishing a late chip buttie lunch and are out front taking nets off the trees and bringing them through the open door. Keef gives me a wave of his spade, sticks up his thumb and points at a plant pot. As I rush around the castle hanging the sprigs, tweaking the last of the tables and easy chairs into place, and adjusting the piles of alpine sledges where the bigger trees are going to go, I'm hopeful we might just do this.

Then Bill arrives in the kitchen with boxes of miniature gin bottles, that all need hanging ribbons attaching. By the time I've tied ribbons to enough bottles to cover a massive tree, I'm kicking myself for this particular bright idea. I'm also wondering where the rest of the tree decorations I ordered are.

When I eventually track Bill down to ask him, is he hard at work? ... is he bollocks. He's in his room hunched over a laptop screen full of figures. Even worse, I get a full-on blast of that body spray again so I get straight down to business.

'Bill, have you seen any tree baubles? There should be quite a few boxes.' Okay, I'll admit, I *might* have got carried away with my ordering, but there's nothing worse than bare branches.

He pulls a face but doesn't look up. 'The pantry's rammed with the latest deliveries ... and the laundry too ...'

It's like pulling teeth. 'Could you possibly track the parcels to check they've arrived?' So many orders, I'm ashamed I'm losing count of what's come. All made harder because the order notifications are all landing in his inbox, and he doesn't always forward them to me.

If I'd asked him to jump off a cliff he couldn't look much more appalled. 'Fine, I'll do it when I finish this, okay?' By which time, no doubt, he'll have forgotten.

'Thanks for all your help.' *Not.* The rest of us are running round like crazy things while he does zilch.

He finally looks up. 'If you need a hand, Miranda and Ambrose are in the hot tub.' His frown deepens. 'They *are* wearing swimmers?' Everything else that's going on and he's still banging on about that.

I refuse to get involved, so I ignore that the tune he's humming under his breath is *Ghostbusters*, and hurry Merwyn out as fast as I can. 'The hot tub's your domain, Bill. Merwyn and I are moving on to tree decorating.'

Or we would be if we could find the damn deccies. If we're talking about boxes, there are just so many, and the stacks are so deep, it's a shame that Merwyn isn't a sniffer dog. What was I saying about if a wall is in your way, knock it down? This time when we get into the laundry it's more a matter of making our way into the box mountain, meticulously opening and checking every box. At times we're so deep in the cardboard fortifications, it feels like we may never emerge. And it's the same again in the pantry.

But you don't just lose thousands of hanging decorations – so long as I look in *every* package they'll turn up in the end. I mean, we'll *have* to find them, because without them the trees just won't work. And time's running out too. In a mere twenty-seven hours Libby will be here, complete with her expectant entourage. All desperate to be wowed. Which is a thought that would make me hyperventilate if I wasn't doing it already.

Except the deccies don't turn up. Instead, as I write the contents on all the boxes in code so as not to give away Libby's present secrets, and try to rearrange them in some kind of order while not passing out from the fumes from the indelible black marker pen, I hit another time slip. When we finally emerge from the cardboard chaos it's with empty hands and paws, and it's almost eight. I've been through every stage of despair, and as I make my way to the kitchen at least there's a lovely tree, its tiny copper wire lights twinkling. The doors to the courtyard are open, my stomach's growling with hunger, Merwyn's so pissed off he isn't even making eye contact, and Miranda's voice is drifting in with the steam wisps.

'Ivy, there you are at last, come out and see us.'

I'm so weary I don't have the will to resist. And Merwyn's so done in, he doesn't even give Ambrose's boxers a second sniff as he waddles past them. From the empty gin bottle in the ice bucket, and the way their Santa hats are slewed sideways on their heads, I'd say these two have had a great afternoon.

Miranda's waving her glass at me. 'So what about those twiggy bunches, don't start without me!'

'I'm afraid they're all finished and hung up now.' That was hours ago.

'Too bad, I was looking forward to doing those.' She's staring at me in that intense way she has. 'Way more important, have you got to work on that handsome caretaker yet? He might be a total pain in the bum, but he's very good looking.'

Merwyn's heard her, and he's giving me his 'hell no! don't even think about it' look, which I pass straight on to Miranda.

'Christian Bale and Ian Somerhalder look fabulous too, but I'm not going there either.' If Miranda's matchmaking I'm wide awake and ready to run, but I'll put this one to bed first.

'Save yourself the trouble, Bill's got a partner, she's a super-model lawyer.'

'That sounds too good to be true, there has to be a catch there. She's not exactly here is she?' Her laugh is soft and throaty. 'It was going to be a surprise, but there might be someone slightly more human and properly single crossing your path in time for Christmas.'

'Who? No! Shit! Miranda, I'm absolutely not here to be set up.' They better bloody not have. But I seriously doubt they would, because every available guy they know has already been hurled at me. At least three times. I used to love getting tagged as Miranda's fourth child back in the day when we visited Brighton, but with this level of motherly interference, not so much.

She's giving me that all-knowing look she does. 'I know times have been hard. But you can't let your past define your future, sweetheart. Every new man is a whole new world of opportunities.'

'Lovely to have your input, Miranda.' But I have a lot less new-age optimism than she does. Hopefully now she'll shut the eff up, and stop meddling in my life.

But this is Miranda, giving up isn't in her nature. 'And just in case that fails, I asked all the hot surfers to keep an eye out on your behalf.'

I let out an appalled squawk. 'Thanks for that, I might as well die now.'

'Take it from me, Christmas is a time for romance, isn't it Ambrose?'

'Hmmmm ...' Ambrose manages a slur and a lopsided grin.

'Ambie, you are such a tease.' Miranda's wiggling her eyebrows and tapping the side of her nose with a spare finger. If she can still find her own nose that's one sobriety test she's passed. 'Let's just say Christmas is the perfect time to take a relationship to the next level.'

This time when she delivers Ambrose one of her significant nudges, he simply slides off his shelf and disappears. I'm counting the seconds, waiting for him to burst back to the surface spluttering. But he doesn't.

'Miranda ...?' I mean, how drunk is she? I know she's careless with men, but Ambrose is breathing in water and she's examining her nail extensions, completely oblivious. It's decades since I got my lifesaver badge, but the images of drowning people are flashing through my head. Libby's Christmas is hanging in the balance as it is, a dripping corpse in the courtyard would finish it off completely. My heart plummets for a second, and then it starts to race – I'm the only non-pissed person here, it's down to me to pull him out!

I take one look at my beautiful pink sparkly sweater then peel it off. As I throw it down on the flags, and toss my phone down on top, I let out a shout. 'Okay, I've got this Ambrose, I'm coming in to s-a-a-a-a-a-a-ve you!'

There's no time to climb up the steps and gently ease myself down into the water. In any case, I'm in full Lois Lane mode now. I'm already launching myself in a full frontal dive over the edge and frig what it's going to do to my messy bob, I only hope my hat stays put. Except what was supposed to be a power packed superwoman swoop ends up as a full belly flop that practically empties the tub. And what looked like just bubbles on the surface turns out to be Ambrose on his way up. As I land on him he lashes out, and we end up in a whole mess of thrashing limbs, slippery skin, curses and flying water.

Then just as we're almost disentangled there's a loud 'woof'. Before we can turn around, Merwyn is jumping off the top of the steps, paws running in mid air. Then he hits the surface sending water splashing upwards in a hundred sparkling arcs under the spotlights.

'Merwyn!' His legs are scrambling frantically as he tries to swim, and as I finally stagger to my feet and haul him out of the water, I'm clinging on as he wriggles.

'What the hell happened there?' Miranda's fished Ambrose's Santa hat out of the water and she's wringing it out. Putting it back on his dripping head as he eases himself back onto the shelf beside her.

The water's sluicing off Merwyn as I clasp him to my waist. 'Ambrose was drowning, I came in to give him CPR, that's all.'

Miranda's laughing. 'However much he'd have enjoyed it, Ambie didn't need the kiss of life. He just likes to scare the bejesus out of me with how long he can stay under.'

'Brilliant. I'm glad we cleared that one up.' And then I hear a low cough by the kitchen doors and my heart goes into free fall. 'Bill, how lovely to see you.' As if it wasn't already awful enough. Seriously, he'd better not start going on about water on the floor.

His lips are twisting. 'So you decided to try the hot tub

after all, Ivy. If you wanted a wet T-shirt competition, you should have said.'

I don't need to look down to know my top's transparent, and I'm cursing my choice of bra.

Miranda's beaming at me. 'Lovely lingerie, sweetheart, you'll have to tell me where you bought it.'

'Very festive colour too.' Bloody Bill should not be joining in. Plus, if he really knows zilch about Christmas, how come he knows scarlet's even a thing?

The ground opening up, me falling in doesn't even begin to cover it.

Bill's swallowing. 'Which reminds me, are you two wearing clothes in there?'

Well, he just had to didn't he? As I back against the other side of the tub I've given up cringing about my underwear being on public display and moved on to shuddering about what I might have accidentally grabbed back there in the struggle.

'Do Santa hats count?' Miranda's lips twitch. 'You're seriously missing the market, Bill, with your private beach, you should be offering naturist breaks.'

Ambrose is slumped sideways. 'We're all guysss together here ... those surfiesss of yourssss don't give a flying f-f-fart ...'

Bill's hands are rising to his hips. 'I'd rather you didn't flash your bits around in front of Ivy, that's all.'

I hoik Merwyn up so he covers my boobs and peer through the waterfall of drips coming off my woolly hat. 'Leave me out of this, I can look after myself thanks!' For my money Ambrose is unlikely to run around naked, I doubt he can even stand.

'Before Ivy gets out, I have a bone to pick with you, Bill.' Miranda's voice has risen so much it's loud enough to be heard in St Aidan. 'In a sub zero castle with paper thin walls, the least I expect is a four poster. So what are you going to do about our substandard bed?'

I'm working out what would be next up the status ladder – a five poster, or a six poster? – and summoning the energy to ask if we can leave this until tomorrow, or at least until I'm back on dry land. Making a mental note to remind her that drinking lowers your core temperature. Not that she'll listen.

From Bill's shrug he doesn't really care. 'They're Hypnos mattresses, we've never had complaints before.'

With an empty gin bottle and Miranda's tenacity, I'm stepping in to smooth this over. 'It's more that it hasn't got enough posts.'

'That's really not my problem.' He might be cursing under his breath, but this is only the beginning.

Miranda's not letting go. 'But we need to discuss alternatives.'

Bill's straight back at her. 'First you stick to the dress codes, *then* I'll think about talking.' Which seems to have worked a treat, because Miranda's opening and shutting her mouth, but nothing's coming out. He turns to me. 'The guys were looking for you before they left.'

'They've gone?'

'It was the Extreme Surfers fancy dress disco, they had to rush off.' He's saying it like it's a completely normal, everyday occurrence. 'They thought you might like to go?'

'*Me?*' I'm screwing my face up in disbelief. '*Why* would I?'

He shrugs but this time the twist to his lips is bigger. 'If you're on the lookout for Ian Somerhalder, why wouldn't you?'

Fuck, fuck and fuck that he heard. And even more fucks that he was brazen enough to admit to listening in.

When you're completely stuffed, there's only one way to go. I pull myself up to my full height, look straight ahead, ignore that Merwyn's tail is hanging down in the water that's lapping around my waist, and clutch him very tight. 'Well, we're going for a shower. And then we'll have supper. And then we're going to check the castle.' As everything else has turned to total shit, I might as well cheer myself up with that. As I turn my scowl onto Bill I hope it's hard enough to drill through him. 'I'll see you in the entrance hall in an hour.'

As if throwing myself into a hot tub fully clothed wasn't embarrassing enough. How am I going to get through Christmas now?

11.

Mwah!

'You do realise, singing the *Ghostbusters* theme isn't actually funny, Bill.'

I'm standing in the castle entrance hall, and the immense branches I'm staring up into reach so high and the lights are so twinkly, even Merwyn's starry eyed. Lucky for Bill, the sight of thousands of tiny studs of light has taken my breath away so much, I'm less cross than I should be about his humming.

'*Is the castle haunted, do ghosts groan with pleasure?* That's going to crack us up for years to come.' He stops smiling, then starts again. 'I could sing a Wet, Wet, Wet song if you'd rather? *I feel it in my fingers, I feel it in my toes* … That's got a festive version too, as a Christmas obsessive you'd have to go with that.'

He – or more to the point, the surfers he bribed with toast – might have pulled off a fabulous tree here, but he's not getting away with cheek like that. 'Bill …' I wait until I have his full attention. 'Frig off.'

He stops in mid hum. 'And we're inside and you've got your hat on. *Again.* Did you know?'

Whatever I said about not being cross, scratch it. 'It's a hat, it's no big deal. My hair was still hanging in rat tails, as I didn't have hours to mess with my drier and my tongs, I took refuge under my pompom. Anything else?' It's fiction made up on the spot, but I'm past caring.

'Maybe a bit more reaction to the tree would have been nice?'

I'm rolling my eyes. 'It's great. Which I'd have mentioned already if you hadn't filled the talking space with your humming bollocks.'

From the faraway look in his eyes, he's talking to himself as much as me. 'We used to love *Ghostbusters*, as kids we acted it out for weeks at a time.' It's strange to think of Bill as a child, somehow he looks like he landed in his fully perfect adult form.

'Good for you – and it's a lovely tree.' If I say how truly wonderful it is he'll only ridicule me, so that's as much as he's getting. As it stands it's only half dressed, I have a serious amount of shell collecting to do before we can fully finish it, but I've already got a butterfly storm in my tummy when I let myself think how it's going to look. I'm finally letting my gaze slide down to the huge wooden barrel it's standing in, the stack of toboggans in front I arranged earlier. Thinking how great a stack of wrapped presents would look too, maybe a couple of gin boxes in the pile to keep the theme going. Then as my eyes drop onto the stone flags I take a step back. 'What the hell is that on the floor?' I stoop down and pick up a brown clod.

Bill takes refuge in one of those all too familiar shrugs. 'Patina – isn't that the word you'd use?'

I'm examining my palm. 'Bill, this isn't patina, it's mud. Earth. Soil.' The main lights are dimmed and as I look more closely, I can see it's spread right across the floor.

'Whatever fancy name you want to call it, there's no need to make a fuss, it's only a bit of dirt.' He's underplaying it.

'It's not only a bit, it's like a bloody ploughed field in here.' There's a scattering of fine soil, then bigger chunks and lumps. 'Look, there are even skid marks.'

He gives a sniff. 'So, they dropped a bit filling the pots, you got your trees, didn't you?'

'And half the grounds too by the looks of it.' As I stare up the stairs the scattered lumps carry on as far up as I can see. 'What's it like further through?' As I follow him into the chilling spaces I should be gasping at the scent of pine needles and the twinkle of another gorgeous undressed tree, feeling excited about the way the chairs look, so cosy and inviting clustered around the fireplace. But instead I'm groaning at the floor. 'Again, a great effort, spoiled by the muddy footprints. It's like you had Young Farmers trampling around here in their wellies, not silver surfers.' And I just know it's going to be like this all over the castle.

He gives a sigh. 'These guys are at home with sea and sand. When it comes to soil or housework, they have less idea.'

Now I've heard it all. 'Is this more of Bill's bollocks?'

He rolls his eyes. 'I wish it was. They're mostly ex-stockbrokers, until they got their Y-O-L-O tattoos and took to the waves, they all had staff. Real life is still a novelty, that's why they're so enthusiastic, but the downside is the gaps.'

'Like the mud?'

'Exactly.' He's looking shifty. 'You must be blinded by the stuff, because you haven't spotted the other deliberate mistake yet.'

I must be too tired to see it, or possibly the mud heaps are too high. 'Tell me.'

'The dining furniture isn't here yet. It depends on the hangovers when that happens.' He pauses to pull a face. 'Since the guys discovered craft cider, Sunday mornings aren't pretty.'

My groan's so loud I could rival Miranda. 'So did you get anywhere tracking the parcels?'

The way his face drops I know the answer before he speaks. 'Shit. Damn. No news there yet.'

My voice soars. 'One thing, and you didn't do it?' He just isn't getting this, what's more, he took one chair upstairs, then didn't lift a finger all day.

He's shuffling from foot to foot. 'It's fine, I'll do it now.'

'Actually Bill, it isn't fine at all. I admit some tiny bits of it are, like the trees. But then even the good bits get stuffed up and suddenly the whole place is full of mud. Do you have any idea how long it's going to take to clean these floors? And what the hell's the point of trees when there aren't any sodding decorations to hang on them? You care *so* little, you can't even be bothered to spend five minutes trying to discover where the effing decorations are!' I'm so angry I'm shaking. I'm also sparing a second to send a silent but heartfelt plea to every Christmas elf in the area to speed the decorations our way. If they arrive first thing we might just be saved. 'The whole of your life for the next two weeks hangs on Libby's first impressions. When we wake up tomorrow morning, we have twelve hours. And it's your choice. Either you step up, take responsibility, and get involved. Or I'm leaving you to it, and you're on your own.'

His eyes are wide. 'Great. I'll bear that in mind.' From the grating wobble in his voice he's shaken. Which has to be a first.

And actually, I'm not going to work my butt off until I know he's committed, because unless he is, there's no point to any of this.

'Right.' I smile down at Merwyn. 'Merwyn and I are going for a walk, then we'll be going to bed. And depending on our hangovers ... and how lazy we're feeling ... and how many pages of figures we find to pore over ... you may see us in the morning ... but you may not see us until lunchtime. Or even later. So over to you, it's your call now, Bill.'

And as we turn and stomp back to the kitchen I can't help noticing how good Merwyn's getting at marching off beside me, right in step, with his nose in the air. And as we make our way out onto the beach and watch the moon's reflection splashing across the sea as we walk, I know whatever I say, I won't be able to stay in bed too long in the morning. Simply because I can't wait to see how Bill's going to play this.

Sunday

15th December

12.

Wrap up!

Me, bribed by baking? I'm really not that shallow. But when we come back from our before-breakfast walk to find a tray of cranberry and cinnamon swirl buns, still warm from the oven, I have to admit, my mouth is watering. When I find a note saying *Ivy, help yourself (not for dogs!)* mainly I'm struck by the writing. It's slightly italic, and despite the *(very bossy!)* condition, it's friendly and relaxed, with neat even letters that are confident and clear, without being showy. Handwriting and cranberry buns can tell you a lot, they're like a secret view into a person's soul. And it's actually fine to exclude Merwyn, because he's only allowed dog specific food anyway.

By the time I've gone through every surfer in my head plus Ambrose and Miranda to guess a match I'm already on my third bun and counting. There's something about the delicious doughy crunch, the snowy drift of icing sugar on the top, the way the juice of the berries is shot through with heat as its tartness hits my tongue. And whatever Bill claimed about hangovers, *someone* is up and about and working all kinds of magic with the Magimix.

Then because I *really* don't want to show up too early, I creep into Bill's room and fire off a couple of 'see you *very* soon' messages to Fliss and Libby, which really mean, 'arrive as late as you like'. When neither of them reply it's fine – we all know what a nightmare last minute packing is. If they haven't even set off yet it means all the more time for us to get the place perfect.

If I'm extra mellow as we finally make our way through to the castle entrance hall, it's because I'm stuffed. Like Merwyn after his favourite turkey dog-dinner blow out, as I swing the bag of shells I collected on the beach and added ribbon loops to last night, I'm waddling rather than walking. I also have zero expectations about what I'm going to find. Let's stay real here – even if Bill's not in his room, why should he pull his finger out with the castle when he hasn't this far?

Then as I push through into the entrance hall my jaw drops. 'Stepladders!' It's one of those times I'm so surprised I end up saying exactly what I'm looking at instead of anything more sensible.

'That's the one, Hat-girl. Wearing the furry pompom indoors five days in a row? We'll be thinking it's deliberate.'

Obviously that was Bill, and obviously I'm not going to reply, especially when he's calling me that. Although if it's a choice between jokes about my hat and jokes about ghostly orgasms, or falling on top of Christmas trees, or my untimely leap into the effing hot tub, or worse still, my supposedly desperate hunt for a man, I'll take the head gear every time.

'And Taj too!' I'm still startled and stating the obvious. 'First one here, working through your hangover?'

He's sliding a second set of steps into place. 'Head's clear as a bell, and I was actually last to arrive. When word got out about those cranberry twirls it caused a surfie stampede.' He dips into a box and pulls out a miniature gin bottle. 'So we're hanging these on here with some shells? How about we make a start and you come back in five minutes and see if we're doing it right?'

'Great.' For once it actually is. I hand him the bag of shells, then I turn to Bill. 'What's that you're leaning on?'

Bill steps back and holds up the stick, to show what's on the end. 'It's a mop, we're all hard at it in there, I can personally guarantee every floor will soon be patina free.' He's pushing on the door. 'There's something through here I know you'll want to work on too.'

As I follow his dark tousled curls past the sofas and fireplace and groups of easy chairs, I'm pinching myself to check I'm not dreaming. Much less productively, I'm mentally tracing the lines of his back muscles through his jumper. Watching the back of his neck flexing as he turns his head to grin at me over his shoulder, and hating myself for it. 'Charcoal – it's a good colour for cashmere.' I've no idea where that blurting came from either.

He glances back at me. 'There you go again, Ivy, completely missing the bigger picture. After all that carrying too.' He steps to one side and takes a breath. 'So what do you think – or are they so transparent they're invisible?'

For a second I don't know what the hell he's talking about and then I see – the three long glass tables from the distillery arranged in the empty space beyond the sofas, surrounded by my favourite perspex chairs. 'Oh my, are they spectacular, or what?' It's like they're there, but they're not. Sure, they're big, but because they're see-through it's as if they don't take up any space.

'Good call of yours, Pom Pom. They actually look so good they may have to stay forever. Are you putting lights on the chairs?'

'I'll do that now.' It's a shock he's even remembered. I dive into a box I left here yesterday, and pull out the sets of the prettiest tiny see-through perspex stars on strands of copper wire along with the tape to stick the battery boxes to the chairs. 'And maybe if you have some larger empty gin bottles, we could have them in clusters down the table centres, with the tea lights in jars.'

As I hear Miranda's laugh approaching I'm expecting her to sweep through in her dressing gown. Instead she's in navy leggings and lots of woolly layers with flashes of brightly flowered silk, all topped off with a shimmery gold puffa coat, and she's carrying pots full of pine branches. 'Had a lovely lie in, sweetheart? We've been at it for hours, where do you think for these, I've got another eight outside?'

I'm picking my jaw up off the floor. Again. For all the reasons. 'How about along the long wall between the trees. They'll be a great way to break up the rockiness of the walls.'

She's purring at me. 'You've got such a good eye, Ivy-leaf, I knew you'd know.' As for being called Ivy-leaf, no one loves a pet name quite as much as Miranda. This one stuck on my very first visit to Brighton when I accidentally blurted that my mum called me Ivy after the ivy-leaved toadflax which grew in our back yard when she was pregnant. They're like tiny purple snapdragon weeds that scramble in nooks and crannies on walls and everyone seemed to think it was hilarious they were the only flowers we had. It could have been worse, they could have called me Toadflax, and at the time I remember loving that I had my own special name.

But getting back to the present, I'm hot on the trail of my mystery baker. 'And those lovely buns in the kitchen, Miranda, were they down to you?' She used to hate cooking, but with Paul Hollywood flexing his pecs in the *Bake Off* tent, she wouldn't be the first hopeless cook to be inspired to brush up on her sponge skills.

She lets out a hoot of laughter. 'I can't take the credit for those, Ambie and I would starve before we switched the oven on.' So that's them out of the running. As she turns to Bill she changes from a velvety purr to a spit. 'So here we all are, *totally* clothed and working our little tushes off for you, have you got anything to say to me?'

Bill shrugs and half closes one eye. 'Your jacket is looking fabulously tinselly?' Is that seriously the only glittery word he knows?

Miranda's not backing off. 'You might like to try again?'

'Nice pine twigs?'

There's a low laugh, a flash of neon orange and the rattle of hair beads, and Keef bursts in. 'Don't listen, he's winding you up.' His joggers are streaked in a shepherd's delight sunset, but there's no sign of any giveaway traces of flour dust. 'If you're after a four poster, Miranda, I'm your man. Say the word, my Milwaukee is at the ready.'

As Miranda unwinds her scarf and readjusts her layers a large expanse of bare chest comes into view. 'It's never too early for cocktails!'

Keef laughs. 'I'm talking about my Milwaukee drill, not my drinks cabinet. Super-fast four poster conversions are my speciality. Do you fancy scaffold poles, ash saplings or rope-tied sail battens?'

Totally entranced doesn't begin to cover her expression. 'It all sounds very hands on! How about you come up and give me a demonstration or two, talk me through the options?'

As he turns to follow her he leans across and pats my arm. 'Stress less, live more, Ivy. You'll be pleased in the long run.'

'*Me, stressed?*' I'm so incensed it comes out as a shriek.

He's wiggling his eyebrows at me as he heads for the door. 'Stop waiting for perfect, don't forget to play, *carpe* those effing *diems*!'

Merwyn and I exchange WTF? glances, then I turn to Bill. 'Would you like to translate?'

Above the corners of his pulled down mouth Bill's eyes are dancing. 'That's just Dad giving you the benefit of his YOLO repertoire. Think yourself lucky you didn't get *You're a diamond, let yourself shine.*' He's rubbing his hands. 'Anyway, no time to lose, we'd best push on, what are you onto next?'

I'm still opening and closing my mouth at the sheer audacity when Taj's head appears around the door. 'We're fine for bottles out here, Ivy, but you're going to need a hell of a lot more shells.'

'Right.' At least this way it sounds like my idea. 'I'll get the lights on these chairs then I'll head straight off to the beach.'

Bill's on his way out but he hasn't quite left. 'I was going to stock up the wood baskets, but I could come with you instead – give you a hand?'

'No, totally not, all your hands are needed here.' Bossing people around. Keeping the crew in order. I'd rather eat my own head than go for a walk with Bill. Just saying.

'Okay, your loss. Well ... busy, busy.' He points to his mop. 'Catch you later, then.'

I sort out the chairs, and there are enough lights left to put them into jars down the tables too. Although I say it myself, as I tiptoe away it looks so amazing and magical I have to go back for another look – three times. Then Merwyn and I hurry out across the sand to collect shells, as I bob to scoop up whelks and cockles, he's chasing sticks and trying to catch the bubbles as the waves rush up the beach. The sea is iron grey, streaked with foam slashes and as we pick our way along the high tide line, and as my stomach starts to growl with hunger and I still haven't filled the bag, I'm slightly cursing myself for being hasty and not accepting Bill's help. But, jeez, spending any more time with the guy than I already have to would simply not be worth the agony.

When we get back to the kitchen it's wonderfully Christmassy, with the lights on the tree and the fairy lights I've strung around the door. As I drill holes in the shells, then thread them with pink and orange hanging ribbons, with my favourite festive playlist on my phone, a frothy hot chocolate, and the rest of the cranberry whirls to dip into, it's the first truly relaxing moment I've had to myself since I arrived. However much bollocks Bill's dad talks, by the time I'm swinging towards the entrance hall with my second bag of shells I'm pretty chilled. Then I open the door, see most of the surfies plus Miranda hanging off the ladders and my jaw hits the floor, followed closely behind by my stomach.

'But what are you wearing?' It comes out as a whimper.

Miranda beams down at me from a top step. 'They're Cockle Shell Castle sweat shirts, aren't they lovely, isn't this a gorgeous shade of yellow?'

Keef's below her, hanging on to her hips, her bum wedged against his chest, but he manages to turn around. 'Bill found a huge box of them in the laundry. #TeamChristmas on the back, that's definitely us!' He's patting his stomach. 'All different colours too! Come and see this gorgeous, glittery writing, it's actually edged in sequins.'

'I don't need to look, I ...' ordered the damn things, spent hours poring over the different fonts, choosing the wording, agonising over whether to pay the massive amount extra for that damned edging '... I saw it when I unpacked them.' They were so beautiful. What's more, they're not meant for random surfies, they were part of my secret stash, my personal thank you to all Libby's guests for sharing their Christmas with me. Also designed to whip out in case of a crisis to pull the party together. Although why the hell I'd think there'd be any of those, I can't imagine.

Miranda's staring down at me. 'You need to join in too or you'll spoil the effect. Even Ambie's wearing one, he's in the tub but he's rolled it up to his armpits to keep it out of the water.' As Bill comes in she's even beaming at him. 'Cockle Shell Castle tops, that's another no brainer you're missing out on, Bill.'

He narrows his eyes. 'Branded clothing for *naturists* – how's that a good fit, Miranda?'

Miranda's laughing. 'You're such a naughty tease. It's a good thing I'm pleased with my bed.'

My eyes are popping in disbelief. 'You actually have your four poster?' When it comes to getting what she wants, Miranda is a human dynamo, we could all do with taking lessons. Although I suspect her methods are probably too 'Hollywood starlet' for anyone in my generation to be comfortable with.

She's nodding like a cat who's had cream *and* fresh red tuna. 'Timber battens lashed with natural hemp rope, draped with twists of muslin. All Keef's design, and so unbelievably floaty, he's doing them for the other rooms too.'

'Astonishing. I mean brilliant!' I pass my bag up to Taj on the other ladders, then incline my head. 'Here's the shells, if I could just have a *private* word with Bill in the kitchen?' It's out before I realise my folly.

As if that wasn't bad enough, Bill compounds it. 'Yes, fine by me, I need that too.'

Miranda's chortling down at me. 'Absolutely, and not before time, sweetheart.' She gives me a wink. 'Take as long as you want, we know the score, we'll all stay out here and give you some space.'

It would matter more if Bill and Miranda weren't daggers drawn. Except, I'm hopeful that now she's got her posts and wispy twists, and with Libby arriving, she'll fade into the background and be less confrontational.

As for confrontation, I'm so silently apoplectic about my

own disappointment, the second we reach the kitchen I turn on Bill.

'So you found the sweatshirts and decided to give them out?'

He's looking sickeningly pleased with himself. 'You pushed me to use my festive initiative and I went the extra mile. Is there a problem?'

'Only that they were meant for a different team entirely. But I'll order more.' And hope they arrive faster than the decorations. Which I'll move on to next.

His eyes are bright. 'They totally worked, everyone's been so much jollier since they put them on. Who knew festive sweatshirts would make such a difference, maybe there's something in your "maxing out the Christmas shit" theory after all.'

If the next bit wasn't so urgent, I'd spend longer basking in the 'I told you so' glory. But it's already two, so I'm moving this on. 'And is there any news on the decorations, have they arrived?' I was at the beach for ages, so surely they must have done.

I watch his throat bulge as he swallows. 'Well yes ...'

My chest drops in sheer relief. In my head I'm punching the air, I'm so happy I almost hug him, but then I notice his expression. 'Yes ... *what*?'

It takes a while for his grating reply to arrive. 'Yes ... and ... er ... no.'

My heart's suddenly banging in my chest and I'm shouting. 'What the hell kind of answer is that? It can't be both.' Except from the deepening hollows in his cheeks, maybe it can.

He clears his throat. 'Well, yes, they have arrived. But not here.'

'Okay, where the eff are they? We can send out a search

party ... let's courier them over.' Whatever it takes, I need those babies, and I need them now.

He blinks, and blows out a long breath. 'They were accidentally sent to my old London address.'

'Great, that's easy then.' Mix ups like that happen all the time, at least we know where they are and I'm sure he said that's where Gemma is. If we go for super-fast delivery, we should get them in seven hours. I can work with that.

Under his stubble his skin is more grey than white. 'I'm sorry, there was a gargantuan mix up, and now they've disappeared from the system completely.'

I'm clinging onto the kitchen island so hard, my knuckles are white. As my heart leaves my chest and slides down to somewhere around my knees, I stagger backwards and sink onto the sofa. In my head an entire castle of empty trees are flashing past my eyes. It's sinking in that as far as Libby goes, an empty tree is way worse than no tree at all. So when I finally speak, it's a whisper. 'What do we do now?'

He flops down on the sofa next to me, pulls up a knee and rubs his chin on the back of his hand. 'It's what my dad would call a FISH moment – frig it, shit happens. Excuse the cliché avalanche but we're going to have to go with the flow, roll with the punches ... and come up with another plan.'

'Right.' I'm almost keeping up with him. 'What kind of *other plan*?'

He pulls a face. 'I haven't got that far yet.' He reaches across to the coffee table and picks up a bun. As he bites into it, it's nice to see that his teeth aren't quite as even as they could be.

As if you could think of eating at times like this. I'm actually thinking how it would feel to run my tongue over those teeth, which is totally unhelpful, and obviously my own completely off-the-wall inappropriate reaction to the trauma of the situation.

He's staring at me expectantly. 'You're the specialist here, what do you suggest?'

I'm racking my brain as I look at the clock. 'We have six hours, maybe even eight. We just need to keep calm ...'

'Keep calm ... and eat cranberry swirls.' He holds up another bun. 'Pom Pom, we've got this.'

In the distance Miranda's peals of laughter are echoing down the hall. And I could be wrong, but I think Bill might have apologised back there. Which isn't like him at all. But there are more voices too. Excited shouts, a shriek or two. Except these ones are coming from beyond the French windows. Bill's holding up his hand in the air, and I'm weighing up if high fiving him is going too far when I hear the wail of a baby, and a louder voice over the rest.

However fast my heart was beating before, I swear it stops dead now. 'Fuck, that's Harriet ... and Libby ... *THEYRE HERE!!!!'*

Bill's up before me, tearing across the kitchen. Then he's back twice as fast, thrusting something soft into my hands. 'Quick, put this on. I saved the pink one for you.'

As I run blindly for the door, and push my arms into the sleeves, I'm letting out a low wail. 'How's a sweatshirt going to help any? We're washed up ... Christmas crackered ... toast.'

And then Libby's at the door, and I know we're totally screwed.

13.

Define good …

'Come on in, Libby, this is Bill, and it's SO GREAT YOU'RE HERE!'

Obviously I'm lying, and over compensating for the shock with volume because when I listen to myself, I'm actually yelling. I'm frantically trying to get everyone past the bare kitchen tree, whooshing them along, hoping if we hurry through the entrance hall will be finished enough to give the impact we need.

As I wave Libby's four kids in it's like pages of Libby's latest earth-friendly child wear catalogue flicking past under my nose. Tomas is the eldest and is almost a teenager, but he's shot up two feet since I last saw him, and seems to have swapped smiley tractor prints for attitude and a black puffa jacket that's so big he could fit a bed inside there as well as himself. He's also keeping his hat on indoors, and it's pulled even further down than mine, so we have an instant bond. Then there are the girls, Tiffany and Tansy, who are ten and eight, and the youngest boy Tarquin who's coming up to five. And if ever I'm confused as to who belongs to who, my clue is – Libby's kids' names all begin with a T.

Fliss's three year old, Oscar, fist bumps me as he bounces past, but it was probably accidental. He's jumping and punching the air, and the stick he's waving around is the size of a small telegraph pole.

Fliss's kiss hits my cheek. 'Okay, Ivy-star?' She's clutching baby Harriet whose squawk rips my ear drum and as Fliss sags into my hug I can feel her weariness. 'We set off yesterday or we might not have got here at all.'

'It's lovely to see you, Fliss.' I mean it this time. She's so much smaller than me, my chin's wedged against her messy up-do and I just know her hair hasn't been brushed in a week. Beyond the tangles I can see Bill dipping in and out of a box like it's a jumble sale, helping the kids out of their coats and into Cockle Shell Castle sweatshirts.

Where Fliss is small, rounded, and soft as an eiderdown, Libby's diminutive frame is as taut as Madonna's in her break dance days when she carried a ghetto blaster round on her shoulder, wore skin tone fishnets and danced the arses off the guys in the street with her skimpy leotard. As I watch Libby peeling off her cashmere roll neck and wiggling into a powder blue version of the Christmas sweatshirt, the diamanté Gucci hair slide is sparkling as she reclips it. 'Getting the freebies in early – Bill, is it? Let's hope it's not downhill from here.'

For now I'll let him claim them. It's just lucky I ordered extras, they have to be running out.

Next thing, Bill's striding over to Fliss. 'Peacock blue okay for you?'

I'm blinking because that's the exact one I'd picked out for her. Then my eyes open wider.

As he scoops Harriet out of Fliss's arms and hands her the sweatshirt, Harriet's wailing stops.

I'm staring at him. 'That baby's cried non-stop for eleven months, how the hell did you do that?'

He gives a shrug. 'Years of practice.' He's balancing Harriet in the crook of his arm and she's cooing at him, poking his cheeks with her pudgy fingers.

I've fallen for his bollocks once too often, he's not getting me again. 'Really ...'

He raises an eyebrow at me. 'Of course not, it's beginners' luck. Desperate times and all that, from now on I'll be keeping out of the way of everyone under eighteen. You take her now.' A second later she lands on my stomach and I slide her onto my hip, then gently ease her back to Fliss.

Then he turns to the rest of them as they pull down their sweatshirts and smile at the sequins. All apart from Libby, obviously. 'So if you'd all like to come this way and follow Ivy, we'll show you the rest of the castle.'

'Here we go, wait for it ...' I'm talking under my breath, pulling a face at Fliss. The tree might be huge but whatever we've done to make the castle better, it's so different from what Libby bought into. When she doesn't get what she orders her eruptions are legendary. So far what she's seen are the good bits, and she's looking really sour. Given the serious lack of luxury in the parts ahead, there *has* to be trouble coming.

With the blast about to break over our heads, as we make

our way towards the hall I'm kicking myself … if only I hadn't gone to bed, if only I'd tracked the orders better, if only I'd argued less with Bill and twigged they were on their way. I mean, after five days I'm almost used to the rocky walls but when you see them for the first time they look seriously cave-like. I've been holding my breath all the way from the kitchen, and as we burst through into the hallway I'm waiting for the light glinting off the miniature bottles and the sea shells spinning on their ribbons. The scent of fresh pine tree as we take in the thousands of tiny stud lights between the branches. Desperate for them to save us.

But mostly what we see are Miranda, Keef and assorted surfies, still swarming over the branches hanging the last of the shells. It's so messy and unprofessional I know we're totally done for.

For once Bill's refined accent's working in our favour, let's hope he's got enough sense to hurry Libby through. 'So this is the entrance hall.'

Libby blinks. 'I see you're making the most of product placement.'

From Bill's frown, he hasn't got a clue what she's talking about. 'Excuse me?'

'Your gin on my Instagram feed – you'll end up owing us if we're not careful.'

Bill sends her an appalled stare. 'Jeez, I hope you're joking, the whole point of a tiny distillery is to keep the brand unknown. Gin lovers discovering the secret for themselves is what keeps the price high.' In which case he really should have said earlier.

I'm rolling my eyes and willing him to shut up. 'With her millions of followers you might have blown that one, shall we move on through?'

Bill shakes himself back. 'Sure, so this leads through to the ...'

Just before he claims it as a chill out space I jump in again. '... these are the family areas. Aren't the log fires amazing?' They certainly are to me, they weren't there when I left for the beach. But burning in the monumental fireplaces, their warmth and the flickering glow has made the whole room come alive, and made the spaces feel ten times more festive and cosy in the fading afternoon light.

Bill's dashing ahead of us. 'We'll put the guards across straight away now you're here.'

Libby's patting the back of a squishy leather chair from the barn. 'I can see why you were horrified, Ivy, it certainly is "less in more".' She lets out a sigh. 'Oh well, it's only two weeks. And if there's nothing to smash we won't have to pay for breakages.'

I should be grateful, her reaction could have been worse. 'How about a nice cup of tea in front of a roaring fire?'

I'm suddenly aware that she's moved, come to a halt in front of the next tree and is frowning at it, so I clear my throat because it's gone completely dry. 'The trees ... you've noticed we've left the smaller ones ...' I'm croaking '... we decided it was much more fun for everyone to help with those and the ones in the bedrooms too. That way everyone gets to personalise their own, it's much more individual.' It goes to show how your brain can come up with the most ridiculous stuff under pressure, and I'm still going. 'We could even make our own decorations too.'

Resting bitch face doesn't begin to cover her expression. 'And that's exactly why we brought you, Ivy.'

Instead of moving through to look at the dining area more closely, she wanders back into the hall, then turns to me again. 'And another surprise! When you mentioned staff, I hadn't imagined so many. Look at this lot, it's like Chatsworth.' What is there to say? Only that she possibly hates this less than the rest.

Beyond Libby's head the whites of Bill's eyes are flashing. 'Our human resources envelope is super-elastic, we bring in the manpower on an "as and when" basis.' At a guess, he's bricking it here.

I'm rolling my eyes at him. 'Really ... nicely put, Bill.'

It doesn't take much to snap Libby back into business-woman mode. 'Great move ... if you can get away with it.'

That tiny bit of encouragement and Bill's flying now. 'We definitely benefit from the seasonal nature of the local economy, it keeps the hired hands hungry. And we also like to maximise the opportunities for the older workforce.' Flying so close to the sun, he's in danger of crashing face down in his own bullshit.

I shoot him a 'shut the hell up' look. I think he's forgetting, he's the man who had seating for ten, a booking for twenty-five and no dining table. He just managed to lose twenty mahoosive boxes of Christmas deccies. However obliging his dad's mates are, he's not about to win Businessman of the Year.

I'm moving this on while we're still ahead. 'So maybe we should bring in the luggage, get that cup of tea.'

Tomas might look like he's old enough to ask for a razor for Christmas, but he's waggling his phone in Libby's face, sticking his bottom lip out like a badly behaved six year old, and whining like he's three. 'Mother ... you do know there's still no signal?'

If it's any consolation, Libby's just as curt with him. 'Your holiday challenge is to find it. Why else do you think we brought all those boxed set DVDs and the vintage Gameboys?'

'Thanks a bunch MUM!!! NOT!!!'

She's totally dismissing his concerns. 'There's a whole beach for you to play on, get on with it.'

'Fuck sandcastles, forget the effing bastard beach, this is the shittest place ever!!!' Tomas wrenches open the enormous front door and slams it behind him.

As the bottles jingle on the tree, and ten mouths drop open, I know exactly how he feels. I've been there. What's more, the other kids are still here, but they're scowling at Libby as if they'd like to nuke her.

'But M-u-u-u-m ...' It's the smaller girl now.

Libby's eyes zone out. 'Don't start, Tansy.'

'But you totally tricked us, you've brought us here by false pretending, it's like kidnapping. If our phones were actually working we'd report you to Childline for lying.' Her eyes are flashing, and she's obviously inherited her resting bitch face *and* her tough talking from her mother.

And there's a strangled echo from the bigger girl. 'How are me and Tansy going to upload our vlogs? All our followers are waiting for updates.' She stares at her mum accusingly. '*Your* products will suffer from this too, you know.'

It's not that I'm judging. And it's true, Fliss has given me enough hints. But they're just *so* lacking in warmth and humanity, *so* tied up in their own little commercial world. And that's just the kids. They're just *SO MUCH* worse than I expected.

The smaller boy pipes up. 'I'm going to tell my dad.'

Libby's granite snap hardens. 'Well good luck with that. It'll be easier to find Cornish wifi *and* a Celtic mermaid than get a line in to him.'

'So maybe, tea now?' I turn to wince at Fliss, but she's fully occupied grappling with Oscar's telegraph pole as he powers towards the tree at a hundred miles an hour. Truly, that boy is a one-man demolition team. I'm picturing the ruination he'd have wreaked on the Osbourne and Little wallpaper and the chandelier candelabras in the Cockle Shell palace up the coast if he'd gone tossing his caber in there. And on balance it feels better we're here, not there.

'Tea?' It's Libby. 'We're not nearly ready for that, we need photos first.'

'We do?' Looking at the kids' angry faces, unless she's brought some spare Santa sacks to drop over their heads we might be best leaving this until later.

'Absolutely. As many combinations as you can of the staff up their ladders, please.' As she hands me her phone she's totally unsmiling. 'And then we'll go for a selfie with us *and* the workforce in front of the tree.'

I have to check. 'Everyone here okay with pictures going

up on Instagram etcetera?' I take it from the way they're holding their poses that they're all in.

As I leap about getting different angles, Libby's shaking her head. 'It's so good we set off a day early, any later we might have missed it.'

With the tree and the staircase, and the ladders and the brightly coloured sweatshirts, it's almost like a scene from *Elf*, but I keep that thought to myself and carry on snapping.

After the selfie with everyone I'm about to hand the phone to Libby when she lets out a cry. 'Mum, is that *you* up there! Come out from behind the man in green *THIS MINUTE*!' She's staring at Miranda as if she's having to look twice. 'What are you doing here, you said you were arriving next weekend?'

Miranda's a lot less prominent than she was on the same step earlier, if you ask me. She's still skulking slightly as she cobbles her reply together.

'I'll say hello properly once we finish here. We came early to give Ivy a hand, and it's a damn good thing we did, we've barely stopped.'

Libby's frown deepens. 'We …?'

Miranda's smile suggests she's completely unbothered by Libby's disapproval and the charm-free interrogation. 'Don't worry, I'll introduce you in a bit, you might have seen him in the hot tub as you came through.' She's still going. 'His Range Rover's out the front, it's the extra-shiny one with the cherished plate.'

Libby lets out a groan. 'You *haven't* got engaged again?'

Miranda hesitates. 'No … at least … not *yet*. At the moment Ambie's just a special friend.'

'Ambie?' Libby whirls round and looks at me expectantly.

'Short for Ambrose.' I can't help thinking about how much she's paying me, which is why I'm filling her in. 'He's great company in the hot tub, drinks gin like a fish and, don't be fooled like I was, he can hold his breath under water for bloody hours.' I take in that Tansy is sending me a dead eye. 'Excuse the swearing.'

Fliss is rolling her eyes at me. 'A husband's for life, not just for Christmas, Mum.'

Miranda's shaking her head. 'Look at you two and your long faces, stop worrying about things that might never happen.'

Fliss lets out a groan. 'But they always do, that's the problem.'

Miranda's smile lights up again as she stares down at the surfies. 'I've met so many new friends here too.' She wrinkles her nose at Keef. 'It's not every day a man makes you your dream four poster.'

It's good to see Fliss finally smile. 'Not even you can marry them all, Miranda.'

And this is why I love spending time with Fliss's family. They're enthralling because they live their lives without limits. They call their mum by her first name. You never know what's going to happen from one moment to the next. I mean, I love my mum and dad, but they're super-predictable and they'd hit the roof if I ever called them Pauline and Harry. For them, every year is the same – they spend a week in the same guest-house in Scarborough in the summer, have a day out at Bridlington in the autumn, a trip to the panto, and that's as much excitement as they can take in a year. Their menus repeat week after week, my dad fishes, my mum knits, and they watch TV. And that's it. When they once swapped Thursday sausage and chips for an M&S ready meal, they talked about it for months afterwards. When I first met Fliss, her noisy, colourful family were a revelation. One weekend at Miranda's and the limitations of my own life exploded. Before, nothing seemed possible, afterwards everything was there for the taking.

I know I'll never be as brave and out there as they are, there will always be a part of where I came from that holds me back and tethers me to the mundane. But, hell, life is so much more interesting since I spent time with them. They gave me courage, made me see what I could do. It's like they showed me what was possible, gave me permission to try new things, to explore and expand my world. And I'm so grateful for that. Without them I'd probably just have slipped back home after uni. At best I'd be a couple of streets away from my mum and dad. At worst I'd still be in my old room, having sausage and mash every Wednesday.

Even if I'll never have a life as lively as theirs, when I'm in their slip stream they pull me to places I wouldn't usually go. Like this castle.

Although right now my bigger picture has shrunk a bit. I over stretched, reached too far, and came crashing down. So for now my courage has diminished. Which is why it's especially lovely to be back in their wake again. Even if this time it's less as a participator, more as a spectator and helper.

Miranda's laughing. 'As Keef told me, we're all diamonds, we just need to be free and let ourselves shine.'

Bill's shaking his head. 'Complimentary life coaching is included in your stay.'

Miranda's eyes are flashing at him from up the ladder. 'Don't undermine your father, Bill. If you had an iota of commercial sense in you and even a tenth of your dad's empathy, you'd offer mindfulness breaks in a heartbeat.'

Bill's groaning too. 'Along with naked beach getaways and the branded hats, then.'

Fliss isn't letting this go. '*Free* – that means *definitely not* tied down, Mum.'

Tiffany's screwing up her face. 'How many husbands has granny had now, then?'

'Why *can't* granny marry all of them … what's a naked beach?' That's Tarkie.

Tansy's musing. 'When you and Dad split up, Mum, are *you* going to marry someone else?'

The way Libby's closing her eyes for a second, she looks like she's beaten. But then she bounces straight back again. 'Guys, give me a break, this is supposed to be a holiday.'

Tansy's sniffing. 'How long before we go home?'

Despite feeling like I'm on repeat, I'm going to try one last time. 'What about that tea?'

Libby's whirling around to me again. 'Ivy, I thought you'd never offer.'

As we make our way back to the kitchen Bill sidles up to me. 'So that went well … wouldn't you say …'

If Libby's so bad it feels like I'm on Bill's team, we *are* in trouble.

Monday

16th December

14.

Everybody's having fun …

After my first five quiet days at the castle, with eight more guests arriving, things were bound to change. First the luggage came in – obviously that was a job for the surfies before they left for Sunday quiz night at the Hungry Shark. Luckily they seem to be as enthusiastic about photo opportunities as they are about everything else in life, and no one queried getting snapped lugging Libby's humungous cases through the door, up the very picturesque staircase, and at many points between. But it went downhill from there onwards. With six children, all unhappy for their own – very real, very individual – reasons, and all *very* vocal, the volume of complaining was off the scale.

When we finally moved on to that tea I'd been talking about for so long, Libby lasted for approximately two sips before she caved in to the kids' nagging. I nipped into Bill's bedroom for two seconds' research, and a nanosecond later she dragged her lot off to the Fun Palace at the Crab and Pilchard down in St Aidan.

If you can believe the website blurb and the GIFs, they

were heading for wifi, turkey nuggets and ball cage play, all watched over by a mechanical Santa, his present-laden sleigh, and eight animated flying reindeer. I pause for a momentary flash-back shudder as I think about that. With staff dressed as Santa's helpers, piped Christmas music, two for one on Festive cocktails, *and* one of those trees where the deccies change colour in gorgeous bands going downwards – an idea that I have completely failed to sell to *Daniels* three Christmases running – well, what's not to like? I was almost sad to be staying home.

Who knows what those *particular* kids will make of it. I get the feeling they've always had 'the best' in unlimited quantities, which is probably why they're particularly hard to please. I mean, they came to a castle on the beach and there wasn't one good thing they found to say about it. Worse still, they couldn't wait to leave again. It isn't exactly promising for the next two weeks for the rest of us either.

But the good part was, with the 'critical moaners in crisis' out of the way Fliss and I managed to separate Oscar from his telegraph pole for long enough for us all to enjoy cheese on toast in front of the fire, and be supremely pleased there were no carpets to scrape the molten cheddar off. Then we all crept off to bed, leaving Miranda and Ambie still waving their glasses around in the hot tub.

After our early night, Merwyn and I were up and out for our walk along the beach early enough to see the dawn spread luminous grey and pink tinges across the clouds above the darkness of the sea as the wind blew our faces off. When we walked back towards the castle, the castellations of the towers were silhouetted against the orange sunrise. We were hoping we'd have the kitchen to ourselves when we got back, but Harriet had woken Fliss and Oscar. They all staggered down in their pyjamas and they're sitting at the table now looking like the walking dead. Except for Harriet who's hurling her breakfast fruit at the French window from her high chair, in between bouts of burying her hands in what looks suspiciously like porridge.

I try not to think how we'll get that out of the cracks between the broad polished floorboards, hand Fliss a coffee, and join them at the long table. 'Are you okay?' She obviously isn't. Oscar used to be so upbeat and rosy, but as Fliss manages to joke, the morning his baby sister arrived he turned into the honey monster from hell.

She blinks at me. 'I'm hanging on, it'll be better once Rob gets here.' Which is her state for most days, not helped by his late working. He's in construction, so the good part is the whole industry shuts down for two weeks over Christmas. The sad part is, that's not until the Friday before Christmas – in exhausted-mother time, it's light years away. And we both know with the trust issues she's had with him lately, a week of him in London and her so far away here could possibly send her round the bend. It was bad enough when he was coming home every night. Him not physically checking in for so long is going to be a total head fuck for her.

'We'll help if we can.' That's actually bollocks. When it comes to mum-support I've turned out to be rubbish because I have no clue what to do. When Bill foisted Harriet onto me when they'd just arrived, my first thought was to pass her on before I dropped her. My best bet is always to talk about something else. And much as I know Fliss will be bursting to discuss Rob, we're always careful not to talk in front of the children. So I opt for neutral but useful. 'So, any ideas for the Christmas tree in here? That's my next job. And as I said last night, I'm making my own decorations.' She won't mind me reminding her, baby brain's a terrible thing, we both know she'll have forgotten.

Fliss opens her eyes again and takes a sip of coffee. 'Well, if it's the kitchen tree something edible would be good.'

I'm grinning at her. 'Thanks for that stroke of genius. We'll have hanging marshmallows!'

She dips a toast finger in Oscar's egg and nudges him. 'Or maybe not marshmallows, Oscar inhales them, don't you? Ten minutes, and there wouldn't be any left and he'd most likely demolish the tree at the same time.' The sad thing is, she's not exaggerating.

'So what *don't* you like, Oscar?'

Fliss is thinking. 'He hates pineapple, and he's not keen on lettuce. Everything else, he devours.'

I'm trying to visualise branches draped with soggy pineapple rings and shredded cos lamella, then I have a really mean thought. 'How about gingerbread stars made with extra strong ginger? He won't try more than one of those will he?'

Fliss's eyes light up. 'That's a great plan – ginger's another thing he's not keen on. We got a warning letter from nursery the other week because he threw his shoe at the St Nikolaus celebration and spat his ginger cake at the class.'

'Poor Oscar, that was a bit harsh.' It's not his first warning letter either.

'Why not have ginger stars *and* gingerbread men?'

I'm nodding. 'Gingerbread men will look *so* cool. There's only one problem, I've never actually done them before.'

Fliss is staring at me like I'm silly. 'You made shortbread heart favours for three hundred when we got married, gingerbread can't be *that* different.'

Rob and Fliss's wedding was something else. His parents are farmers, the family is huge and they insisted on inviting the whole county to a massive marquee in their own meadow. And it's true, I could make shortbreads for England. I smile whenever I think about us in her kitchen, baking trays full of heart biscuits, two days before they got married. How blissful those days were for her compared to now. On every level.

'As soon as Bill gets up, I'll nip in and find a gingerbread recipe, then I'll fly into St Aidan and get the ingredients.'

Fliss looks up. 'It's fine, he already left, we saw him drive off from upstairs. Oscar recognised the sound of the Land Rover.'

Which is great news. Not that I've swapped sides, but I tipped him the wink last night that more of those cranberry swirls might smooth his path with Libby's lot. I mean, they made *my* day better, I'm damn sure I wouldn't have made it through yesterday without them. Fingers crossed he's out now, picking them up from whichever gifted and talented surfer bakes them.

St Aidan isn't far by car, but by the time I've parked, then wandered around the aisles, and picked up candy canes and other bits too, it's all taken far longer than I planned. By the time I'm back, the good news is there's the pile of warm buns I hinted at, and the less good news is that Fliss has gone. But Libby and her kids are all arriving instead.

Libby's darting around, peering into the courtyard. 'I haven't seen anyone, where are all the workers today?'

I smile at her. 'The staff here are a lot like the tide, they come in and out.'

She seems to accept that, so I pick up the bun tray and a stack of plates and bring them over to the table. 'Anyone fancy a warm cinnamon and cranberry swirl?'

I help myself to one, take a bite, and begin unpacking my bags and looking in the cupboards for baking trays and scales. I know what hungry kids are like when it comes to demolishing baking, so I'm wafting past in the hope of snaffling another before they all go. But as I get to the table there's a series of loud moans.

'Totally gross ...'

'Bleugh ...'

'Did we bring Pop-Tarts?'

Libby's tutting. 'For goodness sake Tiff, stop pulling at your tongue.'

Tiff's protesting loudly. 'Those red things are disgusting, I've got to pull to scrape the taste off.'

I'm trying to be friendly. 'My fault, I thought you might like them, I ate my own body weight in them yesterday.' They're staring at me without engaging, looking so supremely pissed off, I'm reaching for my trump card without even meaning to. 'How about we play Elf on the Shelf instead? It's a hunting game.' This was a little gem of an idea I got off Pinterest, on offer because, unlike the baubles, the order of a hundred plastic pixies to hide around the castle *has* arrived. It was meant for when things flagged on Christmas Day, if I'm bringing it out nine days early it's only because I'm desperate.

As they lean back in their chairs they're staring at me blankly. Tansy is first to react, and it's with another grimace and a head shake. 'P-e-r-l-e-a-s-e ...'

'Just no, totally no.' Tiff's got her back. 'I mean why ... just *why* ... would anyone want to look for *elves*?'

'It might have been fun?' I think I get the message about that. 'Well, who likes baking? I'm making gingerbread men in a moment, to hang on the tree. Anyone want to help?'

They don't even say, they just stare at me in total silence as if I'm an alien. I sense I'd actually have got a better reaction if I was.

Libby turns to them. 'Why not go and watch TV in the family room, CBeebies is bound to be on.'

A long groan comes from the gap between Tom's woolly hat and his puffa coat. 'When are you going to get it, Mother, *Postman Pat* isn't doing it for me any more. Why can't I watch *The Wire*? Or *Game of Thrones*? Or *Killing Eve*?'

Libby snaps at him. 'You know why, Tom, twelve is way too young to see women ripping men's whatsits off.'

There's another squawk from Tom's collar. 'THIRTEEN ... in a month.'

Tiff's staring at her mum like she's interrogating her. 'Or you could take us to the cinema?'

Tom's choking. 'I *REFUSE* to watch *Frozen* 2 again.'

Tiff's sniffing. 'One more time, then I'll be ready to do my vlog.'

Tom's voice rises in protest. 'I thought your vlog was about make up?'

Patronising doesn't begin to cover how she sounds. 'Tom, a vlog can be whatever you want it to be. My followers are happy to hear my thoughts on *any subject*.'

'You do know how vommy you sound?'

As Tom launches himself across the table and retches over the edge I totally get where he's coming from. I'm wondering what he's hiding under *his* hat when Libby gets up and pushes a box into my hand.

'An iPhone?'

'It's already set up with all my social media accounts, so you can upload pictures too.' She half closes one eye and her foot lands on my toes and crushes them at the same time. 'We never know when we'll find wifi do we? It's easier for you to slip away than it is for me.'

Bill's been warned – unless he wants the entire house party taking up residence in his room, he needs to keep his door firmly closed. Obviously Libby and I will have to nip in throughout the day, so I've given him a DO NOT DISTURB sign to hang on the door in case he needs private time. If he wants too much of that, we're stuffed.

'Lovely.' It's the latest model, I just hope I can work out how to use it.

'You can kick off with some photos of delicious warm buns. Straight away would be good.' She's clapping her hands, which seems rude even for her, but the claps aren't meant for me. 'Right, guys. Anyone up for breakfast at *Pret*, in the car, *NOW!*'

There's a scrape of chairs, a mass scramble for the French windows, and two seconds later Libby and I are left staring at each other, our jumpers flapping in the gale that's blowing in from the courtyard.

Libby's raising her eyebrows. 'Give them what they know, works every time.' She marches after them, and just before she closes the door she pops her head in again. 'Enjoy the peace while it lasts, the kids coming next are *seriously* hard work.'

'*You mean there's …*' I manage to strangle my *worse!!!!* squeak before it comes out. 'Great,' I say, really, really brightly, and I think I get away with it.

'They're allergic to everything, difficult to please and awkward with it. And they're bilingual.'

Oh my days. 'I'll brace myself while I make my gingerbread men.'

'Unless they're egg free and gluten free, they won't be interested. Best make them gender neutral too, their mother's very hot on equal ops.'

And then the door bangs, and they're gone.

When I nip into Bill's room and look it up, the only *Pret* is an hour away, at the airport. Is it really mean of me to wish that while they're there, they'll get on a plane and fly back to where they came from? And take their even more impossible friends with them.

15.

Deep and crisp and even …

350g/12oz plain flour, plus extra for rolling out
1tsp bicarbonate of soda
2tsp ground ginger (double up to make them Oscar proof)
1tsp ground cinnamon
125g/4½oz butter
175g/6oz soft brown sugar
1 free-range egg
4tbsp golden syrup

I jotted down the bones of the recipe on a scrap of paper in Bill's room, greased the tins, and now I'm weighing out the ingredients and adding them to the Magimix as I work. I'm not sure how many batches I'll need to fill the tree, but I'm doubling the quantities to begin with, and I'll see how I go after that.

It's surprisingly fast to do. Before long I'm wiping my hands on the blue and white stripy apron I borrowed from the back of the pantry door, shaking flour out of a super-posh flour sifter, and dolloping the dough onto the honed granite worktop to knead. Seconds later I'm reaching for the rolling pin.

For a holiday let the drawers are surprisingly well equipped. I mean, who the hell has a flour sifter? I know I don't. Now I'm on my own, I mostly do chocolate cakes for one in a mug in the microwave. They're a lot better than they sound, so long as you eat them hot, they're so totes delish I often have to make a second. Yummy enough to have most evenings in fact. But the kitchen in the flat is so tiny there's barely space for me and my mug, let alone luxuries like flour sifters, so if I do bake I just hurl the flour around.

But that was then, this is now ... I bought my own set of cute Christmas shaped cookie cutters just before while I was out in St Aidan. The scent of cinnamon and ginger is already warming my nose, and – okay, maybe I am getting a bit ahead of myself here, especially as these are for the tree, not for eating – but my mouth's already watering as I anticipate the chewy crunch as I bite into the biscuits, the way the lovely gingery taste will explode on my tongue.

Except when I begin to roll, despite shaking the flour sifter every which way, it's all getting a bit tacky. I whack down more flour, do a bit more kneading, then go to roll again. But this time the mix just ends up rolled around the rolling pin. Then I decide to try stuffing it into the cutters individually, but that's hopeless too. The more I work it, the hotter I'm getting, and the stickier everything is, so I peel off my jumper. It's a good thing I'm down to my T-shirt under the apron because the next time around it ends up in peaks, and instead of sticking to the granite it's sticking to me, all the way up to my elbows.

Staring at my dough smeared arms, letting out a low whimper is not ideally how I'd like to be seen by anyone. So when Bill comes striding through the door, I'm cursing and diving to hide.

'What the eff ...' Behind the kettle's not ideal.

The stack of boxes Bill's looking out over is huge and mismatched. He eases them down, and pushes them onto the island unit. 'I could do with a hand if you've got a ...'

'Yes ...?' I'm hoping he'll carry on but instead he's walking around the unit and coming towards me, his face crumpling in horror.

'Ivy, if you're hell bent on smothering yourself in body butter, wouldn't the bathroom be a better place?'

He's *so* patronising and superior, I'm this close to throwing the rolling pin at him. I probably would if it wasn't completely stuck to my hand.

Usually I hate being so tall I look down on people, but now I'm pulling myself up to my full height. 'If you had any idea about baking, you'd know – I'm making gingerbread, this is a critical stage in the process.'

'Gingerbread?' His voice goes high with surprise. Then he bites his lip, which I wish he wouldn't, because his teeth make my stomach feel funny. 'And that's why you've got a star cutter attached to your elbow?' As he leans over and picks it off he gives me a man-sized burst of his body spray.

'Fuck.' It was bad enough before the teeth and the man scent, but somehow I screw myself back together. 'I'm making decorations for the tree.'

He's pulling down the corners of his mouth, but they keep

twitching back up again. 'Great idea, but you've got two problems –'

'Is that all?' I'm being ironic. From where I'm standing it feels like a lot more. And obviously I don't need him to lecture me on what they are. I mean, who does he think he is, the effing *Bake Off* police?

He's waving the star cutter at me. 'You'll never get perfect biscuits if you use plastic cutters.'

Still talking down. Still sounding like a complete arse. 'Sadly *Spar* in St Aidan didn't stock gold plated ones. So what *should* I have chosen?' It's one of those questions I *really don't* want an answer to, but he's going to tell me anyway.

He shrugs. 'Stainless steel ideally.' He flicks open a drawer, and pulls out a box and flips the lid open. 'Like these.'

The tin I'm staring down at is filled with metal stars and hearts of all sizes, the odd angel, a few different sized snowmen, and blow me if there isn't a whole shiny nest of gingerbread man cutters in there too. Considering the minimalism everywhere else in the castle, the drawers in the kitchen are a complete anomaly, especially the one the cutters came out of. I swear I caught a glimpse of a whole load of kiddy birthday candles and bun cases in there too, which doesn't fit with anything. But I'll have to work out what the hell's going on there later.

Bill's carrying on. 'And second, if you don't chill your dough in the fridge before you begin, it gets too sticky to work with.'

I'm picking my jaw up off the floor. 'Anything else?'

He's glancing at the recipe and the ingredient pile. 'I can

see you've used flour for rolling out, so once your mix is the consistency of Playdoh the rest should work fine.'

Just when I'd closed my mouth it's sagging again. 'Playdoh?'

'You *do* know what Playdoh is?'

'Obviously.' Oscar's Playdoh machine? – totally brilliant, it's the most fun I've had in an afternoon in ages, just saying. But I can't see why child-averse Bill would have the first clue.

He's half closing one eye. 'You wash your hands, I'll get the rest of this lot into the fridge and whizz up another batch.'

It's a measure of how covered I am that by the time I'm de-clagged, he's got a ball of dough in each hand, wrapped in clingfilm, and he's rolling them into the fridge. Giving a completely unnecessary running commentary as he does it.

'Another two batches should be enough. I'll help you make those, then while the dough's cooling we can bring in the rest of the boxes. And afterwards we can roll and cut out together. If we're doing the whole tree we need team work.'

Taking over? Much? Except even though he's sticking as close to my elbow as that offending plastic star cutter as we stand by the Magimix, I'm doing a lot of the work. Actually *all* of the work. While all he's doing is totally putting me off. With his breathing. And those dark chocolate eyes of his looking. Near enough for me to see his individual lashes and be jealous how thick and dark and long they are. So close, our arms keep brushing. Colliding even.

All in all it's a bloody nightmare. And if I'm finding it all a little bit tingly, that's definitely down to festive excitement. Nothing to do with rubbing shoulders with the kind of quality body that would make a topless Aidan Turner look mediocre.

Most probably it's because it's a new situation for me – I can't ever remember cooking with a guy before. I'm not sure I ever saw George even visit any of the kitchens in the places we lived. If I wasn't there to make meals he ate out or went hungry. And sure, I hate Bill ordering me around and being such a know-it-all smart-arse. But someone who passes the spatula *and* manages to produce flat pieces of clingfilm that don't instantly twist into clingy unusable ropes? Just this once I'm not going to grumble, I'll take the help.

Once the dough is safely made and stowed in one of the many gigantic fridges, we rush in and out of the wind unloading the Landy. I'm aching to know what we're carrying, and determined not to ask. By the time we've had a few trips the pile is covering the table and Bill's smug expression has gone up three notches.

I'm eyeing the battered boxes, bursting with curiosity. 'Okay, I give in, tell me what they are.'

'I thought you'd never ask.' He wrinkles his nose. 'Take a look ...'

As I pull open the flaps and catch the shine and shimmer my pulse rate picks up and I let out a gasp. 'Deccies!' I pull open another three boxes, and they're all brimful – baubles of all sizes and colours, no sign of packaging, just thrown in on top of each other. 'So many, too!'

He gives a low laugh. 'You wanted maximalism. Knock yourself out.'

I'm pulling out silvery bells and brass snowflakes, swinging Santas and tiny red glass doves – and I'm dazed. 'But where did you get them?'

'I plundered every charity shop in a twenty mile radius.' He's looking *down* at me, which doesn't often happen. Through those lashes of his too. 'They're definitely *not* what you ordered – but they're *here* and they're *yours*.' His eyebrow goes up. 'If you want more, say the word. Every bauble's different, it won't be hard to get a match.'

I'm musing as I plunge my hand into a box and sift though the pile. 'There are enough here to sort colour themes for different trees. Or we could go totally random.'

He's opening more, and looking in. 'Best of all, we're saving the world one second-hand deccie at a time.'

I'm staring at him. 'Did Keef say that?'

He shakes his head. 'No, that's what they said in the shops.'

I'm being pulled along on the wave. 'Eclectic is good. It's how trees used to be back in the day when people bought their decorations singly and added one or two every Christmas. Before they began buying an entire different coordinating tree's worth every year.' To be fair, without that whole 'buy new and chuck away the old every year' trend, we'd never have scooped such a big haul here.

He pulls a face. 'You're blinding me with festive science again. Let's go back to gingerbread, then I'll know where I am.'

I'm thinking about another hour of shivers, and sizing up the box pile. 'With so many decorations maybe we could skip the gingerbread?'

He's frowning. 'Hell no, it's going to be the best one. No way I'm giving up on a tree you can graze from.'

'Great.' It isn't. But the faster we get on with it, the sooner it'll be over.

By the time Fliss and the kids come back in for a late lunch, there are cooling trays piled with nutty brown gingerbread men – or should that be people? – and Bill's taking the last batch out of the Aga. I look up from where I'm loading up the dishwasher, mostly trying to persuade Merwyn it's not a good idea to let Bill see him licking the wooden spoons. And reminding him for future reference, however tempting and dangly they look, snaffling gingerbread people from the tree is strictly not allowed.

Fliss gets in first. 'Nice move, Ivy, getting yourself a kitchen assistant, in a matching apron too.' She slides Harriet off her hip into the high chair and smiles at the biscuits. 'See, I told you you'd ace them, and you have.'

When Bill doesn't leap in to put her right, I send her a grin. 'It's all in the chilling. We're onto icing next.'

Then I take in Bill's wince as he looks over at Harriet. 'Bill, they're kids, they're here, they won't be leaving for another two weeks. Just get over yourself!'

Strangely he doesn't reply, he just blinks.

Fliss pulls a face at me, then she lets out a sigh. 'If all my hands weren't spoken for, I'd offer to help.'

I'm explaining for Bill's benefit, and moving this on now I've said my piece. 'I'm shortbread queen, Fliss is empress of the piping bag.'

Fliss joins in. 'Not quite. That was in my life BK.'

Bill's eyes narrow. 'B what?'

'Before kids. These days I'm the empress of disarray, swirly icing is a dim and distant memory.'

'Awww, it's not that bad, sweetie.' Except we both know

most days it's worse. She's already extended her maternity leave twice and neither of us know how the hell she's going to get back to *Daniels* in the New Year. Then as I stare at Bill I'm suddenly remembering what I forgot. 'You do have a piping bag?'

'Do bears poop in forests?' Bill's raising an eyebrow at me. When Oscar overhears, breaks into peals of laughter and starts careering round the kitchen whooping about poop, however much I tell him not to, Bill's wincing again. 'All the icing equipment's in the drawers below the cutters.' Which sounds like yet more culinary maximalism. Whoever removed every last object from the castle must have overlooked the kitchen.

Fliss is staring at Bill. 'You seem like a natural with the small ones, how about you clown around while I whizz up some icing?'

I don't know where the hell she's got that idea from. It might sound mean, but I'd rather he left us to it. Him scowling every time the kids make a squeak is frankly a bit of a downer.

'Don't you have work to do ... figures to go through ... stuff to distil?' I'm hurling in every last option in the hope he'll get the hell out of here. Obviously I'm super-grateful for him saving me with his expertise earlier, but now we're moving on.

'What with all the fires to keep going and bakers who need unsticking ...' He's frowning. 'With everyone arriving, you're my priority now.'

Wrong answer. Damn.

Fliss is sounding brighter than I've heard her for ages. 'So does that mean you'd be up for five minutes playing with Oscar?'

If she'd offered him a hand grenade to play with he couldn't look any more horrified. I had no idea she'd be in there so fast, so I'm stepping in for every reason. 'As kids go Oscar and Harriet are hardly a beginner's ride, they'd probably leave Bill for dead before we had the icing sugar weighed.' I let out a sigh. 'You do the icing, Fliss,, this one's mine.'

16.

The more the merrier …

By the time Libby and the kids get back from wherever they've been Fliss has gone off to bed with her two, and Merwyn and I have already had our late night walk.

I say wherever they've been – but thanks to my new phone being hooked up to all Libby's and her family's accounts, I've been following them and their patchwork of posts across the county. Most of them tucked into mac cheese for breakfast at *Pret*, then had fun watching planes before going back to *Pret* again for more of the same. They then went on to the cinema complex in Falmouth to watch *Frozen 2* (again), eat every flavour of Krispy Kreme donut going and buy popcorn from a real live human pop corn dispenser. Quite a few times. Then they called in at Maccie D's.

Obviously these activities weren't aspirational enough to make it onto Libby's feed. She mainly put up floury baking-in-progress shots with arty out-of-focus fairy lights from the castle kitchen that I'd sent her. Then a fast forward video clip of gingerbread people being hung on the tree with the sound of *Feliz Navidad* in the background, occasionally panning out to Oscar and Harriet watching, completely enraptured.

Fliss should enjoy it while she can. Who knew the wonder of Christmas ran out at such an early age these days? If Libby's kids are anything to go by, it's all over by the time they're four. Although as far as captivation with tree decorating went, obviously we didn't load the bit where Oscar helped himself to a gingerbread man then pebble dashed the French windows and a large area of the island unit as he spat it out. But at least from now on he won't be helping himself. And thank Christmas Bill wasn't around to see that bit either.

As Tom and co. amble in late in the evening I'm lounging on the sofa with Merwyn who's having a sneaky sit next to me. We're both in our third best Christmas jumpers because, to be honest, Libby's lot are such a downer we needed to do something to cheer ourselves up. As they trail through, I've already worked out a ploy to hurry their long faces through with the minimum of lingering.

I jump up and put my brightest voice on. 'Hot chocolate to drink by the fire anyone? We have marshmallows, squirty cream, chocolate sprinklies, and sparkly snowflakes for toppings.' It's amazing what they stock in St Aidan *Spar*. Goodies like this are why it took me so long this morning. I'm already at the Aga, milk and mugs at the ready to speed them through to the family space.

Libby's coming towards me. 'Leave the cocoa to me, Ivy. *You go and ask Bill* about interesting days out locally for the kids for tomorrow.'

It's a good thing I'm watching out for her foot coming towards mine. I jump sideways at the last moment and instead of her boot landing and crushing my toe it crashes down on the floorboards. For someone so teensy and slight she's got a stonking left foot on her.

I'm beaming at her from the safety of two yards along the worktop, fishing for more clues. 'What kind of children?'

Over the top of her ice-white cashmere roll neck she's re-knotting the scrunchie on her perfect silky ponytail and hissing at me, 'The vegan moaners are arriving first thing.'

There's some kind of strangled noise coming from inside Tom's hood. 'Get real, Mum, just call them the Twiglets like everyone else does.'

'Tom!' If Libby's amused it hasn't reached her lips as she turns to me. 'The mum's called Willow, they're thin, home schooled and painfully fragile.'

Tarkie's throwing in his contribution. 'They're twiggy like stickmen, they wear dungarees and live in the family tree.'

If these are her friends and she despairs of them, I must remember to ask Fliss why she's invited them.

'Enough, Tarkie!' The glare she turns on him is chilly enough to freeze-blast him. Then she turns back to me again. 'Just find me an Instagram-worthy destination and we'll have a day out with *everyone*. You too.'

I'm nodding furiously. 'Great, got that, two minutes, I'll see what Bill says.' And thank frig that I've left my laptop in there and that Bill's Do Not Disturb sign isn't up yet.

Me hanging onto my super-bright smile for Bill's benefit turns out to be unnecessary. When I knock and Merwyn and

I slip into the bedroom there's enough of his scent around to be disturbing, but no sign of the man himself. As I perch on his bed and open up Google I'm half thinking Bill might come along too. Then I *un*think it just as fast. Because that's the last thing he'd want and the last thing I'd want either. Where kids are concerned, however differently Fliss saw it, I know better. Children in the same county is too close for Bill. You only had to see him earlier, when he collided with the kids he couldn't get away fast enough.

When Mr Google finally comes up with festive delights for kids in the area – well, all I can say is Cornwall's not London. It's a dead cert they'll get rejected, but I note them down anyway and whistle a rather confused Merwyn straight back to the kitchen.

I'm taking a deep breath to announce the list but Tarkie gets in first over the packets of chocolate sprinkles.

'What did she go in there for?'

Libby's warning face tells me what I already know – for everyone's sake, *they must not find out about the wifi*. She opens her mouth to answer them, but Tansy's already eyeing me smugly.

'That's where her boyfriend is, silly, she goes to snog him. You *must* have noticed, she's in there all the time.'

Libby coughs. Hopefully she'll crush this with the same efficiency she uses when she stamps on people's feet. 'Whatever gave you that idea?' For someone in control her voice is rather squeaky.

Tansy's looking triumphant. 'Granny Miranda said it.'

As I wade in to put them right I'm inwardly cursing Libby

for her lightweight challenge and Miranda for blurting her opinions. '*ONE*, he's not *my* boyfriend, his partner is a supermodel barrister, and *TWO*, there won't be snogging, because we don't have mistletoe.'

Tiff's eyes narrow. 'A barrister *and* a supermodel ... like *that* would ever happen. If it was at all real I'd totally need to interview her for the vlog.'

Libby's eyebrows shoot up. 'No mistletoe?! What an oversight! How can you possibly style an Instagram Christmas without *that*?'

The side eye Tiff sends me is worse than Merwyn's, and that's saying something. 'You must think we were born yesterday. Everyone knows, the first rule of having a boyfriend is you never admit it.'

Sometimes you have to quit while you're ahead. With this lot, the only way it can go from here is further downhill. So I let it drop and move on. 'So, days out ... there's a really nice "chop your own Christmas tree" place not far way, with a Winter Wonderland, a snow machine, and LIVE REINDEER! How cool is that?' I admit I'm totally out of my comfort zone here even saying the word, but if they go for it I'll just have to make my excuses – throw up on the way to the car or something.

I'm leaving it to Libby to take it from here. For anyone other than me reindeer have to be exceptionally cute and very shaggy, so I'm really not expecting to hear a mass groan.

Tom's first. 'Reindeer ...? Seriously ...? Surely, *NOT AGAIN*?'

Tarkie's jumping up and down. 'Yawnsville! Yawnsville! Yawnsville!'

Tiff pulls a face. 'But reindeer don't do anything, they're astonishingly non-interactive and disappointing, I already exploded the myth when I did my vlog from Lapland. Whoever wrote that song that makes them sound like they have individual personalities was giving a misrepresentation of the species as found in festive captivity.'

Tansy's in again. 'What about reindeer rights, and animal welfare?'

Libby's joining in too. 'More trees? Don't we have enough?' She's frowning too. 'Solomon, Scout and Sailor have done Lapland every year since the cradle, they were trekking in Bolivia and Peru all last December, they've Christmassed in Australia, Vietnam, New York and Cuba, it's going to be hard to find something fresh to top that lot.'

My heart is plummeting faster than a high speed lift. With three even more cynical, demanding and miserable children due tomorrow, what chance do a few almost-jolly adults stand against this band of fun-suckers?

'How about a visit to the donkey sanctuary?' I'm fighting off the objections before they make them. 'Donkeys have bags of personality and it's a rescue so they should be well looked after.' I'm slightly talking out of my bum here, the only donkey I personally have experience of is Eeyore.

Tom's eyes are up in his hood again. 'And *how* are donkeys festive?'

I've got him there and I'm going for it. 'Remember *Little Donkey, little donkey on a dusty road … sing out those stars tonight with your precious load … Bethlehem, Bethlehem?*'

Tom looks bemused. '*Why*'s she saying *everything twice?*'

At least Tarkie gets it. 'We sing that one. My best song from school is the one about jet planes flying through the air to be refuelled ...' He wrinkles his nose as he thinks about it. 'Can we go back to the airport again?' He's upping the pressure. 'That's where Santa will come in to land, we need to be there.'

As this is the first shout-out Santa's had, I'm not letting it go. 'I reckon Santa might actually land his sleigh on the lawn here.' The thought of a lawn full of sleigh and reindeer in front of the castle is bringing me out in goosebumps and for all the wrong reasons. I banish the thought before I have to run off to be sick.

Tarkie's picking it up. 'Yeah, or he might land on the roof ... or even on the beach.'

Tansy joins in. 'In that case, forget the airport, let's go straight back to the cinema.'

Tiff's frowning too. 'If there's a snow machine can we go skiing?'

'Or snowboarding?' Tom sits up. 'There must be a snow-dome, let's go there.'

If he really wants to freeze his butt off balancing on planks of wood he could just try waterskiing. Just saying. Only not out loud.

'M-u-u-u-m ...' Tom's upping his whine. 'Find us a ski slope *then* we'll smile for your selfies.'

Libby's as oblivious to Tom as she is to the marshmallow heaps and squirty cream exploding across the island unit. But she's taking some control, because she's banging a spoon on the granite. 'That's settled then, as soon as the Twig – I mean the Edmunsons get here tomorrow we'll all go to the donkey sanctuary.'

I've been so busy watching them demolishing the toppings, I've barely noticed that the French window was opening or that there's a guy walking across the kitchen towards us.

'A donkey sanctuary, that sounds like fun.'

He sounds at home enough to belong here, so I'm working through the possibilities of who he is. Even without the rather smart Barbour padded jacket which is so new it's actually still got its tags on, he's much too young for Keef's gang so he has to be a friend of Bill's.

Libby's on this too. 'Are you staff? It's just we haven't seen many around today and we might need more logs bringing in.'

He's got an easy smile, and it breaks across his face now as he laughs. 'No, I don't work here, I've just arrived. I met someone called Bill Markham outside, he told me to come on in.'

So that's *all* my theories scuppered. Which leaves me evaluating the way his boy next door grin lights up all the way to his eyes when he smiles and his nicely cut browny blond hair. His long legs in denim, the flash of a soft checked shirt. Thumbs looped through his belt loops. And some very new wellies, also with hanging tags. By which time, I have to be honest about my first-glance summing up ... if this combo lived next door, and you were in the market in the way, say, Miranda is ... you would not think twice about vaulting the garden fence.

Libby's looking puzzled. What's more, she's paying the

rent here, she's way more invested than me. 'So, if you don't work here and you're not with Bill, then who the hell *are* you?'

He seems completely unbothered by his lack of provenance. In fact he's laughing even more. 'I'm Miles Bentley, here to spend Christmas with my father.' He gives a cough. 'He didn't actually mention there would be other people here. So if you don't mind me returning the question, *who are YOU?*'

For once Libby's silky calm cracks, but her snap sails straight past Mr Bentley. 'For goodness sakes, Tom, you're indoors, take your damned hood down.'

Tom lets out an incensed squawk. 'What?' He's staring straight at me. 'Tell *her* to take *hers* off first, then I might.'

Libby's snipping back at him. 'Leave Ivy out of this, she has a very valid excuse to wear her hat.' And I really wish she hadn't said that.

There's a chorus. '*Why* does she?'

And damn that they're all staring at me now as my hands creep up to my head and pull the woolly edge further down. 'My hat's my thing, that's all.' Despite the sudden focus that's all they're getting.

There's a cough from Miles. 'Still waiting for my answer here ... forget the hats, I'm just not sure how happy my dad will be when he sees *all the mess* you're making with hot chocolate in *his* Christmas rental?'

'I assume you're here to see Ambrose?' Libby's voice is back to pearly smooth. 'To put it in context, he's here as a guest of my mother, Miranda ... who is here because *I* invited her.'

'Right, okay, got that.' Miles takes a step backwards and as his jaw sags he slams his hand on his head. 'How did I get my wires so tangled? And here I am, barging in like I own the place, I'm so sorry, what must you think of me?'

Libby couldn't be any more chilled. 'It's fine, it's an easy mistake to make, it could happen to any of us.' It absolutely isn't and it wouldn't. Which suggests she's picking up on the whole dreamboat thing too.

'And Bill said those two are "otherwise engaged".' The lines on Miles's forehead deepen. 'Has there actually been a proposal?'

'Not that we know of.' Libby's nostrils flare. 'He means it's a choice of two activities – they'll either be dissolving in the hot tub, or bonking the bottom off their new four poster.'

Tansy's smirking behind her hand. 'You said not to say bonking.'

Tarkie's hitting her elbow. 'What's bonking again?'

Miles is bashing on. 'Well, that's all good then. And it looks like the most fabulous place you've got here. If you could possibly find a corner for an extra elf in *the* most ridiculous boots, just until tomorrow, I'd be very grateful to you. Forever.'

Libby's half closing one eye. 'And are you here on your own, or do you have a whole elf family with you too?'

'No, it's just me. Travelling solo ... again.'

He's cocking a self mocking eyebrow at me, and I'm smiling and waggling my head back at him when my heart dives. Solo, meaning on his own? If this is my plus one arriving, scrub the bit about jumping fences, I'll be running ... as fast as I can ... away.

Libby takes a deep breath. 'There's a free room up the back

stairs next to Ivy's, she'll show you the way up. Anyone dressed in surf pants will bring your bags in for you.'

Worse and worse. I close down my smile and dive for cover. 'I hope you like dogs, this is Merwyn.' As Merwyn backs against my legs and flashes me a filthy look, I'm feeling guilty for dodging behind him.

'Better and better.' As Miles's smile broadens we can all see his teeth are as great as the rest of the package. They're also so even and dazzlingly unnatural he has to have had a little help with them. 'If you two are up for an early morning stroll on the beach, just give me a knock.'

Bumping shoulders, picking up shells, dodging the curl of the waves as they roll up the beach, next to a smile full of dental veneers that's been pre-planned for me? As a measure of how appalled I am by that thought, I'd rather ski.

But in the breath it takes me to decide that, Merwyn's gone rogue.

Miles is scratching Merwyn's head and tickling the silky bits of his ears exactly the way he likes it. Two seconds and Merwyn's lapping it up like Miles is his new best friend. Seeing as I rely on him as my main ally here, that's not the best news for me.

As Miles eases up on the tickling his voice is eager. 'If you need wood, I can get that in too.'

With Merwyn the cuteness is all to do with his 'what the eff' glances. Miles is suddenly channelling puppy dog charm by the bucketful too, but his is all about enthusiasm, super-heartfelt looks, and eagerness to please. And it's certainly working with Libby.

'Thanks Miles, wood would be great.' When she breaks off there's the smallest softest sound that might be a laugh. But it's the first since she came. 'Wood-would, you see what I did there?'

'We did.' The appreciative smile that spreads across his face is offered up to all of us. He's holding up a finger. 'One more thing. I'm Miles at work, but to the family – and since we're practically related now, that means all of you too – I'm Milo.'

Milo ... that's ten times more puppyish and so much worse.

Realistically, if Miles slash Milo can march in trying to claim Libby's castle, then not only escape her wrath but thaw her within a sentence, this man has hidden powers. Or looking at him more closely again – not-so-hidden ones. Which could mean we're all in trouble here. For all the reasons.

Not that I'd ever be tempted back into a relationship. But I'm really hoping he's shit in the kitchen.

Tuesday

17th December

17.

Angels with dirty faces

I know our mums spent their lives trying to persuade our dads to try out their stoves, and I'd have loved my ex George to visit our kitchen even one time. But when guys schmooze in and effortlessly ace it, I can't help feeling a little bit WTF? Like they're treading on our toes. Taking over our territory.

I mean, glorious cranberry whirls are one thing, and that was only one (so far anonymous) surfer – with very nice handwriting, don't forget. But coming back from the beach to find yet another guy – well, Miles, I can't quite bring myself to call him Milo yet, however wide and winning his grin is – standing at the Aga like he'd been there his whole life, flipping his perfect triangular cream griddle scones? Then finding out how ridiculously light and fluffy they are. So delectable that when they're split open, spread with oozing hot butter and molten golden syrup, I eat a whole griddleful without even blinking. Disturbing doesn't begin to cover it. Then him being perfect enough to hang round the kitchen to tidy up too, to the point of even washing the mixing bowl. It's really all too much.

So it's a relief when the Edmunson-Twiglets arrive and we finally head off for the donkey sanctuary. Fliss's sporty people carrier dwarfs my little car, but compared to what's ahead of us in the convoy, it's mini. As we wind our way between the high hedges along the narrow lanes behind Ambrose, Libby, Miles and the Twiglets' cars, we're singing along to kiddies' Christmas tunes, in the hope it'll drown out Harriet's bawling.

As some hideous song about a *Marshmallow World* ends I have to comment, 'Those cars in front are so huge it feels more like we're following the Queen than a few friends and family.'

Fliss laughs at me. 'Except royalty would never have glitter decals like Libby or white alloys with diamanté inlays like Ambrose.'

'I hope Donkey Valley is ready to be hit by sixteen out-there townies in the middle of a quiet Tuesday morning.' As we slow by some nicely planed farm gates and see the hand painted donkey pictures on the signs, thinking about the company, I'm truly wishing I'd had the option to stay at the castle.

As it turns out, the donkeys aren't ready for us at all. Miranda's crackly gold coat gets the thumbs down straight away. It's so much like a giant piece of flapping Bacofoil, the woman with a badge that says *Doreen Donkey Welfare* decides it's going to alarm the residents. As Miranda and Ambrose shimmer off towards the cafe they don't look disappointed at all. I'm just hoping the rest of the group see something here to take the scowls off their faces.

Libby hands over what looks like enough cash to buy a whole donkey not just to look at them, then we wander off towards the stables and enclosures. The minute we hit a patch of cobbles Harriet finally drops off. I'm bumping her buggy along while Fliss hangs onto Oscar, still pondering about earlier.

'I know those scones of Miles's were delicious. But at the same time they left me feeling slightly uneasy and a little bit compromised. Squeezed even.'

The donkeys are looking out over the tops of their stable doors and we're stopping at each one, rubbing their huge fluffy ears and bumpy necks, letting them nuzzle our hands with their warm velvety noses. And we're trying not to wrinkle ours at the rather strong scent of donkey.

'Okay, say goodbye to Biscuit and we'll see who's next door.' Fliss lets Oscar have a final pat of the donkey, then she lowers him to the ground and turns to where I'm pushing Harriet.

'More like squeezed into your jeans after eating so much, I've got that too.' She pats her stomach. 'Miles is probably making himself indispensable in the kitchen, hoping Libby won't eject him. That's my theory anyway. If all his cooking's like that, it's not going to help my baby weight is it?'

I'm nodding, but only in partial agreement. 'If Miles can cook, with so many people turning up, Libby's going to hang onto him with both hands. Very tightly.'

She glances across at Miles a few stables ahead of us. 'You have to agree, Miranda's delivered you some choice goods there though, you can't reject this one without dipping your toe in the water.'

My eyes flash open. 'You just watch me.'

She lets out another chortle. 'Adjoining rooms. Libby came through for you there too.'

I look down at Merwyn, hoping he'll add support for my protest. 'Merwyn will tell you, with a tree in there too, there's barely space for us, we definitely can't fit any one else in there too.' I let out a laugh. 'At least Miles is saved from the ghostly noises in your part of the castle.'

Fliss lets out a groan. 'We all heard them again, last night *and* this morning.'

'It's nice that Ambrose and Miranda are enjoying life.' And I'm damn lucky my room's out of earshot.

Fliss pulls a face. 'It's just ironic and a little bit sad when the only person in the house with a decent bonk rate is your mother. You'd think she'd keep it down with the grandchildren around.'

I'm laughing. 'Miranda always expresses herself loudly, I can hear her whoops all the way from the cafe now.'

Fliss shakes her head and lets out a sigh. 'Larger than life and ten times noisier, nothing new there then.'

And this is the funny thing about parents. While I'd have loved mine to be even a teensy bit more expansive and like Miranda, Fliss is completely in love with how quiet and buttoned up mine are. Back when we were twenty we'd have swapped them in a heartbeat, because mine had the reliability and steadiness she craved, while Miranda had all the zest and colour mine lacked. Maybe that's one reason we bonded instantly and stayed so close – because we both found our sanctuary in the other one's home and family.

It's true that Miranda waited until her three girls and their brother left home before she started seriously working her way through husbands. Before that she never gave anyone exclusive rights and the flat just always had a stream of arty types passing through. But at any time of day or night she was only ever a corkscrew away from a party. Which was fabulous for me for a weekend visit, but that's why Fliss was wide eyed and wanting when she came across my parents' level of boring domesticity.

I pass the pushchair to Fliss and pick up Oscar. 'And this is Haribo, you like donkeys don't you?' I watch Oscar's nod. Considering he's usually like a one man demolition team, now he's left his favourite telegraph pole back at the castle, he's remarkably quiet.

Tarkie comes along and Tiff hauls him up on her knee to pat Biscuit. 'You were a donkey in the nursery Christmas play one time weren't you, Tarkie?'

He nods. 'It was crap, my head was good but I didn't have enough legs. My best one was when I was an alien from outer space flying to see Jesus in the stable on a magic carpet.'

Fliss rolls her eyes at me. 'The joys of Nativity have only just started for us. Oscar was a one man flamingo troupe this year, how about you, Tiff?'

Tiffany lets Tarkie slide down to the concrete, and gives a swish of her net skirt above her silver Doc Martens. 'I was head of Mary's personal shopping team one time. We all had Gucci bags, and I got to borrow Mum's special glitter clipboard.'

I grin. 'You have to love teachers, creative casting for the Christmas play is their one way of expressing what they really think of the pupils.'

Fliss wrinkles her nose. 'You're going to be another natural high flyer, Tiff, just like your mum.'

Said completely without bitterness but *with* an entire shed-load of resignedness. And there we've hit Fliss's next hang-up. Libby set her sights on the stars and accidentally reached the moon. All Fliss sees – if she ever actually looks past Libby's size-six jeans which are a fraction of the size of her own large-fit fourteens – is Libby's mega-successful business and her ultra-perfect family. Meanwhile Fliss in her own head is very definitely still stuck at Ground Control, with her flight never really expected to take off and two kids who refuse to conform to any parenting app that's yet been invented.

What Fliss forgets is that she would never in a million years have been happy to take Libby's trajectory, because she's a completely different person. Let's face it, given the choice between teensy trousers or buttercream, *in theory* it's great to say you'd go without and be skinny. But get a hundred per cent real and squishy cupcake in your hand and it's a whole other story. You're mostly left with an empty bun case and a bad case of guilty regret before you even get around to thinking about your choice. I mean, who wants to be strong willed and skinny anyway, it's hideous and boring and everyone despises you for it.

And where Libby's kids might have been perfect leopard cubs once, they appear to have radically changed their spots lately. But now they've both reached their relative thirty-something pinnacles, when Fliss finally stopped to look sideways at Libby, the comparison makes her feel like a failure.

The way Tiff simply absorbs the compliment, she has to get them all the time. 'That Nativity was ages ago, if it was a current production we'd all have iPads. Most probably I'd be a vlogger and come as myself.'

I pull a face at Fliss because Tiff is so sure of herself she's hard to warm to. 'It all sounds very Islington.'

Tiff sniffs. 'That's fine then, because that's actually where the Edmunson-Twiglets are from.'

Damn. But at least I get my chance to ask. 'And how do you know them?'

Tiff's sniffing again. 'Actually we don't, they're Mum's friends not ours.' Which possibly explains why they're at opposite ends of the sanctuary avoiding every kind of contact.

Fliss is filling me in. 'Willow was Libby's bridesmaid and best friend from school, she's very new-age intellectual. They've got absolutely nothing in common other than they sat next to each other on the first day and stuck together ever after.'

Tiff gives an agonised shrug. 'She does this thing where she just waggles her hands around in the air and people pay her.'

'Nice work if you can get it.' Even after the arrival of the Twiglets, I'm still on the 'other side'. The dirty look Tiff gives me is a ten on the Merwyn scale ... where ten is disapproval to the point of me not even registering. But while Merwyn saves his for times of extreme doggy stress, Libby's kids have dished out so many since they arrived I'm almost getting used to them.

Fliss steps in. 'Willow's a reiki master. She's spiritual, sugar-free and non-materialistic, the kids too. She couldn't be more different from Libby, which is why it's strange they were ever friends. And even more of a surprise they're here for a blow out Christmas.'

'No sugar is harsh.' I can't personally envisage a life without buttercream or chocolate pudding. 'I can't believe we're in for so much fun.' Obviously I'm being ironic.

But it's one of those times I'm kicking myself the minute it comes out because a second later the Donkey Welfare Doreen zooms over with a giant wheelbarrow.

'We promised you fun, this is where it starts.' She's shoving a snow shovel thing at me. 'That stable over there is full of donkey droppings and wee-soaked straw, your job is to load them into the barrow.'

I'm opening and closing my mouth, because she doesn't understand. 'Sorry ... we're not hands-on or interactive visitors, we're mainly here for the Instagram opportunities. As soon as we've grabbed a selfie with the elusive baby donkey you promised us, we'll be out of your hair.'

'Nice try.' She's actually pushed the muck barrow into my path and barring my way with the spade handle. 'Big groups like yours always muck out a stable. You'll be surprised how much you enjoy it once you start.'

Not that I'm being reverse sexist or a helpless female ... but where is Bill when we need him? Meaning, with his bashed up Landy and country ways, he might have minded less about *picking up poo*. Looking round the rest of the party, I'm skimming over the super-pristine Twiglets in their earth tone miniature versions of Willow's hand-woven Peruvian alpaca jackets, past Fliss and over Libby's lot who are too stroppy to lift a porridge spoon let alone a mucking out shovel. My eyes finally come to rest where I'd sworn they wouldn't.

'Miles?' Out of all of us, he's the one with the boots for it. I suspect his spotless Hunters might be so new they're still tied together.

He lets go of the donkey's ears he's tickling and turns around to grin at me. 'Please ... call me Milo.'

Fine. And damn that I ever let go of the pushchair, because even though I'm still hanging onto Merwyn I now also seem to have a shovel in my other hand. I might as well hold it up high and wave it. 'Fancy giving those fabulous muscles of yours a work out, Milo?'

Truly, it was meant to come out a thousand times less flirty.

I'm waiting for his reply when Libby marches over. 'Come on, Ivy, we don't need men, someone hold the dog, you and I can handle this.'

'We can?' I'm too flabbergasted to argue, and in any case she's already powering me into the stable.

But Milo's out of his jacket, throwing it to Fliss and he's running over. 'No, I insist, this one's mine.'

The donkey welfare woman obviously thinks all her Christmases have come at once. '*So many* volunteers, I'll go and get more shovels and yard brushes.'

So much for the 'so many'. What actually happens is Milo and me get the shovels, Libby gets to take the photos, and the rest of them peer in from outside the stable and pull faces and wrinkle their noses. For once I'm in agreement – if I'd personally had any idea about the reek of donkey droppings, I'd never have let myself get pushed into this. But thanks to Milo attacking this with the same dedication, awesome pecs and light hands he applied to breakfast, we're soon looking at a clean floor, and a very full barrow.

Libby jumps forward, pushes her phone into my hand and seizes the barrow handles. 'Okay, I'll take it from here, you get me pushing the barrow out of the stable, Ivy.'

She's actually so small, she almost disappears behind the heap of sopping poo and straw in the barrow, but that only adds to the effect. We have to do several tries before we get a take with her hairband straight, a fake smile on her face *and* the donkeys each side watching as she emerges. But I have to agree, for the cuteness factor alone, it was worth the effort.

Then suddenly there's a cry from Fliss. 'Awwww, Oscar, can you see what's coming now?'

Across the yard the fluffiest, dinkiest donkey is being led towards us.

When Libby sees what's coming she drops the barrow in the middle of the yard and rushes over too. Cute doesn't begin to express what I'm looking at – its hooves are tiny, its legs are wobbly, and best of all, it's wearing a Santa hat. And anyone whose heart doesn't instantly melt when they see him can't be human.

Tiff's tutting. 'It's very demeaning to put animals in clothes.'

Merwyn who's rocking his fleece-lined red velvet all-in-one with legs and diamanté trim catches my eye and rolls his.

Tansy joins in. 'It's not animal rights is it?'

As Milo puts down his shovel and goes straight in to tickle the over-sized ears, Libby's clearing her throat. 'Okay, everyone get behind me and the donkey, and let Ivy take our donkey sanctuary selfie.'

I'm holding up the phone trying to fit them all in. 'Okay, all squeeze together ... and smile.' I'm saying it out of politeness, knowing most of them won't. 'Just one or two more ... thanks, all done.'

But Libby's got other ideas. 'Right, put Harriet's buggy on the end, and this time we'll all fan out around the donkey and go again.'

She's made it impossible for me. 'You're too wide to fit on the screen now.'

Libby's barking instructions. 'It's fine, just move back until you get us all in.'

I'm shuffling backwards down the yard. 'Still not working.'

'Keep going ... further away.'

I start with little steps. Then I make them bigger and Tansy and Tiff are still not in the frame. As I step back again I hear Milo call out, 'Watch it, Ivy.'

I'm calling back, looking at the screen. 'Nearly there ... one more step and Tiff should be in.' Then something knocks the back of my knees. And when I try to take another step, instead of moving back, I'm over balancing. As my spine arches backwards into mid air I throw my arms out sideways, and something is braking my fall. As my back and bottom land on something soft and forgiving there's a lurch and the scrape of metal on the concrete of the yard.

'Jeez!' I'm thanking my lucky stars for soft landings. Then

as I ease myself up the wheelbarrow handles come into view somewhere near my flailing feet. And as my bottom sinks deeper, even though it's comfy there's a stench engulfing me. 'Donkey poo? *OMIGOD!*' Only I could manage to land in a wheelbarrow full of muck.

'Wait there, Ivy, don't move!' It's Libby, barking. '*AND FOR CHRISSAKES, DON'T DROP THE PHONE!*'

As if I'd move. Even though there's a dampness creeping around my thighs and back when I try to lever myself up, I'm actually completely stuck, because my knees are hooked over the extra deep barrow edge. And then even though I'm still I realise the stables I'm staring up at are starting to tilt. Very slowly. Then a second later the tipping speeds up, the sky flips, and there's a huge clatter and a massive jolt as the barrow hits the ground. And next thing I know, my shoulder crashes onto the concrete, I'm rolling sideways being ejected from the barrow and a whole shower of soaking straw and donkey droppings are raining down on top of me.

As disasters go, this makes my Christmas tree landing seem like a good day. I'm screwing my eyes closed, pinching my lips together and blowing so I don't get poo in my mouth. Clinging onto the phone for grim death. Working out what to do next.

The first voice to come through the shouts is Milo. 'Ivy, what the hell ... give me your hand ...' They're so poo covered, he must be well brave as well as stunning.

Then Libby. 'Get the phone first, Milo, get the phone ...'

Then someone wrenches it out of my grip, and as I push myself up to sitting I see Fliss looking down at me. She's shaking her head, but I can see from the way her shoulders are wobbling that the laughter's about to explode.

'Don't start ...' I know I've got to get in first.

She lets out a shriek. 'But you should have seen it, it was *so* funny. First the way you sat down in the barrow like it was an armchair. Then the way you tipped sideways ever so slowly and the whole shitload showered down on top of you.' She's laughing at Milo. 'Don't worry, these things happen to Ivy all the time, she's like our own personal stunt woman.' She looks back at me and winks. 'Isn't that right, shit head?'

'Let me.' He's holding out his hand to me. One tug, I'm up on my feet, hobbling around, trying to dance the dirt off.

Tarkie's jumping up and down holding his nose. 'Ewwww, she smells rank.'

Then Oscar joins in, singing, 'Stinky stinky stinky.'

Milo grins at them. 'Thank you guys, we've got that now.' Then he smiles at me. 'We'd better get you home and cleaned up, come on, back to the car.'

I'm picking the straw strands off my furry jacket, trying to brush away the dung clumps without grinding the dirt into the pelt, and I couldn't agree more.

Libby's grimacing. 'No, Milo, I saw your Alcantara seats, they're even more top of the range than ours, donkey manure will ruin them. And ours are non-plasticised Nappa leather, so we can't possibly take her either.'

This is how she's gone so far in business, because she notices things the rest of us don't even know about. I mean, what the eff is Alcan-bloody-tara?

'We've got a full leather interior too.' Willow's like an echo, so maybe she's less vegan than they're all making out.

Milo's nodding. 'Ambrose is the same.'

Libby's eyes are wide with expectation as she turns. 'So that leaves you, Fliss, you don't mind do you?'

I'm already wincing for her. Even if donkey woman gives me a bin bag to sit on, I'm covered – Fliss's sporty utility vehicle will stink of donkey-do forever more. I know what it took for her to scrape together the deposit, I can't do that to her.

I'm truly scraping the barrel here. 'Or we could ask Bill?'

'Great idea, his Land Rover's agricultural, it's designed to be dirty, I'll ring him on the landline from the cafe.' Libby's already half way down the yard. 'Hang on there, Ivy, I'll be back.'

Fliss comes in to give me a squeeze, then gets a whiff and thinks better of it. 'Let's go in the stable out of the wind, we'll get a bale to sit on and have hot chocolates all round. And we'll all wait for Bill together.'

'Thanks, that'll be lovely.' I force out my brightest smile. Somehow I doubt that cocoa is going to take the donkey dung taste away. But however much I'd rather this wasn't happening, it's not like there's a lot of choice.

18.

Looks like rain, dear

'All on your own, Pom Pom?'

By the time Bill's face appears around the stable doorway, Fliss is long gone. I can't fault her solidarity, she'd happily have stayed, but with Harriet and Oscar cold, hungry and howling it was better for us all if I waited by myself.

'There was no point everyone hanging around, they sped off to a multiplex somewhere.' Five minutes of Libby's lot flicking cream at each other off the top of their takeaway hot chocolates was enough for all of us.

As I get up from my straw bale Bill's shaking his head and wincing. 'I see why they called for the farm car. Shall we get off?'

'You might want to see the baby donkey first?' I should have had enough of donkeys for one day, but I'm up for one last ear rub.

'If it's wearing a Santa hat, I already saw it.'

I can't believe he's so unenthusiastic. 'But didn't you love the bells on his lead rope and how fluffy he is? Did you stroke his ears and feel how soft they were?'

Bill's looking down at me. 'It's a donkey. What else is there to say?' As if we needed any more proof that this man is a cold hearted Christmas-phobe, he comes out with this. He shrugs. 'Anyway, I've brought you this.' He tosses me a bag. 'No need to look that worried, it's only overalls.'

'Brown velvet?' The fabric I'm peering at in the bag is way too similar to a donkey's nose for comfort.

'It's a onesie from stag lost property.' He pulls a face. 'To cover up whatever you fell in until we get you into my shower.'

I should be jumping at another chance to get my hands on his scent shelf, but after this morning's assault, I seriously doubt my nose will ever work again.

'Antlers attached to the hood?' I'm shaking out a full Rudolf outfit here and my stomach feels like there are iron hands closing around it. For a moment I just know I'm going to throw up every last griddle scone. And then I get control of my throat, and somehow breathe, and will the vomit wave to go back down again.

'Everything okay there? I can't see much of your face, but the bits I can have gone all green.'

The stable's coming in and out of focus and inside my hat my scalp is prickling with heat. I snort in another breath, and try to smooth out my voice where it's gone all wobbly. All the onesies he might have picked up, and he had to choose a bloody reindeer suit. When Fliss talks about me being unfortunate she's truly not joking. Except that's exactly what I've taught myself to try not to think.

I'm resigned to the world always looking like a different place from the one I knew before the accident, and I know I never deserve to be happy again. But there are so many Christmases ahead of me, and however hard it is, I have to try to move on and hold it together. Which mostly I've managed pretty damned well, until bloody Bill randomly dropped this suit on me. I pull in another breath. Realistically, apart from having antlers, it's nothing like the one I was wearing for the Christmas party the night of the accident anyway. I just have to think of it as a way of enveloping the dirt and pull it on.

Bill shrugs. 'It'll keep you warm, you must be freezing after waiting in the cold.'

'Great.' I'll put this off for as long as I can. 'If I'm parading the whole length of the stable yard I'd rather do it as my dirty self than dressed like I'm about to be harnessed to Santa's sleigh, I'll put it on when we get back to the car.' As we make our way to the Landy, it hits me I'm also forgetting my manners. 'It's very kind of you to come to pick me up. Milo offered me a lift but his upholstery wasn't suitable.'

'Milo the scone baker?' Bill narrows his eyes and jumps the puddles in the gravel as we head towards the car.

'Scone baker extraordinaire …' I look down at Merwyn, pleased we've changed the subject. '… he's a dog lover too.'

Bill sniffs. 'Well, he's not alone there, we all like dogs.'

I'm so indignant my voice is all high. 'No you don't, last week we had to practically beg you to let Merwyn stay.'

He shrugs as he reaches over and unlocks the Land Rover door. 'Here, I'll hold onto him while you climb into your overalls.'

I'm exchanging WTF? glances with Merwyn as I hand over

his lead to Bill. Then I screw up my courage, swallow down the sour saliva in my mouth, tell myself over and over again it's only a reindeer suit, and pull the damn thing on. By the time I'm all in and zipping up Bill and Merwyn are both looking down on me from the bench seat in the front of the Land Rover. As I clamber in and slam the door Bill's looking even more superior than usual.

'Being prissy about his seats, it's exactly what I'd expect from someone like Milo. I bet the car's not even his.'

Whatever's got into Bill, I have to stick up for Milo. 'That wasn't his fault, it was Libby who didn't want me to wreck his interior.'

'And so what, the guy bakes scones. Scone baking's not that special.'

I give Bill a look across the dashboard. 'You obviously didn't taste them or you'd know they were ...' ... all that ... *And more*.

He pulls down the corners of his mouth. 'I'll take your word for it. From where I was standing it looked a lot like showing off.' He looks at me as we come to a T junction. 'You do know you've still got your hat on.'

I send him a look. 'Is there a problem with that?'

'There wouldn't be normally ...' it sounds like there's a but coming '... but as you've got donkey droppings dangling off your pompom, not to mention the other random crusty bits clinging to the woolly parts, maybe you best jump out while we're stopped. You can shake off the worst and put it in the bag too.'

'Shit, sorry.' Here's me thinking it can't possibly get any more embarrassing or impossible, then it does. My heart's tumbling in my chest because I'd really rather not go without my hat. But I can't exactly sit here with donkey crap all over my head.

'If you're cold you can turn up the heater, or put your hood up instead.'

'Great suggestion ... I'll do that ... like right now.' I'm stalling. It's not going to be anything like as surc as my bobble hat for holding my hair in place, but at least it's the cleaner option. And sitting with my antlers up is the last thing I'd choose, but there's no dodging this one. I fling the door open and jump down to do the switch. I pull off my woolly hat and a second later, I flip the hood up. Then I shake the worst off the woolly hat, clamber back in and push it into the bin bag with my jacket. Now all I have to do is to hang onto the neck of my onesie so the hood doesn't slide down, and hold down my breakfast until we get back to the castle.

The umpteenth time Bill glances my way, I challenge him. 'And what the hell's so interesting over here?'

'Nothing.' He's completely lying.

'What's wrong with my antlers?' That's where he keeps glancing.

He's smiling to himself now, as if he's very far away. 'They just reminded me of another time, that's all. How cute they are.'

I'm going to have to tell him. 'Bill, I'm only going to say this once. Don't ever put the word cute and me together in the same sentence, okay?'

'What, even if you are?'

I drag in a breath. 'Especially then.'

'But antlers always look …' As he takes in my searing glare he shuts up.

I'm clutching the fabric under my chin, totally oblivious to the sun glistening off the sea and how pale blue it is today as we head along the road by the beach. And talking randomly to fill the space when it hits me. 'You didn't call Merwyn cute when he was wearing his antlers the other day. You're thinking about Gemma aren't you?'

The way he jumps at the sound of her name, he has to be. 'Actually you're wrong, I'm not.'

'So why did she rush back to London?' It's out there before I know. And jeez knows why, when I really have no interest other than not thinking about bloody reindeer costumes. I mean, it seems idyllic here. If you had the choice, I can't imagine why anyone wouldn't want to stay here forever.

'It's a very long story, remind me to tell it to you some day when we have a few hours to spare.'

My heart sinks, because I'm really not up for details. 'Can we please just get back to the castle and forget we ever had this conversation.'

He's tapping his fingers on the steering wheel, wrenching it around the last corner. 'Fine. In that case you can tell me why you mixed up all the aftershaves last time you were in my bathroom.'

To think I thought my biggest problem was being covered in donkey dung and having the worst flashbacks yet. Now I'm going to have to think of an answer for that.

Wednesday

18th December

19.

Have a banging Christmas …

As shitty days go, they don't come much shittier than yesterday. I actually stripped most of my clothes off outside when we got back to the castle. When Fliss saw the onesie hit the floor she swore under her breath, squeezed my hand so tight my fingers almost went numb. Then she picked it up and marched off inside. She put the clothes through four hot washes before they were anything like clean. Meanwhile I wolfed down three reindeer cupcakes from a tray Fliss had picked up on the way home, simply because the icing was so delicious it seemed like the best way to get my sugar rescue. Which seemed somehow ironic and therapeutic at the same time, as if I was eating my phobia. Then I persevered with Bill's shower on full power, helped by a plastic crate brimming with stags' leftover bathroom products.

I began with a peppercorn scrub, and worked my way through everything from guava to maca root. Past very fragrant bergamot and pear to Scandinavian snowdrop. Then ended up with something called Cowshed Bullocks splash and according to Fliss I still wasn't smelling great.

When Willow passed in a huge bottle of her special organic tomato ketchup from the kitchen, even though Fliss and I were grateful for any help at all, we were still exchanging disbelieving glances. Then she came rushing back in again with sage, muttering about how alarming my aura was and the state of my chakras. Truly, she has no idea. But however much it sounded like she'd got it from some new-age bullshit generator, after sloshing on a whole bottle of ketchup followed by the sage oil, the smell of donkey did actually fade from my skin.

So this morning when Merwyn and I come in from our early morning beach blast and find the table full of baking, it feels like a banging start to a whole new and better day. And I'm peering at the humungous piles on the trays while Bill watches from where he's filling the coffee pot.

'Let me guess – white chocolate chip muffins with raspberry?' They're criss-crossed with snowy white icing dribbles, and the cracks in the golden tops are just wide enough to catch a glimpse of pale gold sponge with scarlet raspberry splashes. And they smell so delectable, I'm sucking back my drool.

He pushes me a plate and a mug of coffee. 'And the darker ones are rum and raisin. Here, grab a knife and tuck in.' In spite of all the cash Libby's paid, Bill's still acting like he owns the place. And despite my growling at him yesterday, he's still giving all the kids dead eyes, especially Harriet and Oscar. As if grumpy kids aren't enough to deal with, it isn't exactly helping the Christmas jolly having him glowering at the kitchen island twenty-four seven.

I'm on the sofa, Merwyn at my feet, munching my way

through my third muffin, when we hear the distant sound of Milo coming down the back stairs. As he pushes through the door, he's looping an apron over his neck. He's got a pinny string in each hand when he spots the muffin pile and comes to a sudden halt by the table.

'What's this? You've done breakfast baking already?'

I'm nodding. 'This must be another batch from whichever of Bill's talented friends is the mystery baker?' I give Bill a searching stare.

His eyes flash open. 'Yeah … right. Another delivery from the Super Surfer Home Bakery.'

Which is a lot less hilarious than the twist of his smile suggests. In fact I can't see the funny side of that at all, but whatever.

Milo punches the air. 'Aw shucks, I was going to make Irish soda bread too, I got a special recipe from Los Angeles.'

Bill raises an eyebrow. 'I'm no expert, but aren't you confusing your culinary credentials there?'

'Worldwide fusion is very current, they're huge on sourdough in LA now.' Milo's overlooking how much of an arse Bill's sounding, flashing me a wide smile, and going in for the argument.

I'm waving my muffin trying to diffuse the testosterone cloud. 'For what it's worth, these have got currants in.'

Milo grins at me. 'That's a completely different kind of current.'

Bill's really channelling his Mr Superior this morning. 'They're actually raisins.'

Milo's sounding less conciliatory, more like he's decided the opposition's talking too much bollocks to bother about. 'It's all good, I'll do my soda bread for lunch instead then.'

At which point Fliss and the kids come in, then Willow and co., so I ignore Bill's even deeper frown, wave at the table and put on my extra bright voice. 'Everyone help yourselves to muffins.'

As far as the Twiglets go, if I'd offered them donkey droppings I'd have got a better reaction. They do a group face pull, then a co-joined shudder and finish with a perfectly choreographed head shake.

Willow's almost transparent, in the palest green silk wrap. 'Thanks all the same, Ivy, but it's important we get our fuel from more natural sources, especially in the morning.'

'Great, lovely.' I'm nodding, but at the same time I'd hate to be one of her kids. I mean, what can be more natural to eat than cake? And I can't help thinking if she ate a tray of muffins she might have more colour. Whenever I've seen pictures of those ridiculously pretty plates full of edible flowers and three calories I've always asked myself who the hell would ever order one, let alone subsist on them. But I bet they'd suit Willow down to the last petal.

Her forehead furrows and she pulls her arms across her chest and stares around the room. 'Oh my, I'm picking up on a lot of negative energy in here, as soon as we've had breakfast I'll bring down a cleansing candle.'

As Fliss looks at me, she's holding in her smile. 'See, very spiritual *and* intuitive.'

I hiss at her under my breath. 'And definitely a pansy eater.' I glance round at Bill and Milo on the stools by the island, looking daggers at each other. 'You don't have to be the psychic chef to pick up the bad vibes in this kitchen, you just need eyes.'

Then Tiff, Tansy and Tarkie shuffle in, which reminds me I need to grab some pictures before the Christmas muffins disappear. As photo opportunities go, this one's a gift. When the kids' mouths are crammed with muffin it's impossible to tell they're scowling not smiling. So, watched by a row of solemn Twiglets over the top of their bowlfuls of gluten free Morning Zen cereal, covered in macadamia milk, I get enough 'happy kids stuffing their faces with delicious Christmassy breakfast' shots against a blurry backdrop of fairy lights and gingerbread on the tree to keep Libby going until mid morning at least.

And before I get chance to send them to her, she's sweeping in, arms waving. 'Okay, this morning we're all heading down to the beach, everyone be back here ready in fifteen minutes. *AND DON'T BE LATE!*'

You can tell why she's gone so far in business. Her tone's so kick-ass, a second later the kitchen's empty. Fifteen mins on, it's bustling with bodies zipping up their puffa jackets, stamping their bright coloured wellies while she snaps her fingers and counts heads.

'Okay, that's all of us except Miranda and Ambrose who are AWOL *yet again*, no surprise there.'

Tarkie pipes up. 'As we came downstairs Granny was calling out.'

Fliss gives me a nudge and mutters. 'Ambrose really is unstoppable.' Then she looks up at Tarkie. 'No need to take any notice of that.'

Tiff's frowning. 'She was actually shouting.'

Libby's eyes go wide. 'Holy smoke, what are those two like?' She turns to Willow. 'I do hope yours weren't upset?'

Willow's beaming around at her three. 'It's fine, we all know –' she stops to make some inverted commas in the air with her fingers '– when "souls touch" it's very fulfilling, but it sometimes gets a bit squeaky, doesn't it?' Three Twiglet heads nod in wholesome agreement.

Tarkie nods, like he knows too. 'That's the bit with the clingon isn't it.'

Tiff rolls her eyes. 'You mean the clitoris, Tarkie.'

Libby lets out a squawk. 'Tarkie, Tiff ...'

'Souls *TOUCHING*? *Really?*' Tom's choking into his sleeve. 'Well these souls had the volume on full, they were literally banging ... like *really, REALLY LOUD*!'

Libby's scowl is fierce enough to turn him to dust. '*ENOUGH, TOMAS!*'

His voice shoots high in protest. 'You were the one who told us to be open and honest about sex and that it was never too early to know where the clitoris is.' He gives a snort. 'I'm only telling it like it is.'

Libby's hissing through her teeth. 'Well DON'T!!!' Then she turns around to everyone. 'Okay, we'll carry on without them. Let's see who can jump in the sea first!'

She has that effect. However determined I am to resist her commands, simply to show I can, when I look down my feet are running, and Merwyn's bounding along beside me. And just beyond him Miles is beaming at me, leaping like a slow motion TV advert as we pass through the garden shrubbery. As we dash out onto the sand, on the other side of him Bill's moving like a winger on a rugby pitch, only without the ball, with the single-minded concentration to match. I mean, truly, why the hell has *he* come along? Okay, he came to the rescue yesterday, but does that mean he's 'friends and family' now? Surely he should be staying at home taking care of the castle or whatever it is he does.

And there's another thing. Libby telling everyone to go and jump into the sea. I mean, why? As Fliss and I watch everyone hurling themselves into the waves like lemmings, splashing the shallows up their jogging bottoms like there's no tomorrow, all I can do is look at her and grimace.

Fliss raises her eyebrows at me as we dodge the worst of the spray. 'She didn't think this one through, did she?'

But Libby's powering towards me through the foam. 'You did get that, Ivy? Everyone running into the winter water, that's a wholly unique image.'

Damn. 'Or maybe we could go again?'

In the end we go the whole way along the beach to St Aidan, running in and out of the sea, by which time the promise of phone signal and warm radiators to dry our soaking wet legs on has become too much, so we all head past the boats bobbing in the harbour, their rigging jangling on their metal masts in the wind gusts, and up the winding cobbled street to the Hungry Shark for some warm apple punch and a wifi fix.

Obviously with a bar full of fairy lights, punch bowls, stacks of mince pie muffins and piles of crusty Cornish pasties topped with festive holly leaves, I'm back in Instagram heaven. From the way they're waving madly from the corner down the end of the bar, this also seems to be where Keef and his mates hang out, when they're not catching half pipes, or whatever it is they do on the beach.

Libby's lot are already at a table, Willow and the Twiglets are having lengthy discussions at the bar, no doubt arguing origins and sugar content.

By the time I get to Fliss and my pasty, Harriet and Oscar are in high chairs, and there's no avoiding Bill who's between them looking hugely grumpy passing out cheese cubes and carrot straws. I'm settling back against my bench seat at the side of Oscar when Milo appears.

'Is there room for a small one?'

It's one of those questions he's not expecting an answer to. Realistically, the answer's no, because the space beside me is child sized. But his glass and pasty are on the table, and his hip hits mine before I can protest. My elbows are clamped to my sides which makes my pasty pointless because I can't get my hand out to eat it. But I take it the wide smile is meant to more than make up for that.

'We haven't had chance to chat yet, I hear we have a lot in common.'

Oh shit. I knew our single status would have to come at some stage, I just hadn't expected it to be so soon or so direct. I can't begin to imagine the build up they'll have been giving me so I need a carefully considered reply here. *So you're single and desperate too?* would work. Or maybe I should go straight for the *desperately NOT seeking …* denial. Instead I take the total cop out and let him do the work. 'We do?'

He's laughing at me. 'Don't tell me you don't know – we both work in retail.'

As I let out a breath of relief my chest deflates entirely. 'Great. Of course, I do styling at *Daniels*, so does Fliss.' Widening it out to three of us is so much less intimate than two.

His eyebrows flash upwards. 'How's that going? I hear they've been having troubles.'

This is one of those painful conversations where I'm on my specialist subject, and I've totally flunked the first question. 'I'm with *Daniels the department store* and everything was fabulous there when I left a week ago.' I add in a cover all just as a talisman. 'As far as I know.' Like not walking under a ladder. Or throwing spilled salt over my shoulder. Or not taking ivy in the house haha. Obviously I break the rules on that one all the time. All those superstitions my granny insisted on so often, I can't do anything else. Not that they saved me trouble in the long term. I turn to Fliss for backup, because suddenly Milo's making me doubt myself. '*Daniels* are doing brilliantly ... *aren't they?*'

Fliss is busy disentangling a soggy spinach puff from her hair and raises an ironic eyebrow. 'Obviously they're struggling without me, it'll all be fine once I start my "back to work" transition.'

He shrugs. 'Well, you're at the sharp end, and what do I know? Investments are what I dabble in, mostly I sell luxury cars.'

However much I'd love to quiz him about the knock on the front passenger side of my Corsa he's not going to be interested, so I'm taking this back to him. 'And how's that going?'

He's smiling again, but this time there's an extra twinkle. 'Terrible, but December always is. That's how I got to sneak away early and come here.' His eyebrows close together again, and he's back to the spotlight and thumb screws. 'Christmas must be *Daniels*' busiest time, how did *you* get time off?'

I'm not going to start on the saga of my outstanding holiday allocation. 'The shop windows get blacked out for the after-Christmas sales, a lot of the sale stock is displayed in boxes, so it was a great time for me too.' I make my smile bright and friendly, but make sure the 'keep out' signals are firmly in place on my metaphorical six foot high razor wire personal defence fence. 'And will your dad and Miranda be joining us for lunch?' It's the best diversion I can think of.

Milo somehow has his arms free, because he's munching his pasty. 'I left them a note, but I guess they've decided on the hot tub instead.'

Thinking of Ambrose alone at the castle, I lean over to Bill. 'I hope you've locked up your gin store.'

Bill treats me to me his best superior eye roll. 'It's fine, my dad's around to keep an eye on things back at the ranch.'

I'm leaning forward to check. 'Actually, I think you'll find your dad's here, I'm sure he waved earlier when I was at the bar.'

Milo frowns. 'There's your answer. The castle and *all* the gin to themselves, they won't be going anywhere.' He grins and pulls a face. 'Talk about a handful, since we lost Mum he's gone right off the rails, I never know what he'll get up to next.'

Fliss gives a groan from along the table. 'Don't say that, I'm relying on Ambrose to keep Miranda out of trouble.'

Despite having zero space Milo manages to nudge me and

his voice drops. 'If babysitting him means I get to meet people like you, I'm not complaining.'

The huskiness in his voice makes my stomach contract. 'Great.' The little bit of sick in my mouth is probably why they call it a gut reaction. And it's all to do with me, and nothing to do with Milo, who I'm sure is lovely so long as he's further away and not turning that dazzly-toothed smile in my direction. Come to think of it, now he's up close, I'm picking up Paco Rabane Million and lots of it, but it's smelling nothing like as nice as it does in the store. I need to speed this up and not only so I can decompress my bum. 'Maybe we should hurry back?'

Milo's smiling at everyone again. 'I'm sure they'll be fine, they're only enjoying a bit of alone time, what can go wrong there?'

Bill catches my eye over Oscar's head. 'Are you worried Ambrose might drown again?'

The glare I send him isn't anything like hard enough. And now I'm hanging my hopes on Oscar and Harriet to give me a fast exit. Whenever Fliss and I venture out for lunch with them we only ever have a two minute window to bolt down our food before one of them starts yelling. But thanks to Milo pulling silly faces at Harriet and making the kind of car noises that send Oscar into peals of helpless laughter, today they're lasting longer. Half an hour later when Harriet's still kicking contentedly, munching chunks of Milo's second pasty I'm despairing of ever leaving when Oscar comes through for me.

Fliss suddenly lets out a shout. 'No, Oscar, don't take the top off your drink, I just filled it up!'

A second later the whole chilly beakerful sloshes out and

into my lap. 'Oh no!' *Thank you, thank you, thank you, Oscar!* As the water soaks my crotch and beads on my pink glittery jumper I'm hoping my gasp of horror hides how delighted I am.

Fliss leaps up and dives back with cloths from the bar. 'So sorry, Ivy-leaf, what was I saying about you being accident prone?'

I'm beaming. 'It's fine, after yesterday you can throw water at me all day long.' And who would think one small cup of the stuff would spread so far and so effectively. The best part is, everyone gets up to help and by the time we've used up most of the Hungry Shark's industrial sized kitchen roll mopping up there's little point sitting down again. So we get our coats on again, Bill's getting as far away from Harriet as he can but Milo comes to pick her up. So with him carrying her and Fliss and I sharing Oscar, we wander up and down the mews and the narrow twisting streets soaking up the twinkle and the golden warmth from the shop windows. And when the older kids' groans get too much to take we wind our way back down past the harbour, out over the dunes, and back down onto the sand.

Thanks to us keeping up with Merwyn's bounds and barks, we reach the castle ahead of the others. As we look back we can see them a long way behind, still trudging around the curve of the bay.

'Here, Oscar, I'll draw you a Christmas tree in the sand, and we can fill it with shells while we wait for the others to catch us up.'

Milo puts Harriet down and she crawls towards us. 'She needs one too.'

Fliss joins in. 'And make one for me.'

Even with a small group of people, there's this wonderful feeling of space and solitude you get on an empty beach that you don't get anywhere else. The wind blowing around my head might be cold even through my hat, but as I pick up a stick and start scraping lines in the flat damp sand, it wraps me in my own cocoon. It doesn't matter that Merwyn's paw marks are scattered across them or that Harriet's throwing handfuls of sand at us. Or even that the sea is the same dull brown as the sky today, with chalky white dashes of foam, instead of blue and glittery. What begins as one tree ends as a long line, wandering and wavy above the foam of the water's edge. As the others come they join in too, as fast as I draw them they're dotting them with shells and stones and seaweed strands.

Libby's marching along the tree line wafting her phone triumphantly. 'A Christmas tree forest on the beach, no one's put one of those up yet this year.'

By the time we eventually get cold and drift our way back to the castle, the masses of grey clouds in the afternoon sky are fading. But as we come into the courtyard, instead of the expected glow spotlights and the steam from the hot tub, the stone flags are unlit, and the tub cover is on.

Fliss shrugs. 'Miranda's had enough of the hot tub! That's a first.'

Libby's marching past, flicking on the lights in the kitchen. 'They've probably gone for champagne supplies.'

Fliss hisses at me under her breath. 'Or more likely, they've run short of Viagra and lube.'

I wink at her. 'Is someone jealous ...?'

Tiff comes out of the kitchen. 'They aren't in the kitchen or the family areas.'

Then I notice Willow, hands across her chest, looking around the courtyard, and have a rush of gratitude for the way her sage oil saved me yesterday. 'Everything okay there?'

She's looking perplexed. 'I'm picking up something ... something unresolved ... something crying out for our attention ...'

Fliss must be feeling helpful too. 'Do we need a candle for that?' She shoots me an eye roll.

Then it hits me. 'All this going out, we still haven't decorated the trees! You'll feel much more settled when we've got those done, Willow, we all will.' So much sensitivity – it's a bit unnerving.

Willow nods. 'Thanks, let's just stay open and vigilant anyway.' As she passes me she puts her hand on my arm. 'We're going to have to do some work together, Ivy, that sage oil I gave you hasn't cleared anything.'

'It sorted the donkey smell.' I grin at her, determined to show myself I'm over yesterday's wobble. 'Let's get the trees done first, I can sort my chakras out any time.'

She's smiling at me over her shoulder as she walks into the house. 'You won't feel right until you do, Ivy.'

'Jeez.' I let out a sigh and shake my head at Fliss. 'What is she going on about, I'm totally fine.'

Fliss pulls a face. 'We both know you're not.' She pulls me into a squeeze. 'You do a bloody good job of hiding it though. I just wish we knew what to do to make things better for you.'

Fliss has been there for me through all the chaos, picking up the pieces. And sometimes I wish she wouldn't do this.

Mostly I'm totally okay. The second someone understands, I crack. My mouth's filling with saliva, and I swallow it down. 'I'm doing Christmas – in a bloody castle – if that doesn't make me feel great, what will?'

She passes me a hanky. 'It's a temporary fix. Like putting a band aid on a fractured femur. What about afterwards, in January?'

She's staring at me really hard. I scrape my hanky over my eyes and dab my nose. 'Hey, I'm not that broken.'

'Aren't you?'

Realistically she's the one who's staring at an impossible January – getting two kids up and out of the house before seven every morning, finding nursery fees, doing a full day's work then going home to thirteen hours of screaming kids again. So long as I stop my flashbacks running riot in my head, I can keep things at bay. Problem solved.

As I hear a loud trundling noise I look around and blow out a breath. 'Saved by the log trolley. It's Keef, bringing in the wood.'

I have to say, he's got excellent timing. What's more, his cornering is way better than Bill's. He sweeps around in a huge curve and pulls the trolley to a neat halt by the back door next to a stack of empty baskets.

'How's it going, Keef?' Oscar scoots up and gives him a fist bump.

'Great thanks, little guy.' Keef turns him upside down, and puts him back on his feet again, then turns to us. 'Is someone having a Dido moment out front?'

'Sorry ...?' I have *no* idea what the hell he's talking about and from the way Fliss is frowning neither has she.

'A white flag over the door? That's what Dido sang about isn't it?'

Fliss gets in first. 'The whole point of *that* song was that Dido said she *wasn't* putting a white flag over her door because she wasn't surrendering and giving in to her broken heart. Why?'

No one's supposed to know, Dido's what she cries herself to sleep to when Rob's really late home. That's why she's so up on the details the rest of us wouldn't have a clue about.

Keef shrugs. 'Well, whether it's Dido or pirates, something like a flag's appeared over ours, I saw it just now. Come round and take a look for yourselves.'

He props the trolley handle against the wall, and we scoop up Harriet and as we follow him out of the courtyard we run into Bill on his way back from the coach house.

I might as well warn him. 'Pirates have taken over the castle, Bill, you might need to come too.'

As we come around the front, sure enough, there's a large piece of white cotton fabric flapping around, its end jammed in the first floor window frame.

I have to say it. 'That's Ambrose and Miranda's room. And this is less Dido, more like people hanging their bedsheets out of the window after their wedding night?'

Fliss lets out a gasp. 'Surely they can't have …?' Then she looks at me. 'Of course they bloody haven't, not even Miranda can claim virgin status when her grandkids are running up and down the landing.'

I'm nodding in agreement. 'Brighton's very continental, Miranda probably just hung the bedding out to air while they went to the wine merchants.'

Keef's tilting his head on one side. 'One problem with that theory – Ambrose's car is right there under our noses, exactly where Libby tells him not to park it.'

As I take in Ambrose's sparkly wheels as close to the front door as he can get without actually parking in the castle porch, my stomach drops. 'They're hardly going to go for a walk, they're not in the hot tub or downstairs ... so where the heck are they?'

'Miranda!' Fliss is cupping her hands around her mouth, shouting up at the window, Keef follows up with a small pebble or two, then we all join in the shouting.

There's a rattle, and as the sash flies up the sheet flops down and lands at our feet. And when we look up again, Miranda's filling the window frame.

'Where *the HELL HAVE YOU BEEN?*'

Fliss shoots me a sideways grimace. 'We walked to St Aidan, then we've been searching for you and Ambrose.'

Miranda's barking. 'Well, we've been stuck up here all bloody day, we even hung out an SOS flag.'

Oscar's stamping around waving a stick. 'All bloody day ... all bloody day ...'

Miranda's still going. 'We locked the door and it jammed, we shouted the place down this morning, why didn't anyone come to help?'

We all know the answer to that, but maybe now's not the best moment to explain.

Keef's calling up. 'Stay where you are, Miranda.' As if she'd do anything else. 'Two minutes, I'll get the ladders.'

In reality it's slightly longer, but then he's back from the side of the castle, and we're hearing the aluminium clinking against the stone as he extends them up the facade. Seeing him shimmying up the rungs in his Aztec print surfie pants, his bead braids flying, to a window filled with Miranda, it's weirdly like watching Rapunzel in reverse.

Then he drops out of sight over the frame edge and a few seconds later there's a shout. 'Yay, we're free!'

When Keef reappears at the window, he's being showered with kisses and adulation from a very appreciative and exceedingly breathy Miranda.

'My hero, my hero, you saved us, you saved us!'

Keef's grinning. 'All in a day's work.' He winks at her. 'You know what they say, Miranda – *before you can be free, first you need to open the door …*'

As she beams back at him her eyes are dancing. '… *and then you need to let go* … then *carpe* those effing *diems*!' She lets out a husky laugh. 'We two should go into partnership ... empowering sound bites from Cockle Shell Castle.'

Bill's shouting up. 'So what was the problem?'

Keef's shaking his head as he finally disentangles himself from Miranda's arms and slides back out onto the ladder. 'Nothing major, these old upside down locks, they'd been turning the key the wrong way, that's all.'

Which probably says something hugely significant, I'm just not quite sure what.

Thursday

19th December

20.

Worth melting for …

I'd somehow pinned my hopes on a day of tree decorating for today. Realistically, if we don't do the damned things soon, Christmas will be over and we'll all be going home again. What I actually mind about more is that if no one wants to decorate them Bill will be proved right about us not needing seventeen trees. And I really, *really*, *REALLY* don't want that to happen.

But as usual, what happens instead is all my own fault. I'd been Googling Instagram opportunities in Bill's bedroom, and came out super-excited because I'd found an evening Christmas Market down at the harbour in St Aidan on Friday. I mean, think of it – is there anything more Christmassy than market stalls, twinkly lights, delicious food, with the added twist of a backdrop of picturesque fishermen's cottages, bobbing boats and reflections off the water? And as if that wasn't enough – pause for a 'squee' at this point – there's going to be ice skating too! I knew I'd unearthed a festive gem, but I hadn't bargained for what Libby did next.

Before we knew it, she'd stopped Keef mid way across the

room with a log basket, turned him straight round and told him to find the event organisers and negotiate a private advance-hire of the rink.

Keef waved away the Amex Centurion card Libby was pressing into his hand, pointed to a wodge of twenties in his surfie pants pocket, tapped his beads against his nose, and said leave it to him, they'd settle up later. Whatever strings or rigging ropes he had to pull, and however much he had to shell out, the end result is, first thing this morning, instead of being elbow deep in vintage baubles and ribbons we're heading off for a spot of exclusive-use skating on the harbour-side outdoor rink.

Which brings me on to the other emerging early-morning castle feature – Bill and Milo's breakfast wars. And the winner of today's battle was ... pause for a drum roll ... Milo!!! He must literally have got up before he went to bed in order to bag his place by the Aga, and stood there most of the night with an industrial sized bowlful of Scotch pancake mixture, poised to cook his drop scones.

If I'm being totally honest, when you think of Bill's breakfasts, brought to the table from wherever he's picked them up, delivered with at best a frown and at worst a scowl like thunder, he's a long way behind in the race. Bill may have the edge on taste, and to be fair Milo does borrow Bill's pinny. But Bill loses out every other way because Milo cooks in person, flapping around the kitchen with his gentle banter, self-mocking jokes, and his easy smile. Breakfast served from the heart with a radiant beam? Steaming-hot dropped pancakes, served with a choice of blueberry or apricot jam and a smile – some of us accept all three – will beat Bill's bad moods hands down every time.

The downside is, by the time we make it to the harbour and the rink side, I'm so full of Scotch pancakes when I bend to do up the ice skating boots they give me, I'm popping my jeans. We're sitting at a cluster of tables at the end of the rink by the skate store and refreshment caravan, watching the fairy lights swinging from the awning edge as the gentle breeze blows in off a sea tinged with deep greens and topaz blue.

I break off to get a really lovely picture of Tiff kneeling down, her tulle skirt spread out across the cobbles, lacing up Tarkie's skating boots. I have no doubt Libby will dismiss it, but I still love the way the two of them were caught in this really sweet sibling moment.

Then I turn back to Fliss and groan at her as I do up my button. 'This has to be why Scottish people wear kilts. I may have to sit this one out until my breakfast goes down.'

She's planned better, and is hauling up the elasticated waistband of her leggings under her huge emerald maternity Elf jumper from last year. 'Don't be silly, get out there on the ice and work it off.'

I saw her looking at her phone a moment ago, so take this second to mouth at her, 'Any news?'

From her grimace it's not the best. 'Rob's pulled yet another all nighter at the office.'

'Right.' That's even worse than I thought. I'm puzzled, because this seems so unlike him. 'Do you believe him? Could he *actually* have been working?'

The sleep deprivation circles under her eyes are even darker than usual. 'Three times in the last week, I can't help but think the worst.'

I sigh because I know how bad I felt when George left. But mostly that was because he dodged saying goodbye and left me hanging for days and I didn't know where he was. When I actually found out he'd landed a mega bucks gig in another continent, no longer needed me, but couldn't face telling me, it came as a relief. But Fliss has so much more at stake. I just had one loser of a boyfriend, she's got the children and this is her soulmate we're talking about. And I know, every day the doubts are getting bigger. It's staring us in the face, we just can't bring ourselves to believe it. Nothing's going to make her feel better, but at least it might take her mind off it.

'Go and skate, I'll look after Harriet and Merwyn while you and Oscar have a go.' I know what I'm doing here, Harriet's in her pushchair, currently sleeping off her own pancake stack. And I'm due a rest. I've already made my contribution to today's Instagram effort by handing out Libby's label stripy scarves for product placement and to make everyone look colourful against the picturesque backdrop of the harbourside cottages. Coaxing the Edmunson-Twiglets into her hats instead of theirs was as exhausting as it sounds. I mean, one trapper hat is effective, four home-made, crocheted and matching is too much of a good thing. Drab brown may be very up and coming in theory, but it's still not bringing in the likes yet on Insta.

Fliss is looking over the barrier to where Brian, Bede, Taj and Slater are already zooming around the ice, their assorted rainbow and palm-tree print trousers flapping as they lean into the corners. 'I thought this was private, what the hell are *they* doing here?'

I have to laugh. 'Libby's hired Keef's mates in as crowd extras to fill the rink for the pictures.' I let out a sigh. 'You have to hand it to Libby, she's phenomenal at nailing the details. She even got them all to turn up in Santa hats and their #TeamChristmas castle sweatshirts.'

Fliss is looking over to where Libby's marching around, ordering everyone onto the ice. 'She doesn't look like she's enjoying it much though does she?'

I give a shrug. 'A Christmas production as big as this is a serious business.' I wrinkle my nose at Fliss as I pull my chair closer to the see-through part of the barrier and push her and Oscar off towards the ice. 'If you think about it, Madonna doesn't smile much either.' I suspect Libby would take the comparison as a compliment.

Not that I'm being critical, but apart from Miranda and Ambrose, and Milo who I suspect is sunny, upbeat and bounding like a puppy even on his darkest days, I don't think anyone's actually having a good time. Sure, we had half an hour yesterday evening with the lights dimmed and tea lights glimmering against the velvety darkness of the windows, sitting in front of the orange glow of log embers, but with Libby always rushing in and out on various missions, it wasn't exactly relaxing.

And the kids have taken a tower alcove for each family, and get holed up in there. Tiff and Tansy seem to mostly film each other on their phones doing earnest pieces to camera, while

Tom disappears inside his coat with his laptop and headphones.

In the other tower, Willow always supervises her crew, and they all talk in Spanish and play Evopolio, which in case you don't know – I certainly didn't – is a kind of Bolivian Monopoly, only better. All while burning their own cleansing candles. Whoop di do. The only times they lapse into English they seem to be saying what a shame it is they aren't actually in South America this year.

And whatever I was saying about Miranda and Ambrose being happy, as Miranda pulls up a chair next to mine, and thuds down onto it with a long groan, I'm having a rethink on that.

'Everything okay there?'

She takes a last drag on her roll up, stubs out the end on the bottom of her sparkly boot, then blows out a cloud of smoke that disappears into the air as it drifts towards the inky water beyond the harbour quayside. When her blue eyes flash towards me, they're troubled. 'Actually, I'm totally pissed off. Yesterday Ambrose completely failed to do something as simple as turning a key to unlock the door he'd just bolted himself. And now he's in a major sulk because he's here and shivering rather than at the castle in the hot tub.' Her nostrils flare. 'To be honest, I could do without the drama.'

As Ambrose wanders over I dip into my bag for the last of Libby's scarves. 'Here, take this, Ambie, you'll feel warmer if you wrap up.'

He coils the scarf around his neck as he sits down. 'Lucky for me, I have other warming strategies.' He pulls out a hip flask, takes a swig. As he offers it to me there's a blast of whisky on the breeze.

'Fabulous, but I'll pass thanks.' I'm toying with letting him into the secret of avoiding alcohol to keep your body temperature up when Keef arrives, towering over us in his skates.

'Morning, campers!' He shakes back his braids, gives Ambrose a gentle fist bump on his shoulder that almost knocks him sideways out of his plastic chair, then turns to Miranda. 'Naughty, naughty! You promised me you'd *carpe* those *diems*, remember – how exactly is settling in as a spectator seizing the day?'

'Er ...' Miranda opens her mouth, and manages to make her eyes sparkle, but unusually for someone so vocal, nothing else comes out.

Keef's already got hold of her hand and pulled her out of her chair. 'You can sit down every day for the rest of your life. But right now we have ice, we *have to* skate!'

Ambrose and I watch as he takes her over to swap her silver doccies for some skates, and a few minutes later he's leading her towards the rink.

Miranda shouts as she passes, 'Won't be long, Ambie.'

I think we all know she will be. I can't help feeling sorry for Ambie, the way the stripy scarf is so incongruous on top of his camel wool overcoat. I smile as I mentally namecheck his shoes. 'Nice loafers, Ambrose.' Then I put my hand on his arm. 'Don't worry, she'll be back.'

Whatever moment Miranda's seizing now this second, later on it's going to come down to a choice between six hundred quid's worth of Horsebit Guccis, or beaten up Animal boarding trainers that look like they could possibly be third hand. Miranda's heart might be momentarily lightened by the whoosh across the ice and Bill's dad's bollock talk of wild moments and free spirits blowing across endless oceans. But with her track record of desperately seeking security, it's no secret where she'll finally end up. Even if her men invariably fall by the wayside, if ever it comes to a choice of two, her head and their bank balance win out over her heart every time. Which is how we all know, however much she's giggling and gazing up at the stars in Keef's eyes as he steers her around, Ambrose will be laughing all the way to the hot tub in the end. I just hope poor Ambrose knows that, because with every circuit of the rink Miranda makes his face is getting longer.

As he takes another swig he lets out a sigh. 'The trouble is, I'm just not used to roughing it. Betty and I always went to places with more stars and a hell of a lot more luxury, I've got wall to wall Axminster at home with double deluxe underlay.'

'Betty?' My heart goes out to how far out of his comfort zone he sounds.

He gives a shrug. 'Betty was my late wife, we were great cruise fans. Once you've had Christmas in a platinum suite with butler service and black tie dining every night at the Captain's table – well, anything less feels like second best.' And a castle with stone walls inside as well as out instead of a stateroom must be about as comfortable as rubbing rough sandpaper on his sun tanned skin. Only made bearable by drinking every last drop of whatever comes his way.

I reach over and give his arm a squeeze. 'I'm sure once

Miranda tries a cruise you'll convert her.' I'm actually less convinced than I sound. I suspect Miranda's a little too naughty to rub shoulders with captains any more than once and if I remember rightly she gets very seasick. She's much more of a boundary pusher and militant protester than someone who rises to expectations. If Ambrose only knew she'd been arrested for a pie in the face incident involving a Tory councillor at the library closure demonstrations in Brighton, we probably wouldn't see his Gucci loafers for dust.

Ambrose hugs his arms and shivers. 'I think we'll definitely head out to Barbados for next Christmas.'

'Lovely.' Even though I'm beaming at him, as a measure of how uncomfortable *I'm* feeling here, I'd actually rather be joining in with Tom and Tarkie at the next table, deciding how likely it is they'll fall over and get their fingers sliced off by a passing ice skate.

Then as I watch Oscar and Fliss wobbling off the ice towards us, a hand closes on my shoulder. I don't have to look. Merwyn jumping up and down, snuffling and even barking – little traitor – is the give-away. I turn around into a Paco Rabane cloud, and a beam the width of St Aidan bay and twice as warm as a summery day. 'Milo, you've made it, and you've already got your skates on.'

If he was Merwyn, the way Milo wrinkles his nose would be adorable. Seeing he's human, it's slightly less cute and frankly a teensy bit unnerving in a 'stomach withering like a prune' kind of way. He's holding out his hand to me. 'Coming for a twirl?'

It's very bad timing. I was ready to stagger on and do a few wobbly rounds on my own, but as I'd rather not join in the pairs skating I'm floundering for excuses. 'Thanks but I think it's time for hot chocolate and Christmas cupcakes.' Not very original, but I'm desperate. 'The skate lady was telling me ... they're home baked from the Little Cornish Kitchen ... that's out beyond the harbour towards the dunes ... they're baked by Clemmie, the receptionist from the solicitors ... they've got every flavour you can imagine ... and they do singles events there too ...'

Milo's looking bemused. 'But we only just had breakfast, I only just finished washing up!' Reminding us all what an angel he is in the kitchen too. 'Come on, twice round, then I'll treat *everyone* to drinks and snacks.' Not that he's manipulating, but now it seems like everyone's elevenses are hanging on me going with him.

Fliss perks up as she arrives. 'Oooo, yes, off you go quickly, Ivy-star, then we'll all have mid-morning cakes.' With besties like this, who needs enemies?

'Fine.' It isn't, but I stand up, pull the edge of my pompom hat down as far as it will go, and grab hold of the barrier side. I used to have all kinds of trouble on roller skates, so how I'm going to attempt to balance on anything as thin as a blade I have no idea. As I begin to haul my way hand over hand around to the gap that leads to the ice I'm regretting all the times I chickened out of the *Daniels*' staff club trips to the ice rink. I'm also watching the guys hanging up the lights and putting the finishing touches to the stalls they're building around the harbour edge, the line of higgledy pastel painted cottages behind them. Thanking my lucky stars that apart from the stall builders who are busy and the odd dog walker making their way down to the beach, the harbour's deserted, and we're doing this without an audience.

I'm determined to do this on my own. Girls Aloud singing *Jingle Bell Rock* is coming out of the speakers, that has to be a good sign. I mean, how hard can it be? Tom and Tarkie have decided to risk their fingers and are staggering around upright more than they're falling over, and the Twiglets are already pirouetting. As I step down onto the ice, Libby strides past on the harbourside cobbles. I nod at Willow's daughter, Scout, who's whizzing round so fast on the spot she's gone all blurry.

'That might be good to upload?' I'm no expert, but from where I'm standing, for a ten year old it's pretty damned impressive. I just hope her scarf doesn't tighten and strangle her due to the sideways gravity forces.

'I don't think so, Ivy, it looks a lot more like showing off than true interpretive free-style skating to me.' Libby lets out a snort. 'That's home schooling in a nutshell – they're outshining Jane Torville with their stupendous spins, they could talk Spanish for bloody Mexico, but their social skills are a total disaster. You must have noticed they have *zero* interaction with *anyone* and look *totally* objectionable *all* of the time.'

I'm too busy thinking she could be talking about her own lot to answer immediately, but she's obviously not expecting one because she's already off across the quay.

So I take it that's a 'no' to the Instagram post then. If she'd said that earlier she'd have saved me forcing the issue with the Twiglets and the hat and scarf sets. I'm concentrating so hard on Libby as I step down onto the rink, my skate hits the ice before I'm ready, and I'm slithering, waving my arms madly, trying to get back to the safety of the barrier when some fingers close around mine.

'No need to panic there, Ivy – just push one foot forwards, let yourself glide, then do the same with the other. You can relax now, I'm here, I've got you.' It's Milo, and his hand is so warm I can feel the heat through my glove. As his other arm extends out across my back I'm suddenly steadier.

'Okay.' It's not. I'm still jerking forwards, trying to divert and make a lunge for the side.

'Keep going, you're completely safe with me.' His voice is calm and encouraging beside me and somehow – don't ask me how – we make juddering progress forwards and we're still standing up. 'Skating's new to you, now *you* know how *I* feel in my ridiculous new country clothes.'

I can't help laughing. 'You do know you've still got the price labels on?'

'Shit, tell me I haven't?'

Somehow I manage to nod and wobble forwards at the same time. 'Hanging out the bottom at the back.'

He lets out a groan. 'Damn. Here's me, trying my darnedest to impress you with how cool and countrified I am and I end up looking like a total loser.'

'So you *are* here for me, then?' It's out before I know, but I care less than I should because we've made it to the barrier at the other end of the rink, and now I've got something to cling on to I can stop worrying about falling arse over ice skate. And as I've blurted, we might as well clear this up.

Milo comes to a halt with his own little flourish, and then suddenly he's smiling beside me. 'You've rumbled me! Is that a problem?'

I drag in a breath. 'I don't know what they've told you ...?'

As he interrupts me his eyes are shining. 'Absolutely loads, but don't worry, it's all really good, I can't wait to get to know you better.'

In the face of so much puppy-eyed warmth, I have to come clean. 'It's only fair to tell you, Milo, whatever they said, the last thing I want is another boyfriend.'

He gives me a nudge, then his face creases as he winks. 'Ivy, it's fine, it's five minutes skating round an ice rink, no one's asking you to sign up for life.'

'You don't mind you've been dragged here on false pretences?'

He's doing the nose wrinkle again. 'Never say never, you don't know what's around the corner.' Then he clears his throat, and pulls a face. 'Actually, I've got my own confession to make ...'

My stomach sinks. 'You have ...?' Girls Aloud have finished, and Bing Crosby's started singing *White Christmas*, and even though he's crooning really slowly he gets through a whole reprise before Milo begins again.

'Dad and Miranda are convinced I'm here looking for love ... but I'm afraid that's mostly a cover.'

I feel my eyes go wide. 'So why *are* you here?'

He drops his voice to a low whisper. 'I'm looking out for Dad.' He wiggles his eyebrows. 'Making sure he doesn't get too involved with Miranda.'

'Really?!' I'm so shocked my voice is a squeak, but I yank it back to normality again. 'And how's that going?'

His mouth is so close to my ear, I can feel the warmth of his breath through my woolly hat. 'She's lovely, but if you had any idea how many husbands she's had, you'd see why I have to put a stop to it.'

Oh my. I'm not going to tell him most of us have lost count. 'So you're here to *break them up*?'

From his sigh he's not thrilled about this either. 'Dad is completely besotted, and Christmas is a very romantic time. I'm simply here to step in – *if the worst comes to the worst* – to save him from himself.'

I'm sure Libby and Fliss would be delighted to know he's got this, but I'm still uneasy. 'I get where you're coming from, but they're adults not teenagers, they should have the right to decide for themselves.' I flash my glare at him. '*Without* interference.'

Milo sighs. 'We only lost my mum last year, he's very vulnerable.' From all the outward signs he's loaded too, but he's skimming over that.

I have to say my piece. 'Happiness isn't easy to find and Miranda's a wonderfully warm and thoughtful, talented and creative, loving human being. If your dad *is* happy with her, is it right to take that away?' It's all very tricky and involved. Obviously Milo doesn't want to see his dad get hurt. And he definitely won't want Miranda ripping her way through his inheritance. And it's true, Miranda's track record is awful. But sometime soon she has to meet Mr Right. And if that is Ambrose, it *has* to be wrong for Milo to wreck their chances.

He gives a shrug. 'I know, I know, it's hard.' His voice drops again. 'You will keep my secret? I'd hate Ambrose and Miranda to feel I'm treading on their toes.'

My voice goes high again. 'But you *are*. And it's not just their toes, you're stamping on their future with your size nine wellies.'

His eyebrow goes up. 'Size tens. Hunters come up very small apparently.'

I nod. 'I should know that, they're always saying that in shoes at *Daniels*.' The number of present returns they get is phenomenal. And we've somehow moved on, but at least he knows where I stand on this.

Then his frown softens and he smiles again. 'Is this a good time to have that cake?'

I sigh. 'Just when I was getting good on here too.' It's ridiculous feeling disappointed we're leaving the ice now. But you know me, if I have to choose between hot chocolate or exercise, there's never a contest. 'Did I see Bailey's cupcakes at the skate hut?'

'You did.' He does the nose thing again. 'We'll skate back to the start nice and slowly so Ambrose and Miranda see us being coupley, then we'll head straight for the cafe.' As he takes my hand again he grins at me. 'Come on then, big beams to show everyone how well we're getting on.'

But for once even the thought of hot chocolate to come isn't quite enough to make me completely smiley.

21.

This way to the North Pole

Okay, it's official. The Little Cornish Kitchen is our new favourite bakery, more so because they do mini cupcake tasters to help you decide which large one you'd like. After my first I would have sworn the Bailey's ones were my new favourite. But then I had a mini chocolate reindeer one, which Fliss decided was good for me. The way she insisted that eating what I have an aversion for should help me regain my power, she sounded more like Willow than Willow. But there again she might have had a point. If all my fears were chocolate flavour, I'd inhale them too. Either way, I closed my eyes, concentrated on the butter cream instead of the antlers and nose, and it scored ten out of ten on our taste chart, and became my new favourite for all of ten seconds before I progressed to the coffee with roasted hazelnuts. Which knocked the others out across the bay. Willow was persuaded too and guess what? – she chose the gluten free low sugar style with the purple petal and the sprig of real lavender, and took a box of six mini ones for the Twiglets for later. Which is progress of a kind.

And then Milo plonked his chair down between Ambrose and Miranda's, which as a separating technique was about as subtle as jumping in there with his size tens. But as he was also holding Harriet who had a very sticky cupcake in each hand and was doing side swipes at Ambie's cashmere overcoat, it did in the end put significant distance between them. The best thing was, with Harriet being looked after, it meant that Fliss, Oscar and I were free to go back to ease our cupcake consciences with a few circuits of the rink. And as Keef had gone to some other pressing engagement that could have had something to do with a meeting at the Happy Shark, at least Ambie and Miranda were back together.

As for Fliss and I, once we hit the ice again you could say we amazed ourselves. When you get your legs and body swinging in time to the Christmas tunes, this skating lark is a lot easier than you'd think, and like the cupcakes, it's very more-ish. Fliss and I always had a thing for Justin from The Darkness – a straight guy who can carry off a sequined jumpsuit and make it ironic at the same time is our kind of hero – so the second his voice comes out over the speakers we're pretty much zooming around singing along to *Christmas Time, don't let the bells ring* at the top of our voices. In fact we're so engrossed by the time we clock that Bill's here too, he's already tearing around the ice. The giveaway is, he's not wearing bashed up borrowed skates like the rest of us, he seems to be wearing his own. Which kind of suggests to mc he must have an ice rink at Downton as well as a stately home.

I break off half way through the chorus to roll my eyes at

Fliss. 'Someone should tell him the Olympic speed skating track is the other way.'

Fliss pulls a face. 'It's a bloody good job he's good at weaving in and out.' She tilts towards me with a low laugh. 'If this is a competition, he's certainly putting old Milo in the shade.'

I shake my head. 'Those two and their baking wars, what are they like?'

She tilts her head and gives me a sideways look. 'That wasn't quite the competition I was talking about.'

'So which one *did* you mean?'

She gives me a wink. 'If you don't already know, it doesn't matter.'

Then I remember. 'How could I forget. Smiley Milo versus Misery Bill. How can he scowl that much and still concentrate on skating?'

And then Justin stops singing, and as if that wasn't enough bad news on its own, I hear some very familiar guitar picking start, and my heart sinks.

Scout lets out a shriek. 'Willow, it's *Feliz Navidad!*' She launches herself into a series of spins, and when she pulls out of the last one she, Sailor and Solomon start whizzing around the ice faster than Bill, all singing in Spanish.

There's a serious scraping sound, a shower of crystals flying up from the ice, and Bill suddenly comes to a halt next to us. He half closes an eye, and when he talks it's somehow obvious he's addressing me, not all of us.

'Did you notice, they're playing our tune, Pom Pom.'

Apart from brushing the ice chips out of my eyes, and off

my jacket, I absolutely don't react. 'Yours maybe, Bill. Mine is Shakin Stevens.'

He's still staring at me. 'I thought you said yours was *I Wish It Could Be Christmas Every Day*?'

I'm holding firm on this. 'No, that's my tag line, not my favourite song.' I'm happy to point out, he doesn't know me as well as he's trying to pretend.

He shakes his head. 'There's a difference?'

Of course there bloody is. 'Absolutely.'

'Jeez, as I'll say, and not for the first time, who knew Christmas was so complicated?' He's holding out his hand. 'Come on, while we're here, you might as well see what it feels like to skate properly.'

'I-I-I-I ...' I'm trying to say *I totally don't think so*, but that's as far as I get. The next thing I know it's as if my feet grew wings and jet packs too. This is nothing like what I was doing when I was rigid with fear and hanging onto Milo. With Bill it's as if he's got the power and the balance for both of us, and as we tear round the ice I'm so shocked and surprised, I actually forget to breathe. By the time we pull up, I'm dizzy, and it has to be from lack of oxygen.

'So how was that?' Bill's staring down at me.

'The music's going on a long time.'

'That's because I asked them to play it on repeat. So how was the skating?'

'Great.' That's probably the closest I've ever come to space travel, but I have to be straight with him. 'To be honest I'd probably have enjoyed it more if you weren't so up yourself, and superior about it all.'

His frown deepens. 'And what do you mean by that?'

I'm looking at his skates. 'Those show-off look-at-me shoes for starters.'

He's looking like he has no idea what I'm talking about. 'They're just my skates.'

I hold my ground. 'Whatever you do, you always have to do it in a way so you look down on everyone else.'

'Now you're being ridiculous.'

The way he says it flatly, as if it's the only opinion there is, and no one else's is valid, completely backs up my point. My chest is tightening. 'And do you always have to look so damned miserable? Here we are, everyone's trying their damnedest to have a good time ...' I know that's not completely true, and no one's actually succeeding, but they might be '... but when you're there like Grinchy McScrooge-face looking down on us all it's *very hard* for everyone *not* to feel like shit.' My voice has gone really high and a lot squeakier than I'd like, and I can sense that the skaters around the rink are sliding to a halt.

His nostrils flare as he blows out a breath. For a moment he looks really dark, then he turns to me. 'Well, I may look miserable, but that's way better than making a fool of myself like you were earlier.'

This is so far away from anything I was expecting, at least the shock has made my voice more low and normal. '*ExCUSE me?*' I really have no idea what he's talking about.

His eyes flash. 'Running round, throwing yourself at a guy like Milo, I'd have thought you'd have more self-respect.'

If my chest was tight before, now it explodes. '*AND WHAT IS THAT SUPPOSED TO MEAN, BILL?*'

His voice is low and steady. 'Believe me, I know.'

'Actually, you know *ZILCH!*' As I look down I realise he's still holding onto my hand, really tightly. So I tug my hand away from him, but he won't let go at first. It's only when I pull really, really hard and his grasp suddenly loosens that I get away. But the force of my jerk sends me lurching backwards which would be fine if we were on the harbourside. But here on the rink things are working against me. One, I'm on ice which when I think about it is the slipperiest surface known to man. And two, I'm wearing sodding great boots and if that wasn't enough, there are also great bits of spikey metal attached to the bottom. One of those, I might have managed, all three to contend with, and I'm staggering backwards. My arms are flailing, I've almost got my balance back but my feet are all over the place. And then the end of my skate catches in the bow of my laces, and that's it. I'm jumping backwards, arcing downwards, as my feet shoot forwards from under me, my back thumps down onto the ice.

One massive thud, and I'm horizontal. Gazing up at the pale grey clouds racing across other darker grey clouds.

Which actually is okay. Everyone's been falling over. It's what you do. It's a bloody skating rink. That's the metaphor, it's the physical embodiment of slick and skiddy surface on which it's impossible to stay upright. In which case, why the hell is there a circle of faces at the edge of the clouds all staring down at me with open mouths, their eyes wide, gasping.

Fliss is staggering towards me across the ice and the way her arms are out she looks a lot like Bill when he was at his most Olympic. 'It's absolutely okay, Ivy, you absolutely don't need to worry, really, *really*, *REALLY*, nobody's going to mind ...'

And that's when I put my hand to my head. And feel the back of my head and my hair resting on the soaking ice. My hat's completely gone. And my long sideways fringe thing that I've grown so carefully to hide the left side of my face has flipped upwards and sideways. Anywhere except where it's supposed to be in other words.

'Shit, where's my ...'

I can see Tom's face looking down at me from inside the comfort of his hoodie. 'So *that's* why she gets to wear a hat inside. Okay, all good, *now* I understand. A scar like that, she has to hide it.'

As I push myself up to sitting Fliss is rushing towards me holding out my bobble hat that's soaking from the layer of water on top of the ice. 'Here ... put it on again ... really, Ivy-leaf, no one minds ... they just don't ...'

Willow's there too. 'It'll all be fine, concealment is *so* confining, exposure is very cleansing, no wonder your chakras are all over the place ...'

Miranda's voice is booming across the harbour as she hurries out onto the ice again. 'Sweetheart, it's only a scar ... and it's so much better than it used to be ... no one minds, darling ... you'll always be beautiful ... we really can't see it now you've grown your hair ...'

And Tiff's there, her eyes flashing, her pink tulle skirt whirling, shouting as she turns on them. 'Will you all stop being horrible, and *LEAVE HER ALONE!!*'

And it's like magic. Suddenly they all shut up and just stare at her. And here's this awful, awful child who I've spent the last few days completely despising. And suddenly I want to hug her.

She and Tarkie are gently helping me to my feet, then Tansy joins in too, but over their heads I can see Bill. As he moves towards me, his face is creased with concern and the way his arms are outstretched, I just know as soon as he reaches me he's going to wrap those arms around me. And even though I also know that's the last thing I would *ever* want, part of me is already anticipating the warmth. His strong hands closing around my back. The whole wonderful scent of him as I bury my nose in that charcoal cashmere. The feeling I used to dream about for months after Chamonix, if not years. Of wanting to be wrapped in those arms forever.

And just for today, I'm not going to fight it. The back of my fur jacket is soaking, my jeans are stuck to my knees, my hair's all damp and straggling out of my sodden hat. But just this once I'm not going to beat myself up, I'm going to lean in and let the wonderful happen. I'm going to drink it in, I'm going to soak up every bit of strength and wellbeing that hug is going to give me. I'm going to *carpe* those effing *diems*, abandon myself and enjoy the goddamn moment.

Somewhere in the midst of my mind ramblings I must have closed my eyes. When I open them again what I'm expecting is the sweet, blissful moment, the impact of my cheek against Bill's jumper. But instead what I get comes careering across the ice out of left field and sends Bill flying out of the frame.

Suddenly, instead of the anticipated warmth of wool, my face is buried in the nylon folds of a brand new Barbour puffa jacket and I'm coughing as the Paco Rabane Million fumes hit the back of my throat. 'Milo?'

'Don't worry, I've got this!' Did I mention his beam? It's wider than the bay and brighter than a thousand watt light-house bulb powered up with lenses.

And then as I push myself free, try to disentangle my hat from his zip, and come across a large lump of buttercream something else hits me. 'Oh my, what the hell did you do with Harriet?'

He's totally unconcerned. 'She's fine, I passed her across to my dad.'

Dumped her on him more like. 'As if you'd trust Ambie with anything as breakable as a child – he has trouble hanging onto a stubbie beer bottle, let alone a squirming baby.'

As if on cue there's a loud squawk. Except it's not Harriet screaming, it's Ambie. 'Will someone come and get this bloomin' kid off me ...'

As Libby strides onto the ice, still in her white trainers, she's clapping her hands and totally ignoring Ambie. 'Okay, I think that's enough ice for one day. Let's all head off for lunch at the Fun Palace at the Crab and Pilchard.'

If we're going there it's like she's totally given up on giving a damn. From what I've seen on the website, she couldn't have picked anywhere more unstylish or less aspirational. All I can think is she has to be going for crass in an ironic way. Or possibly getting her own back on the Edmunson-Twiglets for showing her lot up on the ice with those perfect ten ice spins.

Fighting the fun suckers in a pit full of bright coloured plastic balls and lunch of turkey twizzlers served by people dressed as Disney characters? How is that going to go down with Willow's save-the-earth vegan anti-materialistic multinational-hating pacifists? Worse still for me, there's a sleigh pulled by not just one but eight animated reindeer.

If that's not aversion therapy, I don't know what is.

But as we pile into the cars and wind our way out to the Crab and Pilchard all I can think of is Bill's face as he came towards me earlier. How desperately I wanted that hug. And how sick I feel that the moment's gone, and I'll never have that chance again.

22.

No ski boots …

If my trip to the Fun Palace taught me anything, it's that I shouldn't pre-judge – I should always be ready to be astonished.

I suspect they've been sheltered from anything tacky or commercial, but instead of standing back and looking disgusted, Willow's three hurled themselves in amongst the plastic balls with whoops and jumps, and none of them imploded into ectoplasm due to the toxicity.

As soon as we got our drinks Willow took me off to one side, sipping her still water in a glass bottle through a paper straw. She then dipped into her bag, and devised me my own personal cocktail of flower essence drops. Apparently it was designed to give me an instant post fall-over lift, treat the shock of me exposing my ripped-up face to the entire rink, fight the bruising on my bum, and balance my chakras too.

You have to admit, however much a fan of rescue remedy etc. you are, it's a lot to ask from a few teensy drops of liquid. But I was happy to go along with it. Having someone take an interest in me in such a quiet and thoughtful way was probably as beneficial as a bit of water with petals dissolved in it. Did I feel special? Yes I did. As for whether I would I recommend it, I'll let you know on that one.

When we were finished and Willow went up to take on the menu and the kitchen staff and attempt to order lunch her elbows were sticking out and pointy. But she was back in record time, because it turned out the Crab and Pilchard are big on vegan and veggie options. The vegan beetroot burgers she chose actually looked more meaty than the steak burgers. Just saying. Obviously they weren't.

For my personal challenge, once I'd got my flower essence on board, to pass the time until I was called up for duties with Oscar or Harriet I decided to hunt down as many tasteful photo opportunities as I could, expecting I'd be lucky to get a couple. But once I looked past the really crappy foil-covered cardboard buckles on the staff plimsolls and began zooming in, all I can say is, someone in St Aidan is seriously into their Scandi chic.

Okay, the chunky red and cream hand knit cushions are piled a bit too thickly on the window seats for the true Stockholm simplicity purists but Nordic maximalism as done at the Crab and Pilchard gives a whole new meaning to Christmas cosy. I got enough pretty wood and woolly detail shots to keep Libby going all next Christmas as well as this one. When you come across a driftwood Christmas tree on the bar, totally covered in mini hanging sheep with twigs for legs, you don't think *What the Hygge*? you just think *What's not to love?*

While we were skating Libby had disappeared off up the hill and taken bird's eye views of us skating on the rink between the cottages higher up, which were really effective. And she's certain that the skater close ups of her scarf and hats she uploaded will send her last minute pre-Christmas stocking-filler sales off the scale. Meanwhile, back at the Crab and Pilchard, I gave the Santa and his reindeer a wide berth for my very own good reasons, but Merwyn was entranced. Tiff took this really funny clip of him nodding his head as he watched the animated Santa moving up and down.

It turned out to be one of those rare days when no one had any expectations, but everyone found a bit of what they liked. And I was no exception. By late afternoon when we got back to the castle and I dragged the boxes of charity shop deccies into the kitchen, instead of rolling their eyes Willow's kids pounced on them, and began to sort them into colours. Then they went off into the family areas and started to make the kind of rainbow shaded decorated tree they'd seen at the Crab and Pilchard, which is exactly what I've wanted to have at *Daniels* for years. Except, with the baubles all being slightly different instead of all the same, the effect is going to be stunning.

So seeing they were doing so well with those on their own, with Willow's help – while also watching the DVD of *101 Dálmatas*, which is exactly what it says on the tin except in Spanish, and so acceptable for educational reasons rather than being dismissed as cultural crap – I decided to get on with making some tree deccies for my room. I'd rather Bill didn't know this, but using his beautiful starry gin labels as a starting point, I take some scissors and some sheets of paper I ordered the night I hit on pink and orange as my theme colours. Then I sit down at the table in the kitchen with Merwyn at my feet to make some origami paper stars.

This is just for me. First I make a pentagon template and when I've cut out a pile from each colour, I begin to fold. I know I shouldn't be saying it, but as they pile up the small folded stars are looking unbelievably sweet.

Tiff and Tansy are sorting through the bauble boxes next to me and Tiff reaches over, picks one up and gives that superior sniff thing she does, which I must say I mind a lot less since she stuck up for me earlier today. Then she simply says, 'They're pretty.'

Well, I said it was a day of surprises. I pick my jaw up off the floor, and smile at her. 'They're easy to do, I could show you how to make them if you like?'

Tiff nods. 'We could make silver stars for Mum's tree. And if we make some for ours out of newspaper, we'll be saving the world even more than the Twiglets.' There's definitely some worthiness rivalry going on here, but whatever the reason, I can work with it.

'Great.' For once it is. In fact it's more than that. Absolutely bloody astonishing and brilliant wouldn't be over stating it as I show them the shapes to cut, and the folds. 'You can make them bigger or smaller, just try a few and see which you like.'

They come with me to the laundry for some silver and rose gold paper and we pick up a stack of Ambie's old *Telegraph* newspapers there too. Then I show them what to do again, they tell me how I can do it better, and after that we cut and fold to the usual soundtrack of Christmas tunes.

Tiff makes a couple then she holds one up and looks at me. 'You've still got your hat on.'

I stop my folding and look up at her. 'And?'

'You don't have to wear it for us any more, we all know what's under it now.' She sniffs. 'In any case that scar of yours is nothing like as bad as you think it is.'

Tansy's backing her up. 'You can believe us, we talk the truth not bollocks.'

I smile at them. 'Well thanks for that. Maybe I'll try without.' It's the last thing I feel like doing. But they're children, they're putting the effort in, I want to meet them half way here. As I take off my hat, and shake my fingers through my hair I'm feeling very exposed and strangely bare. But at the same time they're right. Everyone knows, everyone's already had a ring-side view, what the hell does it matter anyway. 'How's that?' I shake out my side fringe as much as I can.

Tiff nods. 'Much better.' She's narrowing her eyes. 'If you like we could try some of our make up later. We've got loads, manufacturers send us it all the time because we vlog.'

'Really?' The make up girls at *Daniels* offered, but somehow I never wanted to let them see, I was always waiting for it to get better.

Tansy's chipping in. 'We get free stuff all the time.'

Tiff sighs as if it's nothing. 'The industry is huge, we're their direct channel to the future generation of make up users.' Then she turns to me. 'For you it's all about confidence. The best vlogs are the ones that help people, it would be really good to vlog about making you feel better – that's if you didn't mind being our guinea pig.'

It's the last thing I'd want. But she's eleven, which makes it easier. There's no expectation because it's like playing. 'Maybe.' I'm tempted to ask if their guinea pigs get animal rights, but I manage to hold it in.

Tiff's nodding. 'You'll see, there's absolutely nothing to be scared of.' She's as persuasive as her mum. 'We'll do some skin tone tests later, if we don't get it right straight away I'll email the technical department and ask for some specialist concealing products, they're very helpful.'

'Right. That sounds brilliant.' I'm not joking. 'I can't believe you're so knowledgeable.'

She wrinkles her nose. 'It's easy when you're interested, that's why you should always work at what you enjoy. Tarkie likes earth moving machines and pile drivers, if you want your basement digging out you'll have to ask him not us.'

Tansy's pursing her lips as she concentrates on her folds. 'My second best thing is laminating.'

Tiff doesn't look up from her folding. 'She's getting a laminating machine for Christmas.'

This is the thing with kids, you never know what they're going to come out with next. 'So what are you going to laminate?'

Tansy frowns. 'Anything that's flat. I just know my life will be so much better with a laminator in it.'

Tiff looks up. 'If she had it now we could laminate stars for the tree. Or gin bottle labels for Bill's product placement.' For eleven she's so tuned in.

'Did I hear my name, does someone need me?' It's Bill, obviously, listening in again, as he crosses the kitchen.

I look up from the pentagon pile I'm rearranging. 'I will have a word in a second. It's nothing important, just an email I wanted to run past you.'

'You know where to find me.' He points towards his room as he heads through the door.

When I turn back to my stars Tiff and Tansy's stares are so intense, I have to challenge them. 'What? I've already told you, he's taken. If ever I go to see him in there it's strictly on Christmas business.'

Tiff's stare doesn't alter. 'But he definitely does like you.'

I'm not letting that go. 'I thought you just told me you didn't talk bollocks.'

Tansy laughs. 'We don't. You should have seen him when Smiley Milo pushed him out of the way and hugged you instead.'

Tiff nods. 'He was well annoyed.'

I push myself up to standing. 'Two words – not happening.'

Tiff grins at me. 'Mum said to tell you, remind Bill to get mistletoe.'

There are a very few times when I like being tall but now is one of them. I pull myself up to my maximum height and try for really scary. 'You two – shut up and make your stars.'

Possibly I failed completely, because as I stride away, they both collapse into giggles. At least I know Bill's expecting me. It's only as I close the bedroom door behind Merwyn that it hits me I'm still without my hat, dammit. I shake my hair across my face, tilt my head and make my smile very bright. 'About the lost baubles ...'

Bill lets out a groan. 'Not those again, I thought we'd moved on.'

'Well it was a huge order, so I raised a query, then elevated it to supervisor level.'

He's standing, holding his hands together. 'But we agreed, we don't need those decorations, we've reduced our carbon footprint by using recycled ones, why are we still discussing this?'

Not that I'm smug, but I've got the trump card here. 'Because apparently they didn't disappear into the ether like you said, they were *SIGNED FOR at the delivery address ...*' I have to hold onto my fingers really hard to stop myself making those little speech marks in the air I hate so much, because it's the one time in my life when they'd work really well '... it means the company won't be refunding. So unless you want to be seriously out of pocket here you *might* want to follow this up?'

'Ivy, maybe just leave this.'

My voice goes all high, because he's *so* annoying. 'But I thought you were counting every penny here, not following this up is like hurling twenty quid notes out across the bay into a force ten gale.'

He's rubbing his thumb across the stubble on his jaw. 'Fine, I'll tell you what happened, but it's not great. They were delivered to my old house in London, and Gemma signed for them.'

I'm nodding. 'So far, so good. The accounts are matching.'

He clears his throat. 'The delivery was so big she assumed it was one of those malicious pranks, like people sending fake pizza orders to the wrong address, or having a load of concrete pumped into your cellar, or ten tons of donkey droppings delivered onto your front lawn.' He stops to roll his eyes.

'Oh no …'

'When she saw it was from me, she dealt with it accordingly.'

'Which was?' I'm puzzled. Surely in that case she'd have sent it on.

'She bought a sledgehammer from B&Q, flattened the lot on the drive, then sent me the bill for the clear up.'

'*WHAT?!!!!* Oh my, I'm sorry, that's so awful.' At the same time, I don't understand. *At ALL*. 'But why, I thought you said you were still together.'

He blows out a breath. 'I think what actually happened was you asked if we were still in touch, and when I said "yes" my answer was an ironic one.'

'Sorry? I was a bit confused before, but you totally lost me there.'

He drags in a breath. 'It's true, I *do* hear from her most days – but lately that's via her solicitor. We're wrangling over property. And the letters are at best unpleasant and often hideous.'

'Oh shit, that's awful.' I really don't want to stick my nose in here, and if I'm secretly whooping inside because she's out of the picture, that's not what I mean at all.

'We never got married, I always hoped that if we parted we'd be civilised. But whatever we agree on, she always comes back for more.' He shakes his head. 'But listen to me, you know how hard it is, I don't have the monopoly on dark times, you've had a break up too.'

'I did, but we were less entangled, we didn't have our own places.' The easy break up was the plus side to George and I not sharing anything. When he left, he literally walked out with a bag and his boxers, because everything else was mine. I'd actually bought most of his clothes and his undies too, but it wasn't like I wanted to keep them.

As for Gemma, I only had two weeks with her. But anyone who filches a mountain size Mont Blanc chestnut meringue one day, and a whole box of my macaroons the next – and then lies about it – is hardly going to be straight in a split up. I shrug. 'Isn't she a lawyer, too ...?'

He lets out a sigh. 'Exactly. That's a good life lesson there – never break up with a barrister.' The hollows in his cheekbones are more pronounced than ever. 'That's how this whole Christmas let fiasco happened. I got yet another demand for cash I didn't have, and an estimate from a solicitor to deal with it and in a very rash moment I threw the castle onto Facebook for a ridiculous amount that would cover the lot and more.'

I pull a face for everything he let himself in for. It was one desperate moment, and he didn't deserve all this. 'Six seconds later, you were committed ... and you've been kicking yourself ever since.' It's not even a question. We know he has, we've all felt his pain and lived with his misery. But at least this explains it.

He shrugs. 'Pretty much.' Then his mouth twists. 'It's not all bad.'

I laugh at him. 'By the end of Christmas you'll have had the kind of free adverts you could only dream of for your gin,

I suspect you're going to eat your own weight in Scotch pancakes and possibly nut roast too. And after this lot, stag parties puking up and wrecking the place will be a walk in the park.'

'You could be right.'

'At the risk of sounding like Keef, you've got three choices – give up, give in or give it all you've got. But I get why you're grumpy.' I put my hand on his arm. 'All those deccies, smashed to *teensy* pieces ... I'd be cross too. Actually I wouldn't, *I'd be effing furious!*'

'Thanks, Pom Pom.' He gives me a nudge with his elbow. 'I couldn't have got this far without you.' He raises his eyebrows, then he drops them again. 'So how about you?'

I lift an eyebrow in query myself, because I wasn't quite ready for this. 'Me?'

'It's good to see you without your hat, that's all.'

I know he's shared a lot more than he needed to. 'And now you're wondering ...?'

'I'm sorry, I can't help being curious ...' The way he's staring at me it's a lot more than that, it's like he's trying to see into my soul. 'You don't drink, you don't date, I give you a onesie to wear and you practically throw up ... yet the first time we met I couldn't get you out of my head because you had this wonderful certainty about you. You were so happy, so much yourself, so different from everyone else in that cabin in Chamonix. So what happened?' he asks gently.

I really didn't come in here for him to be digging this deep. 'Going on a winter sports holiday when I didn't like skiing, that was certainly different. But everyone alters – you grow up, you live life and it changes you.' The way his eyelashes are flickering, I'm going to have to give him something more. 'Okay, I was in a car accident. But I only talk about it to Fliss. So long as I do things for other people and not myself, I'm fine, and I won't ever need to think about it again. So I'm not being mean, but if you don't mind I'd rather not discuss it any more.'

'Whatever gets you through, you go for it.' He tilts his head. 'There I go, sounding like a cliché generator. I'm sad you got hurt, but I'm pleased you're not giving up or giving in.'

I give him a punch on the arm. 'And I'm sad you won't get your refund, and I'm sorry you're having a bad time. But I'm not sorry you broke up with Gemma.' Oh my, where did that come from? I'm scrambling around my head to find something to add to make it sound better. 'What I mean is, she was super-pretty on the outside, but anyone who smashes that many decorations is a lot less pretty on the inside.' But I think we knew that bit already.

I'm suddenly thinking I've been in here for ages and the terrible time the kids are going to give me when I come out. 'I've been in here way too long, Tiff and Tansy are convinced I come in here to snog you, I need to go.'

There's a light dancing in his eyes. 'And that's not why you're here? It seems a shame to disappoint them.'

My eyes are so far open my eyeballs feel like they could drop out.

And then his mouth twists again. 'Only joking. Obviously.' He shakes his head. 'Taffeta and Tulle, what *are* those two like?'

The sweat is running down my spine in rivers not trickles. 'Great, I know.' I'm thinking what else I had to say. 'Oh, and I need to remind you about mistletoe.' And I jumped into that with both feet too.

'So you *do* want the snogging after all?' His eyes are really dancing now. 'I get it, you don't want to ask, and you prefer surprises. I'm sure we can work with that.'

Oh my. To think I marched in here, thinking I was the one who was going to come out on top. What was I saying about needing to be ready to be astonished?

'And another thing ...'

I'm not sure I'm up for any more of Bill's afterthoughts, I haven't got Merwyn in line to march out yet. 'Go on ...'

'I've told Happy Milo to keep his distance.'

I'm taking it in, turning it over in my head, and on reflection, it doesn't sound so bad. 'I know there's been a bit of competition around the Aga the last few mornings, we should definitely work out a rota for the breakfast baking.'

Bill's staring at me like I'm not getting it. 'What the hell has the Aga got to do with anything?'

It turns out he's right, I'm not understanding at all. 'So what *are* you meaning?'

Bill doesn't even look apologetic. 'I've told him to stay away from *you*.'

Friday

20th December

23.

Marshmallows this way ...

Friday begins with another breakfast tussle between Milo and Bill, but this time there's a variation. Bill is nowhere around, but he's bagged his pitch first and left Keef to oversee. Whoever the baker with the cool writing is has sent little labels and jars of home made jams, several cards of instructions on how to make perfect waffles. Then there are bowls full of mixture, six electric waffle makers and flour sifters filled with icing sugar.

There's also a bowl of gluten free and egg free mixture so Scout, Solomon and Sailor have no excuse not to join in. All I can say is, for anyone thinking of giving seven kids waffle irons and strawberry jam and telling them to get on with it – unless you want your kitchen to look like world war three just happened, then don't. It makes the hot chocolate topping destruction that Milo walked in on look like a hiccough.

I wave an instruction card splattered with jam and waffle mix at Tiff and Tansy. 'We could do with your laminator for these.' And they nod back, their mouths bursting with apricot jam and waffles.

As for me, Willow comes gliding by with a strong recommendation for blueberries to balance my aura, so I'm not going to argue. And waffles are one of those things – it's easy to forget how delicious they are. You can go months, or even years without eating them, but once I close my teeth on the crisp golden crunch and get the softness of the icing sugar exploding on my tongue, all complimented by a large clump of blueberry jam – I seriously can't stop eating them. As far as the sugar-free breakfast brigade go, they can't know icing sugar counts because they're shaking it on their waffles like there's no tomorrow.

Whoever thought up this breakfast did not anticipate the clearing up time either. It's a good thing we don't need a fast getaway for the day's activities, because Fliss and I are still wiping jam out of the cracks between the floorboards and waffle mix out of Oscar's hair at lunchtime. But however energetic and unable to switch off Libby is, holidays are about chilling. Today Libby's holed up in the laundry sorting through parcels leaving everyone else free to run on slowmo. And for once, that's okay.

We carry on making our deccies, then Tiff and Tansy come and help me and Merwyn hang the pink and orange stars on our tree. Mostly I think they just want to check I'm telling the truth about not having Bill tucked under my duvet. Obviously I wouldn't have, Keef already told us, he's gone off up towards St Austell making gin deliveries. Next we go up to their room and cover their tree with their super-pretty newspaper stars and fill in the gaps with silver and gold baubles from Bill's boxes of randomness. And then we go to their tower alcove for a little make up trial.

It's very low key. Scraping my hair back out of the way in a headband like Tiff suggests is completely impossible for now. I push my hair back, and offer her my face, just for a few seconds to begin with, because my stomach's wrenching so hard. I manage a touch of foundation, a whisk of powder off a brush. Then Tiff stands back, swishes her lovely pink tulle skirt with sequins in it. She smiles and says, 'Not so bad?' And actually she's right.

And then Willow's lot sit down to watch *101 Dálmatas* again joined by Oscar and Harriet who don't give a damn they can't understand it and are doing a great job pretending to be bilingual. So Fliss comes into the tower room too and we all try out the latest nude lippy shades, and Tansy has a go at our eyebrows, and we all end up looking like we had an accident in the dark with a Sharpie and have to go and scrub them off.

Obviously we're just marking time, letting our appetites build for the big event of today, the night time market. As we pile out of the cars down on the seafront car park in St Aidan later, it's after six but it's been dark for hours. The half moon is spreading its beam across the sky, lighting the clouds from behind, making them luminous, and sending shimmers across the glassy blackness of the sea below. As the wind tosses salt spray in our faces we can hear the waves rolling in and crashing up the beach, randomly splattering out over the railings and onto the promenade. As we make our way along to the harbour, the light strings between the lamp posts are swinging wildly, and below them the wide pavement is heaving with people, most of them wearing Santa hats, all of them shrinking inside the bulk of their padded jackets against the chilly air slicing off the water. As we pass the ice rink full of skaters Fliss and I are bumping a pushchair each over the cobbles.

We push towards the stalls, lured by the smells of sweet caramelised almonds, garlicky cheese and roasting sausages. As I hear a familiar voice behind me, I turn to see Bill. 'No falling over tonight, okay?'

I pull my hat down to stop my ears getting freeze blasted by the cold. 'No more disasters for me, I've had enough, thanks.'

He's got his hands deep in his pockets and as I catch a glimpse of his open jacket for a nanosecond I can't help thinking how it would feel to be wrapped up inside there with him. Knowing he's not with Gemma makes me feel less of a traitor. But I'm kicking myself even more. If I learned one thing from George it was to avoid posh guys who ski. But even if I did want to be with someone like Bill, if he was out of my league before – and he totally was – he'll be out of my universe with my face as it is now. Realistically I'd probably have more chance with Ian Somerhalder. I'm asking myself why the hell I'm wasting brain time with thoughts like that when we come to Miranda and Ambrose, who've stopped right in front of us.

Fliss pulls to a halt next to them. 'Hurry up you two, you don't want to miss those roasted chestnuts.'

Miranda raises her eyebrows. 'Ambie's thinking he'd prefer dinner up at The Harbourside Hotel.'

Fliss lets out a cry. 'I thought Christmas markets were your favourite, we couldn't get you away from the one in Brighton last year.'

Miranda comes in closer and lowers her voice. 'Apparently he's not keen on street vendors or crowds or the salmonella.'

Miranda's whispering, but Fliss's protest is loud. 'Aren't the food and the bustle the best parts? Surely, you can eat at the Harbourside any time, this is only one night.'

Miranda's putting a brave face on this, but her smile is a little too bright to be real. 'It's fine, he's decided, I'd better run.' He's already backing into the shadows without her. If she doesn't go soon, she'll lose him.

As she hurries away, Milo leaps from behind us. 'Actually, I think I'll join them ... if that's okay with everyone?' He's looking at me.

I ignore the double thumbs up Tiff is giving me and answer Milo. 'You need to be there, we totally understand, we'll see you back home.'

Fliss is rolling her eyes. 'Poor Mum. Let's hope they serve gooseberry crumble for you Milo.' I get where she's coming from. What exactly is Milo planning to do if Ambie does propose ... throw himself on top of the ring before Miranda gets it onto her finger?

Bill's straight in with the directions. 'Left through the harbour, and up the hill. There's an exclusive outdoor terrace with a patio heater, you can look down on the rest of us from there.' He turns to us. 'And I have to nip up to the Parrot and Pirate to see about a gin order, so I'll catch you later too.'

Then as Bill wanders off, I catch the ping of Fliss's message tone. 'Hey, and we have signal.'

She pauses, pulls her phone out of her pocket, as she looks at the screen she's hissing under her breath. 'Damn, what the hell is he playing at?'

I check that Tiff and Tansy are far enough in front not to hear, and murmur back over Harriet's head. 'Rob?' He's supposed to be arriving tomorrow.

She lets out a breath. 'That's him saying he's staying on to work Monday, possibly Tuesday too.' Her voice is small and she pulls her hood up further and wipes her cuff across her nose. 'I'm starting to think he won't turn up here at all. All the signs say he's baubles deep in a Christmas fling with someone from the office. I mean, what if this is him leaving us?'

I'm blazing inside on her behalf but despairing too. 'Whatever's going on, you have to fight this. I know you didn't want to upset the kids by seeing their dad when he's not here, but Oscar and Harriet need to Facetime him. If you remind him what he could be losing, it might shock some sense into him before it's too late.'

Her groan is heartfelt. 'You're right. The minute they're both awake and smiling in the morning, we'll be in Bill's room dialling.'

'In the meantime ...' I raise my voice again '... I prescribe German sausage hot dogs all round, with a side of noodles and lashings of melted Swiss cheese and rosti potatoes.' I sound like I'm channelling my inner Willow, but I know Fliss – she always responds to a calorie rescue. 'With a mahoosive mince pie ice cream sundae to finish.'

Her face crumples as she lets out a wail. 'If only I'd lost the baby weight sooner, he might not have ...'

I cut her off, because she really shouldn't be blaming herself here, or beating herself up about her curves which actually look amazing. Again, she's comparing herself to Libby who does so much pointless nervous dashing she probably does ten thousand steps between the kitchen and the pantry before the end of breakfast. But if Fliss's soulmate and best friend has truly gone off the marital rails, it's going to be about much more than a couple of dress sizes. 'Fliss, we're tramping the streets, you're juggling two babies on your own and you got dressed ...'

She coughs. 'A teensy confession, I am still wearing my pyjamas under my clothes here.'

'That absolutely still counts ...' I'm here to build her up not knock her down. '... it's colder than a bloody fish finger factory, you suspect the love of your life is playing away ... for one night only that's four excellent reasons for a free pass to as much comfort food as you can consume.' I pause to let her take that in. 'We're at a Christmas market with the most delicious food smells ever, you need to make the most of this and I'm going to help you.'

'When you put it like that ...' she hesitates, but only for a moment '... point me to the nearest mulled wine stall!'

After how I felt last year, I know how hard it is for Fliss. When each twinkling fairy light and every twirl of ivy, the busker with a trumpet playing *Mad World* in the shopping centre wringing your heart out, and each and every light up snowman on people's porches is resonating to remind you of how happy you should be ... but aren't. Every other time of the year it would just be bad, but thanks to all those TV ads, there's this belief that Christmas should be a perfect, blissfully happy, together-y time. However unreal that expectation, that's what you compare yourself to. The belief that you're failing simply compounds your problems a thousand times, and makes you feel *so* much more tragic and hopeless.

I suppose in a way, that unreal perfection is what Libby's trying to recreate – except she never just tries, she *strives*. And she always does it with ten times more energy and purpose than anyone else in our orbit. But the sad thing is that so far, however much she's poured in the cash, and however much we've heaped in the effort, I can't *honestly* say it's working out. Sure, we're faking it to the world with our Instagram posts and her Twitter feed and the Facebook posts. If you count the success in likes and retweets, she's doing amazingly. But if you judge by the long faces and moans of the people at the castle, thus far she's completely dropped the proverbial ball. Which kind of goes to show, money doesn't necessarily buy you happiness *or* success, not *every* time.

Having said that, I defy anyone to spend time at the St Aidan night market, with the fairy lights reflected in the water, the boat masts etched like dark sticks against the smudgy cloud shadows of the sky, the figures clustered around stalls glowing in the half light, and not feel warm inside. Watching Santa and his elf friend drive through on his cart lit by twinkly fairy lights and laden with presents, with the most wonderful clip clop of hooves and the jingle of bells. Santa pulled by a pony, not reindeer? That definitely works for me.

By the time we're working our way up the twisting streets between the open shops further up the village, we've tried or bought something from most of the stalls, the pushchairs are weighed down with bags of stollen loaves and every kind of stocking filler from soap to tiny wooden toys, and Fliss and I are nibbling on vanilla fudge as a palette cleanser. Our lungs are about to burst with the effort of the push up the hill, so when we reach the mews where the wonderful wedding shop is, we turn along it, drawn by the level ground and the snowy sparkle of the displays.

As Fliss and I press our noses up against the glass and take in the gorgeous white tree, the cream lace dress tumbling like a waterfall, the tiny studs of sequins, she lets out a sigh. 'However wobbly I feel about Rob, looking in here makes me want to get married all over again.'

I can't help laughing. 'Maybe Miranda's long line of ex-husbands are all because she loves wedding dresses.'

As Tiff comes to join us in the soft yellow light from the street lamps, she's nodding at the next window. 'Look, they've got newspaper stars on loopy strings in the background, a lot like ours.'

I grin at her. 'And tulle skirts a lot like yours too. They've stopped short of the mismatched deccies, though.'

As Bill pops up behind her his low voice makes me jump. 'You're spending a long time looking in the wedding shop, is there any significance to that?'

I give a sniff. 'Bill, how lovely you caught us up here …' not '… we're just admiring the display techniques.'

He gives me a high eyebrow. 'A likely story …'

There's nothing worse than being single and caught swooning over wedding dresses. 'We're in the trade, don't forget.'

Tiff who's somehow tagged along with us is looking at Bill. 'My mum says they're both bitching stylists.'

Fliss's eyes flash open. 'Your mum said that?' There's no wonder she can't believe what she's hearing, Libby's not exactly famous for dishing out compliments. Realistically, she's so busy keeping her own balls in the air, she rarely notices anyone else's, and it's rarer still that she says anything nice about them.

Tiff's nodding. 'The minute she gets that proper shop of her own she's going to head hunt you both, for sure.'

I wink at Fliss. 'Whether we want her to or not.' Libby's been dreaming about retail outlets for years according to Fliss, but so far it's always been too big a jump even for her to make.

Tansy's behind Tiff like a disapproving echo. 'Head hunting? That has to be *so* bad for animal rights.'

Bill's there again. 'Well, if you come back when the shop's open, there are four whole floors of bridal gorgeousness waiting for you to sigh over complete with a wedding styling basement and a florist.'

I have to ask. 'How come you're such an authority?'

'Because I specialise in stags?' His lips are twisting. 'Not really, everyone knows, it's Cornwall's most famous wedding emporium, they talk about it on Pirate FM all the time.' In spite of the cold and the rest of us shivering and pulling our scarves over our mouths between fudge chunks, his coat is still unnervingly and invitingly open. 'If you're into beautiful design you need to call in at Plum's Deck Gallery too, further down near the Crusty Cobs cake shop. Come on, it's bursting with great things, they've got local craft stalls out on the deck, and fairy lights too.'

That was a neat move, the way he took control there. I wasn't even aware he was with us, let alone guiding us around town. But as he pulls open the huge glass door of the gallery a few minutes later and we move into a lofty space with white painted walls washed with soft light, I'm actually pleased he did.

As we wheel in the pushchairs and the warmth hits us Fliss takes down her hood and nudges me. 'Willow and her kids are here already. By the looks of the pile at the till they're shopping for England.'

I'm puzzling. 'How does that fit with them being super-non-materialistic and not buying things?'

My aside was meant for Fliss, but Tiff's straight in answering it. 'They do shop, but they're very picky so they don't end up with shedloads of crap.'

'That sounds like the kind of shopping mission statement I could do with myself.'

Tarkie's appeared from somewhere too. 'Our family likes buying crap.'

Tansy rubs her nose. 'So long as it's crap that's kind to animals.'

As Willow turns and sees us she leans and says something to the assistant, then hurries across towards us.

'Ivy, what perfect timing! I've got something to give you.' She's holding out her fist.

I'm kicking myself even more now for not claiming the sparkly sweatshirts as mine. But at least we're in the right place for me to buy them all extra gifts. I make my voice bright. 'Lovely, but aren't we waiting for Christmas?'

Maybe this is a special non-materialist new-age custom to spread the pressies out and lessen the negative impact on the soul due to over indulgence on Christmas Day. But while I can see where they're coming from, I won't ever agree – I'm in retail, overt and spectacular consumption is what keeps me in a job, I rely on people putting worries about principles and credit card bills to one side and going for one glorious gift blitz.

Willow swallows. 'That's a nice festive thought, but this can't wait.'

'It's *that urgent*?' What can be so important?

She's smiling at me. 'The state of your chakras, we need to get to work straight away and this is going to help.'

Oh my. If that's a rabbit's foot she's clutching, when I see it I might just be sick. Although Queen Elizabeth the first used to wear red on her lips to ward off evil spirits. If Willow's homed in on bright lippy, so long as the tone's not too purple, I can possibly work with that.

To be on the safe side I shrink back, hoping I'm not putting Harriet in danger by using her pushchair as a shield. 'So what is it?'

'No need to look so horrified.' Willow's eyes are dancing. 'There's some lovely sea glass over there, the moment I saw this necklace I knew, the blues are exactly what you need, they'll be very healing for you.' It could have been worse. She didn't foresee anything. She isn't claiming it spoke to her.

'Right.' It comes out as a whisper, because I can't remember when a gift was more stressy. Everyone's looking on, rapt. It isn't like I got much practice opening George's, because he bought them so rarely. When he did they were mostly alcohol, and he always forgot I hate whisky then drank it himself.

Willow's eyes are shining. 'I had a feeling I was going to find something beautiful in here, as we came through the door it was literally calling out to me across the room.'

'Oh my.' My stomach withers as I hear that double whammy. She's sounding more excited than I am, which just goes to prove, the pleasure is in the giving. But if her muesli is called Morning Zen, I'm bracing myself for something truly awful here.

'Ivy, just open your eyes and look.'

I didn't even know they were closed. As I force myself to prise my eyelids up I see a fine silver strand of chain. And cupped in her palm, some bright silver stars and chunks of sea glass in the deepest blue, and soft turquoise green. I let out a gasp. 'But it's beautiful.'

Willow's nodding. 'I know, that's why you have to have it. Put it on, the blues will sit on your throat, I promise you'll feel better when they do.'

I unwind my scarf, let her put it around my neck, and turn so she can do up the clasp for me. 'Thank you, Willow.' I drop a kiss on her cheek then hold the stones where they fall just below the hollow of my neck.

Bill's still there, talking to Willow. 'Very fitting, Ivy's second name is Stella, which means star, and her surname is Starforth. She's a very starry woman, you know.'

I turn to him. 'It does, but how do *you* know that?'

He's looking at me like he doesn't know why I'm asking. 'You must have mentioned it in Chamonix.'

'Of course, I tell people all the time, don't I?' I'm staring at Fliss to back me up here and turn this horribly significant claim of his into nothing. And when she doesn't I have to poke her.

'Yeah ... of course ... like every day ... at least twice ...' She's frowning at me. 'Did you ever tell me that?' Then she grins. 'Of course you did, I just lost it when they did the two memory wipes in the labour ward.'

Tiff's bobbing down next to Harriet. 'Tiffany means I'm god, but in the form of a girl.'

I grin at her. 'That's fitting too then.'

Willow's nodding. 'There you go, it's working already. Wearing those blue stones will make it a lot easier for you to express what you're truly feeling.'

Tansy joins in. 'And Tansy means immortal and it's also a yellow flower.'

Tarkie pulls a face. 'A yellow flower that stinks, or a vampire, that's stinky too.'

Tiff rolls her eyes. 'Don't listen, he's always like this when he's had too many hot dogs.'

I'm staring at Willow as the enormity of what she's telling me sinks in. 'And saying what I feel is a good thing?' Even if it was almost true and said in a jokey way, that was a pretty cutting comment I made to Tiff there. From where I'm standing, *right next to Bill* this could turn into a nightmare scenario. I take a step away before I blurt. I mean, really, who here will be better off knowing I'm aching to climb inside his coat with him? Some things need to stay private. Stuff expressing myself, some things need not to be thought in the first place.

Willow's still smiling except now her smile's turned super-serene. 'I'm picking up that you've been repressing yourself for a long time – once you're being true to yourself again, you're going to feel amazing.'

'No, I need to take this off, like straight away.' I'm fumbling inside my collar, desperately trying to find the clasp when Willow's hand lands on my elbow.

'Ivy, it's fine, keep it on.' She's looking at me sideways. 'I know you want to ...'

'It's too scary.' It's coming out as squeaky as a mouse, but it's also the truth. And what I can't get over is how Willow looks like she's about to break, and yet she's so robust. Libby has energy and she's bursting with success and power, but Willow's force is so much deeper and quieter and somehow stronger. More like titanium. Solid, but light at the same time. And even through the thickness of my coat sleeve I can feel the warmth from her fingers. And it's as if some of that strength is passing through to me. Because she's right. 'Actually I don't want to take off my lovely sea glass and stars. Why would I?'

She's nodding. 'That's better, Ivy-leaf.'

I'm nodding back at her. 'And now I need to do some shopping myself.' Which as a statement is totally innocuous. So maybe I don't need to worry after all. Obviously it was all bullshit, I was panicking totally unnecessarily. As if a bit of glass round my neck would do anything. I wiggle my eyebrows at her. 'These people who go buying me gorgeous stuff when I haven't got them anything ...'

Oh fuck.

This can only go one way from here ... downhill faster than a bobsleigh run.

24.

Antlers, angel wings, snowberries and pretty things

Plum's Deck Gallery turns out to have that elusive 'something' every retail outlet aspires to. As soon as I head off to look around I'm overtaken by a compulsion to buy every item in the place, and the others are the same. There are some really cute shopping baskets that look like lobster pots to put things in before you pay, and we fill them to overflowing and then some. The gallery owner, Plum, is there at the till, her dark curls caught up into a ponytail, her paint spattered overalls a lot like her pictures of the sea. She must have a really good eye, because I'm picking up everything from lovely little hand painted signs that say quirky things like *cactus*, to amazing silk scarves that are just so perfect for Miranda I have to get two, and that's before we get to the jewellery and the sea glass and the cute toys.

Once our shopping frenzy – for once that's *not* me exaggerating – is over we all head out for drinks on the deck. Toasting our toes under a pergola covered in pink, blue and orange fairy lights, warmed by the glow of log braziers, sipping from huge mugs of hot chocolate topped with lashings of squirty cream, listening to the distant rush of the waves on the beach far below. Even with the minor hiccup of Tarkie and Tansy almost fighting to the death over the last iced friendship biscuit they were both too full to eat, and Oscar's meltdown when he dropped his toffee apple off the edge of the deck, as evenings go, they don't come much better. By the time we're winding our way back down to the cars again Harriet's fast asleep, and Oscar's nodding too.

Fliss unlocks the car, and starts to load Oscar into the back, and I'm at the other door with Bill looking on, happily showing off how my child skills have improved these last few days. I get Harriet all the way into her car seat, still asleep, before I hit a hitch and step back from the car.

'Okay, you'll have to take it from here, Fliss.'

Bill leans in front of me, pulls on the straps and fiddles with the clip. 'Fine, she's all done and ready to go.' A second later he's out of the car again unhooking the bags from the pushchair. One nudge of his knee, that's folded to nothing, and he sweeps it into the boot.

I'm standing on the car park gravel, blinking at him. 'How the hell did you do that?' Quite apart from the car seat, believe me, I know. Unless you're a fully paid up member of the 'wrecked and desperate parent' brigade, or you've got your Norland Nannies certificate, these pushchairs are damn near impossible to collapse, because that's how they're designed. I've been there, done that, got the hopeless auntie badges to prove it. I've tried, sometimes for ages, and Fliss has always had to come and take over in the end.

Bill gives a shrug. 'It's a man thing, Ivy, anything with moving parts, the instructions are pre-programmed into our DNA.'

'Really.' I'm pleased Merwyn is here because it's great to have someone to exchange WTF? eye rolls with. I'm also quite pleased to say in the battle between me and my sea glass, I managed not to share how much like total Bill bollocks that sounded, although truly, *someone* needs to tell him when he sounds so up himself.

'Anyway ...' He swings the second pushchair into the boot and closes the lid in one fluid movement. '... who's for walking back along the beach?'

Seeing as Libby and her kids are already back in their car, and Fliss is dangling her car keys about to drive her children home, this is what Tarkie would call 'a well stupid' question. But I keep that to myself too. 'The water's splashing onto the promenade, there's hardly any beach left to walk on – somehow I don't think so.'

It's the perfect excuse. There's no way I want to walk back on my own with Bill. Why? Well, knowing what's there and that I'll never have it, for one. It's a lot like pressing your nose up against the window and drooling over the strawberry tarts when the cake shop's closed. On balance, you save yourself a lot of pain if you walk by on the other side of the road and don't look in the first place. And that's before we get to the whole thing about my out of control self expression. Until I'm sure how that's going, it's too dangerous to take the risk. I know my moments of Will-lust were a complete misplaced fantasy from years ago, but blurting anything about it would be catastrophic. If it accidentally came out, that would be

Libby's Insta Christmas up the spout. She'd be on her own, I'd have to leave for London straight away.

The sound that Bill lets out sounds very close to a laugh. 'That was four hours ago, Ivy, that's the thing with the tide, it goes in and out. The sea's miles away now.'

It's a good job I can think on my feet. 'In any case, I really need to go in the car with Fliss.'

Fliss is looking at me strangely. 'We love you very much Aunty Ivy, but we drove all the way from London, I think we can manage half a mile back to the castle.' Whose side is she on here? 'How many times in your life have you had the chance of a moonlight walk along a beach?'

She's got a point. Thinking back to Ibiza with George it was more about crawling back to the hotel at dawn. And then I remember. 'Merwyn and I have had moonlight walks together most evenings since we arrived. And the moon was bigger then too.' Merwyn's sitting up very straight, holding up his paw, and he lets out the tiniest whine when he hears the 'w' word.

Bill's rubbing his hands. 'In that case, what are we waiting for, if you're taking him out later, we might as well all walk back now.' He hesitates for a second. Then he does the unthinkable, and talks to the dog. 'What do you say, Merwyn?'

Merwyn looks from Bill to me, and back again. Then *he* does the unthinkable too, and barks in reply.

Fliss laughs, climbs into the driver's seat. 'I think you got your answer there, we'll see you back at the castle in fifteen.'

'Fuck.' This time the sea glass came off best.

'This way to the beach.' The way Bill's got his arm out,

guiding me down the steps and out onto the sand, I'm half way into his coat already. 'Is everything okay?'

It's not, actually, it couldn't be more crap. I avoid being on my own with Bill in the light for more than a few seconds. Being alone with him in the dark, all the way back to the castle, there's so much potential for me to mess up it's about as comfortable as walking into a minefield blindfold. 'I've got a ton of shopping in my backpack. Apart from that, we're all good, couldn't be better thanks.' And 'yay' to that lie. I bend down and let Merwyn off the lead, and he dashes off along the sand chasing shadows in the half light.

Considering the length of his legs, Bill's walking super-slowly. I'm doing bursts of breathless running as my feet sink into the soft sand, then turning to wait for him. Which is fine, apart from having to watch him come towards me. Put it this way. Somehow the moon shadows on his face make him even more edible than usual. Which is a thought that makes me feel a lot more like Miranda than myself.

'I can carry your bag if you'd like? I saw you loading up with a heap of mini Svens back there.'

'It was all very moreish, it's lucky I got out before I bought a ten foot high sea scape.' My backpack is totally rammed, but I'm puzzled. 'How do you know about Sven?'

'Doesn't everyone know about Sven?'

'Seeing he's a cartoon reindeer, probably only if they've seen *Frozen*.'

He gives a shrug and pulls a face. 'I may have watched it once or twice.'

Okay, I'll admit. I'm picking my jaw up off the floor here

because he just doesn't seem the type. 'Somehow that's *so* unexpected it makes you seem way more endearing and less bad tempered, after all.' *Sea glass alert!*

'I can work with endearing.' He gives a sniff. 'So how come you bought *all* the Svens, I thought reindeer made you jumpy?'

Shit. The lurch of my stomach is so huge I almost bring my hot chocolate back up. I do a couple of big leaps across the sand to cover my confusion and swallow hard. 'This is me working through that. I love Christmas, Santa's sleigh is a huge part, it simply isn't practical to live my life wanting to chuck up every time I see antlers.'

'Having that particular aversion must be awful, especially for you.' His voice goes lower and full of concern. 'So can I ask what brought this on?'

I let out a long sigh because he's already touched on this. 'The crash where I cut up my face happened last December – I was on my way home from a party wearing a reindeer outfit, that's all.' I'm shaking my head. 'Looking on the bright side, when they cut off my clothes in A&E I'd have minded much more if they'd had to cut off my favourite French Connection jeans.' I have to tell him though. 'I sound like I'm making light of it, but that's only because it was all so awful I really can't talk about it.'

That night was probably the lowest point in my life, for so many reasons. If ever I let myself think about it, first I want to die of shame. Then I desperately want to turn back the clock so I can make better decisions. The only way I've found to cope with the guilt and carry on is by never thinking about it deeply at all.

He lets out a low whistle. 'Well, if you've come as far as buying a heap of hand sized furry reindeer, that's progress. And you've taken off your hat inside and everyone's seen what you're hiding under your new hairstyle, so you're moving forward with that too.'

I let out another sigh. 'The counsellors tell you as soon as you learn to love yourself again you'll be free to move on. But I'm so far away from that. It's not just my face, I still have so many other regrets. But it's so much easier to bury my head than deal with them.'

He's reaching out towards me, and before I know it he's caught my hand. 'You've had an awful time, but I promise, you will come through it.' He's squeezing my fingers, and tilting his head upwards. 'Look at the sky ...'

Between the clouds the patches of velvety blackness are literally spattered with thousands of pin pricks of brightness. 'All those stars, the more I look, the more I can see. They're so much brighter than back home.'

He nods. 'You don't get the light pollution here that you get in the city. That's one of the payoffs. What we lack in phone signal we more than make up for with views of the Milky Way.'

I laugh. 'I'll tell that to Tom.'

He's sounding so thoughtful. 'You know the stars are there all the time, but you only get to see them at night.'

I stoop to pick up a clam shell shining white in the moonlight, and rub it between my fingers. 'The first few weeks after the accident I hated the dark. If I turned off the light all I could see was the endless blackness that came after the impact.

I kept reliving how the radio was still playing but no one was coming to help. How Michael who was driving was slumped over the steering wheel and wouldn't answer me. Then the flash of blue lights in the night when the police finally turned up, the noise of the grinders as the firemen cut up the car, the taste of blood in my mouth. I still hate all those flashbacks.'

'You really don't have to talk about it ... not if you don't want to.'

Somehow now I've started it's less hard than I thought. I can't actually stop. 'Gradually, me hating the dark changed and I actually like it now. When it's dark and no one can see my scar, that's when I feel most like myself.'

'You really don't have to hide it.' Bill sighs. 'Dark places aren't always bad, sometimes they feel safe. I used to love hiding in the cupboard under the stairs as a kid. We're both having dark times now, but as Keef would tell us, they won't last forever.'

'So what about *your* dark places, how are they going?' I don't know where that came from, it's not even me speaking my mind.

He clears his throat. 'Well, it's no secret, Gemma was the one who left.'

'Oh my. I'm so sorry.' No one likes to get dumped. But all I can think is that if he'd been mine after Chamonix, how tightly I'd have held onto him and how very much I'd have loved and cared for him. That I wouldn't have been careless enough to let him go. How when I see the lines of anguish in his face because of everything he's lost, my heart is breaking for him.

As a cloud rolls back and the moonlight falls on his face, his smile is rueful. 'I just hadn't counted on how awful the break up fights would be.' His laugh is bitter. 'She took the London house, I kept the castle and the distillery because they belonged to Dad and I anyway.'

My eyes are opening wide. 'So you're definitely not just the caretaker or a leaseholder?'

He lets out a snort. 'A lot of the time with the size of the bills and the maintenance issues, I wish I *was* just the caretaker. You buy these places thinking you're getting a bargain, not knowing how they'll run through your capital. But we'll get there. As you said once before, giving up isn't an option.'

I'm trying to say something to make it seem less bleak. 'The fighting can't go on forever. Once you start to leave the bad bits behind things will feel better.'

He's shaking his head. 'I'm a very long way from that, further than you can ever imagine.' He swallows and looks up.

Except I'm not looking up at all. Instead I'm looking down. Taking in his fingers entwined in mine, feeling the heat from his palm. Listening to his breathing in the dark. The desolation in his voice is making my heart break for him.

'Would a hug help?'

The words hang in the air, then get whooshed off out to sea, before it hits – they came from me. *What? Why THE HELL did I say that?* And of course a hug wouldn't bloody help! The guy's in pieces because his super-hot girlfriend walked out, the last thing he needs right now is to be grabbed by some random do-gooder with a ripped up face. What *was*

I thinking? Well, we all know, I wasn't. It's my sodding necklace talking, it's got nothing to do with me. As I yank my hand out of his and leap sideways I'm gabbling. 'No, you're right, that's the worst idea ever ... I'm the woman who launched herself into a hot tub ... and threw herself into a muck barrow, remember ... you'll have to excuse me ... I stuff up big style ... all the time ... this is just the latest in my long line of *mahoosive* blunders and mistakes ...'

Bill's shaking his head again. 'As you're already so far up the beach you're practically in the castle gardens, I take it you're withdrawing the offer?' He's biting his lip. 'Believe me though, you deserve to be hugged by someone a lot better than I am.'

'P-e-r-lease ...' I'm humming, putting my hands over my ears, sounding like Tiff '... let's just move on ...' Preferably to a suitable hiding place in the bushes where I can lie low until Christmas is entirely over. I need to scrape together a better apology. 'I'm sorry, forget I ever mentioned it – you just sounded so very sad, that's all.'

There's another rueful twist of his lips. 'You have to roll with the bad times. I told you before, Ivy-star, you need the darkness to see the stars. It's not all bad, there are good things in there too.'

As we draw level with the castle, the crenellated edges of the turrets are sharp against the smudges of the sky, the lights in the windows are yellow against the dusky walls, and it all looks so sturdy and strong and safe.

'The castle's a lot like the stars somehow. It's always beautiful, but it's even better at night.'

'Says the star girl who's so mercurial she takes back her hugs before she gives them.' Even in the dark I can still catch the teasing glint in his eye. 'Does this mean you'll be returning all your shopping tomorrow too?'

If this is what sea glass does, I'm glad I only got a couple of chips not a whole neckful. But as I go into the castle, instead of being met by a blast of hot air, I'm still shivering with the cold. And I can't help thinking how much I could have done with the warmth of that hug.

Saturday

21st December

25.

On a cold and frosty morning

'Okay, Ivy, your cheeks are super-rosy, Bill wasn't in his room earlier, add in last night's moonlight stroll – is there something you'd like to share?'

When Fliss launches at me the second I walk into the kitchen from the beach with Merwyn next morning, all I can say is I'm glad Tiff and Tansy aren't here.

'Sadly not.' Oops, spot the deliberate mistake. 'Obviously, what I really mean is – happily not.' Glad we've got that one cleared up. I'm wiggling my eyebrows and winking at her phone. 'I take it this means you've already been in Bill's and made the Facetime call.'

'I did, and now Libby's in there.'

'And how did it go?'

Her messy up do has turned into more of a gluey haystack, and she's fiddling with it as she leans over to check on Oscar who's lying on the floor banging some large metal tool on the table leg. She finally pulls a piece of jigsaw out of her hair, misses the much bigger lump of what looks suspiciously like melted Swiss cheese from last night, passes a piece of something floppy, beige and sticky onto Harriet's high chair tray and wipes her hands down the front of her penguin onesie.

'Total bastard shite.' She's mouthing the words at me silently over Harriet's head.

I roll my eyes. '*That* well ...?'

Tarkie pops his head up from under the table. 'Aunty Fliss is doing *gros mots!*'

'What was that he said?' I'm squinting at Fliss.

Tarkie pops up again. 'It means *big words*, it's French for swearing.'

'Jeez.' I'm rolling my eyes at Fliss. 'Tri-lingual kids, whatever next?

Fliss blows out her cheeks. 'Merwyn talking Tibetan?'

I go back to the important stuff. 'You girls have got your cutest penguin gear on too.'

Fliss pulls at Harriet's babygro. 'Aren't these padded side fins so adorable they make you want to melt? And Oscar's in his lion suit with the cutest tufty tail end and mane, with whiskers drawn on his face.' Right on cue there's a roar from under the table then a whole lot more banging. 'And I put my hood up and got my beak in completely the right place too. At six forty-five with two kids in tow, that's a big ask.'

'So what exactly happened?'

'He was in bed when he picked up his phone.'

My stomach drops. 'You did recognise the pillowcases?' For once it's useful she's still hanging onto her distinctive blue colourway Ikea Cath Kidston cabbage rose rip offs.

'Oh yes.' It's a relief when she nods. 'Then he said, "Shit, is that the time, thank Christmas you woke me, jeez, I've got to go to work." And straight after that he hung up.'

There's a voice from under the table. '*Gros mots*. Again. Final warning.'

That's not much to go on. 'So, how did he look?'

Fliss pulls a face. 'Dishevelled ...'

I'm agonising because she could be describing herself there. 'Rumpled like his wife's been away for a week and he's had to fold his own polo shirts, or ... bed hair like he's been ...' I send her a grimace. '... Jiggin with Jordan.'

'Jiggin with *what*?'

'It's this guy from Florida who fishes and dives and has a YouTube channel with a gazillion followers. George used to watch him in that phase he had when he wanted to be Bear Grylls. Obviously it's a metaphor ... to dodge our *gendarme* under the table.'

Tarkie pipes up. 'What's a *gendarme*?'

Fliss wrinkles her nose and ignores him. 'It's more a substitution than a metaphor. Even if Rob was alone he had to be dashing off for a quickie at the office didn't he? Outside of retail, that's the only reason people ever go into work on a Saturday.'

I suppress a shiver and decide some questions are best without an answer. 'Is anyone else cold?'

Fliss pulls a face. 'The temperature has dropped but it's hard to tell, I've got my dressing gown on under here, I was hoping the padding would give me the wow factor for Rob.'

'Are you sure you're channelling the right look there?' Maybe she and Rob *have* lost their mojo. It's not that long ago, if Rob went away on a site visit she'd Facetime him naked.

She sends me a wink. 'Don't doubt me, I know my audience, Rob loves my Mama Pingu persona – or at least he used to.' She stops short and her wistful sigh turns to a moan. 'Oh shit, what if I'm going to be the first one in the family to get divorced? Libby's so much better than me with her perfect husband and having her kids, and sorting her business. Rob loving me was the one thing I was doing right, I've stuffed up the only thing I had to be proud of.'

At the far end of the kitchen Milo bangs the oven door closed and pops up into view behind the island unit. 'If anyone's wondering, it's boiling over here, but I *am* slaving over a hot Aga.' He brushes back his fringe, and smooths down Bill's apron. 'But it's fab being in the kitchen unimpeded for once.' We all know that's a jibe at Bill.

'Stay nice, Milo, bitching doesn't suit you.'

He gives me a look. 'There's a stack of banana pancakes with maple syrup and whipped cream here, and a pot of coffee whenever you're ready, Ivy-leaf.'

I'm sucking back my drool, making up for being a bit sharp back there by not telling him off for the leaf bit. 'Cool, that's lovely. I'll just grab extra sweaters from upstairs for Merwyn and me, and I'll be with you.'

Fliss's eyes have lit up. 'This onesie is very forgiving, Harriet and I would love more pancakes while you're there please.'

My timing's good. I've just made it back to Fliss at the table with a tray loaded with pancakes when Tom, Tiff and Tansy come in, strangely mute, all wearing headphones, their wires all leading back to the pocket of Tom's jeans. As for the weather, we must be having one of those Arctic blasts from Siberia. The bedroom was so much like a fridge after the warmth of the kitchen that I added my thermal vest as well as my red and pink stripey jumper with mini Christmas trees on it. And Merwyn was super-grateful when I popped his red and white fair isle jumper on him too.

When Willow and her three come in a few minutes later, I stuff my mouth with banana and cream, and brace myself. To be honest, if yesterday's blurting is anything to go by, I'd rather sidestep her suggestions and keep my chakras blocked and my aura up the spout. But luckily I'm spared, because they're deep in conversation in Spanish.

As they come to a natural pause in their gluten free pancakes and in-depth discussion, Fliss leans across to Willow. 'It's colder today, have you noticed?'

Willow's forehead furrows as she considers. 'We make our own inner energy through meditation, and have a fully insulated timber house with passive solar heating, we don't tend to tune in to outside temperature changes.'

'Right.' Fliss and I are looking at each other pulling WTF? faces, then she leans across to me with her eyes shining. 'You do realise, this could mean snow. Can you believe, Oscar hasn't ever seen it.'

A second later there's a shimmer and the unmistakable crackle of expansive gold puffa and Miranda sweeps into the room. '*STUFF SNOW!!! I'LL HAVE YOU KNOW THERE'S ICE CHIPS COMING OUT OF OUR SHOWER!*' She's renowned for enjoying a dramatic entrance. With her arms sticking out and her coat flying behind her like a celestial cape she's certainly pulled one off here.

Fliss wrinkles her nose. 'Morning, Mum, lovely to see you too, but aren't you exaggerating a teensy bit there?'

Miranda's nose goes up in the air. 'Put it this way – you certainly won't be complaining about ghostly banging today because it was too damned chilly for the ghost to show up ...'

Fliss is putting her hands over her ears and shouting, 'Okay, stop ... too much information!!!'

'I had to bring Ambie round with a stiff gin and put him in the hot tub to thaw out. And what does a woman have to do to get a cup of tea round here?'

As Miranda crackles off towards the Aga, I lean so I can see out of the French window, and sure enough, Ambie's submerged all the way up to his Santa hat and waving a pint tumbler at me.

Milo might be making fresh pots of coffee for me, and pouring tea for Fliss, but he's not doing the same for her mum. Instead he arrives at the table with a plate piled with pancakes for the kids, but as he turns to me his mouth is pinched rather than smiley. 'So *very* strident. And *so very* unsuitable for Dad.'

Someone's got to stand up for Miranda, so I nod at Milo's dad outside. 'She stops him being so stuffy, and anyway, I don't see Ambie complaining.'

Miranda's storming back towards us, her pink leopard dressing gown flying out from under her coat, her fluffy stiletto mules clacking on the floorboards although I think she's also wearing Ambie's woolly Argyle socks with them. 'And where's Bill anyway? Always AWOL when we need him.'

Right on cue Bill and Keef appear in the doorway. 'Did someone call us?'

Miranda's got one hand on her hip, and she's waving her tea mug in the other. 'What kind of an establishment are you running here, William? The water's stone cold, the radiators too!'

If my stomach's disappeared slightly, I'm blaming it on the fourth pancake and too much maple syrup, not on the dark circles under Bill's eyes, and the shadows in the hollows of his cheeks. What is it about guys, the more wrecked they look, the more they make your tummy flip?

The way he jerks to a halt and opens his eyes wider, this isn't what he's expecting. 'Ok-a-a-ay – I was out early, I've just come back in, are you *sure* about this?'

Miranda's eyes are flashing. 'What, are you calling me a liar now? I might be over fifty and have been through more husbands than you've had hot dinners ...' note how she neatly subtracted a decade from her age there, she's such a pro '... but I can tell when the bloody heating's broken – I'm freezing my bloody tits off here, Bill.'

The way Bill's blinking he's struggling with the image as much as the rest of us. 'Great ... we might have lost the pilot light on the boiler. It does blow out occasionally if there's a flukey wind.'

Miranda's snapping back. 'And how often is that? It's so unprofessional, what the hell happened to client satisfaction and the customer always being right? You should really get that fixed.'

Tarkie's piping up from under the table. 'Granny Miranda said a *gros mot*, Granny Miranda said a *gros mot*.'

'Shhhh ...' One touch on his head from Willow's super-heated hand and he melts away.

'Give us a moment, we'll see what we can do.'

As he follows Bill out Keef's eyes are popping too, but he pauses in the doorway. 'Y'all, remember, we smile for life, not just the photos.' He's still there, frantically flicking through his brain files to find a better one. 'Stop thinking about what can go wrong, and start getting excited about what can go right!' Then he nods and a grin spreads across his face as he tosses back his braids. 'There are people who would love to have your bad days, Miranda.'

Miranda's running her fingers through her coppery blonde curls as she takes that lot in. Then she twitches her nose, dips into her pocket and pulls out her tobacco. 'So much of Bill bollocks, I need a cigarette.'

If she'd pulled out a hand grenade Willow couldn't have leaped up any faster. 'Absolutely not, Sailor, Scout and Solomon have lived a totally carbon free life so far, you're not tarring their lungs up now.'

Fliss sends Willow a bemused stare. 'How did you manage that when you live so close to the Holloway Road? I heard that's like a pollution superhighway.'

Willow's eyes are flashing. 'We have an air tight home with heat exchangers and filters.'

Fliss is still puzzling. 'So where do scented candles fit into that? I mean, they have flames and smoke don't they?'

Miranda's rolling her eyes as she heads for the French windows. 'Fine, I'll be outside, don't worry, Willow, I'll blow every last carbon particle out to sea.'

Willow's shaking her head. 'So much negativity …'

I'm not up for any more of Willow's wacky interventions, I'd rather smooth this over myself. 'I could bring the juniper sprig off my door down if that would help?'

Willow's eyes are closed, her nostrils are flared and she's holding her outstretched fingers in front of her face. 'Give me a few moments, I'll realign.'

All I can say is, anyone who can rebalance anything with Oscar hammering the hell out of the floorboards and the scrap that erupts between Tiff, Tom and Tansy over their rock-paper-scissors game is a stronger woman than me.

When Willow opens her eyes again she's just in time for a mad rush into the kitchen. Keef and Bill come shuffling back through, Miranda blows in with a wind gust from the French windows that's so huge it sets the gingerbread men on the tree spinning. Then Libby comes in, her hands deep in the pockets of her pristine cream ski jacket.

'Is anyone else feeling cold?'

Tom's detached from his headphones during the last scuffle with Tansy and he pulls a face. 'Keep up, Mother, the boiler's gone out. Everyone's freezing their arses off in here.'

'Tom …' Libby sounds a warning note then blinks at him. 'So why are you sitting there in your T-shirt? For goodness sake put your coat, hoodie and hat back on.'

Miranda drags in a breath, pulls herself up to her full five feet nothing and turns a searing gaze onto Bill. 'But the heating is on again now, you *are* here to tell us you've sorted it?'

'Errr …' The length of the pause, we all know what's coming.

Especially me, because at the last moment Bill catches my eye and gives the smallest shake of his head.

Keef jumps in. 'It's fine, we'll call the engineer, they'll have it mended in no time.'

Miranda's eyes are wide in horror. 'But if it needs mending, that means it's *BROKEN?!*'

Bill blows out his cheeks and when he speaks his voice is extra low. 'That's correct. And you have our word on this, we'll do our best to get it fixed as quickly as we can.'

He sounds so down and defeated, it takes every bit of my will power to stop myself from racing across the kitchen and throwing my arms round him. Which is a *totally* stupid reaction that would be completely counter productive and probably cause complete chaos due to the kids erupting and Bill being mortified. It would be way more helpful to do something practical like phone the engineer and tell him to get his butt round here ASAP. Offer a mahoosive bribe or two. Some gin. A free stag party. A Range Rover or something like that. Ambie's so loaded I'm sure he's got them coming out of his ears.

And I suppose we're all silently asking ourselves the same question – when a boiler crashes this close to Christmas, what are the chances of getting it repaired before the New Year? Even with the heat from the Aga the warmth is seeping away from the kitchen. If the heating stops belting out, every other room in the castle will be completely inhospitable within a few hours, if it isn't already.

Libby narrows her eyes and as she pats down her hair and turns to Bill her voice is calm and measured, but very steely. 'So, what do you suggest we do next?'

I just know. When she moves this on, it'll be to insist he finds us suitable alternative accommodation. And I also know Bill's got no money, that we are his last-ditch attempt to stay afloat. If he has to fund a hotel for twenty people over Christmas, it'll ruin him.

I'm leaning back in my chair, I know they're all looking at me, but for once I don't care. In fact, that's exactly what I want them to do. I take a deep breath, make myself sound super-upbeat, and fire.

'Hey, this is Cockle Shell Castle, we're #TeamChristmas!' Jeez knows where that came from, but I simply know I have to head Libby off and fast. 'What *I* suggest is while you take everyone out for the morning, Libby, we'll get the fires roaring in the family rooms. And when it's warm and toasty you can all come back, and everyone can hunker down. We'll put on our Christmas onesies, roast chestnuts, snuggle under our duvets, eat lashings of delicious home made pizza by the fire and have a mahoosive, record breaking Christmas film-athon.'

If my mouth's still hanging open, it's because I'm staggered at what came out there; I haven't winged it like that for so long, and there were details and everything. I mean, onesies ... records ... chestnuts? How did I think of throwing them in? I didn't mean to do this, I seriously doubt I would have done if Libby hadn't had Bill's back rammed hard up against the wall. I used to be gutsy, always diving in with my ideas at meetings, being inspiring, geeing up our work team. But this last year I've buried myself as far under the table as I could and said nothing. There's a part of me punching the air in my head because it feels so good to have come out of hiding and be doing it again.

'Pizza ...?' It's Willow. 'I take it that will be gluten free?'

Abso – bloody – lutely. 'Of course.'

Fliss is beaming. 'Watching *The Holiday* in the glow from the fire? That's it, I'm in.'

Tiff's eyes are shining. 'Will it last all night, like a giant castle sleepover?'

I'm nodding madly. 'Why not?'

Tansy's jumped up. 'And go all the way into tomorrow?'

I laugh. 'So long as there's a woman standing ... it won't have ended.' I have no idea where the hell we're going to get all the films from when we can't stream them, and then I have a brainwave. 'Everybody bring your favourite DVDs, we'll vote on what to watch.'

Twenty-four hours, we might have to have some repeats. But so long as it gets Libby off Bill's back, we'll make up the rest as we go along. And in the meantime we'll cross everything that we can find an engineer who can get the heating fired up again. Although for now, with this fun afternoon and evening ahead of us, the heating is the last thing anyone's thinking about.

26.

Dashing all the way …

A crisis at Cockle Shell Castle was never going to happen quietly. However much trouble the rest of us have with Cornish communications, Keef and his mates manage fine. Who knows what secret signalling system they use, but as I wave off Fliss, Libby, Willow and the kids not long later, the silver surfies are already rolling in, heading for toast in the kitchen.

Milo was totally determined to join Miranda and Ambie for a morning in the hot tub, but I saved him from himself and sent him off to Falmouth instead to buy chestnut supplies. Between us, we could have sourced them closer, but this way we're spared the sight of him playing gooseberry between Ambie and Miranda in his (newly purchased) swimmers and Santa hat. Someone should tell him, forcing them apart is never going to work. The more he disapproves and tells them not to, the more determined they'll be to stay together.

When I first suggested staying home I assumed I'd be personally throwing on logs and building huge versions of the fires we usually have. But after a second breakfast listening to reminiscences about big wave wipe outs and admiring the pineapple print on Keef's new-to-him surfie joggers, Rip and Brian head off to man the fireplaces. Then while Bede, Taj and Slater ferry massive quantities of wood across from the wood store beyond the coach house, I go into the pantry room to sort out today's first supermarket delivery.

Willow might be appalled by the gender politics, but for once it makes sense. She and Libby have a strict system and even if I mostly avoid cooking I know where they like things put away. Better still, it means that when the engineer arrives and Bill and Keef show him into the boiler room further along the corridor, I'm on hand to listen in. Not that it does me much good. He's there for all of two seconds and three bangs, then he lets out a long whistle, marches off to his van, and drives away again. Then another two loads of shopping arrive and for the next couple of hours I keep warm stacking the fridges.

By the time I'm done, the heap of logs outside by the hot tub is huge. As I wander through to the main part of the castle I can see my breath in the hallway, but when I open the door to the family room I'm met by a wall of warmth and Miranda's shrieks of laughter at some story Keef's telling her.

Lighting the open fires really brought these rooms to life before, but now they're so much bigger the fires are making the heart of the castle beat even more strongly. The firelight's glow brings a warmth to the rooms that's about more than just the heat. And with the rainbow Christmas trees, the fairy lights around the windows and in glass jars on the coffee tables, and Miranda's huge pots of pine branches, it's all so wonderfully sparkly and Christmassy. The leather and velvet chairs by the fireside look so inviting I have to stop myself sitting straight down in them.

'Not in the hot tub, Miranda?' I'm smiling, because laughing helplessly is so much more like the Miranda I know than the tetchy, argumentative one we've seen the last week.

She eases open her scarf, wiggles her eyebrows and waves her tobacco. 'I popped out for a ciggy, bumped into Keef, and one thing led to another.'

Keef's face cracks into a beam. '*She's* been admiring my motor home, and *I've* been extolling the virtues of a wild heart, the freedom of the open road, and being true to yourself.' He breaks off to grin at me. 'You can't do that in two minutes you know.'

'Obviously not.' It's taken these two all morning and then some. 'Any news from the heating man?'

'Who?' It's what everyone else is obsessing about, just not Keef. For a moment he looks bemused then it clicks. 'Oh, that. Nothing concrete, he's coming back tomorrow.'

'Anyway, I'm just going to fill all the jam jars with tea lights ready for later.' I'm holding up a big bag of candles, trying to justify why I'm here even though there's no reason why I should feel like I'm intruding when Keef's only standing around with a box.

There's a rattle of the door handle, then Bill comes striding across to us. 'Great, that's brilliant, candles are just what we need.' He's carrying a box too and he's turning to me. 'You do realise your quick thinking saved me back there, Star-girl.'

'You're welcome, William.' While I try to decide if I mind Star-girl less than Pom Pom I send him a wink across the fireplace where the flames are roaring through a truly enormous fire. 'Who knew everyone would forget about the cold and embrace the filmfest?' I certainly didn't, but I'm pleased they have.

'You totally sold it to them.' He gives a grimace as he slides the wide box down on the coffee table. 'Without you intervening I'd have been toast.'

I suspect he's right, but I'm not going to rub it in. I'm thinking of the last time he came in with the boxes of decorations, how it seems more like a lifetime ago than five days. 'You've been shopping, scouring the charity shops again for DVDs for later?' Except the dull thud the box made as it hits the wood should have told me it isn't right for them.

He shakes his head. 'We've lost the heating, we had to have mistletoe, Libby's already been chasing you on it.' He whips off the lid of the box with a flourish.

'Is that where you've been?' He might have mistletoe, but he's still looking stressed enough to make my heart squish for him.

He's rubbing his hands. 'My mate Rory, from Huntley and Handsome wine merchants and Roaring Waves brewery buys it by the lorry load to give away to his customers with their Christmas deliveries. And since we're his most valued specialist local gin supplier, he was happy to help.'

As I lean in I get the size of the haul. 'Wow! That's a whole lot of Instagram mileage there.' The box is brim full and I can't help smiling as I finger the simple pale green leaves. As

I see the clusters of pretty white berries a thought hits me. 'I'm treading on Miranda's toes making commercial suggestions here, but you really should make Cockle Shell Castle *Christmas* gin. I can already see the labels, a scattering of stars and sprigs of mistletoe ...'

Miranda's eyes are gleaming like topaz, but her naughty glint is back. 'I can see your nudist well-being clients now, Bill, goosepimples on their bums, their heads full of motivational quotes, downing their frankincense gin cocktails on your private beach.'

Bill's shaking his head. 'Thanks, Ivy, your second must-do inspiration for today, I'll definitely work on that ...'

'Anyway, back to the mistletoe.' Before these two come to blows. 'There's enough to deck out an entire castle and then some.'

'That's a whole heap of kisses for someone.' His lips twist as he looks down at Miranda. 'Don't say I never bring you anything, I hope you're going to put it to good use.'

Miranda gives a haughty toss of her head and ignores him entirely.

Keef gives a cough and gives Miranda a hard stare. 'Just be sure you choose the right prince to kiss, Mirry. The wrong one and you'll be throwing your life away.'

Miranda closes her eyes and shakes her head. When she opens them again, she's firing at me. 'I hope you're listening there, Ivy-leaf, whatever I once said about Bill I take it all back. Milo's the catch around here.' She picks up a sprig from the box and as shc passes it to me she's beaming. 'Here, take this, run along and find him. There's no time to lose, not now you're looking so pretty with your lovely new hair on show.'

I'm rolling my eyes at Merwyn, but this time he just looks at me as if he's seen it all before. 'Sorry, Miranda, Milo's gone out.'

Bill's shaking his head and giving me the kind of look I just gave to Merwyn. 'Thank Christmas for that.'

I'm making my smile as bright as I can and frantically moving this on to somewhere less awkward. 'Great, well ... so what's in *your* box Keef?'

He puts it down on the table too, and pulls back the flaps. 'DVDs for our film night.'

'You're coming too?' Jeez knows why I'm surprised.

'It's this or the Gardening Club Christmas Disco. The guys were saying earlier, we've had eighties Christmas discos up to our Santa hats already this December, something new on a Saturday night will shake us up.'

'So all of you, then?' From the way Bill's making throat cutting gestures at me, he's getting totally shown up by his dad here.

Keef's nodding. 'Might as well make the most of the fires, in any case, you'll need us here as stokers.'

On the up side, he *has* brought films. 'We need all the DVDs we can get, so long as they aren't too adult.' They'll have to get past Willow's censorship panel.

Keef looks totally unconcerned. 'These are kiddie ones, I came across them in the coach house earlier.'

As Keef's eyes flash up to Bill's face it crumples. For a

moment he looks distraught, then his expression clears and he goes back to just looking beaten and knackered.

Now Keef's wincing as he turns to Bill. 'That *is* okay? I mean, you don't mind?'

Bill's stammering. 'A-a-absolutely fine ... b-b-brilliant ... why wouldn't it be okay? ... it's a few DVDs ... why ever would I mind?'

I'm peering in, hoping to see where the problem might be. '*Peppa Pig*, ooo, and *The Snowman*, that's a good one for later, *Postman Pat*, *Olaf's Frozen Adventure* ...' As I see the reindeer on the cover I shudder and as I look up at Bill his face is drawn and three shades paler under his stubble.

The whistle he lets out is similar to the one the heating engineer did earlier. 'And despite the reindeer you said that without faltering, Star-girl, that was brilliant.' He's holding his hand up. 'High five for that?'

I lean across and hold up my hand. 'Why not?'

But as soon as my palm collides with his I have my answer. Tingling fingertips and shivers that shoot right up my arm then loop to zip up and down my spine. And not in a good way. That's why not. I write it on my brain so I won't get caught out again. *No more high fives. And stay away from the mistletoe. And the man. End of important health and safety warning.*

There's definitely no shivers on Bill's side, because he's moved right on, his jaw is set square and very rigid and he's nodding at the box. 'If you dig deep enough you should find *Frozen* in there too.'

I'm straight back in, flicking through the cases and sure enough it's there. 'Hey, you're right.'

Miranda taps the pointy toe of her boot and gives a cough. 'If you'll excuse us, we must push on.'

'Fine.' I'm not sure what can be so urgent, although she could be needed in the hot tub.

Keef nods. 'We're bringing extra blankets over from the coach house then pulling in a quick trip back to the motorhome. I promised to show Miranda the wonders of the fold out bed mechanism.'

'Really?' It's my turn to wince and pull a face at Miranda. I'm not judging, just a bit shocked and horrified at the implication.

Miranda sends me a butter wouldn't melt smile as she links arms with Keef and they head for the door again. 'Being free as a bird doesn't happen by itself, Ivy-star, I still have a lot to learn.'

As I'm always telling Milo, she's a grown up, she should be able to make her own decisions. We all have to trust her and let her get on and live her life.

'Don't let us hold up your flying lessons.' Bill's shaking his head at me as they go. 'I'll get the big screen ready and then I'll get the guys to give me a hand rearranging the chairs.'

I grab the Roaring Waves box and whistle Merwyn. 'We'll deal with the mistletoe and bring down the kids' duvets.' Then I have a thought. 'You do know Milo's not completely behind Ambie and Miranda.'

Bill sniffs. 'Milo is a total snake in the grass, I'm pleased you agree.'

Which isn't what I meant at all, but whatever. And I know Miranda hasn't been Bill's easiest guest, but I'm hoping he's big enough to overlook that. 'All I'm saying is, if Miranda and Ambie are happy together, I'd hate Milo to get in the way of that.'

Bill grins at me. 'I can't say too much. But it might put your mind at rest to know I've already been recruited – I'm firmly Team Ambie.' Then his lips twist again. 'And however much I'd like to push Miranda in the sea for winding me up, I'm totally committed to her happy ending.'

I'm so relieved I almost forget myself and give him a fist bump. But I stop myself just in time and pull back my hand. 'Great. You have no idea how pleased I am to hear that.' It doesn't go halfway to expressing my exuberance, but it'll have to do for now. 'So, let's bring on the film fest then.'

Bill's nodding now. 'I owe you big time for all this, Ivy-leaf. And don't forget *Frozen* later.' His lips twist into another even wider smile. 'I'll expect you to be word perfect. It's always best enjoyed with ice cream so best check there's plenty in the freezer.'

If anything was bothering him before with Keef, he's moved on seamlessly. As for his smile, that glimpse of teeth ... my insides turning to hot syrup, really isn't helpful. And of course it isn't a date, so why the hell would my brain be turning it into that? That butterfly storm all the way from my waist to my throat is a total waste of wildlife.

'Just one more thing ...'

What now? I take a breath. 'And?'

'With ice cream ... do you go for *Ben and Jerry's* or *Haagen Dazs?*'

'Does it matter?'

His lips are twisting again. 'It's one of those really important compatibility questions.'

Oh my. 'Haagen Dazs.'

'Because ...?'

I'm being put on the spot, but the answers come straight out because I'm so sure of them I don't even have to think. 'The names are less wacky, and it's more grown up which is not necessarily a good thing, but it's so much creamier and more delish overall. So, that.'

'Right answer. That's because the ingredients are better.' He's grinning now. 'In which case, so long as Milo's nowhere around, I'll leave you to your mistletoe.'

And then he marches out leaving me open mouthed, gazing at the knobbly nails in the door that closed behind him.

27.

Chestnuts roasting on an open fire … with bells on

'Anchovy, mushroom, and brie, and a spicy pepperoni with double cheese coming up.' Bill is giving a running commentary as he pulls the trays of pizza out of the oven later and slides them onto the serving boards on the kitchen work surface.

It's teatime and the film fest is already well underway. We began with *The Snowman*, moved on to *Elf*, and then we left Fliss with a few surfies and the kids in the family room while the rest of us came out to prepare the food. Obviously if she's anywhere within a hundred yards of the action, Libby has to take charge. As she's so mini she can barely see over the island unit, she piled up a couple of Ambie's empty champagne crates and stood on those. Once she'd got an overview of the kitchen she allocated all the jobs in a flash then shouted instructions how to do them as we went along. Willow has been filling huge glass bowls with colourful salads, taking them through to the tables in the family room as she finishes them, I have been rolling out the dough they'd made earlier on the baking sheets, and Milo and Bill have been on toppings – or more to the point they've been fighting over them.

You name it, they've had a stand off about it. Everything from how to de-seed the peppers to whether the tomato sauce should be spread with a spoon or a spatula. They snarled their way through deciding how big to make the brie chunks, Milo was strutting around insisting one bit of the cheese grater was more right than another. I mean, guys, it's cheese, just grate it! Then Bill was getting all superior about how many olives to use and what colour they should be. Please, men, just shut the eff up and throw them on!

Someone needs to tell them, Christmas is the season of goodwill, people are supposed to get on. We're not aiming for Michelin stars here – edible will do. That's the ridiculous part – they both sound like they know what they're doing, but when they lock horns progress stops completely. In the end Libby had to get down from her box and give them a damn good talking to and the same glare she uses for Tarkie when he's cheeking Miranda, and literally draw lines across the worktop and the job list.

Bill's staring at me as he goes in with the pizza wheel to slice the pizza that's come out of the oven. 'How about pineapple? Where do you stand on that?' The man is actually as much a whizz at slicing pizza as he is at getting the toppings on but I have no idea what he's getting at here.

'If you're asking about Keef's joggers, I know the pineapple motifs are pretty huge and hideously bright, but I reckon he's got the panache to carry them off. That's probably why they'd been given away in the first place, someone lost their nerve.'

He's rolling his eyes. 'Ivy-star, we're cooking pizza not trousers – everyone asks these days, and I just wondered, do you take yours with pineapple chunks ... or not?'

Oh that. Why didn't he just say?

'Hell no, I can't stand pineapple – except in cocktails, then I love it – or at least I used to.'

He gives my arm a punch, 'I'm the same, pineapple gets the thumbs down from me on pizzas every time.'

Lucky for me, this time there are two layers of sweater to mop up the tingle where he touches me. 'Which means, in the unlikely event we're ever in the same town again after Christmas, *and* if we happen to be in the same supermarket, *and* we end up hitting the freezer aisles at the same moment, what with liking the same ice cream *and* pizza, we'll probably be looking in the same cabinets.'

He smiles at me. 'Exactly. And when that happens, I promise I'll open the freezer door for you.'

'Thanks, I'll look forward to it.' Except of course it totally won't happen. Not ever. The day after Boxing Day we'll all speed away back to London, and I'll never have to see him again. Which should make me happier than it does. I'd assumed being around him would get easier. You'd think that after ten days the whole good-looks wow-factor tummy-flip thing would have worn off. But if anything it's got worse rather than better. Seriously, the thought of being freed from that and of never seeing him again should be making me jump for joy, so I have no idea why it's giving me a pang in my chest.

As he does the last roll of the pizza cutter he looks across to Milo. 'Okay, where's the pen? I need to make labels for these.'

I give a silent wooohooo, because I can't believe my luck here. All the time hanging round his bedroom and I still haven't seen so much as a scrawled note. And I know I sound a bit obsessive, but I'm still on the look-out for the phantom muffin baker. One glance at Bill's writing and I can rule him out of the search. To be fair, I need all the help I can get with this, I'm running seriously short of suspects.

At the far end of the island unit, Milo gives a snort. 'Nice try, mate. You heard Libby – labels are *my* domain and that's how it's staying.' The taunting way he waggles the pen and pad, he's really enjoying this. 'So you tell me what to write then I'll pass them over to you.'

Damn. So close and yet still so far away. There's no way Milo's backing down on this, so I leave them to it, and turn to Miranda who's coming into the kitchen.

'Hey, you're looking glamourous, are you going to be warm enough?' She's swapped her many layers of jumpers and ladder ripped leggings for a slinky dress and sheer black tights. The strappy high heel boots with studs are the only part of the outfit that looks anything like what she'd normally wear.

'The dress is a present from Ambie, it was meant for Christmas Day, but he asked me to wear it tonight.' She pulls at the fabric. 'It's on the thin side, but I left him on his own a lot today so I didn't want to say no to this.'

I'm smiling to encourage her because she doesn't look completely comfortable in the body skimming, streamlined satin. I've never seen her go for such formalised sequin and beaded embellishment either, she's always been more of a scatter queen. 'It's gorgeous, such a Christmassy colour, and so many sparkles.'

She gives a little shrug and pinches her cheeks. 'Oh dear, red tends to drain me, and it's much more uptight than I'd usually choose, and a lot less forgiving with my bulges. I feel a bit like I'm wearing someone else's clothes not mine.'

I'm still picking up that she needs reassurance. 'You look stunning, and you'll be able to pop a waterfall cardi or two over it later so you feel more like yourself.'

'Thanks, sweetheart.' Her hand lands on my arm. 'Sometimes I feel Ambie wishes I were less quirky and more conventional. He's much more *Marks and Sparks* than *Spanky Dungeon*.'

And I wish my alarm bells weren't clanging so loudly. 'You stay true to yourself, Miranda, I'm sure Ambie will grow to love your bondage biker boots and ironic fairy corset dresses, given time. You could always skip the ripped fishnets.'

She gives a throaty chortle. 'But they're my favourite part.' Then she shrugs away a shudder and starts to smile again. 'It's lovely having you here sticking up for me. And I've been sent to get high chairs for Oscar and Harriet, I'd love a hand with those too.'

'Sure, they're over here, let's take one each, and I'll light the tea lights in the family room at the same time.'

As we make our way across the kitchen Miranda lowers her voice. 'Between us I'd hoped Ambie would help, but he's on the sofa. *Again.*' She pauses to pull a face. 'Once he sits down unless there's a drink on offer, it's as if his bum is superglued to the cushions. If we're talking about people changing, I would not be sorry if he moved once in a while.'

I don't like to notice how rarely he helps. 'Hopefully once he gets to know everyone better he'll get more involved.'

She wrinkles her nose as we get to the high chairs. 'That's the trouble, I'm not sure he will. At my age boyfriends are hard to come by, beggars can't be choosers. He looks after me, he's got a lovely car, and he's here. Asking any more would be unrealistic.' Which is a very sad place to be.

I send her a grin. 'In any case, you've only committed for Christmas. You're free to move on in the New Year if you still haven't bedded in.'

And with that thought we shiver our way out into the chilly hallway and towards the noise from the family room. As we push the high chairs into place next to Fliss's sofa, Willow is coming towards us. Her eyebrows are arched, and she's looking like she breathed in a while ago and forgot to breath out again.

'Everything okay, Willow?'

'Actually, no, it isn't.'

I'd have been more surprised if she'd said yes. Not that this is all about me, but I have to comment. 'You know my auras feel so much better since you gave me the sea glass.'

Her face softens into the smile I was hoping for. 'Aura, Ivy, you only have one, but that's good, I can tell.' She frowns again. 'This is something a lot more global.'

My heart is sinking. 'Oh my ...'

She comes right up to my ear and hisses, 'I just spotted a highly unsuitable DVD on the pile.'

After I warned Keef too. If he's smuggled *Texas Chainsaw Massacre* in I'll personally chop him into little pieces. I hardly dare ask, so take baby steps. 'Are you comfortable to tell me what it is?'

Her mouth comes to my ear. 'It's the one with the pigs.'

'Not *Babe*?' My mind is racing through what else it could be.

She shakes her head. 'It's that pre-school animation, it's so bad I refuse to say the name on principle. It's hugely popular but there are big problems with the gender stereotyping, and the central character *never* wears a seat belt.'

If I remember rightly from watching with Oscar, it's a hand drawn animal, driving a toy car. 'Is that all?' I was sure she'd found something *so* much worse. Surfie porn or something.

Her eyes are flashing. 'It's not a minor issue, Ivy, it's hugely damaging for toddlers to see a father figure lounging around in an armchair reading the paper while the mother does all the domestic chores. We women will never achieve equality in a generation if that's the start in life we give our children.'

'Very true.' Not having children I haven't thought about it before. Maybe this is Ambie's problem – he's been watching too much *Peppa Pig*. I lean towards her. 'Any offending DVDs, bring them to me and I'll put them in Bill's room away from the kids.'

'Lovely.' Her face relaxes again. 'And I'm *so* pleased you got mistletoe, it's a very powerful plant and not only for kissing under.' Her eyes are shining now.

'Really?'

She nods and winks at me. 'It gives you a lot of protection

from werewolves, it's great for fertility, and it stops you having your children swapped for faerie changelings.'

I laugh too and as I go off to light the candles I turn to Fliss sitting on the sofa. 'Did you hear that? Bill bought so much of the stuff it looks like you're going to have to keep Harriet and Oscar after all.'

With so many strong women and opinions this Christmas was never going to be easy. Which is why it's good for me to be on the edge. So long as my tea lights look amazing shining in the dark, sending warm shadows flickering up over the stonework then I'm happy. As I sit down to help Fliss devour the pizza, for a while all I see of Bill are a few grimaces and eye rolls from across the room. When I come back in from the kitchen after clearing away they're well into Wallace and Gromit, and I squeeze down on a sofa between Fliss and Miranda with Merwyn sitting on my feet. To be honest, when it ends we're expecting to move seamlessly into the next Wallace and Gromit film, and then *Home Alone*, but Tiff and Tansy are practising handstands on a duvet. And then Ambie gets up – who said he couldn't move? – and Milo goes out too, and then suddenly Bill's in front of the fire, clapping his hands. He carefully arranges a cushion on the floor and gives a little cough.

'If I could just have everyone's attention there's a slight update to this evening's programme ...'

It takes a while for the acrobats to stop, and for Tom and Tarkie to emerge from their tower room, but we get there in the end. And then the lights dim slightly and some familiar music begins. It's one of those times I know I won't be able to place it until the words begin but before they can Ambie appears, holding a mic in his hand.

Miranda shouts to Bill, 'If you'd told us we were doing *Britain's got Talent*, I'd have brought my belly dancing outfit.' She wiggles her eyebrows at him. 'That's another thing you should think of, Bill, castle erotic dancing weekends.'

Instead of Bill doing his usual answering back he simply puts his finger to his lips.

As I take in Ambie's tux I give Fliss and Miranda a nod of admiration. 'Someone scrubs up well.' I don't think I've ever seen him completely dry before, but now he is he's strikingly tall and distinguished with his tanned cheekbones and his fabulous iron grey curls.

Fliss gives a snort. 'Slightly spoiled by his clip-on bow tie not being straight.'

I hiss at her. 'And I might have given the Santa hat a miss too.' Then I turn to Miranda. 'What's he doing?'

But she's staring at him too hard to reply, and her smile's very bright but strangely fixed.

The moment Ambie starts to sing the words *I've never seen you look so lovely as you did tonight* … I get the song. 'It's *Lady in Red* ... and he's got Chris de Burgh's hip wiggle off to a T too.'

Fliss is hissing across me at Miranda. 'You didn't tell us he did karaoke ...' from her frowns she can't work out what's going on any more than I can '... or is he lip syncing?'

As he slightly misses a note, it's clear it's his own voice. Then he's coming towards us, sliding his shiny black leather-soled shoes across the rug, knees slightly bent as he moves, holding out his hand, still crooning the words. To give him his due, it's astonishing how good he is.

I give Miranda a nudge. 'Good thing you put on the dress.' But she's flapping her fingers in front of her face too hard to reply.

We all know karaoke looks easy, but try to do it and it's a whole different story. Believe me, I know. When I tried singing along to *Somewhere Only We Know, the* karaoke version with lyrics, on YouTube in the kitchen in preparation for Fliss's hen party cocktail night I couldn't even get the first line in the right place. All I can say is thank Christmas I tried it at home first and not in public. It was so hideous I was cringing with embarrassment at myself, and I was the only one there. So I know this is hard, and he's pretty much note perfect, except for the highest bits. And to be fair, even Chris de Burgh cracks on those sometimes. And when he's a yard away I swear I hear Miranda give a low groan and mutter to herself:

'Oh fuck.'

But he's pulling her to her feet, and as she slinks back across the room with him, his hand's slipping over her bottom, and the red dress is riding up slightly. And from the way her eyes are almost popping he's definitely surprised her. He's pulling this off and smashing it, but you have to admit, it's a risky choice of music. This song is like Marmite, it's a lover or a loather. Being a sucker for cheesy romantic I'd go for it every time, but it's the kind of corny Miranda always jokes about. If she was listening to Absolute 80s radio at home and this came on she'd be more likely to throw her slipper at the radio or switch it off than sing along with it.

But Ambie's working it all the way, and he's not going to give up. The way he's looking deeply into her eyes is so sincere, the notes of his voice are so low and deep. As they reverberate around the room it's hard not to be carried away by the romance and the love. And we can see Miranda melting in front of us as she relaxes into this. I mean who wouldn't want to be serenaded by someone who sounds as smooth as James Bond and is suave enough to be Michael Douglas's body double with a sprinkling of Hugh Grant rakishness tossed in for good measure?

From the way he leads her around the room and back to the fireplace with perfect timing it's obvious he's worked on these moves in advance. By the time he's repeated the fifth refrain and is humming his way to the end the last bars of music are fading, and we're all applauding. But he's still gazing into Miranda's eyes, and then his hand's in his pocket, and in one smooth, seamless movement he's pulled out a ring box and popped up the lid.

It's the kind of thing you read about in *OK!* magazine and see in films, but it's the first time I've seen it unfold in real life.

Fliss is murmuring beside me, '*OMIGOD he's proposing!* And *LOOK* at that diamond!'

Even from across the room, I can't believe how huge it is or how brightly it's sparkling as the candlelight catches it. Let's just say, from what I know of *Daniels*' classiest jewellery, it must have cost a packet, and then some.

I'm whispering back, 'She can't turn that one down.' What Ambie lacks in willingness to help, he's more than made up for with carats and the singing.

Fliss is shaking her head, breathing the words behind her hand. 'I'm not sure I want to see my mum getting proposed to, some things should stay behind closed doors, it's a bit like watching my own conception.'

I'm talking back through clenched teeth. 'It is *very* public too, she *can't* turn him down.'

Ambie clears his throat and holds the ring up between his fingers. 'Dearest Miranda, I was a very sad and lonely man when we met, but you came into my life like a storm trooper, and you lit me up from the inside out … we haven't known each other long, but I already know, I *have* to make you mine. And once you're on my arm I'm hoping you'll finally become the lady you deserve to be.'

Fliss gives a snort. 'Condescending much?'

Considering how many times she's sat through similar before, I have to admire Miranda for managing to look like she's not only enraptured, but hearing something totally fresh and new. And you have to hand it to Ambie, he's doing this really well.

Fliss is murmuring again. 'The adrenalin must have sobered him up, for someone who's been downing gin all day he's very coherent.' She lets out a sigh. 'All that drinking, as future husband material he's not ideal.'

I send her a frown. 'Fingers crossed it's fourth time lucky.'

Ambie's carrying on. 'Miranda, I'd love you to do me the honour of being the next Mrs Bentley.' He drops down onto one knee and holds up the ring to her. 'Please, will you marry me?'

A collective ahhhh ripples around the sofas. Then Tarkie

pipes up. 'But Mum, I thought Granny Miranda had too many husbands already?'

Tiff's hissing at him very loudly. 'No, it's totally fine to get another, Tarkie, she's dumped all the others, she got her absolute beginner certificates.'

Tansy's pondering. 'Maybe she should get one that's not old and wrinkly this time.'

Keef's voice cuts in from by the log pile. 'So long as you're sure, Mirry ...'

Miranda looks up at Ambie. 'Dear Ambrose ...' Then she looks over her shoulder. 'Thank you all for your help and concern, this is a big surprise for me too ...' she looks back to Ambie '... but I'm delighted to accept.'

Then as Ambie pushes the ring onto her finger a roaring cheer goes up, mainly from the surfies, and we all clap. And I look round the faces to find Milo. After the way he's been physically forcing his way between them the last few days, I'd have expected him to rugby tackle the ring before he let this happen. I'm pleased he's seen sense, been the bigger man, and backed off at last.

Willow's shouting at anyone who will listen. 'Lovers who kiss under the mistletoe will have lasting happiness.'

As she heads for the happy couple I turn to Fliss. 'So where's Milo?'

Fliss rolls her eyes. 'Who knows, but he's not going to be a happy bunny.'

And then the door opens and he comes in. It takes him a few seconds to take in that we aren't all watching *A Close Shave*, and then his brow creases. 'What's happening here ...?'

Then, as he spots Miranda shaking her left fist like a super-sparkly maraca he comes again. 'What *THE HELL'S GOING ON? IS THAT A RING???*' When Miranda and Ambie are too busy whispering to reply, he rounds on me. '*IVY?*'

I open and close my mouth a few times before I work out exactly how to put it. 'Your dad just asked Miranda to marry him, she accepted, and they just got engaged.' That just about covers it.

'*HE CAN'T HAVE DONE IT, NOT ALREADY!*' It comes out as a roar. '*I TOTALLY REFUSE TO ALLOW IT!*'

Bill's joining in as he heads towards the door. 'It's all done. The best thing you can do now is offer your congratulations.'

Milo's snorting. '*OVER MY DEAD BODY!*'

I can't understand how he missed it. 'But where were you?'

His voice is high in protest. 'Dad sent me out to the car, I was literally away two minutes.'

I feel awful for him, because it sounds like Ambie planned it, so I throw in a few more details. 'Oh, and he sang too.'

'Not *Lady in Red*?' His face crumples in disbelief as he takes in my nod. 'That was my mum's favourite, he learned to sing it especially for her, we had it at her funeral.'

Fliss is deflating more with every blow he strikes. 'I'm so sorry, Milo. But if your dad's moving on with his life it might be a good thing, he wouldn't do it if he didn't feel ready.'

Milo's groaning. 'No offence to your mother, but they're really not right for each other.'

Keef's putting an arm around Milo. 'Don't worry, lad, free birds like Miranda don't take kindly to the kind of cage your dad wants to keep her in. She'll be off before you know it.'

Milo's shaking his head, spitting. 'Not before she fleeces us.'

'Two little words, Milo.' Keef's tapping his nose. '*Pre nup*.'

Milo sniffs. 'Technically I think that's one word not two.'

Keef looks at the ceiling. 'Who gives a damn, Milo, stop being a pedantic prick, cut the moaning, and get one in place.'

'I will.' Milo's staring across to where Willow has seized an enormous bunch of mistletoe from a jug on the table, and is standing on a chair holding it up as Miranda and Ambie dip their heads together underneath. 'Excuse me, I need to run ...' One leap, and he's crossed the room.

He's too late to stop Ambie swooping in to give Miranda the snog of her life. But as he punches the mistletoe out of Willow's hand the bunch explodes, flies in every direction through the air, and scatters all over the floor and the sofas. Which was somehow even more powerful and dramatic than the proposal itself.

So if lovers who kiss under the mistletoe are guaranteed lasting happiness, a couple having the mistletoe snatched away just as their lips are going to meet has to mean something huge and significant. I'm just not sure what, other than Willow looking like she's seriously going to lose it with Milo. It's going to take more than a moment or two of heavy breathing to realign her serenity there.

Which reminds me ... this evening wasn't meant to be hijacked by a proposal. And I refuse to allow it to turn into the full blown family row that could be brewing here. It's our Christmas film fest, and from where I'm sitting there's only one way to get this back on track. And blow all the bossier ladies, I'm going to take charge here. This one's mine.

Before I know it, I'm up on the coffee table and clapping my hands. 'Okay, everyone ... I'm going to tweak the running order here slightly, simply because there's one film that encapsulates every bit of the happiness and *positivity* we should all be feeling now ...' I break off to give Willow and Milo my specially significant 'belt the fuck up and be nice' smile '... so let's all grab our duvets ...' except that might not be necessary, because it's actually baking in here '... put on our Santa hats, reach for the Christmas popping candy and move on with ... ta da ...' I pause to do my jazz hands '... *FROZEN*.'

And for once Libby's kids don't groan, and the Twiglets don't pull faces and start talking Spanish. They all erupt in a cheer and shout 'Bring it on, Ivy-leaf!'

All Merwyn and I can do is to stand back and take the applause and as I scrape the sweat off my forehead and push back the sticky strands of my hair I realise my scar must be in full view. And just for once I really don't give a damn, and no one else does either.

28.

Fifty words for snow

'When you propose to *me*, please promise you won't do it anywhere remotely public.'

As I listen to Bill's laugh in the darkness over the sound of the wind and distant tumble of the waves as they fall lower down the beach I know I shouldn't ever have started this. The smallest murmur of protest from him and I swear I'd have stopped. But the lack of any surprise or chiding at all on his part somehow spurs me on.

'And absolutely no singing. I completely forbid you to sing.'

He gives a grunt. 'That doesn't leave me many options. What the hell am I going to do then?'

As I hear myself speaking, I'm shocked, appalled even, but I carry on anyway. We both know we're joking, but somehow it's like an antidote to the underlying tensions of the evening. Considering Miranda and Ambie getting engaged should have been a truly happy occasion without reservations, there were a hell of a lot of undercurrents from all directions.

'You'll have to be creative. Planes towing banners are definitely out. And I'd hate to have to solve a puzzle, or dig anything up. And it would be a complete nightmare being met off a plane by you holding a piece of cardboard in the arrivals hall. And I'm not thrilled at the idea of a ring buried in a cupcake either.'

He's walking in step beside me, still playing along. 'I had no idea you were so hard to please. How about if I just stick a notice on Merwyn?'

'Perfect.'

'What if you're the one doing the asking?'

So like Bill to push this. 'You'd like that?' We're walking so fast now we're catching our breath between strides.

'I wouldn't be complaining.'

Hmmm. So likely. 'You sound like you've been talking to Willow.'

'We've got gingerbread women on the Christmas tree, it's a logical step.' Simply from the sound of his voice, I can tell his lips have curved into a smile.

Except none of this is logical. Even in my wildest Will-dreams back in the day I never played out a conversation like this in my head. And yet here I am walking along the beach, the sea on our left is moving up the beach, its lines of breaking foam just visible like pale stripes in the blackness, the words tumbling out of my mouth. Absurd doesn't begin to cover it. It's as if once we started we're daring each other to get more and more blatant. Even though I know we're both pretending and talking the biggest load of rubbish I'm still getting the weirdest hot and cold rainbow tingles radiating through my body. I need to watch out, this Bill bollocks could be catching.

I hung a couple of sea glass chunks round my neck yesterday

and said the most outrageous things, and that was before champagne got thrown into the mix. When we toasted Miranda and Ambie earlier the bottles of bubbly kept on coming. I know I've knocked drinking on the head, but my bestie's mum just got proposed to and has a rock on her finger the size of a small house to prove it. Obviously I had to have a tiny glass of fizz to celebrate, I just hadn't expected the alcohol to multiply the sea glass effect exponentially. My only saving grace is that I didn't invite Bill to come with Merwyn and I on our late evening phone-light walk, he was outside at the wood store and somehow just tagged along, so at least I hung onto my self respect there. And the tiny bit of self preservation instinct I have left is stepping in to save me here too so I'm moving this on.

'As you had the champagne on ice and the glasses ready, I take it you were in on all Ambie's plans?' I'm watching Bill, his hands deep in the pockets of his Barbour. He's close enough that every time we bump elbows I get a delicious burst of the oily smell of wax jacket. But we both know he's only close because if he was further away it would be too windy for me to hear what he said.

'He needed help with his backing track, so he had to tell me.' Our eyes have got used to the darkness beyond the light beam from the phone and Bill's looking up at the clouds racing above us, choosing his words before he rolls them out. 'It was supposed to be a Christmas Day proposal, but Ambie's a businessman, he knows the importance of closing a deal early.'

'Milo was hell bent on wrecking things between them.' It

was supposed to be a secret, but anyone with eyes would have known.

Bill laughs. 'That too. But Ambie's biggest worry was losing Miranda to the surf club. If they'd got their boards out, he wouldn't have been able to compete. That's more what the rush was about.'

I can't help feeling sad for Miranda. 'If he couldn't trust her for four more days, he's not very sure of her.'

Bill hesitates as he thinks about it. 'I think he was hoping that once he'd put a ring on it he could relax and enjoy being engaged.'

'More like, if he's her fiancé she'll have to give all her attention to him now.'

Bill's nodding. 'That too. I promise I won't be like that.'

'Like *what*?'

'When we're engaged I won't be possessive.'

I let out a squeak of protest. 'Keep up, we stopped playing that game *way* back.'

He's just looking down at me, unblinking. 'We were *playing*?'

I ignore that my stomach turned a cartwheel, swallow my heart back down from where it leaped and landed in my throat, and give him a play punch on his arm. 'Durr, you know we were.' I know he always does this. Winds me up with a completely dead pan expression. The only way to deal with it is to go in on the attack. 'Anyway, changing the subject ...'

'That's a shame, I was enjoying the other one, Star-girl.'

'I saw you singing along to *Frozen*.'

He lets out a sigh. 'I wondered when we'd get onto that.'

That's the thing, saying he was singing along is understating hugely. 'Put it this way, with you there joining in, Olaf and Sven were finding it hard to get a word in edgeways.' I give it a few strides along the sand for that to sink in. 'Unless you're one of those people who has total language recall, you only get that word perfect from watching a film a gazillion times.' I stop and turn to look up at him. 'So which is it?'

He lets out a breath. 'What comes after a gazillion, then?'

'*Fuck knows.* Maybe a trazillion? Why?'

'As an approximate guess, *that's* the number of times I've seen it.'

'Oh crap.'

'That's not the right reply, Ivy-star, this is where you're supposed to ask me *why?*'

His voice slides so deep it's making my ear drums tremble. There are the same lines on his face I saw earlier in the day, and seeing them sends my stomach plummeting to my knees. That box of DVDs. Keef treading on eggshells asking if we could use them. Was it really only earlier this afternoon? Today seems to have gone on forever. And there's just this void of tragedy opening up in front of me. He was adamant he didn't want kids here, and yet he knows his way round a pushchair back to front and it's not because he's been a mother's help. And he can't stand Christmas. And his house is stripped bare of anything personal. I've walked headlong into this one and there's only one way out.

My scalp is tingling, and my heart is stone cold in my chest. But most of all, I'm really really kicking myself for being so wrapped up in my own dramas that I've failed to notice his.

'You've lost a child haven't you?'

He's biting his lip. 'Yes ... and no.'

'Why didn't you say?'

'It's not as bad as you're thinking, she's in London with Gemma. I just haven't seen her since January so it feels like she's been gone forever.'

He and Gemma had a baby together. It's been staring me in the face, but I chose not to notice; as the truth finally hits it winds me like a kick in the guts. That's so much deeper and more complex than being a boyfriend and girlfriend who split up. I'm swallowing back sour saliva and cursing myself for the pangs of jealousy stabbing in my chest. That it was Gemma, not me. That he'll be tied to her forever now. I know there's nothing rational about the thoughts my mind is throwing up. I drag myself together, and work out the proper reaction a normal, uninvolved person would give.

'But that's almost a year.' As I say it, I can't hide my horror. 'That can't be right!'

He shakes his head. 'At first Gemma didn't want her to get upset by seeing me, and it's ongoing, I'm the idiot for letting it slide.'

'Does she have a name?' I don't want to push him. But at the same time, I'm desperate to know all of it. Right down to the very last detail.

'Arabella, after Gemma's mum, but Abby for short.' His voice is wistful and faraway. 'Saving you the next question, she's almost six.'

'That's pretty.' I'm trying not to think how cute and perfect a mix of him and Gemma will be. And doing the maths. They didn't wait long after they got together, that shows how mad about each other they were, how committed, how head over heels. You don't have a baby unless you're all of those.

'It's all such a mess. And Gemma insists Abby's very settled now. The last thing I want is to upset her because I'm selfishly wanting to see her.' He closes his eyes. 'But I miss her so much – for four years she was the reason I got up in the morning, although to be fair I didn't usually have a choice, she'd be prising my eyelids open. She was such a live wire, her smiles brought the whole castle alive. I can't tell you how empty my life is since she left. How pointless everything feels.'

'And you put everything of hers away?'

There are deep lines on his face in the shadows and he's come to a halt now, staring out around the curve of the bay to the lights of St Aidan, clustered in the distance. 'Gemma literally cleared the place out when she left. The few things Gemma hadn't taken went in the coach house, because I couldn't bear to see them. The only thing that escaped the cull was the shelf of colognes in the bathroom. And the cupboards in the kitchen. The colognes came from Gemma's sister – don't ask me why they're still there.'

I have to say. 'I did notice those and wonder.' It's not the time to ask which he uses. I'm not sure I even want to know any more. It's so much him, it wouldn't be right on anyone else.

'She's a fragrance rep, hence the collection.' He takes a breath. 'I threw myself into work to block out how much I was hurting. So long as I don't allow myself to think about it I can manage to function on a basic level.'

I know exactly where he's coming from there, I'm very familiar with that. Burying the pain. Carrying on as if nothing had happened. Toughing it out, making myself so busy there's no cracks for the past to break through into the current reality. At least this explains why the carefree guy I met that day in the chalet went away and came back so changed.

'So long as I bat away Gemma's demands, I can just about get by. Some days I almost convince myself that part of my life never happened, that this is all there ever was.' He runs his fingers through his hair. 'Then Christmas comes along with a whole heap of memories and expectations and makes everything a gazillion times worse again ...'

He's so broken, my heart is aching for him. 'I'm so sorry. And then we come crashing in with all the kids and make it harder still. If there's anything I can do to help ...' There won't be.

'You did mention ...' he's looking down at me, his gaze steady in the darkness '... the last time we were on the beach ...'

As I see his arms splay my stomach drops so fast I can't breathe. 'You're asking for a ...?' My throat's so dry my voice gives out long before I get to croak the word hug.

'It's a very long time since anyone offered me one.' His head is tilted. 'If you don't mind it's really warm inside my jacket ... you could get out of the wind for a moment ... just as a friend ...'

I swallow, close my eyes, and dive. Lock my arms around his torso, grasp a handful of jumper, drag the scent of cashmere and denim shirt and man deep into my lungs. Bury my head in the hollow underneath his collarbone, listen to the slow primeval clunk of his heart as it bangs against his ribcage. I've waited so long to get here, it won't ever happen again, so I'm loath to let go. Not unless I really have to. Like when the tide comes in and washes over my boots. Or maybe when the water comes up to my waist. Once I'm submerged all the way to my shoulders. Then I might.

He's resting his chin on my head, 'Actually, I haven't minded everyone crashing in ... sometimes it does you good to be shaken up.' There's a grate as he clears his throat and swallows. 'So how about these regrets of yours?'

That's such an unexpected question, I have to open my eyes so I can think better. High above the line of Bill's collar I catch a glimpse of a slender crescent of moon as the clouds part. I'm careful not to let my fingers relax any. That one afternoon by the fire at the chalet got me from there to here. The next few minutes will have to last me the rest of my life. As for being sorry about things that are over, my pile is too high to even begin.

'I wish I'd dyed my hair blonde more often.'

'How often did you?'

'Never.'

'Go on ...'

'That I'd got to a higher level on Tetris before my Gameboy died ... that I hadn't killed so many tamagotchis ... I should definitely have looked after my sea monkeys better ...'

'Those are millennial. Anything more recent?'

We're moving onto very shaky ground here. 'I probably sound like Willow, but regrets are negative, dwelling on them can only be destructive. You need to leave them in the past, because that's where they belong.' I'm pretty much paraphrasing a year's worth of trauma recovery sessions in three sentences here. 'Grasp your life in your hands and head for the future with your head held high. That could work for you too.' I'm watching, hearing the frill of the tide. With each rush the foam is washing closer towards us.

'Now and again it's interesting to look back, compare notes, that's all.' He's musing, chin still resting on my skull. At a guess with his eyes open. 'So far Gemma and I have only dealt with finances. We haven't faced the toughest part yet.'

Then it strikes me. I don't want to interfere, it's his life, it's their broken relationship. But he will regret it if he doesn't do this. 'However hard it is, you mustn't give up on Abby.' I squeeze his back. 'She will still need to see you. You have to find a way.'

His sigh hits my hair. 'I know, thanks for reminding me. I'll try.' His fingers are tucking in my scarf. 'You have to find your way forward too ... how hard is that going to be?'

I've held it in for so long, if I'm pulling it out now it's only to show him why it's impossible. 'Well, with my accident, the driver of the car didn't make it. So before I move on I've got to get past a dead person who wouldn't have lost their life if it wasn't for me.' All I can say is, I'm so pleased it's dark and my head is buried inside Bill's coat.

'Ivy-leaf, I'm so sorry.' His fingers are gentle, catching in the strands of my hair as he brushes them out of the wind. 'Can you bear to tell me how it happened?'

'It's a long story ...'

He's prompting. 'So where does it begin?'

'After George left ...'

'So you were on your own ...'

'That's right, but going out with really random people trying to claw back the years I'd wasted on George. It was all a bit desperate and crazy.' I'm shuddering to think how bad it was. 'I'd met up with someone for a second date at a party in Brighton. Michael. He had a name, and a mum and dad, and two brothers and a whole life ahead of him.'

'How did it happen?'

'Well he – Michael – actually I think mostly his friends called him Mike – that's how little we knew each other, we hadn't even got onto calling each other by our proper names. So Michael – or Mike – offered to drive me back through the lanes to London after the party, and that's where we were when he went off the road.' How did one second of misjudgement turn out to be so shocking and awful? 'One minute he was there next to me, laughing, the next we were sliding off the road, the car was rolling, we hit a tree and his life was over.'

'They can happen so easily on country lanes, you hit a patch of mud and lose control. But how is that your fault?'

'If it hadn't been for me he wouldn't have even been there.'

His voice is slow. 'Ok-a-a-a-y ...'

'But worst of all I didn't realise until afterwards he'd been drinking, probably because I'd been drinking so much myself. I could have stopped him. I should have stopped him. But I didn't. All I keep thinking is, if only we'd never set off he'd still be here.'

'Oh Ivy, it was an accident, that's something that happens by chance that shouldn't have, that's why they're called that. You can't take responsibility for something that really wasn't your fault.'

'His neck snapped with the impact. He was just quietly sitting there next to me, he didn't even cut himself like I did. But he was gone. How unfair is that? That's why it doesn't feel right for me to get on and enjoy my life.' I let out a breath. 'I was so strong to start with, I went back to where the accident happened, but when the anniversary came around, however much I tried to, I couldn't make myself go back. I hate myself even more for that because it feels so wrong and cowardly.'

Bill's chest heaves as he sighs. 'It could just as easily have been the other way round. You were the lucky one, you walked away, and you shouldn't waste that chance. You have to let go of the guilt – beating yourself up for something you can't change is only going to get in the way.' He stops for a while. 'It's more important than ever now for you to have the best time, to get on and live your best life. I'd say you owe it to Michael to do that.'

His jumper is warm against my cheek. 'That helps, thank you, it's a good way of thinking about it.'

'You already go the extra mile for everyone else, it's time you did the same for yourself.'

It's hard to explain. 'It's fine to do things for other people, because it's like paying back.'

'But of everyone I know, Ivy-leaf you're the one who deserves the good things for yourself too. It's time you let yourself have them.'

I swallow away the lump in my throat. 'Maybe.'

I can hear the smile in his voice. 'You need to remember how carefree you were that afternoon by the fire in Chamonix. I'd like to hear you laugh like that again.'

That's the thing, I'm not sure I ever have. 'So, we've both got to work on the hard stuff.'

I can hear his laugh reverberating in his chest, he's probably raising an eyebrow to match. 'How about if we stay here all night and miss the films, will we regret that?'

As a rogue wave comes rushing towards us up the sand, just before it hits my feet I jump. When I look up again he's three feet away, his jacket flapping in the space where I was.

'What – stay here, and get washed out to sea?' There's a sudden chill now I've stepped away from the warmth of his body. However much I'd like to burrow in and go back for more, I won't ever be able to ask. 'You please yourself, but there's no way I'm going to miss Christmas.'

He lets out a groan. 'Tell me you're not going to make me watch *Love Actually*?'

'That's not all. There's *Mama Mia!* too.'

He gives a fake grimace, but he's still hanging around on the spot, barely moving. 'So much to look forward to.'

But I've had my high point, the last ten minutes have been everything I've wished for for the last seven years and more. Being wrapped in his arms was every bit as good as I anticipated. Yes, I was pushing my luck and making the most of his misery, and true, it did have a 'friend' sticker firmly attached before it even began. But even taking all of the above into account, perfect doesn't begin to cover it.

And if Bill's telling me to do something for myself, I just have. At this moment I have to be the happiest woman in Cornwall. And bearing in mind Miranda got the proposal she'd been working for probably since the day she met Ambie, and a rock and a half to match, there's a lot of happy washing around in the county to beat, the Cornish happy-ometer is riding pretty high.

But I'm going to take a second to relive the last ten minutes, wrap them very carefully in tissue paper, and tuck them away in my safest memory box.

Then I need to whistle Merwyn and make a run for the castle before anything happens to spoil it.

Sunday

22nd December

29.

And a partridge in a pear tree …

As a way of keeping a whole lot of people warm, cosy and entertained in a castle that is otherwise like a fridge at best, and at worst feels like fifty below plus wind chill in the Arctic circle, the night of films is a winner. By the end of *Mama Mia! Here We Go Again* it's a long time after midnight and most people have already curled up under their duvets and dropped off to sleep so we dim the lights, heap more logs onto the fires, and settle down for the night.

Merwyn is delighted that I've come to my senses and decided to sleep on the floor at last. And as Fliss and I settle down somewhere between Harriet and Oscar's travelling cots and Tiff and Tansy's gentle snores, Bill has already melted away into the shadows. Due to the 'special (wifi) facilities' Libby allocated his room a priority fan heater and Milo was given a second, due to how small the room is and how devastated he was about his dad. At least this way if he wants to cry himself to sleep, he can do it in private. And she gave Miranda and Ambie the rest of the heaters, supposedly so they don't have to get frostbite on their bits on their engagement night. The real reason is Libby said she could put up with many things, but Ambie's endless moaning about rough sleeping wasn't one of them. As for the silver surfies, they must be used to their camper vans because they're settling down in their sleeping bags without a murmur.

When we're woken next morning by Harriet lobbing her teddies and – more painfully – Postman Pat's large plastic car onto our heads, the dawn sky is streaked with pale pink beyond the small paned castle windows, and Keef's back crouching by the fireplace again. As Fliss, the kids and I tiptoe our way through to the kitchen and gasp at the sunlight shining off the colourless early morning sea, we're welcomed by big piles of what we recognise instantly as Bill & co. muffins.

'Hmmm, nice, cherry ones and blueberry flavour.' I hand one to Harriet on my hip and another to Oscar who's still in yesterday's lion onesie, bouncing like a kangaroo. He's also got a vegetable strainer on his head, and he's banging it with a fish slice. Then I grab a couple of muffins for Fliss and I and follow her through to Bill's room breathing a sigh of relief that the Do Not Disturb sign has already gone.

We heap the kids onto Bill's bed and as Fliss holds up her phone she sounds all breathy. 'Brilliant, I've got a line out and Rob's phone is ringing.' She makes big eyes at Oscar. 'Are you going to talk to Daddy on Facetime?'

It wasn't my best idea to give Harriet a muffin that was bigger than her head, then put her on Bill's duvet cover. I was hoping to show Rob a picture of baby contentment, and as Harriet buries her face in the sponge she certainly sounds happy. The only downside is the cake explosion on the grey Egyptian cotton. Who knew one head-size muffin would spread so far when baby hands collapsed it into a million crumbs and a hundred lumps of blueberry. It only takes Merwyn a second to inhale the bits on the floor, and I'm doing my best to do the same with the ones spread across the bed cover when Rob picks up.

As his face fills the screen, he lets out a loud 'waaaaaaaaaaaaahhhh'. Then he closes his eyes, shakes his head and as he rubs his hair I can't help notice – even though they're hundreds of miles apart, he and Fliss could have walked straight out of the same festival-hair hairdressing tipi. I know they had a huge wedding list, but obviously neither of them thought to put hair brushes on there.

'Hi there, Bubsy Harrie, say hello to Daddy-bunny ...' Rob might sound totally knackered, but he's putting the effort in, wiggling his fingers doing rabbit ears over his head, and the goofy teeth. And it works because Harriet's exploding into peals of laughter.

Fliss is frowning at me. 'Has Oscar been in the dishwasher?'

But then Oscar starts making bunny faces, bashing his colander and screaming with laughter too. There's a moment where Rob breaks off to have a slurp of tea, then they're straight back to the shrieks. Which is all lovely except for one thing. When it comes to mugs, Rob is an engineer and a bit of a purist, he won't have a flowery one in the flat. Which is fine, except when he took his sip of tea back there, I know it was weird in close up, but it definitely looked like roses on the mug rim.

It goes on for a couple of minutes, then Rob lets out a yelp. 'Shit, is that the time, thank Christmas you woke me, jeez, I've got to go to work.' Which sounds a lot like what he said last time.

And then the screen goes blank. But just before it does, he must roll out of bed, because there's a definite flash of pillowcase. Then Oscar starts banging his fish slice on the phone and Fliss whips it away.

She lets out a whistle. 'Well, that went well ... didn't you think?'

My smile is fixed. 'Frigging brilliant.'

She's still going. 'Why have I been tying myself in knots, I should have done this all along. What made me think it would upset them? I feel so much better now.'

Oh my. She's my bestie, she's been to hell and back for weeks over this, she had the proof she's been waiting for in front of her eyes and she missed it. If she didn't spot the alien pastel geometric pillowcases and the floral mug because she was too excited thinking things are okay, I'm not going to rub her nose in them. I mean, my stomach has left the building, I'm too gutted by the implications to start my muffin, so jeez knows how Fliss would feel about this when it's *her husband* in someone else's bed. At least this way she gets a couple of days of ignorant bliss before the shit hits. But I'm not letting it go totally.

'Work on Sunday? Is that a regular thing for Rob?' Of course it bloody isn't.

She gives a shrug. 'Maybe he's just trying to get finished so he can come down tomorrow not Tuesday.' She's so optimistic. Deluded even.

Oscar's gone back to smashing his fish slice on his head. 'Daddy Facetime, Daddy Facetime, Daddy Facetime ...'

I'm busy ignoring my muffin, agonising over the problem, when there's a throaty cough outside the door, and Miranda pushes her way in.

'Here you all are! I've just been out for a ciggy.'

Fliss frowns. 'I didn't think you smoked before lunch.'

Miranda's eyebrows shoot up. 'It's the holidays, rules are for breaking, *carpe* those effing *diems*, shine like a diamond and all that jizz.'

Fliss stares at her. 'Jeez Mother, listen to yourself, you sound like you bumped into Keef and had a bullshit top up. And I've told you before, saying jizz is not okay.'

'Jizz ... jazz ... it's only one letter, how can it matter?'

Fliss sends me her 'give me strength' look. 'Believe me, it does.'

I didn't have Miranda down as a blusher, but her cheeks are suddenly very pink and she's flapping her fingers in front of her face and talking really fast. 'And if Keef was at the woodpile it was a total coincidence.'

I'm smiling at Miranda to move this on. 'It's a shame you missed Rob, two minutes earlier you could have told him your news and showed him how sparkly your ring is.'

Her right hand slaps over her left one and if she's trying to hide her empty finger it's worked. 'I left it upstairs for now, it's a little loose – I'd hate for it to fall off and get lost.'

As if that would happen. Now she comes to mention it, it hits me what her diamond reminds me of. You know when people have bunches of keys with tennis balls attached, so they don't get misplaced? Well, that. A tennis ball's about the size of it anyway. Just saying. She might not want to wear it, but if she tied it to her key ring at least she'd always be able to find her keys.

Fliss grins at her. 'Don't be ridiculous Mum, it's such a rock, if you dropped it you'd be more likely to cause an obstruction in the street or break a leg falling over the thing than lose it.'

It's one thing thinking it, and quite another saying it. Maybe I'm not the only one Willow's hit with a truth collar.

'Let's go and get you a tea, Miranda, there are lots of delicious muffins in the kitchen too.'

She pulls a face. 'Tea would be lovely, sweetheart, but I'd better give the muffins a miss.'

Fliss rounds on her. 'Why?'

'You know Ambie, he'll definitely want a slender bride.' When did Miranda ever have a tiny voice? She usually booms like a fog horn. If sea glass makes you blurty, it's like Ambie's diamond has turned her into the Queen with a teensy voice overnight. 'He's always telling me, when Betty turned sideways she was so thin she used to disappear.'

Fliss lets out a squawk. 'Jeez Mother, Betty died of cancer, that's why there was nothing of her. You've always been curvy, that's why you've got guys buzzing round your boobs like ...'

'Like surfies round a big wave?' That was me, with an effing great push from my necklace. 'Or, if you don't mind a honey pot cliché, bees work just as well.' As I hear a door slam and footsteps in the corridor, I pick up Harriet and push her at

Miranda, and shoo Fliss and Oscar towards the door. 'This could be Bill – you make tea, I'll clean up in here. Hurry up, off you go.' I can hear Oscar yelling his Daddy Facetime chant all the way back to the kitchen.

We were talking about regrets last night. As the others leave and I take in the enormity of the muffin spread I'm certainly regretting this particular tidying offer.

I look down at Merwyn and let out a loud groan. 'Jeez, blueberry muffins knee-ed into a white duvet cover! *Quel désastre.*'

He looks up at me, puts his front paws up on the bed, then looks at me again. If he were Tom, he'd be saying, *Mother, it's bloody obvious, stop messing, just do it.*

I'm looking back at him. 'I don't know, Merwyn, if Tansy catches me using you like a hoover, I'll never hear the last of it.'

I nip and close the door and wedge a stool in front of it. A second later I've scooped him up by the bottom, lowered his nose to duvet level, and I'm skimming him around the bed. I let out a sigh. 'Sorry, Merwyn, desperate times and all that ... we'll call this your one Christmas treat ... after this you're back to your Lily's Kitchen Rise and Shine Doggy Specials all the way to New Year.'

Then despite the stool, the door bursts open, and as Bill appears I'm kicking myself for not using the Do Not Disturb sign, and pulling Merwyn close to my chest so it looks like Bill just walked in on us having a quiet Sunday morning cuddle.

'Were you talking French back there?'

'I didn't mean to – it must be catching.' Like a lot of other things round here.

He's scrutinising me now. 'Are you okay? You look a bit pale that's all. And you've been in here ages, yet there's a completely unstarted muffin next to your laptop. That's very telling.'

I'm going to have to give him something here. 'Someone I know in London is possibly making a huge mistake. If I were there I'd be straight round to sort them out. But as I'm not I'll just have to forget about it, and get on with my day.'

He's screwing up his face. 'And are those wet splodges on the bed?'

I'm hoping he won't be too cross. 'Ooops, sorry, Fliss's tinies were in here with breakfast earlier Facetiming their dad.' I'm kicking myself. 'Ooops, sorry again ... shouldn't have said that. Lovely muffins by the way, please pass my compliments on to whoever does your baking.'

'You don't have to tiptoe around me, Pom Pom.'

He has no idea what a relief it is to hear that. 'In that case, as we're here ... I've been thinking ...'

He drags in a breath. 'Yes?'

'It's Christmas, it's the season of goodwill, it's the perfect opportunity to ask Gemma to let you see Abby. I mean, from what you said everything's still informal between you, technically you're both still looking after her.'

'What?' He blinks. 'It's Sunday today, they're flying out to Davos early Tuesday until after New Year.'

'Which leaves you plenty of time, then.' I grin at him.

He stares up at the ceiling. 'How well do you know Gemma?'

However difficult Gemma is, I'm going to have to throw something else in here. 'Fliss's dad died when she was ten, she hated growing up without him, please don't do that to Abby. You're actually really lucky to have the choice here, so don't throw it away.'

Even after he swallows his voice is still extra gravelly. 'Thanks, Ivy-star, I know I need to wake up. A whole year on, I still haven't made it happen.'

I do understand how hard it is but he's going to have to accept that things have changed forever. 'I know it's gutting that you and Abby might never live together full time any more. But you have to find a way to spend time with each other – make new patterns, be sure to spend the holidays together, use Facetime for the bits in between, things like that.' It's so tough, but there's no point him just wishing things are as they were, because they never will be again. 'You're the only person who can fight for this, it has to be you. And you need to get on with it, the longer you put it off the harder it will be.'

'I know you're right.' At least he's nodding. 'We have arranged things – holidays, weekend visits, trips. But every time something more important has come up, or they've been ill. Every time Gemma's found an excuse to put them off.'

It's so important, I have to push him. 'So spring a surprise, it'll be over before she has time to change her mind. You don't have to ask for a lot, keep it low key and she's more likely to agree. Just message or text, and be really clear about what you want – ask for a couple of hours to take Abby out. You'll feel so much better once you have. It'll be like a Christmas present for both of you.' I know if it happens it'll mean him being away when I don't have much time left here, but that's a sacrifice I'll have to deal with. I can count the days we've got left here on one hand now, that's how fast it's whizzing by.

'Great idea, I'll get onto it now.'

I smile at him and put Merwyn back on the floor. 'And I'll go and make some coffee, if you're hoping for a muffin with yours, don't leave it too long.'

He's already opening his laptop. 'I won't.'

In fact, the kids take ages to wake, and when they do, they just roll over and go straight into watching CBeebies with Oscar and Harriet and eating a pile of last night's leftover pizza. Which leaves Merwyn and I sitting together on the kitchen sofa, watching the waves sliding up the beach in the distance as I work my way through the muffin stack single handed. I'm saved from bursting when the latest Waitrose delivery arrives and I head off to the pantry to put away the cratefuls of shopping.

I'm drooling over sides of smoked salmon, hampers of wax covered cheeses, and cartons of thick cream flavoured with brandy as I stack them into the fridge, when Keef arrives.

'Anything I can help with?'

For someone who rides the wave of life whilst giving absolutely no fucks whatsoever, his forehead has a lot of deep furrows.

He's tapping his bead braids on his teeth. 'I don't know ...'

'Live more, stress less, Keef.' I can't believe this is the same laid back, chilled out guy who told *me* not to be uptight not so long ago. 'What the hell's the matter?'

He hitches up his harlequin check jogging pants and pulls a face. 'It's Miranda, she's really not happy, but I can't help without looking like I've got an ulterior motive.'

'And have you?' Damn, that one was hundred per cent sea glass.

'What a question, Ivy. I stay fit running away from relationships, my middle name is no-commitment.'

I stare at him. 'Commitment is an act, not a word, Keef.' It's fun seeing how far his eyebrows shoot up as I tease him. Then I take pity. 'It's okay, you can care about someone without wanting to get involved. Would you like me to have a word?'

His face relaxes. 'I'd feel a lot better if I knew she was getting proper support from a good place.'

'Leave it with me, I'll have a chat.' I'm leaning down to pick up a humungous luxury Christmas pudding, tied in authentic muslin when I hear Bill.

'Dad, what are you doing in here?'

Keef makes a zip sign across his mouth to me, then turns round to Bill. 'The heating engineer just rang, I came to give Ivy an update.'

Bills eyes are popping. 'And? I wouldn't mind knowing too if it's not too much trouble.'

Keef blinks. 'Sure, of course. Well the good news is, he's finally tracked down the boiler part he needs.' He wiggles his eyebrows at me. 'It's good going too, it's the only one in the country.'

Bill's nodding. 'Great, so what's the hold up?'

'It's at a plumbers' merchants in London, they're open tomorrow morning, then they're shut until the New Year. With couriers flat out, it's going to be touch and go.'

Bill nods. 'No worries, I'll pick it up myself, I've got to go anyway.'

My heart does a leap. 'You've heard back already?'

There's no mistaking the shine in his eyes, or the width of his beam as he turns to Keef. 'With Ivy's help I'm doing lunch with Abby tomorrow, and we're hanging out for a couple of hours before, while Gemma packs for the holiday.'

Keef makes the hang loose sign, waggles his hand at Bill and goes all Australian. 'Rippa, mate, that's beaut, well done Ivy-leaf, that's the best news we've had on Ramsay Street all day.' He pauses then he qualifies that as he pulls Bill in for a hug and pats him on the back. 'Even better than the boiler part.'

Bill's still grinning as he turns to me. 'So, are you up for a quick trip to the shops, Store-girl?'

'Sure.' It's nice to be asked and I'm desperately trying not to mind how long he'll be disappearing for. Realistically, he stokes the fires and fails to mend the boiler quickly. We can completely manage without him and that disgustingly amazing smile of his. And it's coming back to me now. When he really smiles it's not just creases in his cheeks – there are dimples too. And eff, shit, bollocks for what those are doing to my back-flipping stomach. And obviously his first thought is the presents he's going to take with him for Abby. 'The Deck Gallery? They had nice things.'

He wrinkles his nose. 'I wasn't thinking of St Aidan, Pom Pom, I meant are you coming to London?'

Fuck. I try to ignore that my insides just left the building. And that my voice has turned to a squeak. 'Really?'

'Didn't you say you had business to sort out there? This way you can. Merwyn can come too, we can share the driving if you want, I'm sure Libby can manage her own Instagram for one day, we'll be back before you know.'

Seeing as the sea in Yorkshire is made from melted igloos, and I come from a family that only recently succumbed to oven chips, items like wetsuits never featured in my childhood. So the nearest I ever got to surfing was doggy paddling on a float in the local swimming pool which dated back to Victorian times. But the surge in my insides at the thought of this trip to London is so enormous, in my head I'm upright on my surf board, and riding one of those huge waves you see on YouTube, the height of a house, that stretches for miles, and goes on forever. I know it's stupid, it's every kind of irrational, I'd always promised myself I'd never get my hopes up. Yes, I know all of the above, that my chances are totally zilch etc. etc. And yet I still feel like I won the lottery. Better actually. Everybody knows money only takes you so far, it's no guarantee you'll be happy. What I'm feeling now is a happy rush that's closer to ecstatic. Or beyond.

And all the time I'm riding this *MAHOOSIVE* wave, I'm working my way backwards trying to find another reason for him asking. And I just can't think. And then suddenly, there's a flash in my head, and it hits me. 'You want me to take my Corsa because it's easier than the Landy?'

And shit shit shit, because we're talking dimples again. Bill just laughs and says one word. 'Rumbled.'

That brings me crashing down to earth again faster than a tumbling wave. Which, once I pick myself up ... and spend quite a while having imaginary CPR due to the fake water in my sodden lungs ... is actually no bad thing.

Three guesses who the lifeguard is? I really promise when January comes I'm going to reassert my grip on reality. For now, I'm a bit stuffed.

30.

Cocoa served here

Have I ever been on a road trip with Bill before? Only about a hundred times. Always in my head, and strangely ... never in my Corsa. They were always in an unnamed super-comfy car, obviously one a lot less 'eff off' and blingy than Ambie's, and I don't think I even specified a leather interior. But they always had the kind of inordinately huge back seats where the making out could easily slide into so much more.

And it's funny how the minute Bill gets into my Corsa I'm seeing marks on the seat covers I never even noticed in the previous six years. And then there's the passenger side knock. Obviously Merwyn – bless his little Tibetan paws – his bed, blankets, food, and enough clothes to keep him going for the next thirty-six hours are taking up the entire back seat anyway, not that I begrudge him the space. That's the other embarrassment – the car is way too old have Bluetooth, so I'm stuck with the CD player. When I loaded up the stacker before I set off it was with all five CDs from one of those really cheap 100 Hits sets that I bought for a fiver in the supermarket. I was thinking of singing along when my Christmas tunes CD and Pirate Radio got too much. I certainly wasn't thinking of showing my best self to anyone at all other than Merwyn. And definitely not Will-Bill.

We get as far as the second bend and I decide to come clean. 'You'll notice that knock on the front passenger side?'

Bill grins. 'Nothing to worry about, it's probably only a grumbling wheel bearing, we'll soon have that sorted once we get back.' Truly, we won't, by the time the parts departments open up again I'll be long gone.

When Celine Dion's *My Heart Will Go On* comes on, Bill shoots me a look and I manage to hold in my singing, even though it's almost bursting out.

Instead I give a sniff. 'I'm hoping the classy dashboard fairy lights will make up for the terrible choice of music.' Then as Celine finishes and Bonnie Tyler starts to croak I say, 'Yay, *Total Eclipse of the Heart*!'

Bill looks across at me. 'On balance, would that have been better or worse as Ambie's proposal song?'

I look back at him. 'Oh my, how long have you got?'

And, call us shallow, but that's what we pass the next three hundred miles discussing. Every time a new song comes on, there are so many things to say, the next song's starting before we've finished. And it's sweetened by many packets of gummy bears and Haribo Christmas mix, all washed down with bottles of Pepsi Max. The time flies by so fast, we're half way, at Yeovil and stopping for petrol and we're barely half way through the CD stack. Bill swaps into the driving seat, Merwyn and I have a dash around the car park for a comfort halt, then we set off again.

It's one of those journeys where everyone is in their own bubble of happiness for completely different reasons. Bill's all smiley because he's going to see Abby, Merwyn always pretends he's disapproving, but once you get to know him well enough to see past the side eye, he's a sunny character who's just happy to be with you whatever adventure you're on. And we all know about me. From where I'm sitting, the A30 and the A303 never looked better. As we skim past Dorset fields, the daylight's fading to dusk, by the time we're zooming along the M3 towards London all we're seeing is the white flash of headlights in the dark although those dimples of Bill's are so deep I can still see them in the shadows across the car.

And we've got a plan. There was no point paying for two rooms at a Premier Inn when we could stay at mine for free. Did anyone mention all my dreams, in the world, ever, coming true? It's good that I'm grounded by the whole friends label, because if it wasn't there, I'd have probably exploded already.

As James Blunt starts singing *You're Beautiful*, I let out a groan. A lot of these songs are my oldest faves, but the minute I imagine Ambie wiggling his hips to them, they change entirely. 'Oh my, if Ambie had sung this we'd have had to pass round the sicky buckets before he started. Can you imagine?'

Bill rubs the stubble on his chin and taps the steering wheel. 'Listening to the lyrics there, for a moment they sounded really fitting – you're not getting that?'

I'm staring at the slices down his cheeks in the darkness, then I get it. He does this to me every time and I never realise. 'You're joking me, aren't you?'

My steering wheel ... it's hard to believe we made such a big leap he's actually got his hands on it. And after all these hours driving, the car's going to smell of him so much, I won't be able to sell it. Probably not ever. Which might be really inconvenient eventually if this one breaks and I have to get another car because that'll mean I'll need a second parking space. And they're like gold dust where I live. I suppose I could always leave the car outside my parents' house, but my dad isn't that keen on me parking there when I'm visiting, and realistically how often would I get to smell it if it was in Yorkshire?

As Bill glances across at me, one eyebrow lifts. 'Why would I be joking?'

What a question. 'Of course you bloody are, you do it all the time.'

He's biting his lip. 'In that case it's a good thing the coach house is full of spare buckets then isn't it?' He laughs. 'So many romantic songs, it reminds me of that day I couldn't prise you away from the wedding shop window.'

I throw a gummy bear at him for that.

By the time we're pulling up in the car park outside my flat it's so long since our lunch back at the castle that my stomach's growling. But being hungry is great, because the desperate need to sort out food stops any awkwardness. Merwyn's rushing up the stairs, barking to let us know how delighted he is to be back, but for me it's like the marks on the car seat. Once I see the stairwell through Bill's eyes I'm dying, and it's the same in the flat but worse. As soon as I get over the worry of switching the heating on, and flicking the fairy lights on everywhere, after the big spaces at the castle it looks so much more minute than when I left it.

'Come in, this is my *totally teensy* living room.' As I do half a step and arrive in the middle of it I'm kicking myself for not doing better with the Christmas tree. To be honest, I reckon his wardrobe is bigger than my living room. 'The good part is when I paint the walls I can do the whole room without moving my feet.' I'm praying to my fairy godmother that he isn't noticing the scratches on the waxed floorboards, or how scratty and bashed up they are compared to his. Or how un-smart the stripy rug is and how unmatched the cushions are. For someone who should be super-stylish at home, I'm failing at every judgement. I'm also desperate for him to ignore the line of black and white photos of Fliss and me drinking one of every kind of cocktail in the world ever when we were at uni. And specially not to look at the little one of me the day I was Fliss's bridesmaid. Even though the dress she made me wear was my favourite ever, I'd just rather he didn't have an excuse to get back onto weddings.

'I like the dark blue.' Bill's nodding as he takes it all in. 'And the way the stars scatter up the wall and across the ceiling.'

I blow with relief. Of everything he could have landed on, my Farrow and Ball Hague blue estate emulsion walls and ceiling are the best. 'I was going to get sticky stars and take them off again. Then I thought, bugger it, why can't it be

Christmas all year round, so I painted them on instead. That was three years ago, and I'm still in love with them now.'

He smiles. 'I love how unfailingly festive and optimistic you are. And how the stars are tiny like the ones in the sky.'

I block out how much his teeth are killing me. 'But mostly you're laughing at the way I say bugger not bogger, like everyone else from London does.'

'I admit, it's an attractive trait.' His grin stretches and his eyes dance as he moves back to safer ground. 'Silver and rose gold for the stars too, they're like the Cockle Shell gin labels.'

'Are you ready to go and pick up that pizza we talked about? And let Merwyn have a walk on the way.' Poor Merwyn, he's going to miss tearing along the beach trying to catch the sea as it comes in, a park with grass is going to seem so dull after that.

Bill's still smiling. 'I thought you'd never ask about pizza. I was beginning to think you were going to wait until I fainted, then tie me up and take me prisoner and keep me here forever.'

I narrow my eyes. 'And would you be complaining?'

There's that spark again. 'Probably not.'

'So what happened to you, Mr Markham, you're suddenly very jokey?' Flirty would be a better word, but I'm not saying it.

He twitches his lips. 'I just walked away from my responsibilities for a day, it feels like playtime.'

Fuck. First my stomach leaves my body then it hits me, the trouble I could be in here. 'So definitely without pineapple then?'

He frowns as if he's puzzled. 'Is that code for a kink then ... like vanilla?'

'No, Bill, nothing so exciting.' When I look into his eyes they're dark brown with tiny yellow flecks. 'I'm talking about pizza toppings.'

He smashes his hand on his head. 'Oh crap. Country boy coming back to the city, I'm way out of my depth here. Maybe we better had go and get them then.'

Pizza, garlic bread and cheesy chips on the sofa, bottles of Peroni, *Love Actually* on DVD, then *Breakfast at Tiffany's*. Why ever did I think this was going to be hard? So long as I keep two cushions between us, however irresistible his thighs look with the jeans stretched tight over them, I'm pretty confident – so long as I sit on my hands I'm not going to grab him unexpectedly. Now I've got over the immediate emotional stress of him being here, I'm starting to enjoy it more. Soak it all in. Savour the tiny electric charges of excitement zithering up and down my spine. The whole unexpected, delicious indulgence of it all. What an amazing treat it is.

It's all going really, really well. And then I reach into my bag to get my sparkly cashmere jumper to put over my knees, and as I pull it out a big sprig of mistletoe flops out onto the coffee table with it.

'Shit, where the hell did that come from? I swear it wasn't me who put it in there.'

Bill smiles. 'I know, I got one too, it was Willow.' He stretches down and pulls a twist of stem and crushed leaves out of the front pocket of his jeans. 'She told me, a sprig on your person will make sure you get good luck, protection and fertility.'

Willow was going straight for the target there then with his front jeans pocket, but I'm not going to say that.

'How does it work if it's in your bag not your pocket?'

He seems to find that funny, because there are crinkles at the corners of his eyes. 'I'd guess it'll still do the job or she wouldn't have bothered to put it in there.' He gets up, grabs a handful from the table and heads for the door. 'Alternatively, you can hang it in doorways, like this.' He fiddles for a moment, picks a pin off the pinboard and then it's there. Dangling in the air. Tantalising and very dangerous. 'Still giving good luck, but also handy for when you're walking past.'

'Great, thanks for that.'

'Kissing underneath it is also good. You probably know that already though.' He raises an eyebrow, turns, and holds out his hand to me. 'Maybe you should come and try it out?'

'Totally not.' He's already pulled me to my feet. That's the trouble with tiny rooms, everything's so easy to reach. If we'd touched lips on the sofa it would probably still have counted.

'So what's the problem, Star-girl? There's stars on the ceiling and it's light enough for me to look at you.'

'Arrrgghhh ...'

He ignores my groan, and spins me round to face him. 'It's true, you are so like Audrey, but you're so much more beautiful because you're real and more kick-ass, and so much more special and unique because you're you.'

I'm dragging in that scent, his warmth, the smell of worn denim. Taking in the strength of his body, how wonderfully vital and alive and real *he* is. I let out another squawk. 'Hair!

Oh my, it's days since I washed it, because of the broken boiler.'

As he looks down at me his eyes go darker, and his finger lands on my lips. 'Shhh, Ivy-star ... we've got one night all on our own ... there's no need to panic ... let's just see where it takes us.'

I'm buying time. 'Do you mind the other people at the castle?'

He laughs. 'With Taffeta and Tulle lurking round every corner giving me side eye or trying to grill me about my taste in girlfriends and Libby glued to her phone sitting on my pillow there's not too much opportunity for privacy.'

I don't take any notice of Merwyn as he opens one eye on the rug and catches mine. But I have to protest because even without my spoiled face I'm not the kind of woman Bill would choose. He's completely out of my league. 'I really don't want to be your one night stand.'

Even as I say it, my finger has landed on the button of his shirt on his sternum. And I know I'm totally and utterly lying here. I wouldn't even ask for a whole night, I'd happily settle for half an hour. Five minutes even. My whole body is thrumming with anticipation. I've thought about how this would feel for so long. And now for some completely unknown stroke of luck, it's been handed to me. All I have to do is let myself accept, and go for it. Grab five minutes to last me the rest of my life.

'That's totally ridiculous, Ivy, why would you think that?'

'B-b-b-e-c-ause ...' There are so many reasons it's pointless even beginning.

My palms are on his chest now, and he's looking down on me. Gently brushing aside the hair that's hanging across my eye. Looping it back with his finger. He's looking, just looking. Swallowing. So close I can feel his breath on my cheek, see the pin pricks of the pores, each spike of stubble. Then he lowers his face towards my forehead, and I feel his lips featherlight on my skin. As they brush across the twists of thin scarred tissue I shiver.

'Are you okay with that?' His voice is very low as his fingers barely trace a line along my cut, and his eyes are amazingly tender and soft as he looks down. 'This is part of who you are, always remember, it's every bit as beautiful as the rest of you.'

And even if it isn't true, my insides are melting because he's thought to say the words at all – my heart is bursting with gratitude because he wants to reassure me. Then my hands are reaching up, sliding round the back of his head, I'm tugging my fingers through his hair. As I close my fingers on his scalp, his head is warm, I'm pulling his lips down towards mine, hearing the thud of his heart against his ribs.

The fairy lights on the tree blur as my eyes go out of focus, and as the room starts to spin, for the first time since the accident, the past is going hazy too. There's a fleeting moment when I think about the future enough to remember I don't have any condoms. Then I push that away too and all that matters is being here in this moment, his mouth colliding with mine. How amazingly hot and soft and sweet it is, how he tastes of starlight and chocolate. How fast the room is spinning. How very right it feels, how it's so amazing I want to climb inside him. And a long time later when my lips finally slide away from his as I clasp my hand to my mouth it feels like I've lost a part of myself.

'Not so bad then, Ivy-star?'

All I can manage is to moan for more. And as I press my hips hard against him, and I crash my mouth onto his all over again my whole body explodes.

Monday

23rd December

31.

This way to the North Pole

'I certainly won't miss the London traffic when we go back to Cornwall.'

It's Bill, and he's tapping his fingers on my steering wheel – again. Just saying. It's a novelty I could get used to.

I take a sip of my third coffee and laugh across at him. 'Ten minutes to get a hundred yards? It makes the three car queue at the roundabout by St Aidan station feel like nothing.'

It's one of those mornings after the night before, when there's so much to do you can't sit round talking about what happened, or even carry on doing it – you just have to leap out of bed and get on with the next thing. But as we inch our way along in a sea of cars on Hackney Road and watch the people on the pavements pulling up their collars to keep out the cold as they hurry to work, it almost feels like the last twelve hours didn't happen at all. I might just have dreamed them. Then Bill's hand comes across and squeezes mine, and as I look down at those beautiful knuckles and grin across at him I know I didn't.

When Bill woke me with coffee and toast at seven it felt as

if we'd only just gone to sleep. Let's just say, I finally found out what 'chemistry' is last night. For the record, we only made it to third base. Two healthy adults, a flat to themselves, and no protection – somehow rather than being a logistical disaster, it was nice to find out that no one was making assumptions.

The bathroom cabinet was stuffed with the things at one time, but they must have left with George. Not all things are transferrable though. You could hardly wear someone else's size nine wellies if your feet were a size ten. Not that I would compare, because what I had last night wasn't like anything I've ever had before. Amazing doesn't begin to cover it. As I sit here in my post-orgasmic daze I'm marvelling that I got so far into my thirties without knowing sex could be this good. Nothing I've experienced came even half way to getting close to this.

Bill's focused on the list of jobs because it ends with him getting to see Abby. 'So, we've ticked off the boiler part, the next stop is Rob's office on Islington Green. According to my phone we're closing in.'

'Brilliant, there's parking around the back.' If I'd been less busy cavorting under the mistletoe etc. I'd have been really worrying about this next bit. I've texted Rob and he's expecting me. But even though I didn't say why I was coming it's pretty obvious I'm not dropping round for a chat about beams, bending moments and structural loading or whatever engineers spend their time obsessing about. When we finally get there I take Bill in too with the excuse that he'll be cold in the car, but it's more because I'm cacking it. Also, when you're on delicate business trying to uncover your bestie's other half playing away you never know when an extra pair of eyes will come in handy. As we walk in and the girl on reception looks up Bill's right behind me murmuring.

'Nice green plastic pixie ears.'

He's not wrong there. There's a champagne glass and a bottle of Baileys on the desk in front of her, and as she smiles and takes a slug I'm wondering if it's her bed Bill's been sleeping in. As work is where he spends all his time, everyone female in the building is under suspicion here.

'We're here to see Rob.' As I take in how pretty she is and the sequins on her pointy fake shell-pink nails I can't help shuddering at the image of them raking down Rob's back. I make a mental note to look for scratches on his neck as well as love bites and Baileys stains on his shirt.

'Two floors up, you can't miss it, there's only him and Jane up there today.'

Bugger. 'Great.' Who said engineering was a man's game, there's a woman round every corner in here. I scrub everything in my head already, and take the stairs two at a time.

When Rob staggers across the office towards us as we walk in, with his bed hair, crumpled shirt and the dark circles under his eyes, he definitely looks knackered enough to have come straight into work after an all night shagging session. Although maybe I'm not in the best position to be sounding judgemental about that.

'Ivy, and I assume this must be Bill from the castle, so hi, Bill. How can I help?' Rob rumples his hair even more, just like he did on Facetime then he looks at me more closely and frowns. 'Jeez, you look rough, is everything okay?'

I raise an eyebrow. 'And I love you too, Rob.'

'Sorry, I just ...' As he does a whole lot more hair rubbing it strikes me how much he looks Oscar, just without the colander.

I sniff. 'Well, *we've* had a long journey.' That's my excuse out of the way. 'And what's *your* reason for looking like shite?'

He lets out a sigh. 'Working all the hours, unfortunately I can't share why right now.'

Nice try. 'I'm sorry, Rob, but I'm not going to stand back while you cheat on Fliss. Working weekends – as if engineers do that! Hanging round in London when you should be in Cornwall.' The calm voice I'd sworn I'd hold onto has already risen to a growl. 'Well, unluckily for you I saw those pillow-cases on Facetime that weren't yours, Rob. You've been found out, the game's up!' It's a complete yell now, because I'm *so* annoyed for Fliss, so gutted that he'll wreck all their lives for a bit of sordid sex. 'What have you got to say for yourself?'

'Oh jeez.' Rob's face crumples and he puts his hands over his head. 'You think I'm cheating on Fliss?'

The fact that he's not coming clean is making my angry yell flare to a roar. 'Don't play the innocent with me, Rob! Why else would you have your head on someone else's sodding pillow on a bleeding Sunday morning?'

He lets out a sigh. 'Because I was staying with a colleague round the corner to save making the trek home. So we could be back in at the crack to get this extra contract we've taken on – for Fliss's benefit – finished and out.'

My mouth's gone dry. I hadn't expected him to put up this much resistance. 'A *colleague*?'

'Yes – she's called Jane, and she's sitting over there.' Rob rolls his eyes and points at the woman across the room. 'She also happens to be gay.'

The woman looks up, gives a teensy four finger wave, points at her Pride mug full of pens and pencils, and goes back to working on her laptop again and pretending to be deaf.

'Oh fuck.' Even though I've got my hat on, I'm doing the head rubbing thing myself now. I take a huge breath to fully inflate my lungs because if I don't I might just crumple in a heap on the floor. 'So what the hell's going on?'

Rob lets out a long whistle. 'On the up side, I'm not shagging my way around Islington. But I'd rather not be the one to break it to you why I'm doing what I am. I'm afraid it's not the best news for you or Fliss.'

'Whatever it is, I'll find out soon.' If I was feeling deflated before, this flattens me. I edge my bum onto a spare swivel chair and lock my fingers around the seat edge. 'Go on, I'm sitting down, tell me ...'

Rob's nostrils flare. 'It's all confidential, the official emails aren't going out until after Christmas ... and I got it from someone at the squash club who found out by accident, so please don't pass this on ...'

I'm beside myself now. 'But *WHAT* ...?'

'*Daniels* are closing their doors at the beginning of January, straight after the Christmas sales. They've sold the site, and they aren't opening up anywhere else.'

OH FUCK!!! I mean to say the words, but nothing comes out because my insides have dematerialised. For a moment the room spins, then I think I'm going to be sick. Then that passes, and I start to shake. And what Milo said that day in the pub is suddenly making sense – it wasn't bollocks after all. Eventually I croak a whisper. 'So is *everyone* losing their jobs?'

Rob's expression is pained. 'I'm afraid they are.' From the way he's hugging himself and hanging onto his own arms he's as stressed about this as I am. 'They'll be paying redundancy, but with High Street retail in crisis and so many lay offs from other stores, no one's going to walk into a new job, especially not someone in Fliss's position.'

As a returning mum with baby brain she'll struggle to get herself to an interview, let alone answer the questions. I'm also thinking of how humungous the rent is for my flat, the payments on my car, the gas, the electricity, Merwyn's treats. I spend every penny I earn. But even my cupcake bill is huge if there's no money coming in.

I dig really deep and find a tiny voice. 'I'm sorry for misjudging you so badly, Rob. And sorry for you and Fliss too.'

He shrugs. 'No hard feelings at all. But this was me, trying to get my hands on all the cash I could for when we need it later. I was lucky, they offered me a rush contract and loads of overtime, so I grabbed it. I just wish there was a happier ending for you and Fliss.'

I nod. 'If it makes sense, I think Fliss will just be very happy you're not about to walk out on her.'

And to be honest, I am too.

What a day for epic revelations. Discovering why people have sex *and* finding out I'm not going to have a job in the

New Year, all in the space of twelve hours. One of the suppliers had sent in a hamper so Rob offers us coffee or brandy to bring me round. But once he's agreed to ring the landline to tell Fliss what's going on we accept a box of luxury mince pies instead, and hurry down past the receptionist who's still swigging her Baileys, but is now firmly off the suspect list.

So we sit in the front of the car and this time it's me tapping on the steering wheel. Then we hit the pastry and for one day only I give no shits at all about the crumbs getting ground into the carpet even though suddenly this car's got to last a whole lot longer than it might have done otherwise.

Bill folds his tin foil container into tiny squares. 'I'm really sorry. What a difference ten minutes makes, hey, Pom Pom.'

I bite into another pie, because the sticky filling and thick but deliciously light and buttery icing-sugar dusted pastry is definitely picking me up. 'Truly, I couldn't be any more gutted.' Mostly for now I'm relieved to know that Fliss and Rob are okay. I send Bill my best WTF? face. 'But if I let this spoil Christmas, I lose that as well as my job. So I'm going to go very Keef on you, and worry about the rest very soon. Just not now.'

He gives me a play punch on my arm. 'Here's wishing for lots of stars in the dark times then.'

And I punch him back. 'Okay, so ... on to the next destination ...'

He fiddles with his phone, sticks it onto the dashboard magnet, then blows. 'Two point six miles, fifteen minutes to Camden.'

I grin at him as I start up the engine and ease the car out

of the car park and towards the road. 'You have to admit, the traffic's bad round here but it's great to have wifi. And how are you feeling about your big moment?'

He pulls a face. 'Happy, but about as nervous as you were going to talk to Rob.'

'Shitting bricks then?'

He gives a nod. 'Times by ten, you'll be getting close.'

'You're going to be fine, I promise.' I reach over and touch his hand for a second.

'I hope so.'

'You've got your mistletoe for luck?'

'Totally.' He points to his pocket. 'After how it worked last night, I'm never going out without it. I sent Willow a "thank you" text when I was making breakfast.'

My jaw drops. 'Tell me you didn't?' Then I see his lips twist. 'You better not have done. What happens in London stays in London.' I'll let him off that one then. 'And you've got the little presents that Tansy and Tiff wrapped up for Abby? And the baby Sven, and the antlers on a hairband?' Once word got out at the castle, everyone wanted to send something.

'Yep.' He nods to a carrier in the footwell.

'In that case, put *Feliz Navidad* on repeat, and by the time we get there you'll be all good.' I grin across at him. 'I don't offer this to many people, but would it help to sing along?'

He manages to laugh. 'You always know how to make me feel better, do you know how much I appreciate that?'

When you're singing along, there's no point doing it by halves. It has to be top of your voice or nothing. So we yell our way across town, and by the time we reach the part where the houses are seriously nice I'm practically fluent in festive Spanish. We're winding our way between elegant Georgian terraces, and then we're turning into a street where the houses all have front gardens and Christmas trees flanking the entrances, and wreaths the size of car tyres on their front doors. And over the sound of the music the phone app tells me I've reached my destination.

'Anywhere along here would be good, thanks.' Bill lifts his eyebrows. 'It's okay, Ivy-star, you can say what you're thinking.'

I'm glad he said that, because I can't keep this one in. 'This is a seriously fabulous road.' I should have known, the guy has a castle on the beach for chrissakes. Even if it's a bit beaten up and he shares it with his dad, it should have been a clue. 'I understand why you and Gemma might be fighting now. Seriously loaded people always do.'

'It's not quite how it looks, I bought it as a wreck years ago when houses were cheaper and did it up on a shoestring. I made a lot in the city, but it came at a price, I was glad to get out.'

I can imagine. That would be the kind of diamond-studded shoestring the rest of us ordinary mortals can only dream of. If anything it's good to have a reminder. That's the second metaphorical ton of bricks to come cascading down on my head in half an hour. This man might be gifted in bed. But it's not just about him being so much prettier than me, he also belongs to another world. A world where people wrangle over beautiful four storey town houses, with pale pastel stucco walls and basements and authentic small paned sash windows and really wide pavements and front gardens big enough to park their cars in.

My whole rented flat would fit into their boot porch with room to spare. This is the lifestyle George aspired to, which is how I collided with Will in the first place. But George was a pretender, he actually had nothing and was happy to live off me until something better came along. But Bill is the real deal. And that's galaxies away from me. Gemma's mum's called Arabella for chrissakes, mine's called Pauline. Standing on a beach, snuggling under the duvet, it's easy to forget the differences. But when you see them laid out here, they're huge. But at least I've had my night. No one can take that away from me, that star will shine forever.

Bill picks his phone off the dashboard, taps out a message, and slips it into his pocket. He's very pale under his stubble, and as I catch the tension shadows under his cheekbones my heart goes out to him.

He's waiting, quietly breathing, looking further along the street. And then he suddenly sits up straight. 'She's here!' He's biting his lip, scraping a tear away from the corner of his eye, then he leans over and kisses my cheek. 'Thank you for this, Ivy-star, I owe you ...'

It was only a brush, but I'm melting inside all over again at the touch of his lips. But mostly I'm pushing him out of the car. 'I'll pick you up back here around two. Go, on, go! Go! Go! Go!'

And then he's walking away from me down the street, and I'm watching his broad shoulders, his soft jeans and his scuffed Timberland boots, his arms stretching outwards. And there's a small girl walking along the pavement towards him, who looks so much like he does with her brown curls and her long legs. And as she sees him she starts to run, and she's hurtling along towards him, shouting. And then he scoops her up, closes his arms around her, and spins.

And as he puts his forehead down to meet hers, there are tears running down my face, and I'm swallowing down my saliva and sniffing away my snot, and I'm murmuring, '... and give her a hug from me ...'

32.

The strongest blizzards start with a single snowflake …

I'd planned to wander around Camden Lock while Bill was with Abby, pick up a few extra goodies, maybe another Christmas jumper or two, have something delicious for lunch. But after Rob's bombshell I head home for a packet of crisps and a nap instead. Then I whizz Merwyn round the park, throw the bags into the car, and by two we're back on Bill's road in Camden all ready to pick him up and head back to Cornwall.

Seriously, pet fashion statements in this area are second to none. While we wait Merwyn and I are passing the time scoring the outfits of the pampered pooches that walk past. We're both picking our jaws up off the floor at a Scottie in a full kilt, then there's a Frenchie with a shimmery pink and turquoise outfit and a unicorn horn. We're so busy exclaiming about the Chihuahua dressed as a Christmas tree, complete with baubles and chaser lights, that the first we notice of anyone outside the car is the sharp rap on the window.

By the time I turn on the ignition and begin to wind down

the window the person in the white ski jacket has her nose on the glass. Then she stands up so she can swish her long blonde hair without hitting her head on the car and knocking herself out and I get to take in a horribly flat stomach, the skinniest, perfectly toned thighs, super-expensive studded ankle boots and the kind of heels that are understated but at the same time take proper effort to walk in. It's when I get the blast of Miss Dior in my face that I finally realise.

'Gemma!' The smell's distinctive and sophisticated, and for a minute I'm right back there by the fridge in the chalet kitchen in Chamonix, arguing about missing profiteroles. 'Great to see you again.'

As I pull my hair across my eye I'm kicking myself for getting caught with my bad side facing her, but breathing a sigh of relief that I took the time to use Tiff's special kit earlier. It's no surprise that Gemma's make up is flawless, but I can tell her skin underneath is too. And when I see how many layers of barely-there lippy she's wearing I'm wishing I'd paid more attention to mine. Like me putting on any would have made me feel slightly less of a loser. Slightly better equipped to deal with her. I know she never had the sweetest expression back then, but even for someone who was big on sour faces, the glare she's giving me now is searing.

'You're sleeping with him, aren't you?' That's all she says, and her voice is low and menacing.

As every bit of breath leaves my body I don't have a hope in hell of getting any words out as I consider – one accidental night, with very little sleep at all, and we didn't actually – ahem. On balance I'm thinking once I can talk again the correct and truthful answer to that exact question with it's ongoing implications would be 'no'.

Her perfectly shaded eyebrows are a jagged line across her forehead. 'Don't bother to answer that, it's written all over your face.' She's spitting the words. 'Before you go helping yourself to what's not yours, you might like to consider his family.'

She turns and as she goes clicking off down the pavement I still haven't managed a word. Then further along the street Bill and Abby come into view walking hand in hand, and as she jumps from one pavement stone to the next they're both laughing. Then Gemma meets them too, and for a moment I watch as they stand in a huddle on the pavement. Then my phone rings and it's Bill.

As he speaks he's waving at me from along the road. 'I'll just say goodbye to Abby and I'll be with you.' And then they all go through the gate and disappear through the front door, and Merwyn and I are back to dog outfits.

Bill doesn't keep us long. Two identical Daxis in mediocre Santa suits and a Cockerpoo in a snowman suit several sizes too small. Someone should tell him, as a look, it's not flattering. There's just enough time for me to swap across to the passenger seat, and Bill's opening the door and swinging into the driver's seat and pushing his coat into the back. And when his scent wipes out every last bit of the Miss Dior it's a big relief.

'How did it go?' I don't really have to ask, the depth of his dimples and relaxed satisfaction on his face as he looks down at his phone and programmes the navigation app are the giveaway.

'Good.' He raises his eyebrows and squeezes my hand. 'It was so amazing to see her, we got her a phone so we can talk. I can't tell you how happy I am, I'm so grateful to you for the push ... or the monumental shove, more like.'

I smile at him. 'Any time, it's all in a day's work for your favourite fairy godmother.'

He wrinkles his face. 'Bittersweet too, it was very hard to say goodbye again.'

I'm getting that from the depth of his sigh.

As he comes to the end of the road and pulls out into the traffic he frowns. 'Gemma said she had a word, was she okay?'

I'm making my smile really bright. 'Fine.' If I give him the gory details no one will come out of it looking great. I lean forward and flick on the radio, then bundle my jacket under my head. 'I thought maybe I'd have a snooze if that's okay.'

'Great, I'm taking a slightly different route back, I'll wake you in a bit.' He flashes me a smile. 'I'll wait until you're awake again before I sing along.'

I'd actually only meant to close my eyes and pretend to sleep. But as I wake up to Bill shaking my shoulder, the last thing I remember is Maria Carey singing *All I Want For Christmas is You*, and we hadn't even got on the motorway.

'So where are we?' From the village green and a pub, some pretty cottages and houses we're in the countryside.

He sniffs. 'You've done so much to help me, I wanted to help you too. We're not far from whcre you had the crash.'

My stomach contracts. 'How did you know where it was?'

'It wasn't hard, I knew the approximate date, Google did the rest.' His hand is on my knee and his eyes are dark and full of concern. 'I hoped that if you came back it might help you move on, begin to do things for yourself again instead of only for other people.' He reaches for a carrier from the back of the car. 'I bought this for you too, in case you wanted something to leave.'

I dip my hand into the bag and pull out a small circle of twigs. 'That's so pretty, with the ivy and white berries.'

He nods. 'The twigs are vine stems, I asked them to weave some extra ivy and mistletoe in – Willow was telling me, it's meant to be very healing, so it felt right.'

'Thanks, it's beautiful.' I smile at him. 'It's a whole lot smaller than the door wreathes on your road in Camden.'

He laughs. 'Everyone tries to out-bling the neighbours. If you think the wreaths are bad, you should see their designer dog clothes.'

I glance at Merwyn who lifts one ear up when he hears the 'd' word. 'We already did – we were shocked and delighted in equal measure.'

'So how about this wreath – are you up for dropping it off? It's only a couple of hundred yards down the lane there.'

If he'd asked me before I might have hated the idea. But now we're here, and I've got the vine circle in my hand, it doesn't feel hard, it just feels right. And as it hits me how close I am to where the crash was my eyes are full of tears, and I'm swallowing, but it's more about how kind and thoughtful he's being than about any of the rest. And I'm nodding before I realise I'm doing it.

Bill's completely right. It's barely any distance away. And then we're out on the verge, by a hedge full of holly, the wind whipping across our faces and blowing so hard Merwyn's ears are flattened. And the most there is to show of the crash is a splintered fence post in amongst the tangled stems of the hedge.

'So this is the tree?' I let out a breath and look down at a bunch of white roses in cellophane propped by the base of the trunk. 'It's so strange, just one random tree on a roadside, one moment in time. Michael and I will always be always bound together by that second, but I'm here, and he isn't.' I'm swallowing down my tears, but it's not working. 'Him dying always felt so random. I mean, why him and not me?'

Bill shrugs. 'There's never a reason, it's just how things happen.'

'If only we hadn't set off, if only I'd thought ...' It's what I always think.

'But it changed you. If you'd been as you are now, it wouldn't have happened. That has to be some comfort?' He's holding onto my fingers, and he squeezes my hand tightly. 'But you're the one who came out of it, you owe it to him to live life for both of you – no holding back.' He's fumbling in another bag and reaching up the trunk. 'I brought a hammer and a nail, tell me where you think.'

I'm laughing and crying at the same time. 'For a guy who worked in the city you're very practical.'

He laughs too. 'Years of battling with an unruly castle, I have to be.'

'That's perfect.' He taps in the nail, then I reach up and hang up the wreath.

'There's a label in there too, in case you'd like to write anything.' He passes me a pen, and a piece of card.

So squatting by the roadside, on a blustery day before Christmas, in the fading light of a December afternoon I write my goodbye note to someone I barely knew but will never forget.

Michael,

I will always look for you when the stars shine, and I promise to live life for both of us,

all my love, Ivy xx.

Bill smiles at me as he reads it, then I tie the string to the circle with fumbling fingers. And as I step back, Bill passes me a tissue and I blow my nose. Then his arm slides around me, and as I lean into him all I can feel is his warmth and strength and his goodness.

'I'd like to come back every year and do this.'

'That's a good idea, we'll make sure we do.' He pulls me closer and squeezes away my shiver. 'There's a tea shop in the village, let's warm up with a hot chocolate before we set off again.'

And just for a moment, there's a sureness and a certainty in his voice that's nothing to do with arrogance. It's simply a deep and calm reassurance. And the thought that he'll still be here to come with me again next year is like a blanket being wrapped around me. As we get back into the car, it does feel like a new beginning. But it's not about what I'm leaving behind, it's more that there's someone who wants to be here for me. To support me. And it's as if by being here, he's passing on his strength, making me stronger. It's not anything spoken, it's just a feeling deep inside. Whatever doubts I was having, I *know* I can rely on him, just as he can rely on me.

It's not anything we mention or talk about, it's like an unspoken understanding. As we sit by the teashop fire and munch on deep slices of sticky ginger cake and drink our hot chocolate we're quiet. Together, but reflecting. It's been a day of big emotions, sometimes it's better *not* to talk.

By the time we set off again it's dark, and the lights on the Christmas trees in the cottage windows around the village are shining out into the night, and the festive CD is playing quietly in the darkness, breaking the journey into tune sized fragments.

Bill's musing in the dark. 'Not long to Christmas now, Pom Pom.'

As I count on my fingers I let out a heartfelt sigh for how few days there are left. 'That's the trouble with holidays, you look forward to them forever, then they're over so fast.'

He clears his throat, and I watch the shadow of his Adams apple as he swallows. 'So do you ever think about Chamonix?'

There's no hope of answering that one and keeping my dignity intact so I send this back to him: 'It was a really significant holiday for you, wasn't that where you got to know Gemma properly?'

There's a few beats of silence. 'I've been meaning to tell you what happened with Gemma.'

'Really?' I can't imagine why.

'When she went back to London last January it was with the marketing manager who'd been working on the gin account.'

I raise my eyebrows. 'So that explains your patchy promotion.'

He shakes his head. 'I didn't get around to replacing him. He and Gemma didn't make a go of it though, they aren't together any more.'

'Right.' I'm sounding doubtful because I still don't know why he's telling me this.

'I want to be honest and open going forward, some background might help put things into context.'

'Great.' He's sounding so much like Libby now I might have been better to go with Chamonix. 'Shall we put the volume up now and sing along to the Christmas tunes? Get in the mood.'

'What, to *Christmas Wrapping* by the Waitresses?' His voice is high with disbelief. 'Good luck with that, of all the songs to choose that one's impossible to join in with.'

I sigh. 'Okay, fine, we'll sing as soon as the next one comes on.'

He glances across at me. 'If we're going to see more of each other I don't want to hide anything, that's all.'

It comes out as a choke as I catch my breath. 'More ...?'

He's glancing across at me. 'That's what I was hoping, so long as you'd like that too?'

I'm opening and closing my mouth and nothing's coming out. The Waitresses are singing about their happy ending, and I'm not quite ready to believe that mine is happening too. And as I'm deciding whether to say, fine shall we get married this week or next, or thinking if I should ask if this is just another wind up, his phone beeps.

He sounds excited. 'Can you check that and read it out for me, it could be from Abby.'

I pick up his phone and look. 'It's from Gemma.'

'So what does she say?'

'She says, *Great to see you earlier, Abby's so excited you'll be coming to live with us again. Why wait til January, why not come with us to Davos for Christmas?*'

'What?' He frowns across at me. 'Are you *sure*?'

Considering my chest just imploded, I'm doing well to reply. 'I'd hardly have made that up, would I?'

'Oh crap.' He lets out a long breath and hits his head. 'I'm so sorry, Ivy.'

I'm muttering under my breath. 'Not half as sorry as I am.'

He's tapping the steering wheel, shaking his head. 'You shouldn't be caught in the middle of this, it's not fair.'

Except that's the whole thing, no one's actually caught anywhere. He's been generous enough to try to help me past the accident, but that's obviously as a friend. We had one amazing night together. For me that night happened to be the best few hours of my life so far. But as I realised earlier, we come from very different places. For him it probably only served to confirm everything better he's been missing. We all know, it's the first rule of choosing guys to see – anyone who's fresh out of a relationship is likely to boomerang right back into it given half a chance.

Bill has just seen the partner and child he's been pining for for an entire year – if Gemma's asking him back, why wouldn't he want to give it another go?

As he stares across at me in the darkness his voice is so strained I sense he's gone pale. 'There are things I should explain ...'

'I'd actually rather you didn't.' This way at least I get to keep my pride. If we skip the excuses about why I'm second best, I can walk away with my head held high, wishing him well.

He's blowing out his lips. 'I've got a lot of sorting out to do here.'

He's not joking there. But if he's got another chance of being a full time dad to that amazing little girl, he has to take it.

As for me, I'm back to pretty much where I was this time yesterday. Obviously there's the added irritation of being without a job. But there's absolutely zero reason to feel like my whole world has folded to nothing. I went to the top of the emotional roller coaster. And then to the bottom again. All in the course of a few hours. Now I've got off altogether. More fool me for letting my delusions get the better of me.

So all I can think to myself is – *Let's get on with Christmas. Yay!*

But admittedly, the Yay! is very feeble. And somehow I can't bring myself to say anything else, and neither can Bill. And we sit in silence the whole way back to Cornwall.

Tuesday

24th December

33.

With love …

When I wake up next morning the first thing I hear is Merwyn huffing and as I get out of bed to go to the bathroom the temperature in the bedroom feels positively tropical. The heating engineer was waiting as we arrived back at the castle last night and he had the boiler working again within the hour, so when bedtime came everyone was okay to take their duvets and go off to sleep upstairs again. So when Merwyn and I come in from our not-so-early morning walk on the beach everyone in the kitchen has shed their extra jumpers, and Milo is by the Aga cooking his crusty golden triangular griddle scones with only a T-shirt under his stripy apron. I have to say, just as we were leaving for the beach, Bill knocked on the bedroom door, but I couldn't talk. And luckily when I get to the kitchen he isn't there.

I make a large pot of coffee, pick up a loaded plate and an extra wide smile from Milo and go to join Fliss and the little ones at the table. I may be shouting on the beach where the wind can whoosh my howls out to join the white streaks of sea horses on the expanse of the diesel blue sea, but in public

I'm determined not to let anyone see I'm anything other than fabulous.

However much I'm aching inside after yesterday, I can't help smile at Harriet leaning back and rubbing her tummy in her high chair. 'Someone's enjoying their syrup.' Her cheeks are slicked with the shine of grease and she's got a chunk of scone stuck to her ear. The clang of fish slice on colander tells me Oscar is in his usual place under the table, but the rest of the chairs are empty. 'So where is everyone?'

Fliss's reaction to yesterday's news from Rob was much the same as mine. The immediate relief that he wasn't about to desert her eclipsed the awful, but more distant, news about *Daniels* and our disappearing jobs. When she grinned at me and said 'Phew, don't need to wash my hair after all then', I took it as a joke, but from this morning's haystack where her messy ponytail should be, she was telling it like it is. As she thinks about my question she's rearranging her hair pins.

'So many changes since you left.' Then she grins at me. 'The wifi secret's out, everyone's in Bill's room watching YouTube clips.'

'After all our efforts! Who told?'

She peers under the table. 'Oscar was chanting about Facetiming, Tom and Tarkie heard, grilled him and that was it.'

I'm even more puzzled. 'But Libby had promised them a day at the ski slope today, surely they should have left by now.'

'Keep up.' Fliss laughs. 'They're in there with Rip, Brian,

Bede, Taj and Slater watching big wave clips. Who wants fake skiing when winter waves are on offer. They're all picking up wet suits and going in later.'

'Oh my. Rather them than me. So what else have I missed?'

Fliss's smile stretches. 'With everyone in the family room the barriers tumbled. Tiff and Tansy abandoned their tulle and swapped into Scout's spare dungarees.'

'You're joking. I bet Willow loved that?'

'She wasn't so keen on the red lippy. But Tiff insisted they needed that to maximise their girl power.'

'What a great couple of days.'

'That's not all.' Fliss's eyes are dancing. 'When Solomon, Scout and Sailor's dad arrived for Christmas, he took them into the tower room and his treat was that they all did calculus.'

'What?!!' I can't conceal my horror. 'Jeez, I'm pleased I missed that.'

Fliss is on a roll. 'And Libby did a deal with Taj and the guys. They get to stay for the whole of Christmas so long as they help with cooking and clearing and put on their pixie hats and elf waistcoats whenever she does a photocall. They're proving very popular on Instagram, she's got this ongoing story thing going.'

I'm not sure if that's progress or not. I look up as Milo comes with another plate of scones. 'Delicious baking, Milo, as usual.'

He pulls up a chair. 'We missed you, Ivy, but on the upside it was bliss to have the run of the kitchen.'

I take it he's meaning without Bill's interference. 'It's good to see you looking happier.'

He dips his head towards Fliss and I, but as his voice drops to a confidential whisper I'm the one he ends up touching fringes with. 'There's very little I can do about Dad and Miranda.' He smiles and wiggles his eyebrows at me. 'But if the castle is such a romantic venue, maybe it's *my* time after all?'

Fliss leans over and gives him a punch on the arm. 'Yay, good to hear, knock yourself out, Milo.' Instead of reacting to my sharp kick on her shin she laughs. 'Sorry, as of yesterday morning, I'm definitely off the market again. But I can't speak for anyone else – just saying.' Considering I went all the way to London to sort out her husband, her wink is *so* not funny. Obviously I haven't shared any of what happened at mine.

I'm opening my mouth to clarify this once and for all with my own jokey climb down when I look up and see Bill in the doorway, with a scowl like thunder.

'Hey, welcome back, Mr Happy.' Milo sends him a dead eye, so that has to be ironic.

Fliss's eyes narrow, then she grins again. 'Anyway, for anyone not surfing today why don't we *mix things up* with a *baking competition*?'

It's so fab to hear her so upbeat but I still let out a groan. 'That pun was awful.'

Milo doesn't care, he's already up and punching the air. 'Absolutely. A Cockle Shell Castle Christmas Bake Off ...' he's sending Bill a mocking stare '... let's finally sort the professionals from the pretenders.'

Fliss is in her element here. 'Okay, anyone can enter, it can be any kind of cake or sweet biscuit. Everyone gets a vote, the one with the most votes wins.' She sends me a knowing wink. 'And teams can enter.'

'That's a good idea. We'll be the Gilmore Girls, like the TV show.'

Milo's joining in glaring at Bill, his chin jutting. 'No outsourcing allowed. Cakes must be *ALL YOUR OWN WORK*.'

Fliss is laughing. 'Nipping out to Crusty Cobs and The Little Cornish Kitchen isn't allowed.'

'Entries on the dining tables, judging starts at half past two.' As I add my piece my mouth is already watering. 'And the judges get to taste!'

Bill's still filling the doorway, head tilted, eyes narrowed. 'And may the best man win, Milo.'

I ignore what the low notes in his voice just did to my insides, hold up my finger and cough. 'May the best *person* win – I think that's what you mean, Bill.' I mean to avoid speaking to him, but it had to be said, in the interests of getting equality in a generation. And who knows, once Fliss and I get our butter cream icing heads on, we could be serious contenders here. I rub my hands together. 'So what are we waiting for, let's get started before the rush!'

We have to stay real here – neither of us is Cherish Finden. Even if I have Nigella's curves and the temporary use of a pantry I'm seriously lacking her pizazz in the kitchen. On balance we decide the *Frozen* cake with five tiers and pale turquoise icing we fall in love with on Google Images is too ambitious. But delish is achievable, so long as we keep it simple and Oscar doesn't drop too many foreign bodies into the mixing bowl. So in the end we plump for a simple sticky dark chocolate sponge with snowy swirls of vanilla buttercream and glittery snowflake sprinklies.

As baking goes this one's not hard. It's my mum's foolproof recipe, even I'd find it hard to mess up. Bish bash bosh and it's done. Milo's still agonising over what to cook, and our sponges are in the oven. With Oscar quiet under the table licking mixture off a wooden spoon and Harriet busy rubbing Nutella into her hair, Fliss and I lick the bowl out ourselves then get straight on with the icing. Giving the bowl to the kids? Truly, being an adult has many downsides, getting to keep the bowl to lick yourself is one of the only good bits.

So we move on to the buttercream and we've covered the table in a snowy cloud of powdery icing sugar and we're just getting the perfect consistency for piped rosettes, when Miranda appears. She pops a cigarette butt into her tobacco tin, slips off her shimmery coat and flops down at the table next to us.

Fliss takes in her long sigh and gives her a questioning stare. 'Not in the hot tub this morning, Mum?'

Miranda shakes out the layers of her chiffon top and sniffs. 'Ambie's sulking, we've had *another* tiff.' She drags in a breath. 'Yesterday he was arguing over which side of the bed to get out of, this morning it's my top he hates.'

I give her arm a squeeze. 'I can see that Ambie might find the print unconventional, but it really suits you, the silk is so light it's almost not there.'

As Miranda gives a snort her feathery top flutters. 'Roses, chains and barbed wire, the pattern says it all. Ambie seems to think now we're engaged he's got the right to fence me in, tie me down, and tell me what to think.' Her eyes flash.

I'm worried. 'I'm not judging, or interfering, but that doesn't sound too healthy.' I love Miranda, she should have so much more. When she has the capacity to be really happy, anything less is a waste.

The flames go out of Miranda's eyes and she gives a resigned sigh. 'Relationships are about give and take.'

Fliss's face wrinkles. 'But do you want to be fenced in?'

Miranda winces and dips in for another spoonful of icing. 'It's not as if there are lines of men all shaking engagement rings at me.'

I have to be realistic. 'On the other hand, looking at the signs, it could be a quick ride back to the divorce court.'

Fliss blows out a sigh of exasperation. 'But why are you so obsessed with husbands?'

Miranda sucks the icing off the spoon. 'It was such a shock when we lost your dad, Fliss. All those years with you four children, you've no idea what a struggle it was on my own with all that responsibility. There were so many nights when I'd lie awake desperately wishing your dad could be there to take care of me.'

I'm squeezing her hand really hard, and Fliss groans at her. 'Oh, Mum.'

Miranda dips in her leggings waistband for a hanky and dabs the corners of her eyes. 'Once you'd all left home all I wanted was to be secure and to be married again. But I messed that up three times now, I'm ten years older than I was when I started. If I've got one last chance, I have to take it.'

My heart goes out to her. 'You've been toughing it out on your own for so long, it's bound to have made you strong and independent. When you've been used to making all your own decisions, it's hard to change, especially when someone's asking you to be like someone else, not yourself.'

Miranda lets out a little sigh. 'It's true, I often feel that Ambie wants me to be Betty.' She slurps down another spoonful of icing then frowns at the spoon. 'If I'm trying to be thin eating all this icing isn't good.'

It's hard to watch her trying to be something she's not. 'Maybe you need to stop looking for marriage – it's the marrying types who always want to change you, and you never like that. You don't have to be on your own, maybe a relationship with less ties would suit you better?'

Fliss is waving both thumbs at me. 'If you're willing take a chance on a man who's not truly happy with who you are, surely you're brave enough to try something different?'

Miranda doesn't look convinced. 'It's the ring that I *like* – that's what makes me feel safe.'

I'm laughing. 'Don't forget the wedding dress too, we all love a fabulous dress. And a blingy wedding.'

Fliss is nodding at her. 'Far from being the answer, it could be the ring that's the start of your problems. Maybe you'll only be happy when you ditch the idea of getting hitched.'

I smile at her. 'Of everyone here Miranda, I'd say you're the one who knows your own mind. You're in an excellent position to make your choice – but only you know what that should be.'

'I've got to shine like a diamond.' Her voice has gone very small now.

I'm nodding. 'Sure, but you need a partner who thinks you shine just as you are. You shouldn't have to be polished before they appreciate you.'

Fliss grunts. 'If you were a diamond I suspect Ambie wouldn't be happy until he'd had you re-cut.'

I wince at Fliss. 'That's harsh.'

Fliss pulls a face. 'Harsh but true.'

Miranda's next spoonful is smaller, and she savours rather than gulps it. 'You've given me a lot to think about there girls – thank you for being so honest and open.'

As my phone beeps and I get up and cross to the Aga I'm hoping we have. 'Our cakes are ready.' It's not lost on me, I'm hardly the best person to be dishing the relationship advice. I slide my hands into the oven gloves, pull out the cake tins, and as I test the sponge with my finger it's firm and springy. I wait a couple of minutes, then turn them out onto a wire cooling rack. 'This smells so chocolatey, we have to be in with a chance of being the Bake Off champions. As soon as these are cool, we'll get the icing on.'

Miranda coughs. 'Does this mean I'm on your team?'

I'm grinning as I bring the cakes across. 'We can always use another Gilmore Girl, Miranda.' I catch Oscar staring up at me from the gap between the table and the chair. 'We're actually the Gilmore People. So for your first job, Miranda, pass the icing.'

She's peering into an empty bowl. 'Er – we may need to make some more of that.'

It may have taken most of the batch of buttercream, but if it's made her see things more clearly, it's a small price to pay.

34.

Sledges at dawn ...

Christmas Eve has to be one of my all time favourite times of the year. It's the twinkliest sparkliest day when months of anticipation build to the biggest excitement storm ever, and I, for one, will be rocking it.

Except for when I close my eyes, because whenever I do there's this clip on repeat in my brain. First I see Abby running into Bill's arms. Then their beautiful little family huddled on the pavement. Then they all disappear into their lovely house and the front door shuts.

Deep in my heart I've always known that Bill was only ever on offer in my head, and I completely understand the only right place for him is together with Abby and Gemma. I also know I'll completely come to terms with it, given time. But right now it doesn't stop the aching hole in my chest. And every time the front door of their home slams in my head, it hurts all over again. Which is why it's lovely to have Merwyn. There's something very comforting about that worried sideways look he gives me. I can tell he cares and he's completely happy for me to bury my face in his fur and fair isle jumper for as long as it takes for me to feel better.

But luckily for Merwyn and his tear-dampened knitwear there's not too much time for snivelling because there's still so much to get ready for tomorrow. After we've spread the word about the Bake Off we leave Willow pondering over recipe books on the kitchen sofa.

Then I get to open the florist's boxes which arrive, gasp at how beautiful the orange and pink roses are, and cut the stems to length. Then with a jug in hand, one by one I put them in water in the numerous gin bottles around the family room. By the time I'm finished I've used gallons of water and the alternating colours really pop as the roses line up down the centre of the tables and along all the window sills.

Then I nip upstairs to catch up on the last of my present wrapping and wrap a stack of empty delivery boxes in pink and orange paper as a piece of final scene setting. I tie them up with pink and orange ribbons and big bows and pile them on the sledges under the downstairs Christmas trees and take ages getting them to look just right for the photos. I'm expecting to have to fight my way through the crowds to reach Bill's room to grab some wifi to upload them, but when I get there the big-wave crowd has gone. I know I was cynical when we first arrived, but when I watch the rush of 'likes' that come in as soon as the latest parcels-under-the-tree pictures come up on Libby's Instagram account I'm thinking how much I'll miss this in a couple of days' time when I don't have to do it any more.

As I go back through the kitchen Milo has taken over the

whole central island unit is cooking up a storm. I laugh at him. 'Hey Milo, how's it going?' If an entire sack of flour had exploded the mess wouldn't be any more huge. 'You haven't left much space for poor Willow.' She and her other half have bagged a tiny spot by the toaster.

Milo's voice is high and unusually strangled. 'Ivy, I'm working on a show stopper with five different elements here, I can't be limited by space restrictions.'

Libby's at the kettle smiling one of those indulgent smiles she only ever brings out for Milo. 'No need to stress, Petal, it's going to be amazing, you've got my vote already.' Which totally undermines the competition for the rest of us when she hasn't even had a taste, but whatever.

As I catch Willow's eye I note that she's not jumping in to help, offering her usual homeopathic stress busters. 'Is this the Edmunson Team corner?'

She laughs. 'Absolutely not, it's every person for themselves over here. Mine's vegan lemon and elderflower with chia spice and Nigel's doing a gluten-free Mexican carrot cake and he might try some boozy truffles too.'

Nigel pushes his on-trend specs back up his nose. 'Then I'll do some marshmallow snowmen cupcakes with the children later.'

I'm having a sea glass moment here. 'But don't marshmallows have animals in them? And what's with the snow*men*, surely it should be snow people?'

He grins. 'No need to panic, Ivy, the Dandies' marshmallows are all good. And obviously we'll have equal numbers of snow women too.'

I'm smiling back. 'Great, I'm glad to hear it, in that case I'll head off to the beach with Fliss and catch you later.' I turn to Libby. 'Are you coming too?'

She's perched on a bar stool now, looking totally teensy beside Milo, and if I didn't know better I'd say she was positioned to take maximum advantage of the tanned and honed forearms at work here.

She wrinkles her nose. 'You know what, I think I'll take a second to relax ... come along in a bit.'

I'm picking my jaw up off the floor because when does she ever not rush? Chilling is not in her remit. 'What about all the fabulous surfers in Santa hats waiting to have their pictures taken?' Three of them are her kids, after all.

She cocks an eyebrow at me. 'Can you handle those? Just this once ...'

Nigel wiggles his eyebrows at me. 'No need for Libby to get cold, I'll come down and help as soon as my cake's cooked.'

Seriously, I have no idea what the frantic eyebrow action is about. If Libby's happy to miss the once in a lifetime opportunity to watch her kids having a Christmas dip in some Cornish sea, that's up to her.

As we walk down onto the sand a few minutes later, Fliss has Harriet in a sling carrier, I've got Oscar by the hand, Merwyn's running up and down the sand alongside me and I'm soaking up the way the sunstreaks on the water are breaking up into a thousand silvery fragments as the wind blows.

Fliss turns to me, her hair blowing across her face. 'You're looking very thoughtful today?'

I wrinkle my nose. 'When we go home I'm really going to miss just walking out of the door and being on the beach, that's all.' I dip down and pick up a cockle shell, and then another, then another – simply because I can. When I'm back in my tiny flat if they're there on the coffee table they'll help me believe these two weeks actually happened and I didn't just imagine them.

She gives me a harder stare. 'Are you sure it's not more than that?'

I'm fighting the sea glass, because I'd love to share. And I will, once we get back and everything's safely in the past again. 'I'm good.'

'Well, Aunty Fliss is here if you need to talk.'

I pat her arm. 'Thanks, I'll definitely take you up on that one day soon. Just not now.'

I pull Oscar's hood up, and turn my collar up against the wind, and we make our way along to where Keef, Taj and the gang have swapped their elf clothes for wetsuits and are messing around in the shallows with the rest of the kids and some body boards. Even I know the waves aren't anything like big enough for surfing, but there's enough screaming and splashing going on to make up for that.

'Okay, who's up for some Christmas at Bondi beach shots?'

By the time I've taken every variation of poses and boards in and out of the water, it's a long time later and Fliss and the littlies are long gone. I should have known from the skating that Sailor, Scout and Solomon would have some tricks up their home-school jumper sleeves. It turns out they're acrobatic enough to be in the Cirque du Soleil, so we end up with some fabulous shots of surfie towers and flick flacks into the sea, as well as all the rest. When Libby finally tears herself away from the Aga and comes down she's happy to use the human tower shot, because her kids are the important bottom layer. As she said, the high flyers couldn't show off without the people in the base. And then she hurries off again, with the excuse of getting the pictures uploaded. But spot the deliberate mistake – she left without taking the phone with the photos on.

There's another nice surprise when we get back to the castle – Rob has arrived early, and he's just putting the finishing touches to the cake that he just speed baked. Between us, you have to love a guy who can build bridges, drive three hundred plus miles and dash off his signature Squishy Black Forest Gateau before he even stops for tea. But that's Rob for you. Which was why it was so weird when we thought he was going off the rails.

So we leave Milo in the kitchen spinning sugar – really! – with Libby watching him wide eyed. First observation – truly, if we'd only known, the rest of us needn't have wasted our time. And second – when did Libby ever take this much interest in cooking? Just saying. Then Fliss and I tuck up in the family room with Rob and the kids and watch *The Holiday*, apparently for the third time since Saturday. Some films are like that, however many times you watch them you can always watch them again. And as we sit there the entries for the competition are arriving on the dining tables one by one.

As we go through to get our Gilmore People's cake we get held up by a nappy change which we pop up to my room for because it's closer. So we're only back at the table with five minutes to go to the deadline, by which time everyone's gathered in the dining area standing staring hopefully at the laden table. Then at one minute to half past the door opens and Milo staggers through carrying a cake the size of a mountain. It's so heavy, as he slides it onto the centre stage position I swear I hear the table groan.

As I scan the faces, it's a full house. Miranda's somehow managed to persuade Ambie out of the hot tub, Taj and co. are standing with their arms folded poised to taste, Willow and Nigel are looking ethereal enough to have fallen off a serenity advert, the kids are all exchanging very loud opinions. In fact everyone seems to be here except Bill.

Milo's pushing to the front. 'Just to tell you, mine has a coconut sponge base, and Malibu buttercream, on an ombré bottom tier ...'

There's a ring of defeated sighs as he pauses.

'... followed by a rocky outcrop of cream filled profiteroles and macaroon haystacks ... which gives way to a mini meringue pavlova mountain ... topped with a Baileys cupcake ... all encased in a golden spin drift crackle of spun sugar.'

There's a gentle whisper of open mouthed curses from the surfers, and Nigel mutters. 'I'm late to the party here, but is he trying to prove something?'

Fliss turns to Milo. 'Red card for you there, you wrecked the anonymity, judges' decision is final, you're out of the competition.'

As Milo's face falls I open my mouth to jump in, but Libby's there before me.

'It's a bit of Christmas fun, *NO ONE'S* going to be disqualified.' Not that you'd ever argue with Libby, but her mouth's a total 'don't you *DARE* disagree' straight line here.

I'm coming in under the radar. 'And after all that, Bill didn't enter either!'

Milo's hissing and punching the air. 'Couldn't make the standard, I knew it.'

Nigel's looking at me. 'Yes, he did, I saw Bill bring his in earlier but he had to rush off.'

I'm looking along the entries and I come to a plate of gingerbread men. Sorry – *people*. And I start to smile because there's no mistaking Bill's handiwork there. He might as well have left a sign on them saying *BILL MADE THESE*. It's just extra poignant to think the day we found the cutters and made the gingerbread men for the kitchen tree we had no idea he had a child. Thinking how he must have used those cutters with Abby, I don't know how his heart didn't break that day. But it won't need to break any more now.

I'm moving this on before Libby jumps in and declares Milo is the winner without any voting. 'So, if everyone except for Milo has left their name in secret underneath their cakes, shall we move on to the tasting and judging? Fliss is giving everyone a bead and putting out saucers, put your bead in the saucer in front of the cake you want to vote for.'

Fliss beams. 'And while I'm giving out the beads, Ivy will cut a slice out of each cake so everyone can taste.'

It's funny there are so many cakes here. There are some gorgeous Christmas tree cupcakes with bright green buttercream and coloured baubles. There are some eye-catching round iced shortbreads with fairy light strands across them, our snowy chocolate cake, Rob's Black Forest gateau, oozing cream, Willow and Nigel's plus some extra truffles, and then the kids' cupcakes, and some Nutella brownies, which I suspect from the way they're giggling at them, are Tiff, Tansy and Scout's. And then at the very end of the line, my heart melts.

I point to Fliss. 'Oh my, someone's baked a Merwyn cake with matching Merwyn cupcakes.' It's basically a chocolate Swiss roll, with lashings of chocolate buttercream spiked to look like fur with a face on the end. But the expression in the eyes, it's the very spit of the dog himself. And each cupcake is a furry Merwyn face too.

All the kids dash to the end of the table and there's a collective 'Ahhhhh ...' and the clink of beads hitting the saucer in front.

I'm frowning. 'But how can you lot vote, you haven't even tasted yet?'

Tiff gives me a side eye. 'We don't have to taste, we already *know* what's best.'

I know I should give my bead to Rob for being awesome, but I have a sea glass moment, so the Merwyns get my bead too.

Fliss gives Rob's cake her bead and Harriet's, Oscar insists on giving his to Merwyn, and Willow and Nigel give theirs to the kids' snowpeople. By the time everyone else has tasted and dropped their beads in the saucers Milo's mountain has got two beads, and I suspect one of those came from Milo himself. And why did we forget to say you couldn't vote for your own cake?

Fliss is clapping her hands. 'Great, so the winner with twelve beads is the Merwyn ensemble. There's a little note attached to the collar of the main cake ... which I'm guessing will say who baked it?'

Tiff snatches it up. 'It's got Ivy's name on ...'

She hands it to me and as I unfold it I see some very familiar pointy writing. 'Okay, so the note says, there's a cupcake for everyone, and if *I* go to the coach house now I'll find out who the *secret baker* is.'

I'm not sure why my heart is beating so fast as I grab my coat and cross the back courtyard. That's the other thing – I might be going in search of the secret baker, but this was never going to be a secret *mission*. As I hurry through the shrubbery and out towards the coach house I'm flanked by seven children all shouting. By the time we see the light shining through the glass door of the distillery we're running and breathless.

As I push my way in there's a figure by the end window, and as he turns and I take in the Aztec print joggers I gasp.

'Keef?' I have no idea why my heart sank there, but I pick myself up again really fast. 'Hey, so you're the one who's been thrilling us with your cranberry swirls?'

He purses his lips. 'Not exactly ...'

'As an answer that's no good at all. Surely it's yes or no?'

He lets out a sigh. 'Actually this has very little to do with baking, and it's more about Bill than me. He's trying to talk to you but apparently you keep avoiding him ...'

'So this is a trick?'

Keef's shaking his head. 'Don't be too hard on him, he

hasn't had it easy. He's very sorry for the position he put you in, it'll be good to clear the air before Christmas. He baked the Merwyn cakes and he'd like a word if that's okay?'

'Fine.' It's not at all. But obviously Bill can't afford ambiguity, if I'd let him do this in the car yesterday or let him say his piece early this morning we wouldn't be here now.

Keef pushes back his bead braids and squeezes my arm. 'He's waiting on the beach, it won't take long.'

As I turn for the door, the kids turn too.

'Not so fast! You lot wait here with me.' Keef puts his finger up, then he winks at me. 'Remember, *carpe* those effing *diems*, Ivy, and cut the boy some slack.'

There are times when I'd like to stuff his *carpes* and all the rest. If I wasn't in such a hurry, now would be one of them.

As I make my way out onto the empty sand the sea has turned to the colour of dark slate in the fading afternoon light and this morning's sun has given way to a heavy leaden sky. It's not helpful that when I see Bill's shoulders hunched against the wind, his hands deep in his jacket pockets, my first instinct is to throw my arms around him. As an icy gust blows inside my furry jacket I'm kicking myself for not bringing my hat. I draw near to him, cough, and he turns.

'Ivy, you came.'

I try to move past how one glimpse of that smile of his is lighting me up inside. 'If we could make this quick ...'

'Of course. I just want to set things straight, let you know how things stand.'

'Great.' I can't help my ironic tone.

'I don't want to speak badly of Gemma, but a wider view

may help you understand.' He frowns. 'I know you didn't want to know this, but I'm going to tell you anyway. It makes sense to start at the beginning, which was when Gemma and I were on the same flight back from Chamonix. We shared a taxi home to mine, one thing led to another, and two weeks later she told me she was pregnant.' He blows out a breath. 'It wasn't a great start. It certainly wasn't what I'd planned, but she moved in and we took it from there.'

'So that was Abby ...'

He's staring out across the water. 'In fact ... no. That first pregnancy didn't *actually* work out, but by the time I knew that, Abby *was* on the way.'

'Wow.' We all knew she was determined to get him, but we didn't think she'd go that far.

Bill gives a shrug. 'Gemma and I both had different priorities, different reasons to make the relationship work, but it wasn't ever easy. When Abby arrived she made everything worthwhile for me, but the rest was always hard work. We did our best for five years. But when Gemma wanted to move on with someone else last year it felt like at least one of us was getting the chance to be happy.'

'But that didn't last.'

'Maybe it was too optimistic of me to hope it would.' He sighs. 'I'm so sorry, it was wrong of me to take you anywhere near the house. When Gemma saw you she reacted.'

'But if Gemma wants to try again, surely you have to, for Abby?'

As his face folds the lines are pained. 'It was the first time Gemma had mentioned a reconciliation, and I wanted to clarify things with her, and make sure I was doing the best for Abby.'

'I understand.' Really I do. He doesn't have to keep going.

'But I've thought about it a lot – how good is it being brought up by parents who never loved each other and don't get on?'

That wasn't the impression I had. 'But Gemma was crazy about you, she pursued you the whole time in Chamonix.'

'I'm not pretending I'm perfect. But with Gemma, there's no give and take, no sense of partnership, it's only ever about her. It's fair to say, Gemma loved my house and earning capacity a lot more than she ever loved me.' Bill winces. 'As we are now Abby won't get to see both parents every day, but if she gets to see the two of us being happy on our own, being the people we want to be instead of being miserable together, that has to be more positive for her.

'Gemma didn't want me back until the moment she thought I might have moved on. And then she came in with the wrecking ball. And I'm truly sorry I caused you to be caught up in that, it was very demeaning.'

I let out a murmur. 'It was horrible.'

'There you go. I maybe made it hard for her when Dad and I found the castle and I wanted to move here. But she was the one who made the choice for us to go our separate ways, but now she has, I'm standing by that. I'll always be there for Abby as much as she wants me to be, but I won't be going back to Gemma.'

'Okay, well thanks for telling me.' I'm letting it all sink in. 'Is there anything else you'd like to clear up while we're here?'

His eyes go wide. 'In case you hadn't already guessed, when you saw the note on the Merwyn cake collar ... I'm your secret baker.'

I'm laughing now. 'And I almost thought it was Keef. Are you going to tell me why?'

'Milo was there, pretending how good he was, I had to throw something into the mix to show you he wasn't "all that". And it was my way of trying to help the Christmas cause too. You weren't exactly thinking the best of me at that point, if I'd come clean about the baking you'd have only disliked me more.'

'Why were you ever worried about Milo?'

'He's attractive, I'd missed my chance with you once, I was damned if I was going to let it happen again.'

'Milo's not *that* handsome. It's not about looks anyway ...' Looking at Bill, and feeling my stomach disintegrate, I could be lying here. 'For me it's much more about what we talk about, how much you make me laugh, how you smell ...' which reminds me '... what aftershave do you wear?'

He rolls his eyes. 'All those bottles in my bathroom, how do you ever expect me to know that? It might be a browny one ...'

'I don't believe it.' I give him a play punch on his arm. 'You're joking me?'

There's a twist to his lips. 'It's Dior Fahrenheit.' His lips curve more. 'Do I get a kiss for telling you that?'

I roll my eyes. Because, hell, I don't want to look like a pushover here. 'Do you have mistletoe?'

His face falls. 'Shit.' Then he grins again, and wriggles into his jeans pocket. 'Of course I have mistletoe, I told you before, from now on I'm never going to be without.' He holds up the tiniest wiltiest sprig that's obviously been all the way to London and back.

I can't help laughing. 'You call *that* mistletoe? It's not very impressive.'

'Well try this first, and *then* we'll see if you're still grumbling.'

One moment I'm laughing, the next I've turned, his arms are around me, and the dark, sweet, coffee warmth of his mouth hits mine. And as I close my eyes and drag the delicious scent of Dior Fahrenheit deep into my lungs, and fling myself against the wall of his chest the world starts to spin. If there's a distant cheer and something that sounds a lot like Tiff and Tansy screaming, I hear it for a moment, then the rush of the waves falls over it and the battering of the wind blows it out to sea. And it's a long time later when we finally part. I'm left with my mouth aching for more.

As I stagger backwards he grabs me again. 'I refuse to let you fall in the sea here.'

So instead I press my cheek against the cashmere of his jumper, and listen as he starts to talk again.

'This was never about choosing between you and Gemma. I was here, living my pretty shit life and the minute you walked around that corner and found me in the hot tub, everything changed. Up until then even in a relationship I'd been completely alone. And then you marched in, and started to help.'

'Started to order you around you mean.'

He rolls his eyes. 'I had no idea what I'd signed up for. But I'm really pleased I did. But I'd have been in *such* big trouble without you. You shook me up, and made the most amazing things happen, but most of all we worked as a partnership. When things went wrong, you were there to haul me out of the mess. You made me stand up to Gemma and made me strong enough to see Abby. And through all of it you've been wonderful to be with, in a way that makes me never want to be without you again. You're incredibly beautiful inside and out, and I can't thank you enough for all of it.'

For some reason there are tears running down my face, because my cheeks are wet against the wool. 'Actually, I'm the one who needs to thank you. You made me feel beautiful when I didn't think that would ever be possible. And you made me see I don't have to be sad forever.'

He sniffs and swallows. 'You give so much to everyone, unconditionally. Of everyone I've ever met, you're the person who most deserves to be happy, Ivy. I've never been in love before, but I'm completely in love with you now. It's like my life turned upside down these last two weeks. I love you, Ivy, I just want us to be happy together, if you're up for giving it a try?'

I push my hand upwards, slide my fingers through his hair and tug. 'And I love you too, Bill.' However strong the sea glass, I can't let on how long I've felt that for. 'This is like a dream come true.' There. I'm saying the same thing in a different way.

'There is one more thing ...'

He always does this and it's not always good. 'And ...?'

'That sky ...'

I look upwards past his ear. 'There are stars, I know they're there, we just can't see them yet ...'

He laughs. 'For once I didn't mean stars, I was thinking more that the sky looks full of snow ...'

I have to check. 'Are you joking me again?'

He's smiling down at me. 'Would I joke about something *that* serious?'

If he's trying to give me a reason to snog the pants of him in gratitude, I'm very happy to do it.

But when we go out much later to take Merwyn for his phone-light walk along the beach it still hasn't snowed and if anything the icy blast off the sea is less cold not more.

'Still no snow then? What did your famous BBC weatherman say about that?'

He wrinkles his nose. 'Tomasz said it would snow when it warmed up.'

And as I huddle inside Bill's coat the sky I'm looking up at is very dark.

'It's too cloudy for stars tonight too.'

'So many disappointments.' Bill laughs. 'We can't see the stars, but if you look really carefully can you see those tiny flecks falling out of the sky?'

'If I half close my eyes I think I can.'

'They're little pieces of falling stars.'

'Is that a Cornish thing, then?

In the half light I see him biting his lip. 'Only teasing. I don't want to get your hopes up ... but I think they might be snowflakes ...'

Wednesday

25th December

35.

Tinsel, sprouts, turkey, snow!

'Snow on Christmas morning, it's official, I'll love you forever for this Mr Markham ...' I'm looking down from my bedroom window, catching my breath with excitement as I take in the snow in deep drifts across the lawn, clinging to the branches of the shrubbery, and in clumps across the beach all the way down to the water's edge.

'I hope that's the kind of forever that goes on to the end of time, Ms Starforth, not the kind that melts when the snow goes away.' Bill's lips twist as he eases his tanned shoulders back on the pillow pile. 'So are you coming back to bed so I can give you a happy *white* Christmas kiss?'

After our first proper night together I doubt we'd have been getting up at all if it hadn't been Christmas Day. But Christmas Days with snow are the kind of thing that happen in stories. In real life they're so rare, however delicious and warm it is under the duvet and however sad I am to let Bill cover up that smoking hot body of his with clothes, we *have* to get up. By the time we hurry down to take Merwyn for his early walk, everyone else is already out in the garden.

Fliss calls across to us. 'Hey, lazy bones, what time do you call this? We've already opened our stockings, had breakfast and built an entire family of snow people.' She's hauling Oscar across the lawn on one of the sledges from under the Christmas trees, dodging the snowballs that Tiff, Tansy and Scout are pelting at the boys.

As I dip into my pocket for my phone Bill gets in first and pulls me towards him. 'Come on Ivy, smile for our first ever Christmas morning selfie together.'

I do as he asks, sneak a quick and very discreet brush of his lips then bob down. 'And we need one with Merwyn too! And then some of the castle in the snow.' It's beyond picturesque with the snow-capped turrets stark against a bright blue sky, the snowy expanse of lawn and the dark trees highlighted in white where the snow is sticking to the bark. If Libby had ordered up the scene of so many people in bright coloured coats and scarves and wellies, playing in the snow in front of the castle she couldn't have asked for any more. Even Miranda and Ambie make it outside, and Ambie donates his hat for the grandad snowman.

Once Merwyn has had a run along the beach and we're pretty much snowballed out, we all head inside for hot chocolate, freshly cooked croissants and Milo's ever popular griddle scones. Then Keef, Taj and the guys get going with lunch while the rest of us go into the family room to watch the children start on their present opening. Its amazing how an operation that's taken literally weeks to prepare – I'm thinking off all Libby's deliveries, the hours she's been holed up in the laundry working on the gift wrapping – is demolished so fast. In minutes it's all over and the room looks like a bomb went off in a paper recycling factory, and the kids head to Bill's room to set up the new iPhones Libby gave them all. As soon as they've done that the girls come back and set up a production line in one of the tower rooms with Tansy's new laminator and a stack of Bill's gin labels. Before long they're calling Keef out of the kitchen to get his step ladders and they're sending him up the tree in the hall to hang the glossy labels in the branches alongside the shells and the miniature gin bottles.

So as Fliss and I get some after-lunch games ready and start to help lay the tables we're already popping the corks on the Bucks Fizz, and I'm frantically dashing around taking photos because wherever I look there's an Insta-worthy shot. Everything from the glow of the fires to the twinkle of the fairy lights is there, all given an extra brilliance because it's Christmas Day today.

By the time we're ready to sit down for lunch the serving table is groaning under the weight of a huge turkey and various veggie alternatives. There are dishes piled high with crispy potatoes and creamy mash whisked into peaks, there are more stuffings than I can count, towers of crusty golden Yorkshire puddings, crispy Cumberland sausages, veggie sausages, pigs in blankets, veggie pigs in vegan sleeping bags, sprouts, peas, carrots, asparagus, celery, baked squash and parsnips and peppers, jugfuls of gravy. By the time I put Libby's phone away and sit down between Fliss and Bill and hold my glass up for Keef to fill with Prosecco I feel like a food photographer. And whatever people say about sex making you extra hungry … I'm ravenous.

The platefuls of food are so large, it takes ages to finish, but every mouthful is so delicious I can't bear to leave any. Then just as I'm thinking I might need to get up and help clear the tables there's the sound of a knife tapping on a glass.

As we all stop talking and look around, Miranda stands up and gives a little cough.

'Er ... Ambie and I have a little announcement to make.'

I hear Libby's groan from further down the table. 'Oh no, what now?'

Fliss mutters too. 'Please may it not be Gretna Green or Vegas ...'

Miranda ignores her, breathes in so deeply that her boobs practically burst out of the top of her black lacy bustier, and carries on. 'As you all know Ambie and I got engaged a few days ago and you all helped us celebrate.'

Along the table Keef blinks at the pop of cleavage, then shakes his head.

'Well ...' Miranda does another little cough '... today's news is, we've decided to put our plans on hold ...'

Fliss looks bemused. 'On hold ... *how?*'

Miranda's beaming. 'On hold, as in we're getting *un-engaged for now*, with a view to re-visiting the ring thing at some point in the *very distant* future. We've talked about it for many hours in the hot tub and we *both* feel more comfortable that way.'

Libby's eyebrows have gone high. 'Congratulations, Mum, it's so much better to wait until you know each other better.'

Milo's picked his jaw up off the floor. 'No need to rush things ... isn't that what we've always said?'

As I grin at Miranda she's beaming back at me. 'Well done, Miranda, high fives to both of you.' I give her hers and then look around. 'Where's Ambie?'

Miranda gives a little wince. 'In the hot tub having a liquid lunch. But he's fine with it.'

Tiff looks at Tansy. 'What the fuck? How the hell are we kids meant to keep up with who our step-grandparents are going to be when they change their minds all the time?'

'*LANGUAGE, TIFFANY!*' The glare that Libby sends Tiff is fierce enough to nuke her, but she can't hold it. A second later she's back to grinning again.

Fliss is holding up her glass. 'So let's all drink to *good* decisions – and being sensible in your sixties!'

Miranda sends Fliss a saccharine smile. 'Fifties, sweetheart ...'

Tom mutters, 'Fifties, my arse.'

But this time Libby doesn't sweep in to correct him, she just quietly murmurs, 'Too right.'

Tarkie frowns at Tom. 'Does that mean they'll be having safe sex then?'

Tom's face crinkles. 'Senior railcards, more like.'

Tiff turns to Tarkie. 'If you start banging on about the clitoris Tarkie, I'm going to mash you.'

Tarkie groans. 'How will I, that's the one I can't remember!'

Fliss tries again. 'So let's drink ... to *MUM and AMBIE* and their *DISENGAGEMENT*!'

There's a roar of applause, and everybody bangs on the

tables so hard I'm hoping the plastic molecules are going to hold up. And as Keef catches my eye he's got his elf waistcoat off and he's twirling it around in the air. And then he grabs hold of Miranda and waltzes her off around the room.

Then as the mayhem dies down Libby claps her hands. 'Okay, so how about you kids clear the tables then?'

If you want something doing, ask someone young. There's the scraping of chair legs on the floor, and the stampede of feet and before we know it the tables are spotless, the kids are back in their seats again, and we're watching Keef, Taj and Bede carrying in flaming Christmas puddings, followed by Slater with a tray of home made rum and toffee ice cream, Brian with a tray of vegan-friendly sorbets, and Nigel with jugs of rum sauce and cream and mince pies. And we all settle in for the next round.

And just when we really think we can't possibly eat another thing, Keef comes around with coffees and brandy in glasses followed by Bill with a tray of hand made chocolates and truffles, with Kinder eggs for the kids.

By the time Willow comes round with her mini scoops of cucumber and ginger sorbet end-of-meal palate-cleanser-digestives, we are certain that one last mouthful will make us burst. But as usual, she's right – they might look and smell disgusting, but the end result makes us pleased we went along with her, held our noses, and swallowed.

Then Libby stands up and coughs. 'Okay, kids. While we clear away, just before you go back to your laminating, you're going to play *Elf on the shelf*. There are a hundred elves hidden all over the castle. Your job is to find them all, you can each take one of these baskets to collect them in.' She nods to the pile in front of her.

I'm holding my breath because the last time I mentioned this game, they were so unimpressed they didn't even bother to roll their eyes. But this time they don't do that. Instead they throw up their arms, shout 'yay' and all grab a basket and dash off.

She sends me a smile. 'Just another one of your little Christmas life-savers, Ivy.'

'You're welcome.' As I grin back at her Fliss sends me a wink. Now we're here, there's something else I've been meaning to ask. 'By the way, Libby, has Nathan been delayed?' I double checked earlier. According to her hour by hour calendar he was pencilled in to arrive twenty-five hours ago.

For a moment her eyes go wide. There's enough silence for Oscar to get down from the table, and start to bang on the table leg with a pepper mill. And when she replies she's smiling but her voice is even more brittle than usual. 'I'm pleased you asked that Ivy, you're the first person who has. It's strange, even the kids haven't noticed he's missing.' She takes a breath. 'Although seeing how little he's been home these last few years, it's probably business as usual for them.'

Fliss's eyes are like saucers. 'So where is he?'

Libby takes a breath. 'He's in St Moritz with his personal assistant, Gloria.' She gives a shrug. 'He's been seeing her for years. At least this way it's honest.'

Fliss is pulling a face. 'I thought Gloria was old enough to be his mum?'

Miranda's nodding. 'Sexy, single and sixty! Old doesn't mean we can't rock their socks off!'

Libby looks appalled. 'Obviously that's not you, Mum, you're way too young.'

I'm frowning. 'And here's me thinking he got you the castle for Christmas for romantic reasons – it shows you how wrong you can be looking in from the outside.'

Libby pulls a face. 'It was simply the most expensive Christmas rental I'd seen before or since so I grabbed it. He had to pay somehow. He was invited, but he declined to come. At least this way we all got to enjoy it.'

Fliss is blinking at Rob. 'So who else knows about this ... I mean, what happens next ... are you getting divorced?'

Libby shrugs. 'I doubt we'll bother with that. But Willow and Nigel have known for years and been very supportive.'

Fliss is blowing. 'I'm sorry, Libs. How did I not know? I always thought you had it all.'

Libby's smile is rueful. 'I certainly put the work into making it look as if I do. And there's nothing like a cheating husband to make you determined to make a success of your business.' She smiles and catches Milo's eye across the room. 'And it hasn't all been bad here. Have you ever tasted a coconut sponge as good as Milo's?'

Miranda's choking. 'But how can you and Milo possibly be compatible when Ambie's so wrong for me?'

Libby shakes her head. 'Mum, he's nice to be around, I enjoyed his pavlova. I didn't say I'm rushing off to marry him – or even thinking about it.'

Fliss is shaking her head. 'We can't complain about romance and the castle – it worked its magic for Bill and Ivy, me and Rob are back on track, Libby's got as far as enjoying someone's company, and Miranda's found six surfie admirers. I bet none of them would throw her out of their camper vans if they were given half a chance.'

Libby's expression is pained. 'But *Christmas* is what matters – we *are* all enjoying it – *aren't we*?'

This is the woman who had no doubts. The one who was so far above us her oxygen came from another stratosphere. The one who was so super-sure of herself while the rest of us stuffed up. And suddenly she's here, looking small and sad and lost. And she's asking *us* for reassurance. And somehow even though her superiority has annoyed us so much for so long, now she's down at our level all I want to do is to help her.

I'm counting on my fingers. 'You know Libby, I'm looking across the room at Milo, and he's *really* smiling at you. The kids are all tearing round the castle searching for plastic elves, of all things. Then there are the surfies who've *begged* to come and join us. Bill and I couldn't be more ecstatic. Fliss, Rob and the kids all know they love each other. Willow and Nigel know all the secrets anyway. Miranda's just been brave enough to save herself. Merwyn pretends he's pissed off, but it's all an act to hide how much he loves it here. Even Ambie's euphoric in his own way in the hot tub. So that only leaves one person. Libby – are *you* happy?'

Libby's pulling a face. 'I never thought I'd say this, because it never felt as if I would be – but – yes, I actually think I am.'

I'm laughing at her. 'I never thought we'd say this either. When everyone arrived I couldn't see how it could be anything other than a train wreck Christmas. But for this year, I reckon, we cracked it, it's job done!'

And as Libby high fives me and pulls me into a dewey eyed hug, I'm so happy for her, I'm wiping my eyes and sniffing too.

And then the kids come careering through. 'Ninety-nine elves, Ivy, we've counted them all up and we've got ninety-nine – where the heck did you hide the last one?'

Fliss is looking at them. 'If you think about it rationally, you'll realise – before Ivy and I can answer that question you're going to have to tell us every place you found the ninety-nine.'

And then I smile. 'No. It's fine, I've remembered where the hundredth one is –' And somehow this is really fitting too, but it gives me a lump in my throat at the same time. 'Bill took one to Abby, remember.'

Tiff nods. 'So he did. That's nice, but it's a shame she's not here.'

'It is.' I smile. 'She'll be having a nice time though, she's gone skiing.'

Scout nods. 'Well I've been skiing. I've been to lots of exotic places at Christmas, because that's just what happens when your dad is a green travel writer. But none of them were as good as it is here.'

I'm catching Libby's eye, and giving her the thumbs up behind Scout's back, and I'm so happy I'm grinning. 'Bill did well with the snow.'

Tansy's staring at me. 'Did he make it happen?'

I'm smiling. 'He had a special word with this guy he knows – Tomas Schafernaker.'

Scout pulls a face. 'The weatherman?'

I'm nodding because she's so on the ball. 'That's the one.'

Scout's frowning. 'So how does that work then?'

I do my best 'who knows?' face. 'I'm not sure. It could be something to do with mistletoe ... or sea glass?'

Scout's nodding. 'Yes, probably that, they're both very powerful.'

'So that's good then, if we're all done at ninety-nine.' Tiff, Tansy and Scout are swishing their tulle and sequined skirts, and Tiff turns to them. 'We should have timed ourselves. Then next year we'll be able to see if we can beat it.'

Tansy's shrugging. 'No need to worry, we'll do it all over again tomorrow and get a time.'

Tiff narrows her eyes. 'What's that weird noise?'

Bill's come in and he's pulling back the fire guard and he's piling more logs on the fire. 'Bill ... any idea what the noise is? It's really jingly ... a bit like bells ...'

He's laughing at me. 'Not *entirely*. But I'd say it might be no bad thing to pull your boots and coats on and get out to the front of the castle – like *right now*.'

36.

Jingle bells and cockle shells

'Santa and his elf and his pony and cart? Was this you or Libby?'

I'm looking at Bill, we're out in the crisp afternoon sun, and if I thought the snowy castle couldn't be any more pretty, I was wrong. Santa arriving with his little pony stamping his hoofs and tossing his head with bells jingling on his reins, and the cart twinkling with fairy lights, just made it even more magical.

Bill's cheeks are creased where he's smiling. 'I have to put my hands up, this one's down to me, with a lot of help from Keef, obviously. Definitely no reindeer, I thought you'd like it.'

'It's perfect. But how did you know? Two weeks ago you didn't have the first clue about Christmas, and then you pull this off?'

'I'm a fast learner, I had this ace instructor who showed me how worthwhile it was to go the extra mile every time when it comes to Christmas.' He gives a smug smile as he swings first Tarkie then Solomon up onto the cart as the older ones scramble into the back of the cart themselves.

Tansy's looking at me as she rubs the pony's nose. 'Do you think it's okay, Ivy, is it kind to animals?'

Bill smiles. 'This pony is called Nutty, short for Nutella. He's very well looked after, he has a stable with lots of sweet hay to eat, and carrots and pony nuts.'

Santa's elf leans over. 'But not too much, it's not good for him to get fat.'

As the elf was rubbing his rather large tummy earlier, I don't think he has any room to talk.

I smile at her. 'From the look on his face, I'd say he loves pulling the cart as much as you like laminating and I like making things look pretty.'

She's taking that in. 'In that case, I'll go for the ride.'

Santa leans down. 'Why don't you come up on the front between us, and you can have a go taking the reins.'

Tiff's mouthing at me. 'Has Santa got eyeliner on?'

I go in for a closer look and nod at her. 'I think he has. And Mr Elf too.'

Tiff's grinning at me. 'Nice job.'

Bill's hissing at me from behind his hand, 'That's not Mr Elf, that's actually Santa's husband – so he's technically Mr *Santa*.'

Willow's standing next to me and she lets out a gasp. 'Has *Scout* got eyeliner on?'

I grin at her. 'Forbidden things are fascinating and compelling, Willow, available things aren't. Once she knows what it is and how to use it she'll be able to make an informed choice for herself.'

Willow sniffs, and then she smiles. 'Well said, Ivy. It's

wonderful how far everyone's come this holiday, especially you.'

'I'm working on it,' I laugh, but at the same time I'm bursting with pride inside.

Mr Elf leans forward. 'Hey, you down there in the blue coat with the very cute dog ... Ivy, is it?'

Willow gives me a nudge. 'That's you ...'

As I turn to look up I could hug him. Because he's just shown me, I'm not defined as the woman with the cut up face who had the accident any more. Somewhere in the last two weeks I've left her behind and gone back to being my plain old self in the blue coat again. And if it's taken Santa's elf to make me finally see that, I'm happy to go with it.

'Yes?' As I turn my face up to him I'm not even thinking about my scar.

He's nodding. 'We heard Bill spent years lusting after you, now we completely understand why.'

My mouth's fallen open. 'Excuse me?'

'Bill's been a favourite heart throb of ours ever since he arrived, it's lovely to see someone finally put a smile on his face.'

Bill's hissing in my ear. 'We all go to the St Aidan Chamber of Commerce, if I'd known they were going to be this rude and outrageous, truly I'd have brought in the real guy with the reindeer instead.'

Mr Elf's laughing at Bill. 'Us, outrageous? As if! Sometimes it's good to tell people your secrets.'

Santa's clearing his throat now. 'Okay, girls and boys, if everyone's aboard and holding on tight, we'll set off. Come on Nutty, trot on.' There's a jingle as he shakes the reins, the pony tosses his head, steam comes out of his nostrils into the cold air and the cart draws away. As they pick up speed and turn down the drive there's snow flying off the wheels, the children are cheering and waving, and my heart is flying.

Bill's arm slides around me. 'So about Chamonix ...'

'Yes ...?' The less I say about this the better.

'Every time I mention it you change the subject, but I have to tell you what Mr Elf says is completely true – I spent the whole holiday waiting for you to break up with George so *I* could ask you out.'

I feel my eyes snap open in surprise. 'Really?'

'That first afternoon when we were the only ones there ... I've kicked myself so often since for not telling you how I felt that day ...' He's frowning at me. 'When I sounded George out at the end of the holiday he was so adamant you were already unofficially engaged it felt wrong for me to intervene. That's why I assumed you were married.'

I sigh. 'As I discovered, George lied a lot more often than he told the truth.'

Bill's voice is low. 'You *do* remember that afternoon though, tell me you've thought about it occasionally?'

I grab my courage and my dignity in both hands and go for it. 'Only most days since.' It would probably be too much to tell him that lately it's been more like every hour.

'Ditto.' He lets out a long sigh. 'You've no idea how pleased I am to hear that. Or how over the moon I was when you walked round the corner and found me in the hot tub.'

'We still haven't found where Merwyn buried your boxers.'

'Who needs those?' He laughs and pulls me closer. 'So many lost years, this time I won't be letting go.' As he looks down at me, his eyes are so dark, and it's wonderful to know the shadows of his stubble are mine to touch whenever I want. 'You are going to stay on after the others go home? We can work together at the castle, there's so much you could do with the gin, or find another job if you'd rather?'

I smile. 'Thanks, I'd love that.'

He's squeezing me even tighter. 'A whole new adventure – together.'

We look up as the rumble of the wheels and the jingle of the bells comes closer again. And as Nutty comes to a halt snorting in front of us, Tansy's waving down at us.

Tiff grins. 'Well however much Granny Miranda changes her mind, Ivy and Bill are in love, we always knew they were.' She turns to Libby standing beside us, her hand shading her eyes from the bright afternoon sun. 'Can we come back here for Christmas every year, Mum?'

Libby laughs and turns to Bill. 'Is it too early to book in for next Christmas? Same great rates, Nathan's treat.'

I give Bill a jab in the ribs. 'Can you face doing it all over again in twelve months' time?'

Bill shrugs inside his Barbour. 'If you'll be here to help me ... then, hell, yes!'

Tom's frowning at Libby from under his hat in the back of the cart. 'In that case, why are we even going home, we could all just stay here ...'

Libby holds up her finger and nods at Tom. 'Funny you should say that, I've been checking out the local rental rates and the fabulous visitor numbers here in summer, it might be a great place for my first shop. Just saying.'

Fliss and I roll our eyes at each other. 'This is Libby, she's never going to stop.'

Libby's looking straight at us. 'If you two are looking for work, I'd happily take you on – you could do worse.' Considering the huge Christmas lunch she just ate there's a scarily lean and hungry look in her eye.

Fliss gives her a hug. 'Thanks, Libs, that's fab. Let's talk about it after we've had our ride with Santa.'

I smile up at Bill. 'You see, Christmas comes first, every time.'

He laughs down at me. 'I'm with you on that!'

As he pulls me against him, I'm talking into his new stripy scarf. 'This has to be my best Christmas ever, for so many reasons – but mostly because of you.'

'Mine too.' He's rubbing his cheek against mine. 'No pressure – but should we be planning for next year?'

My cheeks are tight because I'm smiling so hard. 'Totally. But let's have one more snog first.'

And as he pulls me into the longest Christmas kiss ever, with the snowy turrets sharp against the diesel blue sky, and Merwyn snuffling at my feet, I have to be the happiest woman in Cornwall if not the world.

37.

PS …

So another Christmas came and went so very fast. But I think it's fair to say, everyone had their own wonderful times, and no one went home from Cockle Shell Castle quite the same person as when they arrived. Some places are like that. But I think it was the company too. We were all very different people, but after two weeks together we'd somehow all changed each other for the better. And all had a fabulous Christmas too. And those memories of torchlight sledging on Christmas night will stay with us forever.

I now have a lovely silver starfish bracelet to wear – my present from Bill – and a Chamonix key ring on the key to the castle I use, as well as my sea glass necklace. And when we head back to London after New Year Merwyn's seashell necktie gets a lot of admiring looks in the park. But everyone can tell – we've both left our hearts at the castle on the beach. And as Tatiana's working abroad more, I agree to have Merwyn full time. Merwyn pretends to be sad, but we get along so well, we're both giving secret cheers.

When I come back to *Daniels* for the last few weeks, Bill

comes for weekends, and sees Abby. A friend of Willow's is happy to take over my flat for a while, so this time when I wave goodbye to my starry ceiling and get in my little Corsa I'm not just going away for Christmas – I'm going to a whole new beginning under the Cornish stars.

With Merwyn sitting in the back and Bill waiting for us at the castle, I couldn't have two better guys to love me. I'm almost too excited to breathe, and I can't wait to find out what's going to happen next ... all I can say is, watch this space ... I'll let you know.

THE END

Acknowledgements

A big thank you ... To my editor and friend Charlotte Ledger, for her inspiration, support, brilliance and all round loveliness. This is our eleventh book together, and it never gets any less exciting. To Kimberley Young and the team at HarperCollins and One More Chapter, for their fabulous covers, and all round expertise and support. To my agent, Amanda Preston for her warmth and brilliance, her vision and encouragement, for sparkling and for always being there.

To my writing friends across the world ... To the fabulous book bloggers, who spread the word. To all my wonderful Facebook friends.

To my wonderful readers ... these books are all for you, thank you so much for enjoying them – I love hearing from you and meeting up with you.

And last of all, huge hugs to my family, for cheering me on all the way. And big love to my own hero, Phil ... thank you for never letting me give up.